Kendall Bl...

THE LITTLE TOWN THAT SAW IT ALL

AUSTIN MACAULEY PUBLISHERS
LONDON * CAMBRIDGE * NEW YORK * SHARJAH

Copyright © Kendall Blanchard 2026

All rights reserved. No part of this publication may be reproduced, distributed, or transmitted in any form or by any means, including photocopying, recording, or other electronic or mechanical methods, without the prior written permission of the publisher, except in the case of brief quotations embodied in critical reviews and certain other non-commercial uses permitted by copyright law. For permission requests, write to the publisher.

Any person who commits any unauthorized act in relation to this publication may be liable to criminal prosecution and civil claims for damages.

This is a work of fiction. Names, characters, businesses, places, events, locales, and incidents are either the products of the author's imagination or used in a fictitious manner. Any resemblance to actual persons, living or dead, or actual events is purely coincidental.

Ordering Information
Quantity sales: Special discounts are available on quantity purchases by corporations, associations, and others. For details, contact the publisher at the address below.

Publisher's Cataloging-in-Publication data
Blanchard, Kendall
The Little Town That Saw It All

ISBN 9798891557239 (Paperback)
ISBN 9798891557246 (ePub e-book)

Library of Congress Control Number: 2025927348

www.austinmacauleyusa.com

First Published 2026
Austin Macauley Publishers LLC
40 Wall Street, 33rd Floor, Suite 3302
New York, NY 10005
USA

mail-usa@austinmacauley.com
+1 (646) 5125767

I cannot thank my wife, Connie Blanchard, enough, for using her skills as a literature professor and literary critic in providing suggestions and guidance on this and everything I write. I am also indebted to Jan Reasonover, a friend from my childhood days, for her reading and editing an early version of the book. Also, I appreciate the work of Nathaniel Hansen in using his talents as a professional editor to help me find and flesh out the flaws of the final draft. Then of course, there are my long-time friends who have read much of what I've written and continue to encourage me: Jean Ouler and Clayton Kallman, friends and members of my high school graduating class; Eugene Sadler, a high school friend; Paul Beckwith, a friend from my college days, John Neuenschwander, a friend from our post-doc days at Johns Hopkins, and Phillips Stevens, friend and fellow anthropologist.

Table of Contents

Author's Note	10
Chapter One: Why Me, Lord?	11
Crossroads, Kansas, June 1948	*11*
Chapter Two: The Rural Community Myth	24
Crossroads, 1948	*24*
Chapter Three: Divine Plan or Magic?	34
Chapter Four: Hormones	42
Chapter Five: Witchcraft and Sorcery	58
Chapter Six: Who's Cheating Whom?	81
Chapter Seven: When a Secret Is Not a Secret	87
Chapter Eight: Peru Comes to Crossroads	92
Chapter Nine: Surprise!	107
Chapter Ten: Basketball Bewitched	110
Chapter Eleven: Spring 1949	112
Chapter Twelve: The Plan	118
Chapter Thirteen: Missionary Turned Terrorist	121
Chapter Fourteen: Big Brother to the Rescue	130
Chapter Fifteen: The Unwanted Rescue	136
Chapter Sixteen: Finding Love in Strange Places	147
Chapter Seventeen: Murder in a Small Town	161

Chapter Eighteen: An Unsuspecting Suspect   **168**

Chapter Nineteen: The Trial   **171**

   Murder and Prostitution in Rural Kansas   *196*

Chapter Twenty: An Outside Perspective   **202**

Chapter Twenty-One: A New Suspect   **235**

Chapter Twenty-Two: The Lombardi Trial   **240**

Chapter Twenty-Three: The Truth Shall Set Thee Free   **276**

Epilogue   **284**

I'm going out to clean the pasture spring
I'll only stop to rake the leaves away
And wait to watch the water clear, I may
I shan't be gone long
You come too
I'm going out to fetch the little calf
That's standing by the mother
It's so young
It totters when she licks it with her tongue
I shan't be gone long
You come too

(Robert Frost)

Author's Note

I lived in a small town in Kansas for three years as a child. To this day, I remember those times as some of the most exciting, enjoyable, and fun-filled years of my life. But I was only a child, naïve and sheltered from the ugly truth. What follows is a story set largely in two of the years I spent in a similar town: 1948 and 1949. The characters in some cases are based on real people—people I knew, that I went to school with, who belonged to my church, whose farms I knew well. But all the descriptions, like the story, are concocted, and the names I use are completely fictional in this tale of tragedy, hypocrisy, deceit, and self-delusion.

Residents of this town, which I am calling Crossroads, seem certain that their town, like all other small towns in America, is immune to the ailments that afflict life in the city. They tout the virtues of rural life and rail against the sins of urbanity. At the same time, they feel cheated, convinced that Uncle Sam spends a disproportionate amount of his tax revenues on the cities, and that rural America only gets the scraps. Most of this is not true, but these are myths that make Crossroads residents feel better about where they live.

Chapter One
Why Me, Lord?

Crossroads, Kansas, June 1948

Life is a precarious balance between the expected and the unexpected. If human existence were comprised of all expected events, it would be as ho-hum as watching the sand dribble through a bottomless hourglass. Of course, the unexpected, when the hourglass explodes in your face, can make one long for the boredom of the expected.

Many small rural towns in America are like pumpkins carved for the holidays, sitting on the porch a few weeks after Halloween. On the outside, they still look firm and fresh and they still have those cut-out eyes and toothy smiles on the surface, but inside they are slowly rotting away. Economically, these out-of-the-way places are usually dependent on the farmers and the land by which they are surrounded. But over time, the farmers become part of the corporate world, the communities' major sources of income dry up, and the little towns are reduced to rural ghettos.

As they die, they tend to breed more crime, drug use, and alcohol addiction. They invite more unemployed squatters. Residents beat their wives and girlfriends and ignore the law. And yet, the myth of small-town America lives on. Listen to the rhetoric. They bill themselves as paragons of virtue, patriotism, and godliness. At best, it is self-delusion; at worst, it is pure mendacity. And yet, there is still something compelling and intriguing about rural life. These towns, though small and isolated, have seen it all.

*****

It's hot, hotter than usual for this time of year. And dry. The ripe and ready stalks of wheat sway gently in the soft warm breeze; the fields look like thick, brownish-yellow undulating wool blankets, randomly tossing reflected rays of sun into the summer sky. The spring wheat is ready for harvest. Karl Miller stands beside the long, heavy metal gate that breaks the monotony of the lengthy, almost endless, row of wooden posts and barbed wire that run along the edges of his largest wheat field. The fence is there to keep out the cattle and any other animal impostors that might damage the wheat.

Of course, for the deer, the fence is no challenge. But, in some cases, their leap across that fence and into Miller's wheat has cost them their lives. Karl has a reputation as a marksman. He has a gun cabinet that houses a Winchester 30–30, a bolt-action 38 rifle, a single-shot 22 rifle, and two 12-gauge shotguns, one of which is a double-barrel. His weapon of choice is the 30–30. His skills are almost legendary. His friends joke, "Miller could knock a horsefly off a cow's back at 100 yards." Whether true or not, the middle-aged farmer has a history of using his rifle in almost artful fashion.

As an illustration: a couple years ago, it was late at night. He and his wife were in bed when he thought he heard a commotion out in the large metal Quonset hut, where he keeps most of his equipment. He grabbed his rifle and threw open a window facing the direction of the noise. He hollered and two men bolted out of the makeshift barn and headed toward a beat-up, early 1940s Chevrolet pickup truck. Karl could have shot their eyes out, but instead, fired a shot over their heads and let them get into their vehicle and take off. But just as they were about to exit the property and hit the gravel road that ran in front of the farm, he steadied his gun and shot out both the pickup truck's rear tires.

The intruders kept driving their wounded vehicle down the road, the back tires flopping and slapping noisily against the gravel until they destroyed themselves. The two would-be burglars abandoned their now two transportation and were eventually apprehended. They served time while Farmer Miller basked in his embellished reputation as a guy not to be messed with.

Today is a big day. Time to start harvesting the spring wheat. The wheat is ripe and must be harvested before it dries out. Timing? It's critical. Farmer Miller's hired hand—a scrawny, well-weathered white man of undetermined age—will manage the process. He is called "Pete". That's it. No one knows his last name or even if he ever had one. Where he is from is a mystery. He just showed up one day looking for work. For years now, he has lived in one of the older barns on the property, having carved out a space for himself in the back corner of the facility.

Pete lives a hermetic life. He's a confirmed loner, but a hard and dedicated worker. He rarely bathes and his strong, pungent body odor has become a consistent part of his identity. His wardrobe consists of a few tattered sweatshirts, a couple tee-shirts, two pairs of bib overalls, and some scratched-up boots. He sometimes eats with the Miller family, but for the most part manages to scavenge food from here and there. He says very little and reads even less. Apparently, he dropped out of elementary school early and never learned the three Rs required of school children of his generation.

Shortly after 5:00, Pete climbs out of bed, pulls on his boots and his straw hat, and goes out to join his boss.

"Good morning, Pete."

"Good morning, Sir." The hired hand, though often thought of as part of the Miller family, still maintains a status distance from the man to whom he answers.

"I think we need to get started. Why don't you go get the reaper?"

The reaping machine is a wide tangle of metal blades and fork-like, curved tines that is pulled behind plow-horses or a tractor, and cuts down the grain and leaves the stalks lying in neatly aligned piles. Miller is one of the few men in the community with a tractor. Most of the farmers in the area still rely on their broad-backed workhorses or mules.

Karl Miller is 49 years old; large for his generation—six-foot-one and 200 pounds with a body of pure steel. He is thought to be the strongest man in the entire northeast corner of Kansas. He consistently wins strongman and weightlifting contests at county and state fairs, cookouts, and other entertaining public gatherings. His once blond hair is now several shades darker and gradually receding. His face, once handsome, is still attractive but rough and worn, the result of years of exposure to the vicissitudes of outdoor life. His dull green eyes lie quietly beneath heavy dark eyebrows and thick wire-rimmed glasses made necessary by his acute nearsightedness. Despite his premature aging, he remains a convincingly charismatic figure who, for all practical purposes, is the informal head honcho of the area's farming community. His neighbors turn him for advice; come to him when they need help, and listen to him when he speaks.

Karl is a quiet person who rarely opens up about anything personal. In fact, he is slow to talk about anything other than what is necessary in the process of running a large farming operation or helping a fellow farmer solve a problem. He plays it close to the chest, and it is always difficult to gauge his reaction by watching his stern, stoic face. Life has been good to him. He is grateful but does not take anything for granted. In many ways, he is the prototypical Kansas farmer.

Karl is the eldest of four brothers, the children of parents who emigrated from Germany in 1890. They were hardworking, ambitious, thrifty, and energetic scrappers who managed to buy and farm several hundred acres of good farm land before passing it on to their sons. The sons in turn bought and leased additional properties so that now, between the four of them, they own or lease over 3,000 acres.

When the parents landed at Ellis Island, the young couple signed in as the Muellers, but immediately changed their last name to Miller to minimize the chances of always being known as German. Growing up, the children were forbidden to speak German at home, even though their parents struggled with English. Karl graduated from the local high school but never considered college, even though there was no doubt he was qualified. He was confident he was cut out to be a farmer and saw no reason to believe that a degree from Kansas State or any other institution would be that useful in his chosen career.

Pete pulls up on the tractor, dragging the reaper behind him. "What now, Boss?"

"I tell you what," Karl responds, as he strokes his chin and stares out across his bountiful crop, "let's start on the north end, up over the bluff there, and work back this way."

That's all Pete needs to hear. Without a word, he pulls through the gate and heads north, leaving in his wake a powerful trail of gas, oil, and body odors. Karl watches quietly, knowing that in an hour or so a diverse crew of laborers will be here to pitch in; neighboring farmers who are always there to help each other out, young men out of school for the summer who are trying to earn a little spending money, the preacher of the local Methodist Church where Karl and his family worship, and a few boys who spend their summers doing odd jobs, like bringing water and supplies to the men in the field. There is no other time in the course of the year that is witness to the kind of neighborliness for which rural America is known. It seems that wheat harvesting season brings out the best of country folk.

When the crew arrives, it will walk along, following Pete's trail, picking up and baling the wheat into shocks, tying up the shocks, and standing them up as sheafs, where they will be left to dry for a few days before being picked up and brought into the threshing machine.

*****

It's lunch time, what all the men and boys have been waiting for. The crew hears the dinner bell ring, drops what it is doing, and heads for the Miller's front yard. Four worn and stained wooden picnic tables have been brought around for this occasion. Ample shade is provided by two large oak trees and a soft breeze takes the edge off summer's heat. A serving table has been moved to the yard and is weighted down with enough food to feed a professional football team.

There is corn on the cob, platters stacked high with fried chicken, fresh green peas in cream sauce, steamed green beans, fresh sliced tomatoes straight from the garden, vegetable goulash, cornbread and a mountain of German potato salad that would make Pikes Peak quake with envy. All of this, with scrumptious desserts to follow: chocolate pie, carrot cake, raspberry crumble bars, and homemade ice cream. Those who have volunteered today and are expecting no wage compensation remind themselves that this meal and the camaraderie alone are more than ample rewards.

Several of the crew-members' wives have come to help, in most cases bringing with them their own kitchen creations to add to the feast, but Thelma, Karl's wife, is in charge. Thelma, like Karl, is of German descent. She is one year younger than he. They went to the local high school together when there were only 45 students in the four grades, 9–12, combined. It was impossible for them not to have known each other.

As in a classic high-school romance, Karl was a star on the basketball team and Thelma a cheerleader. Thelma was cute and curvy in her teens, but her years of being a farm wife and giving birth to four children have taken its toll on her body. She is still a pleasant-looking woman: a light-skinned, blemish-free face, dark brown hair that she keeps in a short bob, and crystal-blue eyes that continue to sparkle despite the hardships of being a farm wife. But her weight has given her a large shapeless figure that makes it impossible to even imagine the body she once had. She used to worry that Karl had lost interest in her; indeed, maybe looking for a heifer in another pasture. Now, she really does not care. But the two of them have kept turning out children, so apparently Thelma still knows how to light his fire, at least that is the assumption of those who know the Millers.

Members of the voluntary crew file past the serving table and pile their paper plates high with the bounty of their gardens and their wives' and mothers' culinary talents. As they sit down, they grab their utensils and begin shoving food into their mouths. On many occasions like this, someone says grace before everyone starts eating, but even the preacher, who is chewing happily on a fried chicken leg, knows that today is about work and any kind of prayer would only take valuable time and throw the day off its rhythm.

When the women finish serving, they help themselves and settle at an empty table, along with the three young Miller daughters. The older men and younger men are segregated into separate groups, with the pre-adolescent boys scattered among them. Pete is seated at the far end of the fourth table, downwind from the rest of the diners. As usual, he is sitting quietly by himself. He is not much of a talker. But, seated across from him is Karl Miller Junior, better known by his nickname "Sonny". Sonny, who is six and soon to be seven, has just finished the first grade. He is the only son and enjoys having three older sisters, who dote on him, yet at times complain that he gets a disproportionate amount of their parents' attention and affection.

Karl, like most farmers, always wanted a large family of boys; boys who would help him manage the farm and someday take it over. But after hearing, for three times, the announcement, "It's a girl", he had been ready to give up. His brothers sometimes teased him about not having enough lead in his pencil, although no one else in the community would have dared. So, he and Thelma apparently kept trying, and it was with great joy that Karl finally heard those coveted words, "It's a boy!"

Sonny remains special in many ways; he is not like the other boys his age. He has inherited his father's blond hair and his mother's blue eyes. A small, pug-like nose and soft olive-colored skin and a perfectly shaped face. He remains cute, but is on what seems an inevitable path to being handsome. He is also "smart as a whip", as folks who know him say. The school principal tried to convince his parents to let him skip the second grade, but Karl and

Thelma did not think that was a good idea, being concerned about his social as well as intellectual development.

Like many of the farm wives in the community, Thelma plays the piano and spends a lot of her time teaching her daughters. All but the eldest have taken the challenge of mastering the black-and-white keys seriously. Meanwhile, at age four, little Karl watched his sisters making music and when alone with the piano began tapping the keys and pecking out simple melodies. The following year, he told his mother he wanted to learn to play, but while gentle in her response, Thelma put her foot down—"playing the piano is like sewing and cooking; it's an art reserved for girls, not boys." But Sonny persisted. Finally, Thelma and her husband discussed the matter, and Karl thought it through and decided it was fine, noting, "What if he's a child prodigy—a modern-day Mendelsohn? To take away what might be a gift from God would in my mind be an act of defiance. Going against God's will is a sin, you know."

Thelma's response, "What if he becomes a sissy and ends up like the Lockwood brothers?"

The Lockwoods are two attractive and effeminate middle-aged men who claim to be siblings and live together in one of the nicest homes in Crossroads, indeed, in the county. No one knows exactly what they do for a living, but there are rumors that they are really not brothers and are actually "homos". This is a farming community and homosexuality is viewed as a venial sin and a choice made by individuals who make that choice because they are unhappy with the body God gave them; it's a lifestyle not to be tolerated.

Karl smiles at his wife's anxious query, "Come on, Honey. Playing the piano ain't gonna turn our boy into no queer."

Sonny has been taking lessons from his mother for over a year now, and his innate talent has already begun to show. He has already advanced to a level above that of any of his sisters. Thelma has decided to sign him up for piano lessons at the local school when he begins the second grade in the fall.

Karl Junior is different in other ways. He has a special affection for Pete. His sisters, on the other hand, find the hired hand spooky, weird, and sometimes frightening. And of course, added to that is the issue of his body odor. As one of the sisters notes, "He stinks. He smells like a dead rat. Oooh!"

But Sonny has grown to think of Pete as his friend. Sometimes in the evening, after supper, he will walk out to the hired hand's makeshift living quarters in one of the barns and visit. When asked about these meetings, Sonny will defend himself vigorously. "I don't understand why you hate Pete. He's a nice man. He tells great stories. He also does magic."

"What do you mean?" one of his skeptical sisters will ask.

"Like finding quarters in my ears or hiding them in his hands. He can do amazing card tricks. He also makes things disappear."

The girls shake their heads in puzzlement and dismiss Sonny's claims and affection for the strange man that stinks, as just another little boy's fantasy.

As everyone sits, chatting and enjoying today's feast, there are those who glance in the direction of Pete and Sonny and wonder what is it about that boy that seems to bring something out of the quiet hired hand that never happens with anyone else. At times, Pete seems uncharacteristically animated, as he and Sonny chat vigorously, all about who knows what. Some speculate that the relationship is rooted in Pete's stunted maturity. In many ways he is still a child, perhaps still living in an inner world not unlike that of Sonny and other pre-adolescents.

When lunch is over, the men and boys go back to work; the women clean up but not before they are thanked profusely by their sons and husbands. Gratitude is a moral compunction among farming folks in the area. Nothing good that happens to you, just happens. Somewhere, somehow, someone, whether it be a friend, a family member, or God, has helped. Being thankful is the least you can do to repay your benefactor.

*****

A week has gone by and the sheaves are dry enough to be collected and taken to the thresher to complete the process of turning the crop into grain that in turn will be taken to a place like St. Joseph, Missouri, or Atchison, Kansas, to a large silo next to the railroad station from where it will eventually be shipped to markets around the country and around the world. Kansas remains the breadbasket of America, and farmers like the Millers take that as both a responsibility and a source of patriotic pride.

As the sun creeps up over the eastern horizon, members of the work crew begin showing up. Pete has the Miller hay wagon swept and ready to roll with the aging plow-horse couple, Ferd and Dolly obediently waiting to go to work. As usual, they are harnessed to the wagon and to each other, the breast collars and bridles gently in place, with the harness aligned in a way to distribute the workload evenly. The traces are connected to the drawbar which hangs behind and below the muscular rear-ends of the horses. The reins are draped across their backs and over the front side of the wagon.

A couple of the other farmers will bring their own hay wagons and beasts of burden, a staple of every farm of any size in the county. The Miller threshing machine is in place not far from the main gate to the field. The Millers are one of only two families in the area that have this equipment. In keeping with the ethic of cooperation that ties farming families together, the Millers are generous in letting others use their thresher. But, they do so, making sure whoever uses it understands the risks.

The large mouth or the feeder at the rear of the machine is like a hungry monster tearing up and swallowing whatever comes its way; its appetite is boundless and its tastes without limits. It can chop a man or parts of his torso into hamburger meat in seconds, so great care must be taken to keep at a distance from the spinning cylinder as it flashes its sharp teeth. One must be especially careful about keeping their clothing at a distance from the monster.

Two years ago, Karl let a neighbor use his threshing machine, and as part of making sure the borrower knew how it worked, he stressed the need to be careful; this thing was not a toy. As luck would have it, in the process of throwing sheaves of wheat into the thresher, the neighbor's shirt sleeve got caught in the rotor and his arm was pulled into the mouth of the monster and ripped from his shoulder. The farmer was fortunate that his whole body was not dragged through the powerful grinder. The neighbor lost his arm, but survived. However, in an uncharacteristic display of ingratitude, he threatened to sue the Millers, claiming Karl had not warned him of the dangers that came with using the threshing machine. The reaction of the rest of the farming community in the area was one of shock, disappointment, and anger. To take advantage of a man's generosity and then go after him when you screwed up? Unheard of! Unacceptable! The social pressure was intense, causing the would-be plaintiff to back off.

As summer temperatures begin to rise, the wagons head out into the field, each with one man at the reins guiding the horses forward while others walk along beside with pitchforks, tossing the sheaves over the wagon railings and onto the growing pile of wheat stalks that are soon to be fed to the hungry threshing machine. Wielding the pitchforks is hard work and only for those among the strong and hardy. And, the job comes with occasional surprises. A field mouse may come running out from under what was its temporary shelter and scurry away in terror. Or, there are the occasional snakes: usually harmless ones like rat snakes, chicken snakes, garter snakes, or king snakes. Much rarer are the poisonous vipers like the copperhead and western rattler.

But it seems there is an unarticulated but generally shared religious-like tenet that defines all snakes as evil. Women find them terrifying; men are less fearful but see the belly crawlers as a threat. Then there are the superstitions: a snake crawling across ones porch is an omen of bad things to come; that snakes like milk and are drawn to babies; that snakes can crawl up a man's pants leg and attack his genitals. So, pity the poor, innocent garter snake who has been napping under a sheaf of wheat when his shelter is suddenly lifted off him and he must flee for his life, only to have a farmer—who feels violated—stab him with his pitchfork or grab a hoe and chop off his head. It's one of the anomalies of farming, that you would kill an animal ally with such impunity. After all, snakes eat mice, rats, and other varmints that are the real threat to the farmer. It is like killing a friend, but don't tell that to Karl and his neighbors.

As the day wears on, the horses seem to tire, as do the men who keep feeding the bundles of dried wheat to the wagons. In general, the field's rows run north and south, bounded in the north by barbed-wire fence and on the south the banks of the Lazy River. For much of the year, the river is more of a creek as it weaves its way east to the Missouri River. But, after heavy rains that occur once every few years, the slow-moving creek becomes a torrent and a wall of swirling water up to 50 feet in depth that can overflow its banks and flood adjacent farmland.

The last time there was a flood in the area, a section of the bridge that connects the Miller farm and the town collapsed. It happened only seconds after a school bus full of students on their way home rolled across the bridge. To this day, folks talk about the wall of water that knocked out the bridge and speculate as to what might have happened had the bus driven onto that bridge only a moment later.

Over time, water has worn away at the soft soil that lines the banks of the river and now there are what amounts to steep cliffs on both sides. The height varies from 30 to as much as 60 feet from the surface of the creek to the edge of the banks up above. The river runs along beside the Miller wheat field. It is a popular place for kids to play and splash around in water that is normally no more than three feet deep at the most. Karl has built a rope ladder that hangs from secure wooden posts about six feet from the edge of the drop-off. Few folks in the county, young or old, know how to swim and parents worry about their children drowning, but their anxieties are mollified by the awareness of the non-threatening shallowness of the so-called Lazy River.

The waggoneers climb up behind the horses, gently slap the reins on their backs. The horses react with an instinctive shudder and go to work. The three wagon teams head in different directions and began moving up and down the rows. The first wagon is filled and it returns to the gate and pulls up to the back of the threshing machine, its cylinder turning rapidly in anticipation of the incoming sheaves of wheat. The thresher is attached to the Miller tractor by means of a large rubber pulley that is connected to a power take-off (PTO) drive shaft that extends from the transmission of the tractor. The pulley is responsible for turning the gears of the threshing machine and ultimately turning the cylinder.

As the members of the crew toss the wheat into the feeder, the machine grinds away as the tractor and pulley mechanism chug along with the loud rhythmic sound of *thuck, thuck, thuck*. After the stalks of wheat are ripped to shreds by the sharp teeth of the cylinder, they are thrown into another part of the thresher where the heads of grain fall through a screen and the remaining chaff or straw is blown out the side of the machine and into a pile. It will eventually be used to feed livestock.

The day goes on without incident. Karl studies the grain output and tries to calculate the return in comparison to that of previous years. His sense is that this may be one of the best wheat crops he's ever had. The crew leaves their pitchforks, wagons, and horses behind while they enjoy another noon-time feast, not unlike that of the previous week. As they burp, rub their tummies, and stretch their legs, they return to the task at hand. There is still a lot of wheat to be harvested.

It's mid-afternoon. The heat has taken its toll. The field crew is tired, hot, and sweating. The team working behind Ferd and Dolly stop for a breather. Sonny has come running up with a small bucket of cold water and a single metal dipper that the men take turns sharing. As they are resting, Aubrey Gorman, the man driving the Miller team of horses, steps down from the wagon and tells Karl, "Look, man, I'm sorry, but I've got to leave. My son-in-law is driving in from Troy with a truckload of cattle feed in a little bit, and I need to be there to help him unload it."

Karl reaches out and shakes his hand. "I understand. No problem. But I hope you know how much I appreciate your help. I owe you one."

As Farmer Gorman walks away, Karl turns to the rest of the crew and asks for a volunteer; someone to put down their pitchfork and drive the horses. Before anyone steps forward, Sonny runs up to his dad. "I can do it. Let me do it. Please! Please!" he begs as he gives his father a look of irresistible innocence and affection.

Karl looks down at him as he ponders the request. Karl Jr. knows Ferd and Dolly well. He has ridden both of them from time to time; bareback and moving at a slow speed; nothing like the Kentucky Derby. He has helped rub them down and feed them. The team knows him well.

"Okay. Why not? You're a big boy now. And you know what to do, right? When you want the team to move forward, you slap the reins on their back. When you want them to stop, you pull back on the reins. And when you want them to turn in one direction, you slap the back of the horse on the side you want to turn to."

"I know that, Daddy. I've done it before."

So, with that, Sonny climbs up into a half-full hay wagon, grabs the reins, and smiling in a way that says "look at me", he is ready to go. Moments later, he slaps Ferd and Dolly on their backs and they ramble a few yards forward as the sheaves of hay begin once again flying up over the railings of the four-wheeled, roughly constructed, wooden, hay wagon.

Things go smoothly, in spite of the intense heat from a scorching sun that burns into the exposed skin of the crew. This is not new. This happens every summer, and sunburn is viewed as no more serious than a random tick-bite. The faces and arms of the older men reflect the years of being cooked by a merciless sun—leather-like and weather-beaten. They know it makes them look older than they really are; what they do not know are the long-term effects. In many cases, serious skin cancer will be their reward. But it is a chance they must take; it comes with the occupation.

As Sonny and the team of pitch-forkers move down its fifth or sixth row since he took the reins, the team is headed south, toward the river bank, where it will turn around and head back toward the north and probably to the threshing machine, since the wagon is already nearly full, piled high with the results of the bountiful harvest, a painting-like picture of plenty. Sonny taps the horses on their backs with the leather reins and says something like "Okay, let's giddy-up."

Suddenly, Ferd and Dolly's ears perk up, they bolt, and break into a fast trot, jerking the wagon forward and rolling rapidly toward the edge of the Lazy River embankment. The crew, including Sonny's dad, see what is happening; some holler, "pull back on the reins!" But the horses continue galloping ahead as though in a race with each other. Karl sees what is going on, but is confident the horses will stop when they get close to the drop-off down to the river. They know better. Seconds go by, and suddenly time stands still.

Then the unthinkable happens. Ferd, Dolly, the hay wagon, and Sonny disappear as they sail over the edge of the embankment.

Before the reality of what the men have just seen sinks in, there is a sickening explosion of sound from the riverbed; the sound of metal, wood, and flesh being dashed against the river's sandy shore. Karl watches and listens in horror as he runs toward the river. He is muttering loudly, "Please, Lord, no. Please, Lord no." He dashes toward the rope ladder and starts down, looking down to his right at the heap of horses, shattered wood and scattered wheat stalks. He does not see Sonny.

When he reaches the bottom of the ladder, he runs toward the wreckage in a panic. Ferd and Dolly are still alive, but writhing in pain with what is probably broken legs, perhaps necks. As he climbs over the wreckage, he sees his son lying face-down at the water's edge, held in place by a piece of the wagon's metal frame.

As Karl pulls his son from the water, he is crying in desperation. He keeps muttering "No. No. No." With a horrible premonition of what he is going to find, he reaches for Sonny's neck to check for a pulse. There is nothing there. Knowing not what to do next, he began giving his lifeless son mouth-to-mouth resuscitation. Finally, he gives up, realizing that his beloved and special son is dead. His body goes limp and he falls backward onto the sandy band with Sonny's dead body stretched across his chest. As he stares up into the sunny blue sky, he screams in an agonizing and wordless torrent of anguish. "Absalom, my Absalom!" The sound echoes off the soft-soiled cliffs of the river and into the dispassionate space above him.

Chapter Two
The Rural Community Myth

Crossroads, 1948

The small farming town of Crossroads lies comfortably in the middle of Doniphan County, the most northeasterly county of Kansas. It is located on the south side of Lazy River, less than a mile from the Miller household. It has a population of 110 people; at least it did until old man Gunderson and his wife left and moved to St. Joseph, Missouri, to live out their last years with their oldest son. The Gunderson home, just a block from the center of Crossroads, sits empty and surrounded by a jungle of weeds that threaten to engulf and bury the house, a small clapboard building that is falling apart. It was built probably 40 years ago, just after the turn of the century. There is no "For Sale" sign in the front yard. The Gundersons are old but smart enough to know that no one is interested in buying a house in a place that people are leaving without looking back, like rats from a sinking ship.

The Gunderson story is the story of Crossroads. It was once a small but thriving metropolis. That was in the last century. It was actually founded in the 1860s and named Crossroads because two state roads happened to intersect where the center of the town is now located. The location was also chosen in part because of the proximity to the railroad and Lazy River. From the beginning it was an agricultural community; its economy dependent on the many farms in the area and what they produced, primarily wheat, corn, milo, and livestock.

The town that eventually took shape had a variety of thriving businesses, on or close to Main Street, which ran north and south for about 200 yards from one end of town to the other. There was a bank, a post office, a hardware store, a small grocery store, two taverns, a smithy, a restaurant, a clothing store, s small hotel, a small jail with three separate cells now sitting empty and unused, and a municipal building with offices for the mayor and his staff and a courtroom and judge's quarters, a school, and two churches. There was also a small depot beside the railroad track where people might catch a ride on the train that ran from St. Joseph, Missouri, to Topeka, with multiple stops in-between.

The streets in the town were all unpaved, and with every rain of any size, the streets turned to mud. The only law enforcement in Crossroads at the time was a justice of the peace who had the authority to arrest or detain anyone suspected of breaking the law. Otherwise, the town depended on the police force of nearby Troy. Likewise, they were dependent on the larger community's fire department for help if and when circumstances demanded it. Needless to say, over the years there were many buildings in Crossroads that burned to the ground while locals threw buckets of water on the fire in desperation, waiting for the outside help which invariably arrived after it was too late, just in time to watch the last gray wisps of smoke curl lazily up into the air.

Crossroads grew during the last three decades of the 19th century. By 1900, it had a population of 380 and life was good. When local folks began having automobiles and tractors, Texaco added a gas station to the town's business district. But, as was the fate of many American small towns, Crossroads began a slow decline, hit hard by falling farm revenues, the exit of young people going elsewhere to find work, and the Depression. So now, the town is a skeleton of what it once was. The bank building is abandoned; filled with boxes of paper, blank checks, deposit slips, and other paper scattered throughout the building. The post office is gone. The depot is still here but without function, since the train no longer stops at Crossroads. Some locals joke that their community is the crossroad between nowhere and nowhere.

The school is still here but with less than 100 students, grades one through 12. In 1900, there were 28 students in the graduating class at Crossroads High. Last year there were exactly four members of that class; one was class president, one vice president, another secretary, and the fourth, class treasurer. It's called making the most of what you've got, a basic principle among Kansas farmers.

The downtown area of Crossroads is still alive and well, but in some ways, barely hanging on. Ward's store is still open and selling everything from diapers and toilet paper to canned peas and cheddar cheese. Mr. Ward is getting up in age, but still has a pair of hawkish eyes that make sure no one walks out with things not paid for. On occasion, he will catch kids trying to steal a candy bar or a pack of gum. Rather than call the law, which is virtually non-existent in Crossroads these days, he slaps them around a little bit. Rarely does he get pushback from angry parents. The kids know better than to go home and admit they've been shoplifting.

There's a small hardware store and a bar in downtown Crossroads, Louie's' Tavern, an interesting place. Most of the religious folks in the community see it as a den of iniquity and speculate as to all the shady and seamy things that go on there. Yet, Louis Lombardi, the owner and proprietor, does a booming business; his tavern is rarely at a loss for patrons, drinking adult beverages, smoking, and playing cards. It is likely that there are occasional things that go on there that are not exactly on the up-and-up, like the slot machine that is rigged to take your fifty cents and give you back a quarter.

Louie himself is an enigma. Of obvious Italian descent, he is overweight, swarthy, and loud. No one knows how or why he ended up in Crossroads, but they love to speculate about him and his shady business. He is married and has one son. However, the rumor is that Louie's crotch is devoid of testicles. So, it is said, either his wife did the thing with another man; or jokingly, it is called a case of an immaculate conception.

While locals make fun of Louie behind his back, they are afraid of him. No one would dare call him "ball-less" to his face. It would be safer to jerk a pit bull by its tail. Rumor has it that the legendary tavern-owner beat some guy to death in his younger days while still in Sicily. More recently, what is not a rumor is that late one night while he and his wife were in bed in their apartment upstairs over the bar, he heard someone moving around downstairs. He grabbed his bat and crept down the stairs and saw someone behind the bar, fumbling around with the cash register.

Apparently, the intruder did not hear Louie creeping up on him and before he knew what hit him, the about-to-be "robbee" slammed the intended robber in the back of the head and then, when the guy collapsed to the floor, continued to batter the burglar's torso. Next, Louis dragged the unconscious thief out the front door and left him lying on the street. The next day, Louis called the police in Troy and within 24 hours the intruder had been arrested. The would-be thief eventually served five years in Leavenworth Prison. However, when he got out, he tried to sue Louis for assault and battery, a lawsuit that went nowhere, but it got the tavern-owner a lot of publicity. For these and many other reasons, if you are in Crossroads, you don't want to get on Mr. Lombardi's bad side.

On the other end of the sin-to-righteousness scale, there are two churches in Crossroads—one Methodist, the other Catholic. The Methodist Church was founded in 1872 and a small wooden building with a steeple over the front door was constructed. This was razed in 1915 and a much larger, more impressive brick building was erected in same location. At that time the church boasted a membership of 120. Most of the members were from farming families, like the Millers, and many of them with roots in other Protestant denominations, primarily Lutheran. But, for the latter, the Methodist Church was the only game in town.

The church today has a membership of just over 100. Weekly attendance for Sunday School is about half of that, with perhaps 50 or so attending the main service. The current pastor is a man named Craig Butler, a young man who is working on a seminary degree in Kansas City while living in Crossroads. He and his wife and two sons live in a small wooden frame parsonage that was built in 1880 and now lies adjacent to and west of the church.

Rev. Butler is a heavy-set man, just over six feet tall, with a head of thick black hair. His turquoise eyes are set close together over a large nose that seems to work in his case. Despite his obvious history of acne issues, most would say he was an attractive man. But his real strength is his compelling personality. Everything considered, he seems cut out for the role of Methodist preacher. His deep bass voice rumbles with an impressive authority. His warmth and teddy bear aura make him a comforting counselor and leader. The charisma he exudes not only draws strangers into his circle of friends and congregates, but also works to make people trust him.

Rev. Butler is also a musician who plays the piano and the trombone, and, in addition, charms audiences with his sonorous bass voice. It is thus no surprise that attendance at the Methodist Church has increased since he was named pastor.

The Catholic church is located on the eastern edge of town. It is a small white wooden building that has been there for over 50 years. The priest who serves the small Catholic population in Crossroads lives in Troy and makes only occasional visits to supervise mass and to listen to confessions. Most of the local Catholics actually live within the town limits of Crossroads. There may be one or two farming families that identify themselves as Catholic, but it seems their devotion is not that deep and they rarely attend events at the church in town.

Though not open and outright, there is a strong anti-Catholic bias among Protestants throughout the county. Rumors about the church and its congregants abound. For example, it is said by some that the small church has a lime pit in its basement where the priest brings the bodies of fetuses aborted by nuns in Troy, Atchison, and other larger towns in the area, to be quietly decomposed and forgotten. Some claim they have seen the itinerant priest giving candy and getting way-too-friendly with some of the younger boys in town. They also make fun of their Catholic neighbors for not eating meat on Friday, a bias that makes sense, since cattle and hog raising are basic to the local farming community.

It is speculated that the antipapal attitude in Crossroads is so strong that there is always the possibility of violence or vandalism; that the hatred might lead to something like the torching of the church. Perhaps the only thing standing between the Catholic church and Protestant-based violence is the fact that Louis Lombardi is a papist and the unofficial head of the local Catholic congregation.

The people of Crossroads, indeed across the county, think of themselves as rural, and while they occasionally enjoy the opportunities provided by the bigger cities (e.g., St. Joseph and Kansas City), they see urban communities as lawless dens of iniquity; modern-day Sodom and Gomorrah's.

Crossroads folks are convinced that life in rural America is special. They see cities having easy liquor, strip joints, adult bookstores, prostitutes, drugs, ghettos, and rampant crime. In addition, they believe that cities are the breeding grounds for liberal extremes and godless intellectual elites who corrupt their young by promoting anti-American and anti-Christian ideologies like socialism or communism.

In contrast, the rural folks of Northeast Kansas see their communities as rooted in traditional Christian values and democratic and capitalistic models that the fore-fathers intended America to be. And, because of their commitment to the teachings of Christ, their communities are relatively free of crime, alcohol, or drugs; at least that's what locals want you to believe. If you ask a Crossroads resident if he or she can remember the last time a crime was committed, it is likely they will answer with a story of a reasonably innocent misdemeanor.

Take, for example, the case of the two teenagers who decided to pull a trick on their old-maid English teacher. They hung a dead black snake that was over four feet long above the front door of her house. They knocked on the door and then ran. When the woman opened the door and saw the snake, she fainted dead away and hit her head on an adjacent cadenza, which resulted in a cut to the side of her head and a serious concussion. Fortunately, a passerby saw the wounded teacher lying in front of her open door with the snake still dangling from the frame. The teacher ended up being rushed to the hospital in St. Joe. She survived. The two boys were apprehended and tried as juveniles. They were put on a one-year probation and required to do 50 hours each of community service.

These are the kind of stories you will hear when you ask local residents or farmers who live in the other areas of the county.

My neighbors, they done moved to town;
But me, I plan to hunker down.
While other folks may go, I'll stay
It's cause I love the country way.
Why everyone in these here parts,
They've got the biggest, warmest hearts.
They are so nice, so very kind;
And only their own business mind.
While youngsters prank from time to time,
But here, it's true, there ain't no crime.
Nice clean streets; no urban blight
No need to lock your doors at night.
It matters not, you're poor or rich,
If your old ox be in a ditch,
Your neighbors, they will be right there
To help you out; they really care.
God-fearing, Bible readers we,
Who take religion seriously.
Sundays find us in our pew
And forkin' out them tithes that's due.

Those city types are crass; they're rude;
They lack our moral fortitude.
Left-wing kooks and Jesus haters,
Sinners, drunks and fornicaters,
While we're workin', doin' chores.
They're slammin' doors and bangin' whores
So it is, me and the wife,
Will always choose the country life.

Clyde Miller, December 1947

But what these country folks conveniently fail to remember are the more serious events that fly in the face of the community's glorified self-image. There are the town drunks that can sometimes be found sleeping on a park bench or lying in the street on Sunday morning. There are the occasional hold-ups; thieves with guns robbing businesses and sometimes homes. There is the fact that many of the Crossroads high-school graduates have served time for a variety of offenses: armed robbery, breaking and entering, assault, cattle rustling, and more. Statistically, a greater percentage of the graduates of the local school are convicted of either misdemeanors or felonies than is true of either of the two high schools in St. Joe.

Then, there are the drug problems. As of today, there are at least four individuals in the town who are seriously addicted to heroin. Where and how they get it is a mystery. The other deviant behavior that mars Crossroads' self-image as a model Christian community is spouse abuse. Men beating their wives or verbally assaulting them is widespread among the residents of Crossroads, more so among the townies than among the farmers, although it happens there on occasion. However, it is true that divorce rates in Crossroads and other small towns in Kansas are relatively low, perhaps because residents feel trapped and cannot imagine life without their respective spouses. Also, it seems there is a greater stigma attached to being divorced here than is the case in the city.

The problem is that a large portion of the Crossroads population is made up of unemployed or under-employed individuals who have moved here from somewhere else. In many cases, they have come because housing was cheap.

In fact, some live in homes, like the Gunderson home, that have been abandoned. Without electricity or water, they still survive.

Nevertheless, there is a solid core of good folk who for whatever reason have chosen to live here: merchants, retirees, artists, and commuters who drive to work in adjacent towns or in the city either daily or once a week. Some folks live elsewhere but maintain second homes in Crossroads, spending their summers here while returning to their primary residence during the school year.

Despite what Crossroads citizens might like to imagine, the county's population is socially stratified. There are the drunks, the law-breakers, and the desperately poor who occupy society's lowest rung. Above them are the working-class Catholics who are ranked below the working-class Protestants. In both groups there are men like Pete who work for some form of financial support on a local farm. Next up the ladder are those who own and work small farms and the merchants and professionals. At the top of the pecking order are those, like Karl Miller, who own large farms, and a couple of those folks in town who are deemed wealthy.

Life in Crossroads is not without its entertaining community events. Each summer the carnival comes to town and sets up in the park and along Main Street. There's a Ferris wheel, a merry-go-round, and other riding equipment. There are also various side-shows and booths that allow one to shoot an air gun at a moving target, throw softballs at bottle shaped targets, toss a basketball into the net, take a large hammer and try to ring the bell at the top of the tower. There is cotton candy and other sweets available to all those with money in their pockets. Also, as a way of making money for the church, the Methodists set up a hamburger and hotdog stand in the old abandoned bank building.

Carnival time in Crossroads is in many ways a ritual of reversal, meaning that cultural and religious values are shoved to one side. It's a time when men and women do things they would not do at any point in the rest of the year. Men who do not normally imbibe, drink until their plastered. A couple women who travel with the carnival lure men into their small travel trailers and for 20 dollars they have several organismic options. Normally-very-proper women dress in provocative ways, wear more make-up than usual, and flirt like they were teenagers again. Men and women dance with other men's spouses and single adults. Unexpected liaisons happen. It is not unusual for a married man, a farmer who may be straight as an arrow the rest of the year, to hook up with a woman, single or married. Together, they sneak into the woods on the east side of town and have sex standing up against a large oak tree, quietly and with the understanding that what happens at the carnival stays at the carnival.

Another summer time entertainment option is provided by the community band, a group organized by Rev. Butler. On five or six nights during the summer, the band sets up in the park downtown and puts on a concert made up largely of march tunes. The locals bring their own folding chairs and listen and applause politely to performances that would not cut it in the city, but are enough to entertain small-town and country folk.

Also, on most Saturday evenings in the summer, the mayor sponsors a movie night. A large screen is erected in the middle of Main Street downtown. Folks come in, again with their own seating arrangements, and watch whatever black-and-white film the mayor is able to rent.

There are also church picnics, which along with the other summer events give community and farm folk chances to get together, chitchat, joke, and catch up on the latest gossip. It also gives young people a chance to meet up in liaisons that sometimes morph into serious relationships.

During the winter months community activities revolve around events at the school. Boys' basketball is the only formal, interscholastic sport, and the games draw reasonably large crowds. Then there is the annual cake walk, the major fundraising event for the school. After paying a small entry fee, country and community residents gather in the Crossroads school gym where there is a large folding table laden with a host of lovely, and sometimes artistically, decorated cakes. On a cue from the master of ceremonies, the music starts and attendees begin walking around in an oval path around the basketball court. A different cake is placed somewhere around the oval circle for each procession.

The usual musical performance is Mrs. Butler playing a popular tune like "Nola" on the piano. She plays until there's a signal from the emcee. Everyone stops, and the person standing nearest to the latest cake is the winner. The evening includes musical entertainment: performances by school groups or individuals. For the past few years, the crowd has been entertained by Rev. Butler, in his deep, rafter-shaking voice, doing a special rendition of "Old Man River", accompanied by his wife on one of the school's aging upright pianos.

In short, Crossroads is a small but still reasonably vibrant community. It is shrinking as the number of newcomers cannot keep up with the number of residents dying or moving away. Yet, despite the image it has of itself as a wholesome All-American community relatively free of the sins of its urban counterparts, the facts tell a different story. As is true across most of America, small, farming communities are in no position to be throwing stones. Even though the residents of the greater Crossroads area want to ignore them, the warts are there. And yet, it is hard to be a part of this small farming village and not feel its charm and the sense that it's a world apart. It's hard to believe bad things happen here, but they do. But why do they happen? And that's where, for a simple community, the answers can be amazingly varied and complex.

Chapter Three
Divine Plan or Magic?

The mood at the Miller house is an extension of the weather outside—dark, cloudy, and foreboding. Karl and Thelma have just returned from the funeral home in Troy where they have left the body of their beloved six-year-old son. Thelma cannot stop weeping and muttering softly to no one in particular, "Sonny, Sonny, Sonny." Karl has withdrawn into the silent, rigidly stoic shell that is an integral part of his personality. That moment that he held his dead son's body and fell into the shallows of the Lazy River, the explosion of the heart-wrenching cries of agony expressed all the emotions that were his to express. Even now, he feels empty, drained, as though he will never feel anything again. Quietly, he blames himself, and the guilt exacerbates his sorrow. Still, he cannot bring himself to admit that guilt to anyone, not even his wife.

The Miller girls are in the small bedroom upstairs, the bedroom that they share. They are quiet. They know what has happened but are not sure how they are supposed to react. It seems they are more worried for and about their parents now, than saddened by the death of their brother. Children in many ways are a barometer of their parents' relationship. Perhaps unconsciously, they are more aware of the dynamics of the marriage than the adults realize. Somehow, they sense that the stability of that relationship is tied to their survival; like small, helpless chicks in the nest, when there are signs that mama or papa may not be coming back to fill their hungry mouths, they get nervous.

The last few days have been beyond difficult for the whole family. Amidst her heaving sobs of sorrow, Thelma cannot help herself; she shouts in anger, "Why? Why? Why did you let him drive the team? You knew; you knew he was a child. Why?"

Karl just continues staring at the floor. He is asking himself the same question. He's angry at himself and yet, he remains at a loss to explain how Ferd and Dolly would bolt like that and throw themselves into the emptiness over the edge of the river's embankment. They knew that terrain like they knew the feed trough at the back end of their respective stalls in the barn, where they had spent most of their adult lives. It makes no sense. The grieving father tries to shake himself from the conundrum of confusion that seems to have taken control of his mind. But then, he falls back into the dead-end plight of second-guessing, wishing he could go back and tell Sonny "No". But it's too late and there is no way of freeing himself from the pain, a pain he cannot imagine ever going away.

Dinner time, and two of Thelma's sisters-in-law have come to handle responsibilities in the kitchen. The hostess tries to help, but is gently guided back into the living room. By now, Karl has retired to one of the barns and is doing maintenance work on a rusty harrow, hoping this might divert his attention from the nightmare he is living and reliving.

Pete, who has been silently grieving in his own way, walks past the barn door and sees his boss with his attention focused on twisting a loose bolt into place on a large multi-tine harrow. Unsure as to whether he should interfere or not, he cautiously asks, "Can I help?"

Farmer Miller's reaction is curt and nasty. "No! Get the hell out of here!" he barks, without looking up.

Pete is stunned. He stands there, trying to deal with the shock of the unexpected rebuttal. It seems no one understands that he is also in mourning. He loved Sonny as though he were his own son; he would gladly have taken his place in the plunge over the riverbank. But no one else seems to see that. Unlike the others, he must grieve alone.

Pete turns and goes back to the job of organizing the chaos that was left in the wake of Sonny's death. The threshing machine lies quietly like a resting monster, impotent and helpless; its life dependent on its now silent power source, the Miller tractor, which itself seems wrapped in sadness. Stalks of wheat lie on the ground waiting to be stripped of their grains. The field remains littered with sheaves standing like orphaned produce ready to be claimed. The neighbors who had volunteered to help with the harvest left as soon as they were struck by the reality of the tragedy. To carry on and finish the job would have been to belittle, indeed to sacrilege, the gravity of their friend and neighbor's son's death.

Pete is getting things together, with the assumption that the team of neighbors will return tomorrow to finish the job. While no one has said, he realizes he must take the leadership on this. The man he answers to is obviously incapacitated by sorrow. As he struggles to adjust to a role quite foreign to him, he continues to puzzle over the causes of the fatal accident. He knew Ferd and Dolly probably better than anyone else. He has fed them, brushed them down, talked to them; even slept beside them in their stalls on occasion. They were dear to him and even though he realizes Sonny's life should take precedent over theirs, he mourns them with a similar intensity.

But, why? Why did they not do as they always did; come to the end of the row and stop, waiting the command to turn right or left and onto the next row? It makes no more sense than if one of the feral cats that hangs around the farm started talking to him in Spanish. Impossible. Yet, it happened. The more he ponders this dilemma, the more he is convinced that: one, they were spooked, or two, they were the subjects of witchcraft. Someone with magical powers who envied the Millers for their power, money, and influence cast a spell on the two, ever-faithful drays, and they raced themselves to their own deaths, unaware that they were being driven by the forces of the occult.

But who could have done such a thing? And who is going to believe him? To suggest such a thing may only add to the suspicion that he is not only slow-witted but daft. The crazy hired hand has gone off the rail with a conspiracy theory that makes no sense. Perhaps, but how else can this terrible tragedy be explained? Regardless of the potential consequences, he must tell someone.

*****

Three days have passed since the Millers' idyllic farm life was ripped asunder by an event too terrible to describe, much less explain. Karl and Thelma are at the church, sitting in Rev. Butler's small study. They are here to discuss final funeral arrangements. Services are scheduled for tomorrow. There will be an open casket. The pastor will deliver the eulogy. It will not be easy. Karl Jr. was special and in many ways like a son to Craig Butler and his wife. He was the same age as one of the Butler boys and had spent many a night at the parsonage, while at other times the Butler boys had been the overnight guests of the Millers. Though not formally so, Sonny's death and his interment are Butler family business.

There is little to say about the funeral. The pastor's request, if there is anything in particular they would like him to say about their son, is met with a softly uttered, "We trust you to say the right thing." There are a few moments of awkward silence broken only by the occasional sobbing of the heart-broken woman. Craig feels he should say something, but worries that it might be the wrong thing.

Finally, Thelma looks up and as the tears run in small rivulets down both sides of her nose, she asks the inevitable question, "How can God allow something like this to happen?" She raises her voice as she blurts out in unmasked anger, "He's supposed to be a God of love. How can he do this to us?" Her anger intensifies her crying.

The pastor feels compelled to answer. "Thelma, I can't speak for God. None of us understand his ways. They are beyond our ability to comprehend. But, at the same time, I'm not going to argue that this makes sense. And I'm not going to give you the standard, canned response to your questions about why this happened; that this is part of a larger plan that you will understand someday; or that Sonny is now in a better place. No, Sonny is dead and it makes no sense. As much as it pains me to say it, you have a right to be angry with God."

"Any way you look at this, he let you down. He robbed you of one of your most valuable possessions and he robbed your son of a lifetime; a lifetime of promise; and he robbed this community and the world of the contributions that Sonny was destined to make. Believe me, I'm angry too, and at times like these, I wonder if I'm in the right profession. I should be defending God, but I can't. This whole thing is insane, pointless, and without purpose; and there is not now, or will there ever be an explanation."

At this point, a speechless, foggy-minded, and beaten-down Farmer Miller raises his head and softly asserts. "You're wrong, Craig. There is a reason."

"What do you mean?" the pastor asks with genuine sincerity. Thelma turns her head toward her husband, somewhat surprised to hear him speak, and curious as to what he has to say.

"There's no way Ferd and Dolly would have charged over the embankment like that without something extraordinary occurring."

"What do you mean?"

"I mean someone put a spell on them; caused them to go crazy, out of their heads suicidal."

"Who would do that? Who could do that?" the preacher asks, as Thelma remains transfixed by her husband's outburst.

"A witch; a sorcerer; someone with magical powers and someone who had it in for me."

"Where'd you get this idea?" Craig asks.

"Actually, it was Pete. He's a bit slow and quiet. He's also strange. But he does magic tricks and seems to understand the other world. Anyhow, he didn't say anything to me, but he told one of my brothers what he thought. My brother told me and at first, I thought it was pure foolishness—ole Pete foaming at the mouth again. But, the more I thought about it, the more it made sense."

"Come on, Karl, you don't believe in that witchcraft stuff, do you? That's pure, unfounded, ridiculous superstition. It doesn't explain anything."

"But what about religion?" the desperate farmer responds. "What is different about asking God to do something for you and having a witch cast a spell? They both are in some ways appeals to the supernatural."

"I can't believe you don't understand the difference, Karl." The suddenly defensive pastor responds. "Magic is based on pure, unfounded superstition; religion is based on history and the very real presence of God."

"I'm sorry, Reverend, but I look around here and I don't see God hanging out any more than I see someone next door who has supernatural powers; someone who's probably a lot more real than God."

"Be careful, Karl. You're toying with something really dangerous here. Sacrilege is a deadly sin, and to compare the workings of God with the results of witchcraft is sacrilege at its most dangerous. You may rue the day."

"No, I won't. I can't rest until I figure out why my son had to die. There has to be more to it than pure circumstance. More than simply a part of one of God's strange, unknowable plans. So, if you really want to help me, Craig, then ask your God to lead me to the person behind my son's death; the person who cast a spell on my well-trained draft horses and tricked them into charging headlong into Lazy River."

The now puzzled pastor knows there is no point in trying to dissuade his desperate friend. It is clear he's convinced himself that his son's death is the work of an enemy with the power to affect fate; to actually put a spell on dumb animals and cause them to do things that are in stark contrast to their usual well-trained behavior. Thelma, on the other hand, seems taken in by her husband's explanation. She had not thought of this before, but maybe this is the case. She has heard and believed other stories about witches and their evil ways. So, perhaps Karl is right; they should not be blaming God but rather looking for the evil soul who used his or her satanic powers to end the life of Karl Miller Jr., the intended heir to the family farm and fortune.

*****

The church is packed; the largest crowd since presidential-hopeful William Jennings Bryant came to Crossroads to talk about his plan for midwestern farmers. Standing-room only. The wooden pews are stuffed, hip to hip, shoulder to shoulder, crammed together like passengers on the New York City rush-hour subway. Today, the usual "there's always room for one more" expression has been replaced with "I'm sorry." Children are seated on parents' laps. Men, young and old, are standing at the back of the sanctuary. The crowding is dangerous and were there a fire marshal present, the building would be immediately evacuated.

The air is still and warm, smelling of sweat, dirty shoes, horse shit, and testosterone, with occasional whiffs of cheap perfume, used by some of the farm women in lieu of bathing. The silence tells the story. Sonny's body lies in the open casket in front of the pulpit, dressed like he was on the first day of school the previous fall. The make-up accentuates his angelic face. His perpetual smile belies the solemnity of the occasion yet reminds folks of what the world is missing as a result of his untimely departure.

Rev. Butler steps up to the pulpit. For perhaps the first time in his life, he is suffering stage fright. He knows that there is nothing he can say to heal the wounds of family and friends. He also knows that he cannot use this occasion to promote the Gospel, to use Sonny's death as an opportunity to evangelize. He has seen this many times before, and it is disgusting. He must focus on the deceased. Yet he worries that he will break down emotionally if he talks too much about this amazing little kid whose death has pulled the community together in ways he never would have expected.

So, with an uncharacteristic temerity, he launches into his prepared remarks. "We are gathered here today to remember and celebrate the short but impressive life of Karl Miller Jr. Unlike other boys his age, Sonny was someone who stood apart, was mature beyond his age, and who wreaked with the promise of greatness. And there was a contagious kindness about him. To know him was to love him."

At this point, tears have welled up in the preacher's eyes. His voice cracks. He tries to fight back the show of emotion, but to no avail. He fights the urge to let go and weep; to let his feelings take charge. But after a few moments of awkward delay, he continues. "Today, as we come together to say goodbye to young Sonny Miller, the question we are all asking ourselves is 'why?' Why would God allow a tragedy of this proportion to happen? I wish I knew. I wish I could stand here before you today and tell you that Sonny's death was part of a larger plan; that there was logic behind what has happened. I'm afraid there is no plan; there is no logic; it was a random, senseless event, and none of us will ever know why it happened. We can only mourn our loss and remember this beautiful young boy for who he was and for what he might have become."

Suddenly, without warning, Karl Miller leaps from his seat on the front pew and hollers "Liar! Liar! Liar!" His booming voice reverberates off the walls and ceilings of the crowded church as he storms out the side door and into the hot afternoon. His outburst stuns the crowd. As the reality of what they all have seen begins to settle in, members of the congregation begin looking at each other in disbelief, but also with a puzzlement that seems to be asking "please tell me I didn't see what I just saw."

But just as the audience is coming to grips with the reality of the explosive exit of the departed ones father, the silence is broken by the sudden shaking and shifting of the entire building. The chandeliers sway carelessly back and forth; there are creaking sounds as the pews strain against the bolts that tie them to the floor; members of the congregation slide slowly in one direction and then another. The casket shifts slightly from left to right and then back. There are screams and shouts of terror as the lights go off. The trembling stops and the light that streams through the stained-glass windows bathes the audience in an eerie array of colors.

"What happened?" everyone is asking.

Rev. Butler is as shocked as anyone else in the now structurally compromised sanctuary. Fearful, lest the crowd erupt and stampede toward the exits, his first words are words of caution, "Please, everyone, please remain calm. Everything is okay." Down deep, he knows he is lying. Everything is not okay.

He continues ad-libbing, "I'm not sure what has just happened, but I think we must reschedule this event." He looks at Thelma, making sure she is okay with this. She is staring straight ahead as though she were in a trance. Rev. Butler is confident she is in no condition to approve, or make any decision, for that matter.

"Ladies and gentlemen, the Miller family is grateful for your being here to support them as they say goodbye to their beautiful young son, Karl Miller Jr. But, at this point, they think it best, in the interest of safety, to cut this ceremony short; to be conducted at a later date. So, may the Lord bless each of you. Please be careful and take your time as you leave the building."

Despite his instructions, the crowd panics and people begin pushing and shoving as they funnel through the main door of the church. Fortunately, there is no stampede and no one is injured, but the turmoil of the mass exit only adds to the string of strange events surrounding Sonny's death. Even Craig Butler is beginning to wonder, perhaps Pete was right. Maybe there are forces at work here that exist outside the scope of the natural world; forces that actually compete with the workings of God and his son, Jesus Christ. But who, and why?

Chapter Four
Hormones

The excessively warm Kansas summer is approximately half over. The Millers have buried their son in a quiet, graveside ceremony and are trying to keep their grief from continuing to dominate their lives and destroying their marriage. The tremor that cut short Sonny's funeral did a little damage to the church, the school, and a few other brick and stone structures in the area, but seismologists have not yet been able to explain it. Some, like Karl Miller, see it as one more manifestation of the supernatural powers that lay behind the tragic death of his son.

The spring wheat is in and now in large silos next to the railroad in St. Joe, waiting to be shipped to parts unknown. Farmers across the Midwest have in many areas struggled with drought so that production levels are down, which means prices are up. Karl anticipates a larger-than-usual pay-off this year. Right now, he is debating whether or not to replace Ferd and Dolly and the wagon that was destroyed in the June disaster with another larger wagon and another tractor.

At the moment, the big news is that it is carnival time in Crossroads. The traveling group is rolling into town; by train, by bus, and by truck. A few broad-backed workmen, who double as construction workers and performers or hawkers, are setting up the equipment—the Ferris wheel, the merry-go-round, the kiddy train—and driving large stakes into the ground to tie down the large tents. Some of the local kids are hanging around the now busy, downtown park, watching with palpable anticipation. They can already feel the thrill of the rides and taste the sweet nothingness of the cotton candy.

Two of the Miller girls are among the kids being entertained by the sweating carnival crew. However, the oldest of the three, Marlene, is working with several members of the Methodist Church who are setting up the hotdog and hamburger stand in the old bank building. Marlene is 14 years old and will start the ninth grade at Crossroads school next month. She is, by any measure, a pretty young lady. She has her mother's brunette hair and the body Thelma had when she was young. Marlene has matured a little earlier than most of her peers. She stands at five feet and four inches, which means she will be taller than most of the other girls in her freshman class. Of course, more noticeable than her height is her large, fully developed chest. Already, young men are prone to stare at her and drool, dreaming of burying their faces in the warmth and silky softness of the space between her "large, luscious tits".

Karl and Thelma are aware of Marlene's maturity and sex appeal, but still have a hard time thinking of her as anything but their little girl. They have never talked to her about the "birds and the bees", assuming that growing up on a farm and watching the cows, horses, sheep, pigs, and dogs reproduce is the only lesson their children need. Perhaps, but it is clear in her conversations with her girlfriends that Marlene is still unaware of her body's power and still unacquainted with the ins and outs of human sexual behavior. She thinks of herself as homely and is embarrassed by the obviousness of her large breasts.

It is late afternoon. The bank building has been successfully converted to a refreshment stand and the small team of volunteers is ready to feed the carnival crew and the many locals and out-of-towners who will be working up an appetite as they enjoy the festivities. Marlene, who has been helping out with getting the improvised refreshment stand ready for the carnival, is standing across the street from the park and watching as the "really big show" takes shape. She will be walking home, which is less than a mile from "downtown" Crossroads.

The road crosses the tracks and Lazy River; an easy stroll for a healthy teenager. As she turns to begin her short trek home, a car pulls up beside her and stops. It's Walt Zimmerman in his 1945 apple-red Chevrolet convertible. Walt is an only child. His parents operate a small farm about five miles west of Crossroads. They also have a lucrative chinchilla-raising business that allows them to dote on their son. Walt is nineteen, soon to be twenty, and a junior at Kansas State University, where he is majoring in agronomy and minoring in business administration. He is one of the best-looking young men in the county and one of the few recent graduates of Crossroads High who have gone on to college. Many of the young ladies in the area have a crush on Walt, and giggle among themselves as they swap stories about the handsome young man in the sleek, red, top-down vehicle cruising the streets, showing off, and purposely tugging at their heartstrings.

"Hey. What's up, Miller?" Walt calls to Marlene.

She turns and walks to the passenger side of the car that admiring, often jealous, young men in the area call a "pussy magnet". "Not much," she responds. "And what are you doing here? I thought you'd be home playing with your chinchillas."

"Hah, hah! I'm serious; what are you up to?"

"Well, right now, I'm on my way home."

"You walking?"

"Of course; how else am I going to get there?"

At this point, Walt tips his baseball cap in Marlene's direction and quips in a corny, feigned formality, "Well, my good lady, let me do the honors and give thee a ride to thy destination. Step thou into my carriage and we shalt be on our way."

Marlene laughs and hesitates. This is the first time she's had a chance to ride in Walt's convertible; indeed, the first time she's had a chance to ride in any convertible. Why not?

Walt pushes the door open and Marlene slides into the passenger seat, at this point feeling a bit nervous but also privileged to have been picked up by Crossroads' number one heartthrob. The driver shifts into first gear, shoves the throttle to the floor, and pops the clutch. The eight-cylinder Chevy jerks forward with a roar and a cloud of dust. His passenger giggles with excitement. This is almost as much fun as a carnival ride.

They pull out of town and head west. However, a short distance down the road, they are to turn to the right and head north across Lazy River. But Walt races past the intersection and continues heading west.

"What are you doing?" Marlene hollers over the roar of the engine, the blaring of pop music on the radio, and the wild whoosh of the wind whipping through her hair. "You missed the turn!"

"No, I didn't," Walt hollers back. "I want to show you something!"

"What?"

"Hang on; you'll see. I guarantee you'll like it."

A few minutes later, the car slows and Walt steers gently onto a narrow, grass-covered lane that snakes along the river. Several hundred yards from the main road, the driver slows to a stop, parking under a large tree on a bluff with a scenic view of the gorge and its meandering flow of muddy water. He cuts the engine, but leaves the radio on.

"What are you doing?" Walt's increasingly nervous passenger queries.

"Come on, Marlene. You gotta love this view, the shade, the breeze. It's like heaven, right?"

"Maybe."

Then Walt leans toward his unwary passenger and puts his right hand on her left thigh. "Look, girl, you've got to know I've had my eye on you for a long time; I guess you'd say, I have a thing about you."

Marlene's first impulse is to push his hand away, but the instinctive thrill of being told that she is desirable overrides her common sense.

Walt scoots closer and puts his head on his captive companion's shoulder with his nose in her hair and his lips on her neck. Her earthy, late-afternoon smell is intoxicating. He whispers into Marlene's ear, "You know I really like you, don't you?"

Afraid to move, but warming to the attention of one of the most attractive young men in Doniphan County, Marlene does not respond.

Walt makes his second move. Pulling back a bit, grabbing her head with both hands, he stares her in the eyes and asks, "What if I told you I was in love with you? As far as I'm concerned, you are the most beautiful girl on the planet."

Marlene blushes to the point that she is almost as red as Walt's shiny convertible. She stammers, "I-I-I don't know," as the sound of the Mills Brothers and their *You Always Hurt the One You Love* streams from the radio. Walt continues trying to create a romantic atmosphere and craft a line his young companion cannot resist.

"Come on, sweetheart," he whispers, "you know you wanna kiss me, don't you?"

Marlene pulls her head back with the look of a frightened mouse. She knows she shouldn't, but she also knows she would love it. "Okay, but…"

Before she can complete a sentence, Walt thrusts his face forward and plants his lips on hers. She doesn't resist, but keeps her mouth closed and her lips locked tightly together.

Walt pulls back a few inches and mumbles, "Relax, sweetheart; you can do better than that." This time, Marlene is more receptive and lets her lips part as his press firmly against her slightly open and wet mouth.

"Um. That's more like it." And as he stares into her eyes, he lets his hands roam over the contours of her fully developed breasts. His female companion is becoming increasingly nervous. She is not certain, but thinks she knows where this is going. The question she is asking herself is how she should respond. If she resists, it might make Walt mad and she would lose this opportunity to be his girlfriend. But if…

Suddenly, she realizes her erstwhile lover is unbuttoning her blouse. "What are you doing?" she blurts out as she grabs his hand to stop him.

Walt ignores her reluctance to give him access to a private part of her body. "Come on, sugar," he whispers, "God didn't give you these beautiful things to be kept hidden away. They're like perfect soccer balls that are at their best when they're played with."

And before the innocent young lady realizes what is happening, her new boyfriend has his left hand up under her brassiere kneading one of her fleshy breasts and tickling its nipple. No one has ever touched her like this. She knows this is probably not something she should be doing, but then, it feels good. She senses her body warming up, as though she's blushing all over.

With the deftness of one who has done this before, Walt reaches around to Marlene's back and unhooks her brassiere. It slides off her breasts and settles at the bottom of her blouse just above her waist. The young farm girl has heard of something called "petting" and has the impression that this is something of little consequence; just what teenagers do. She rationalizes and decides not to resist as her male companion continues grabbing at and massaging her chest.

Suddenly, Walt pulls away, slides back to his side of the car, opens the door, strides to the back of the vehicle and opens the trunk. He reaches in and pulls out a large plaid blanket that looks disgustingly nasty, like a family of rats has been nesting on it for months. It smells of the farm. Dragging it behind him, he moves around to the passenger side and opens the door with a command-like invitation, "Let's do this right." He reaches in and pulls Marlene toward him and out of the car.

Together they walk a few feet, Marlene stumbling along beside her insistent lover. Walt spreads the thick, filthy blanket on a grassy area under a large black walnut tree whose fruits have yet to start falling. With forced guidance from Walt, the couple lowers themselves to sitting positions and the "making out" continues. The kissing gets more intense; Walt's tongue explores the inside of his "date's" mouth and saliva is exchanged. All the while, his hand is groping without resistance across Marlene's upper body. Then he lays her on her back, gets on his knees, reaches up under her pleated skirt and pulls down her panties. This unexpected move sends her into a frightened and defensive mode. She knows enough about these things to know this is moving beyond the petting stage. She freezes and lies rigidly in what might be described as a catatonic trance.

By now, Walt's ardor has made him oblivious to the mood of his young victim. He puts his head under Marlene's skirt and licks the inside of her thighs while he runs his hand over her warm belly and through her soft, freshly sprouted pubic hair. He is engulfed with a complex mixture of smells; the scent that reminds him of warm cow's milk, the aroma of Jergen's body lotion, and the earthy smell of the juices that are leaking from between her aroused labia minora. His fingers explore the tightness of her vagina.

Marlene is now terrified. She wants to scream, but can't. What began as a fun ride in a cool convertible with a good-looking young man, has turned into a veritable nightmare. She wants to ward off her attacker and push him away, but the fear is constraining her. He might turn violent and really hurt her.

Walt backs away from between her legs and pushes himself up onto his feet, standing at Marlene's feet and facing her. In what seems like seconds, he undoes his belt, unzips his Levis, and lets them fall to his ankles. Then, smiling at his quietly horrified companion, he slowly slides his jockey shorts to his knees, exposing his rock-hard and throbbing penis. For a few seconds, Marlene's fear turns to curiosity. This is the first time she's ever seen anything like this. Until now, the only penis she has seen is that of her only brother. But this thing? Amazing and interesting.

But as Walt drops to his knees and scoots up between her legs, the realization of what is about to happen provokes a different emotion, and she begins to cry. The young man who is about to mount her and rob her of her virginity sees the tears, but selfishly reads them as an invitation to greater intimacy, rather than the sign of horror and emotional pain. As he lowers himself onto her body, his privates rub against her tummy and between her legs. As Marlene grits her teeth and awaits the painful thrust of Walt's engorged manhood into her wet but not-ready-for-love private parts, she is startled by his sudden, explosive grunt as he collapses with all his weight onto her rigid body and trembles like a horse shaking off a stinging horsefly. Her first thought is that he is having a seizure. Then she feels a warm wetness across her stomach. She assumes with disgust: *this guy has just pissed on me*. Based on her limited knowledge of intercourse, this assumption makes sense.

As Walt recovers from his premature ejaculation, he pushes back and up off his would-be lover's body. He stands up and awkwardly pulls up his shorts and his blue jeans. Marlene sits up and begins dressing herself and getting her clothes back in place. As she pulls her panties on, she rubs her hand across her lower belly and feels the sticky liquid of Walt's semen and realizes what has happened. She has heard the older girls in town talking of how boys sometimes "shoot their wad". Right now, she is feeling ashamed, used, violated, and yet fortunate. Thanks to Walt's over-anxiousness, she is still a virgin.

Walt tosses his blanket into the trunk. They climb into the bright red "pussy magnet". He turns the key and starts the engine, but before he shifts into gear, he looks at Marlene and says, "I hope you won't tell anybody about this."

She does not respond as she sits with her head down and staring at the rubber mat on the floorboard.

Walt raises his voice, "You understand, right? You don't tell anyone. No one!"

Marlene answers with a slight, almost imperceptible nod.

"Listen, I'm telling you, if you talk about this, bad things might happen. Remember what happened to Sonny."

This veiled threat jerks Marlene out of her stupor. She whirls in Walt's direction and barks, "What do you mean?"

"You know what I mean. We have our ways."

"Why did you say that about Sonny?"

"Because I want you to be careful, you know; don't say anything about what just happened."

"But why did you have to bring up what happened to my brother?"

"Look. I've said all I'm going to say about that. But I remind you; you better keep your mouth shut."

With that, Walt pulls away from the secluded parking space and drives back toward town and then north to the Miller farm. He steers his fancy convertible into the driveway next to the large, two-story white-frame house. Without a word, Marlene gets out of the car and walks to the front steps and through the front door. She is hoping to get to her bedroom and into the shower before running into one of her parents. But before she can get through the living room and to the steps upstairs, her mother shouts from the kitchen, "Marlene.

Where have you been? I thought you'd been home earlier. I hope you haven't been hanging out with that carn-evil crowd."

"No, Mom. Don't worry. I haven't."

"So how did you get home?"

"I walked."

"Now, don't lie, dear. I saw you get out of that Zimmerman boy's fancy car."

"Well, I started walking, but he stopped and offered me a ride."

"You sure you're all right? You look a little messy, like you've been in a fight."

"No, Mom. I just had to do some heavy work while we set up things at the bank; carrying boxes, moving chairs, you know. And it was hot, really hot."

"Well, go freshen up and get back down here. I need your help in the kitchen."

*****

Several days have passed since Marlene's misfortunate encounter with Walt Zimmerman. She cannot seem to think of anything else. The affair has left her feeling dirty and it's a dirt she can't seem to wash away. Even though her assailant warned her against telling anyone about what happened, she feels she needs to talk to someone about it; get it off her chest and get the nasty taste out of her mouth and move on.

The carnival is in full swing. Marlene walks into the bank building where several members of the Methodist Church are busy waiting on customers. Her pastor's wife, Mrs. Butler, Lois, is standing by the portable electric grill tossing burgers. When she sees Marlene, she waves her spatula. "Well, hello young lady. Could I offer you a genuine Methodist hamburger or perhaps a Methodist hot dog?" They chuckle.

But, somehow, there is more to the exchange. The chemistry is there. Marlene feels it. At this moment, she knows she has to talk to the preacher's wife who is also one of her mother's best friends. She knows she can trust her. So, she walks up to the smiling woman wielding the spatula and with an air of obvious sincerity, blurts out a plea for help. "Mrs. B., I need to talk to you."

The preacher's wife sees the desperation in Marlene's demeanor and immediately turns to another woman who is working to keep their customers fed. "Can you take over, Jan? Thank you, honey. I've got to take care of something." She pulls off her apron and walks up to Marlene. "Okay, sweetheart, what's the matter?"

The troubled teenager says nothing but points to the front door and nods in that direction. Lois follows her outside. They find an empty park bench and sit down together.

"Okay," the older of the pair asks, "do you want to tell me what this is all about?"

Marlene sits quietly for a few moments, not sure how to proceed. Finally, she tells her the whole story, every sleazy detail. Mrs. Butler listens carefully, but by the time the entire tale has been told, she is in tears, "You poor girl. This should never have happened. I'm so sorry. Marlene. Marlene. You poor girl." Her sympathy is genuine, not like that she feigns when a sloppy, overweight, and smelly farm wife comes to her complaining that her husband is not showing her enough attention.

As she wipes her eyes, she puts her arm around her young confessor's shoulder and continues, "I know he told you not to tell anyone, and I can see why. This is a multidimensional crime: sex with a minor; statutory rape, sex abuse… But you must say something. I like Walt, but he has crossed the line here and justice must be done. He did it to you and he will do it to other young women."

"But, I'm afraid."

"Afraid of what?" The pastor's wife asks.

"That when people find out, they will see me as spoiled goods. No decent boy out there is going to want to date me. I will be ostracized. Even my closest friends won't want to have anything to do with me. And what if Walt says I asked for it; that I did things that made him want to do what he did? I don't think I could handle that."

"Listen, Marlene. No one is going to think the less of you for what happened. None of this is your fault. You were abused by a cruel and thoughtless young man who must pay for what he's done to you."

"But I wasn't actually raped, you know. He put his fingers in me, but didn't, you know? So I guess I'm still a virgin. You know what I mean, don't you?"

"I do, but that does not lessen the seriousness of what he did. It was only an accident that kept him from hurting you and stealing your virginity."

"So, what should I do?"

"Let's start with your giving me permission to speak to your mother. I think she and your father are the ones who need to decide how they handle this. I'm confident they'll do the right thing. After all, you're their daughter, and anything they do will be done with your best interests at heart. I promise you; everything is going to be fine."

"Okay."

Lois turns toward Marlene, wraps her arms around her, and whispers in her ear, "Everything is going to be okay. I love you. We all love you."

*****

The next morning, Lois Butler knocks on the front door of the Miller home, unannounced but certain she is doing the right thing. Thelma answers the door. Her hair is in curlers and she is garbed in a flowered housedress and an apron tied around her waist. She is surprised to see her friend at this hour of the morning, but senses something must be wrong. "Good morning, Lois. But what's up?"

The pastor's wife is dressed in a pair of washed-thin pair of green slacks and a faded yellow blouse. Her hair is tied up in a bun and partially covered with a small green scarf. It is clear she is not planning to make a public appearance. She gets right to the point. "Thelma, I've got to talk to you. I wouldn't drop in on you like this, but it's important."

With a look of bewilderment on her face, the farm wife invites the preacher's wife inside. The latter hesitates and suggests, "I think it would be best if we just sit out here on the porch, alone. What I have to say is for your ears only."

Still with a look of mild puzzlement, Thelma shuts the front door and points to the porch swing. Lois pushes herself up on the swing while her hostess sits in an upright wooden chair beside her, both of them facing west into the cattle barn across the road and beyond. The wooden floor of the porch is dark with age and stained with blotches of chicken shit. The morning breeze is pleasant, bringing with it the smells of the farm; a combination of animal droppings, pine bushes, freshly turned earth, and chemical fertilizer.

"What is Karl up to this morning?" the unexpected visitor asks.

"He and Pete are out there somewhere," Thelma points toward the west, "repairing a fence and dealing with an unhappy neighbor."

"What happened?"

"Apparently, some of our herd found its way through or over the fence and spent the night wreaking havoc on Oscar Riley's cornfield."

"So what do you do in cases like this?"

"Well, there's an unwritten rule among farmers. It is a given that things like this are going to happen. So, when they do, you do the neighborly thing and find some way to compensate any losses that may have been suffered. I'm not sure, but I suspect Karl will give Oscar one of the calves from this year's crop. That should settle matters, but if not, they will find a way. They have to, because farmers must, whenever possible, put cooperation ahead of competition. Regardless of how large or small your farm, you depend on each other. It is the ethic we live by, even though there are sometimes farmers who chose to ignore the rule and refuse to cooperate. I guess you could call them 'isolationists'. That's their right, but it's not smart; it's like driving a new car without insurance."

Thelma interrupts her commentary on farm ethics to ask, "Can I get you some coffee, Lois?"

"No thanks. I've had my two-cup quota for the morning. And, to be honest, I'm anxious enough about what I have to tell you; coffee would only make it worse."

"Wow! Okay! Maybe you better tell me what's on your mind."

The preacher's wife leans toward her friend. She hesitates for a moment, as though making sure her words sound more like professional advice than idle gossip. "It's about Marlene."

"What about Marlene?"

"She came to me the other day. I was working at the burger stand in the old bank. She said she needed to talk to me. I could tell she was really upset and needed for someone to listen. I dropped what I was doing. We found an empty park bench and she told me her story."

"Her story? What story?"

At this point, Lois reaches out and puts her right hand on Thelma's leg. "It's about something horrible that happened to her last week."

"What!"

The bearer of bad news launches into Marlene's story. Her friend and hostess sits with her mouth hanging open and staring in disbelief, as though in a state of shock. At several points, she mutters a soft "Oh, no. Oh no."

By the time Lois brings the narrative to a close, both of them are crying openly.

As she wipes the tears from her wet cheeks, Thelma admits, "I saw her when the Zimmerman boy brought her home that day and she looked disheveled and distraught, but she blamed the work she was doing in preparation for carnival week. Oh my God, my God. Poor girl. My sweet Marlene. Look, Lois, I appreciate your telling me, but now I wonder what I should do."

"Well, I'm not a lawyer, but I know that having sex with a minor, statutory rape, and sexual abuse are punishable crimes; not just misdemeanors, but serious felonies. So, like I told Marlene, something must be done or Walt will keep this up and other young women are going to get hurt."

As she stares out toward the cattle barn, still struggling to get her arms around the reality of what she has just heard, about what has happened to her oldest daughter, Thelma mutters, "I have to tell Karl, but I dread it."

"Why?" Lois asks rhetorically. She has a pretty good idea how the country's unofficial godfather will react. It won't be pretty. This on top of Sonny's death, which is still an unsolved mystery for him, believing the person behind that death is still out there somewhere evading their deserved justice. It eats on him like a perpetual stomach ulcer.

"You know Karl," is all Thelma will say. After a few moments of reflection, she adds, "Poor Marlene. I can't imagine what she is going through. I must talk to her right away. She spent last night with a girlfriend but should be home soon. I must talk to her."

Before Lois can get in another word, the farmer's wife leaps to her feet and heads for the front door. The well-intentioned informant sits for a few minutes, but realizing there is little more she can do or say now, gets up, steps off the porch, and heads for her car.

*****

Later in the day, Karl has come back to the house for lunch. The girls have already eaten and are outside playing games and enjoying the unusually pleasant July afternoon. As he and Thelma sit down together to eat, as has been the case almost every day since Sonny's death, they say very little to each other. But today, that silence is broken. His wife tells her husband the story of their oldest daughter. Before she finishes with the last detail, he reacts.

Karl leaps up out of his chair. "I am going to kill that bastard!" he shouts as he heads for his gun rack. "That slimy little son-of-a-bitch is gonna rue the day he was born and wish he'd never even seen my daughter!"

"Karl. Karl. Please. Calm down. I think we've got to let the law handle this," Thelma pleads.

"The law; what law? You know what will happen. The Zimmerman kid will lie; say that Marlene seduced him; that she wanted it and that what happened was her fault. Eventually, he'll get off with at best a slap on the wrist. I can't let that happen."

"So, what are you going to do, Karl? You can't just go over there and put a bullet in Walt's head. That would be premeditated murder, and you would spend the rest of your life behind bars. I don't think you want that."

Karl returns to his seat at the table, holding a rifle in his left hand. He stares out across the yard, thinking about how he should handle this. A few moments go by, then he jumps out of his chair and heads outside. "I need time," he grunts as he slams the door behind him.

*****

It's six o'clock in the evening. A car pulls up in front of the Zimmerman home. The driver turns off the engine and the five occupants climb out into the late-afternoon air. Karl Miller, with a baseball bat in his right hand, walks across the yard and up to the front door of the house. Pete and one of Karl's brothers hurry around to the back of the house. The other two men, another Miller brother and a neighbor, stand in the front yard, waiting to deal with whatever happens.

The aggrieved father knocks on the door, gently, so as not to spook his prey. Mr. Zimmerman gets up from the family dinner table and opens the door. Cluelessly, he greets his fellow farmer with a friendly, "Hey, Karl." It is obvious he has no idea what has happened.

"I'm here to see your son."

"My son? Walt? Why?"

"I'll explain later," Karl says politely, trying hard not to show his anger and put his neighbor into a defensive mode. "So, could you go get him and bring him out here? It's important."

Meanwhile, Walt hears the exchange at the front door and realizes immediately what this is about. Without a word, he jumps up from the dinner table and races out the backdoor in an effort to escape confronting the father of the young lady he abused. But, having anticipated this move, Pete and Karl's brother are waiting and grab him before he can get away. They drag their prey around to the front of the house as he struggles and screams, "I didn't do anything! Let me go! What do you think you're doing. You can't do this!"

His captors remain silent.

Karl steps off the porch, followed by Walt's confused and concerned father. He walks up and looks Walt in the eye. "You raped my daughter and I should kill you. But if I did that, you would not have time to think about and regret what you did when you took advantage of a 14-year-old GIRL!"

"No! No!" Walt screams. "I don't know what you're talking about!"

"Oh yes, you do, you worthless little piece of shit. You raped my oldest daughter and you know it," Karl growls as he grips Walt's shirt collar and pulls his face up under his.

"I didn't rape her. She wanted it. She was asking for it."

With that, Karl's big right hand lets the baseball bat fall to the ground and slams, with a resounding 'smack', the front-left side of Walt's face with his huge fist. The blow splits the culprit's lip and blood begins trickling down over his chin.

Walt's father is now pulling at his son and begging the band of vigilantes to leave his son alone. "Look," he cries, "if my son has done something like this, I will make sure he's punished; really. Please, don't hurt him."

Meanwhile, the wife has come outside and standing on the porch watching the drama unfold. She is holding a dish towel over her mouth and looking on in horror, instinctively anticipating what is soon to happen to her only child.

Seeing his wife, the father is emboldened and hollers, "You do anything, and we're calling the law; I'm sure the sheriff is not going to stand by and let you hurt my son."

Karl turns to Mr. Zimmerman. "Why don't you do that? The sheriff would be happy to arrest and put the cuffs on this sorry-ass bastard you call a son.

The charges, for a starter: statutory rape, sex with a minor, sexual abuse, assault and battery... So, yeah, go ahead and get the law out here."

The protesting father backs off a step or two, not certain now what to do or say. Karl has had it with him and tells him in a way everyone knows he means business, "You and your wife, go back in the house, NOW! Do you understand? This is between your son and me. So get out of my face before we decide to hurt you!"

Reluctantly, Farmer Zimmerman backs away, walks slowly toward the porch and up the stairs, grabbing his wife's arm and retreating into the living room of their small two-story frame house. The husband watches the action through the front window; the wife cannot bear to watch and sits on the couch, holding her head in her hands and sobbing.

The oldest of the Miller brothers reaches down and picks up his baseball bat and orders Walt to lie down on the ground. He refuses and tries to spit in his captor's face. Bad idea. In seconds, Karl's bat slams into his daughter's abuser's knees and he screams in pain as he sinks to the ground. As he lies there groaning and sobbing, his judge and prosecutor makes sure the spoiled little college boy knows what is happening, and why. "We could have you arrested and thrown in jail where you'd rot away for years. The courts don't fancy men who sexually assault children. But, we're here to save you from that. We are going to beat you till you hurt so bad you'll wish you were in prison. You'll probably pass out before we're finished, but you and your broken body will long remember this day and you'll regret forever that you ever met my daughter. This is my way of seeing that justice is done."

Walt continues to groan and whimper. Karl slams the bat across the young man's back and the beating begins. He is kicked and beaten until he passes out. The attackers deliberately avoided hitting him in the head. The goal is to put him in the hospital and leave him crippled, perhaps for life—not kill him.

After the damage is done, Karl shouts, "That's enough."

Nothing else is said. They walk back to the car, get in, and drive away. As they drive away, they see Walt's parents come racing out the front door and to their son's side. The mother kneels down beside her unconscious son, stroking his lifeless body and repeating, "Oh Walt. Oh Walt. My boy. This is not right." Then she looks up at her husband and hollers angrily, "Why didn't you do something? Stop them? You're his father. You're supposed to protect him!"

The father sees that as a question so idiotic that it does not deserve an answer. He is much less emotional than she, even though what has happened angers him to the point of wanting to go after Karl Miller with a gun. But he also is not happy with his son. He realizes Walt brought this on himself. In some ways he deserved it. He has brought shame on the family.

The father turns and walks back into the house and calls the EMT from the nearby town of Troy. An ambulance arrives within the hour and Walt's limp, bruised, bloody, and broken body is taken to the emergency room at the Troy hospital. The mother and father following their own vehicle.

As they sit and anxiously await the doctor's prognosis, questions are asked. But, the Zimmermans are afraid to tell the real story, claiming that their son was injured when their cattle herd had stampeded and stormed over him before he could get out of the way.

As soon as they are by themselves in the waiting room, Mrs. Zimmerman begs her husband to tell the truth and turn the matter over to the police. He, however, knows that it might make matters even worse for his son, given the uncertainty as to how the matter might play out in court. He also realizes down deep that they have been too lax in raising their son, giving him everything and demanding nothing in return. And finally, most importantly, he does not want to go to war with the most powerful man in the county.

Walt is in the hospital for a week and, as might be expected, he is nothing like the handsome young man he was when that week is over and he is released. While his face is intact, the rest of his body is not the same. While the bruises and the pain may eventually go away, the broken and cracked bones, even though they heal, will limit his mobility for the rest of his life. As Karl predicted, he will forever rue the day he took advantage of his 14-year-old daughter. Justice done.

Chapter Five
Witchcraft and Sorcery

It is said that farmers and farming communities are more superstitious than folks who live in cities. And it makes sense. Afterall, farmers are dependent on or victims of so many unpredictable events or conditions; drought or too much rain; insect infestations; plant diseases; animal illness; wind; ice storms; or personal illness or injuries that limit the farmer's ability to keep up with the work that needs to be done in order to pay the bills and feed his family. In many ways, the life of the farming family is a crap shoot. A good crop, a good price for livestock, a surplus of marketable produce: means money in the bank and a vacation in Florida. A poor crop, low-ball prices, a garden destroyed by grasshoppers and potato bugs, *ergo*, no money in the bank, numerous unpaid bills, and no vacation.

The story is told of a daughter of a Kansas farmer coming home from school one day excited about a poem she'd been required to memorize. The proud mother insisted she recite it that night at the dinner table. The poem: William Ernest Henley's *Invictus*. The young lady finished the last lines with a poignant emphasis:

It matters not, how strait the gate,
How charged with punishment the scroll,
I am the master of my fate;
I am the captain of my soul.

The father joined the others in clapping for the performance and then quipped, "I tell you what. Whoever wrote that poem weren't no farmer."

In dealing with the uncertainties of a farming economy, what options does the farmer have? He may get on his knees and ask God for help, knowing that help may or may not be forthcoming. In all cases, there must be an explanation. Things happen or do not happen for a reason. But those reasons are not always readily knowable; at least not to human beings, who are, after all, just that—human beings.

But there are superhumans that exist in a semi-supernatural world who have the power to reshape or interrupt the natural course of nature. And, sometimes they work through real people; real people who have extraordinary powers. In the eyes of many farmers in the greater Crossroads area, there are witches and there are sorcerers. Witches are real people who can be good or bad and may use black or white magic, depending on their intent; beneficent or evil. Witches can fly, they can levitate, they can take on the look of any person they wish. They can put curses on people or they can heap blessings upon them. And evil witches can be put to death.

Being a witch in Northeast Kansas is an unofficial capital offense, at least in the eyes of those who believe witches exist. The problem is that it is difficult to discover who among the many people in the area are witches. And in the hunt to make that discovery, one must be careful. For accusing someone of being a witch is a dangerous thing, because if they are bona fide witches and fear they may be outed, they can do horrible things to their accuser. Or, if they are not, real witches in the area may be offended by your attributing their deeds to an ordinary person and then take out their anger at being offended on you, themselves. Either way, calling someone a witch, despite what evidence you might have, is a dangerous enterprise, and sensible people leave it alone.

At the same time, there have been persons in the county who had achieved such notoriety that they openly bragged about being a witch, knowing that ordinary people were too afraid of them to bring charges against them. It's an accepted paradox in these parts. A witch is vulnerable and can, theoretically, be put to death for being a witch, unless and until that witch establishes a reputation that frightens even the most zealous of witch-hunters.

Sorcerers, on the other hand, cannot be divided into good and bad. Everything they do is evil—the devil's work. Sorcerers in the greater Crossroads area are considered the scum of the earth and a continuing threat to the health and well-being of every normal human being who lives and works here. And, like witches, sorcerers can be indicted and convicted of their evil deeds and then punished, most likely by execution, at least theoretically. The so-called laws that govern the treatment of known or self-confessed sorcerers are not actually codified in writing. They are simply principles passed from generation to generation as a part of oral history that carry with them the same authority as that of written law; again, among those who believe. And there are and have been many of those.

Not that long ago, the county, indeed the whole Northeast Kansas area, was hit by a devastating plague of mad-cow disease. Every farmer in Doniphan County lost his herd, except one, a fellow named Polinsky who was a first-generation Ukrainian-American and still not fluent in English. His two children found themselves often having to translate and interpret for their monolingual father. When it was discovered that his cattle had remained untouched by the epidemic, red flags went up all over the county. Why? It was true; the guy was strange. He spoke a funny language and seemed to be a loner, without friends, without church affiliation, and with only minimal participation in or contribution to community events. Rumors flew, and soon farmers across the region had the answer. Polinsky was a sorcerer and had rained down the terror of mad-cow disease on all the other farmers in the area in order to ensure that he got a phenomenally good return when he took his cows to market later in the summer. As the rumor spread, so too did the anger.

Finally, under the leadership of the head of the local cattleman's association, a mob was assembled, although the participants claimed it was simply a peaceful protest, and it descended on Mr. Polinsky's modest farm house. Fortunately, the family was forewarned and had left. The angry farmers searched the home. The only thing they found was a witch's tall black, pointed hat that was stored along with other Halloween paraphernalia. It turned out it was several sizes too large for a child's head; the assumption then was that this was part of Sorcerer Polinsky's professional get-up. After the search for evidence was completed, one of the "protesters" set fire to the house and it burned to the ground. Fearing for his life, Mr. Polinsky went to the sheriff in Troy and asked to be locked up for a while in order to protect himself from his neighbors' wrath.

So, the haplessly accused victim was put into protective custody, which was fine until the original mob found out. This time they assaulted the jail, overpowered the one guard, and pulled Polinsky out of his cell, dragged him across the street from the jail, and hung him. Then they left him there with a sign hanging from his neck with the scribbled words: "Sourcers [sic] are not Welcome Here."

Needless to say, the sheriff looked into the matter, but to be fair, every one of the men in the mob would have to have been charged and then be proven guilty. It was not worth the effort. The case was dropped, despite the outcry from the Polinsky family.

The lynching is something everyone, including most members of the mob, would like to forget. But, many of them still believe that they were right; that Polinsky was a wicked sorcerer and used his supernatural powers to interfere with the lives of his neighbors.

The belief in a mysterious otherworld with witches and sorcerers persists. One of the signs of this is the fact that most of the people in the greater Crossroads area, in particular the farmers, do not feel fully dressed if they are not carrying their favorite amulet or good-luck piece. For many, this is a rabbit's foot that is usually carried on a keychain. Some have special coins, a small smoothly finished piece of quartz, a horse-hair lariat or an "Indian arrowhead" they may have found in a recently plowed field. Ladies tend to prefer four-leaf clovers. Most of them have a healthy supply of these, carefully pressed and dried, and left in a book, often the family Bible. In addition, there are things like a horseshoe hanging over a barn door.

One German family, recently having moved to Crossroads from Pennsylvania, have what they call barn stars mounted over all their barn doors. And then there are bits of clothing that must be worn on certain occasions. When Karl Miller wants to ensure that his day goes well, he dons his old K-State cap, which was once a deep purple, but not having been so many washings it looks almost white, with a light tint of purple remaining. Karl still believes that had he been wearing his lucky cap on the day of Sonny's death, things might have turned out differently. But, for some reason, that day he opted for an old straw hat that he had found lying in his front yard. When no one came by to claim it, he concluded that fate had intended for that hat to be his.

Most family and friends who have chosen to live in the city, find the beliefs and superstitions of the farm folk they left behind silly and a terrible waste of spleen and energy. They are usually kind in their ribbing, but the true believers see it as one more difference between the farm life and life in the big city. If you are a "townie" you really cannot understand what it is like to be a farmer and cope with the myriad uncertainties that complicate their lives.

Often, they tell stories of witchcraft and sorcery that they have seen or heard about. One of the favorite tales of the supernatural at work in the real world is that of a basketball game, several years ago. Crossroads High was hosting a team from Atchison. It was a close game and with only seconds to go, Crossroads had a one-point lead. The other team had the ball at their end of the court and one of their players, the only black player on either team, slung the ball from about as far away as he could have been from the bucket. The ball skyrocketed into the air, bounced on the foul line at the other end of the court, caromed upward, and "swooshed" through the basket just as the final buzzer went off. Crossroads High lost the game.

However, the next day, some of the Crossroads parents decided to look into this "miracle" shot, convinced that it would have been impossible without some form of magical assistance. It turns out the black boy who made the amazing shot was an immigrant from Swaziland. Missionaries had helped his family resettle on a farm just outside of Atchison. This is all the angry parents needed to know. The suspicion was that the boy's mother was most likely a voodoo witch and had put a spell on the basketball that night causing it to find its way into the bucket on the Crossroads end of the court just as the clock signaled the end of the game.

A couple of players on the Crossroads team told the investigators that they had seen her rubbing some stones together and chanting in a language they did not understand. That was it. The next day, the parents went to the school superintendent, told him their story, and demanded that the game be forfeited by the winning team and played again. This time, they would keep their eyes on the strange black kid from Swaziland.

The superintendent and the school board took the complaints seriously, and the game was replayed. This time, Crossroads lost by 15 points. There was still talk of witchcraft affecting the outcome, but the hometown team in many ways defeated itself with turnovers, missed shots, and stupid fouls. No one protested the results, but at the same time, no one has forgotten how their boys were defeated by the miracle shot that could only have been made by the supernatural.

*****

Two months have gone by since Karl Jr. plunged to his death over the edge of the steep embankment and into the Lazy River gorge. The father remains convinced that this tragic accident did not just happen; it was not an accident; there had to be witchcraft behind it and there is someone out there who knows this and is responsible for Sonny's death. It has to be a person who hates him, perhaps a person who is jealous of his wealth and power, or someone with powers they use at random, finding satisfaction in destroying peoples' lives, ruining their crop, or sickening their entire cattle herd.

He has wondered if Pete were behind this. Afterall, Sonny has often talked about how he could do magic tricks; with cards, with coins, with sticks. He was convinced that Pete was a magician and then, quite possibly, a witch. The things he did could not be explained by ordinary means. They had to be supernatural. But, Sonny reasoned, if Pete were a witch, he was a white witch; a good one; who only did fun things or good things for people. Nevertheless, Karl continues to suspect Pete. It was obvious his hired hand had a way with Ferd and Dolly. He knew them better than anyone else and was capable of making them do anything he wanted. What if he had spooked the two of them that day; making them do something they would never do under normal circumstances; pull the hay wagon over the edge of the river bank and plunge to their deaths.

Then there's the woman in Atchison, the mother of the black basketball player. The person who emigrated from Swaziland last summer, who speaks Swahili most of the time. It is still widely believed that she was a voodoo artist in her home country. The missionaries who engineered their moving to the United States insist that voodoo is the work of the devil, and that when the family members converted to Christianity the Lord forgave them for their past sins and the wife, who once may have been considered a witch, has put that life behind her and is no longer doing the work of the devil. But Karl still remembers the basketball game whose outcome could only be explained by the work of evil forces beyond the control of ordinary people.

But, even if she had the powers of the occult, why would she target him and his son? Perhaps it was because he was head of the Crossroads school board and one who voted to support the superintendent when he proposed forfeiting the game, because he was convinced that the final moment of the game was orchestrated by evil powers, not fate.

He has discussed this with Thelma and with Rev. Butler. He has been seeing his preacher in a counseling relationship for some time. The preacher is pleased that Karl would confide in him this way, but feels he is being used; spending many hours of unbillable time with a member of his church whom he really likes as a friend, but is not comfortable seeing as a patient. Also, these sessions seem to be going nowhere. Despite the clergyman's advice and his efforts to make his erstwhile patient understand that there is absolutely no evidence that witches exist, Karl continues to cling to the idea that his son's death was the result of occultic forces put into play by someone who wanted to hurt him.

Just this past year, a couple of middle-aged sisters moved into Crossroads. They decided to rent an abandoned building on Main Street and turn it into a hair salon. Barbara Creighton has a two-year degree in cosmetology. She has also completed with a few basic business courses. When her old aunt told her she was leaving Crossroads to move into a retirement community in St. Joe, Barbara convinced her to let her have her house; one of the nicer homes and yards in Crossroads, but again, not one that would be easy to move.

Now Barbara and her sister, Estelle, are living in their old aunt's house while Barbara tries to stir up business for her salon. As it happens, Estelle is not right in the head; by any definition she is "retarded" and arguably crazy. Like her sister, she is reasonably attractive, but is a brunette; Barbara is a natural blond. Estelle has blue green eyes that constantly dart from one subject to another. And, she is always talking to herself; at least that is what it seems. In the heat of the summer, she puts on a heavy fur coat and wanders around town mumbling in a language few can understand. She is frequently the butt of jokes or pranks orchestrated by boys in town with nothing better to do.

Once, the Butler boys killed a large black snake, almost six feet in length. They saw Estelle coming down the sidewalk in front of their house, so they climbed up into a large maple tree whose branches spread out over the walkway in front of the parsonage. As she walked under the tree, they dropped the dead snake, which fell neatly across Estelle's right shoulder. She kept walking and talking to herself. The snake eventually slid down her back and on to the ground. She never had a clue. Sometimes young pranksters would stop her on the street and tell her that someone, usually in a house close by, was going to give her and her sisters a lot of money; all she had to do was knock on the door and ask. Which she did, while the boys were crouched down in the background, laughing raucously as they watched the awkward and confusing conversation.

One time, on a Halloween night, the Butler boys were dressed for trick-or-treating, the older as a scar-faced monster; the younger as a rabbit; a scary face versus an innocent bunny-looking creature. As luck would have it, as they were hanging around in their front yard, Estelle came walking by in front of the church and then the parsonage. This time, she was carrying a cat and involved in an energetic conversation with her feline friend. As she got closer, the older boy jumped on his younger brother and began growling and pretending to beat him up. Estelle reacted immediately, throwing her cat on the back of the older boy and screaming, "Get out of here, you gloat-eyed devil!"

Then she jumped on the older boy's back and began beating the every-living shit out of him. It was brutal and before the boy could divest himself of his costume and show himself for who he really was, Estelle had pounded him into mincemeat and given him ample reason to regret everything he'd ever done to her.

Karl Miller knows about Estelle. She is the "retarded" lady who talks to herself. But he has also heard stories; stories about how she has supernatural powers. A couple of the high-school boys that delighted in picking on her, claim they were once in the back yard of the house the sisters had inherited from their aunt and saw Estelle levitate. They say she was sitting on a chair on the porch and when she was ready to get up, she floated up off the chair, still in a seating position and her feet lifting off the floor She then floated forward, lowered her feet, and stood up. They also tell of a time they saw her standing in their backyard with an empty glass in her hand. She told her sister, Barbara, that she would like some milk. But before her sister had time to move, Estelle's glass was magically filled with milk.

Karl has heard of situations like this; 'idiot savants' was what they called them. On the surface, Estelle Creighton comes across as someone who is not all there; having only one oar in the water, so to speak. But, underneath that ostensibly vacuous shell, there lurks a creature endowed with amazing supernatural powers. Perhaps she is the one responsible for what happened to his horses and his son. But why? What has he done to her? The only thing the desperate farmer can think of are a few comments he made as the Creighton sisters were moving into Crossroads. He had told several people that the town didn't need a hair salon. But that was well after Sonny's death. Could it be that

Estelle is capable of time-travel—using events still to come as the justification for current or future acts of witchcraft?

*****

The fall semester has begun at Crossroads school. The teachers get ready for a new year, which here is not an easy task, at least not for the elementary and junior high teachers. There are two elementary classes, grades 1–3 and 4–6, with one junior high class, grades 7 and 8. The high-school grades are specific to disciplines (e.g., English, American History, Science, Biology, Algebra). Latin is the only language taught other than English.

Eighty-seven students enroll on opening day. They have seen a lot of each other during the summer months, so it is not a matter of every one getting reacquainted or catching up. There's a lot of horseplay, particularly among the boys. The girls split into different groups, usually by age and status. The main topics of discussion in these little cliques this year are Sonny's death, the tremor that interrupted the funeral, and what happened to his sister over the summer. As Marlene feared, the stories do not portray her in good light. No matter how the tale is spun, she is rarely seen as the victim; rather, the collaborator. The usual narrative is that she really wanted it and actually enticed her older partner into "doing it". Of course, this makes her in some circles not only damaged goods, but a common whore.

And then there are the rumors about the other party to this story, every pubescent female's heartthrob, the charming young Walt Zimmerman. But it is now clear that he has lost his charm.

Marlene has refused to speak to her dad for over a month now, having heard through the grapevine what he, Pete, and her uncles had done. One of the girls whose family farm abuts the Zimmerman place reports that Walt is on crutches and having to sit out the fall semester at Kansas State. Also, his father has taken and sold his Chevy convertible. The rumor mill got the attention of the county sheriff. But, when he approached Mr. Zimmerman, the aggrieved father refused to file charges against his son's attackers, continuing to stand by his story that Walt had been the victim of a cattle stampede.

Today is shaping up as a slow day at the farm, so Karl has decided to drive up to St. Joe, ostensibly to take care of a couple business matters related to this year's wheat harvest. But, the real purpose of his trip is to consult a fortune-teller and tarot card reader as part of his effort to explain the freak accident that took his son's life. He is determined to get to the bottom of this, and to that end will do anything.

The fortune-teller he calls on is a middle-aged woman who calls herself Cleopatra. She lives in a small, one-story wooden frame house that she rents in a run-down part of St. Joe. She is tall for her generation: 5'7", a bit overweight, with a rugged yet interesting face, long black hair that she pins in a way that allows it to fall behind her shoulders and down her back. Her dark brown eyes have a mildly menacing look about them. Today she's dressed in a bright red, paisley patterned, sleeveless dress with hems that almost touch the floor, covering up her sneakers that she wears without socks.

Karl knocks on the door. She opens it, greets him, and quickly escorts him to the dining room table which is in a small alcove off to the side of the kitchen. The air is thick with the smell of cheap perfume and the smoke from several sandalwood incense sticks that she has lit and placed in the middle of the table. She has been expecting him. He called earlier.

As they sit down facing each other across the table, Cleopatra gets the essential business matters out of the way. She hands Karl a mimeographed sheet of paper that lists all her services and their respective costs. Tarot card reading, $12.00; crystal ball consultation, $12.00; palm reading, $12.00. As Karl reads down the list, the nature of the services changes dramatically and the costs jump up accordingly: hand job, $15.00; nude hand job, $20.00; blow job, $25.00; a date (meaning sexual intercourse), $40.00.

Cleopatra is a prostitute as well as a fortune-teller. Prostitution is illegal in Missouri, but that has not kept her from remaining gainfully employed for over seven years now. Apparently, she has an arrangement with the local police. Free samples for looking the other way. Also, there are many who are afraid of her; afraid of what they believe are her supernatural powers. So, she is still in business.

Karl has come here today as a part of his continuing effort to solve the mystery of his son's death. He remains convinced that his death was the result of foul play on the part of someone who had the power to manipulate supernatural forces and someone who had an ax to grind with the largest land owner in Northeast Kansas. He spells it out for his "counselor". She knows the story, and perhaps in the interest of keeping her profession respectable, she has bolstered his unorthodox explanation. True believers are essential to her continued success as a "seer".

"So, what should I know about who may have perpetrated this evil act?" the colorful fortune-teller asks. "Do you have any ideas?"

"I do. In fact, I have a list of suspects."

"Anyone on that list that is the most likely suspect at this time?"

"Yes, lately one person has become more and more likely as I have worked to figure all this out. It's a women named Estelle Creighton."

"Who's she?"

"She's this strange 'RE-tard' who may not be as daft as she pretends. She happens to be a sister to the new hairdresser in Crossroads."

"Why her?"

"Well, I've heard stories and have come to think there is more to her than what you see. She's strange and apparently also does strange things; things that cannot be explained by simple scientific measures. They defy the laws of nature; the laws of God." He tells her about the levitation event.

"I'm not sure I've ever heard anything quite like that," Cleopatra responds, after mulling over the details of Karl's story. "Most of the people I have known who have supernatural powers are pretty damn smart. So, unless this Estelle is playing some game, acting like she is dafter than she really is, I have a hard time believing she could be responsible for what happened to you a few months ago."

"So, if not her, who?" Karl queries.

"Good question, and I'm sure that's why you're here."

Karl nods without saying anything.

"Okay, where do we start?"

"Wha'da you mean?"

"I mean, you need to decide which of my methods of invoking the world of the occult is most likely to give you the answer you want?"

"You're the professional," Karl replies, not really having a clue.

"I'd suggest the crystal ball. Let's see if looking into its exceptional ways of enlightening seers regarding past events can provide any clues as to who might be responsible for what happened to your son."

"If that's what you think is best, then let's go for it." Karl continues to live in a state of quiet desperation, obsessed with finding the someone who essentially ruined his life by taking away his promising young son. He is always willing to do anything that might help him get answers, put all this behind him, and move on.

Cleopatra then asks, "you see the charge for that, don't you?" as she points to the item on the printed list of "services." Afterall, she is a businesswoman as well as a seer.

"Sure I do," Karl responds with a note of annoyance in his voice. "You'll get your money," he mumbles.

With that, the diviner gets up, pulls down the two paper shades covering the kitchen windows, turns off the light, and brings out the crystal ball from a cabinet next to the table. Using only the light from the burning incense, she plugs her globe-shaped window on the supernatural into a wall socket, and hits the switch.

As Karl stares across the table into the face of his unconventional adviser, he is struck by the way the light from the crystal ball gives her such an eerie look. He is not sure if it is angelic or demonic. Either way, there is something otherworldly about it, giving him an additional bit of confidence that his hostess is capable of otherworldly things.

"Put your hands on the top of the table," Cleopatra commands, having now a deeper voice and a more compelling tone of authority.

He does and she puts her hands on top of his and is quiet for a few moments as she stares into the glowing sphere that lights the space between them. She asks him to state his full name.

"Karl Gunter Miller."

"What is your profession and where to you work?"

"I'm a farmer and I live just outside of Crossroads, Kansas?"

"Can you tell me as concisely as you can, why you are here?"

"I want to know who is responsible for the death of my son, Karl Miller Junior."

"Can you describe how his death happened?"

"Certainly! We were collecting and threshing the sheaves of dry wheat from a field that is bounded on the south side by the Lazy River. I let Sonny take the reins of our horses who were pulling the hay wagon up and down the rows of wheat. And, suddenly, out of nowhere the horses took off at a gallop, and despite Sonny's efforts to stop them they plunged over the embankment and…" He stops here, as tears well up in his eyes and fog up his glasses. This happens frequently when he remembers or recounts the events of that horrible day.

"And when did this happen?"

"On the early afternoon of July 2, 1948."

"And you believe that this event was not just a horrible accident; that it was the result of an evil act by a person with supernatural powers; a witch or a sorcerer, perhaps?"

"Yes."

"Sonny is dead and now his body lies in the ground. But his soul is still alive. Do you believe that?"

"Yes."

"Then we must reach out and see if we can speak to him. It is possible he knows something we don't know and can help us solve your problem." The fortune-teller continues staring intently into the crystal ball.

Moments go by. It is quiet. Then she gives him new instructions. "Mr. Miller, you must join me as we try to reach your son's spirit. You must close your eyes and repeat the following. 'Sonny, can you hear me?'"

Karl responds immediately, closing his eyes and with a pleading voice repeats the question at least ten times before Cleopatra intervenes. The table shakes ominously as she tells her client to stop. "I am getting a message; I think it's Sonny trying to tell me something."

Again, all is quiet for a moment. Eyes are still closed. Then the soothsayer begins to mumble, "Yes, yes, yes,...is that you, Sonny?" "We are listening. You must tell us what you know. Your father cannot rest until he knows who is responsible for your death."

Silence follows. Moments later, "I hear you, Sonny. I see the picture. It's a man; perhaps a man who is different; one who speaks a language other than English; a man who has a history of challenging fate with his unusual powers. But why?"

Keeping her eyes closed, she tightens her grip on Karl's hands, and then, as though responding to a voice he cannot her, she asks, "Resentment? But resentment of what, Sonny? Where is the resentment coming from?"

Nothing happens for a few moments and then Cleopatra begins acting as though someone has just hung up the phone on her. "Sonny. Are you there? We can't hear you, Sonny. Sonny?"

At this point, she releases Karl's hands, leans back in her chair, looking into the ceiling and breathing heavily, as though exhausted from this brief encounter with the other world and the spirit of the now deceased son.

Finally, she comes out of her trance and leans into her customer's face. "Well, does that mean anything to you?"

"Not really. I don't know a man like what you've just described, and—"

The fortune-teller interrupts him, "Look, that was not me describing him; it was your son."

"Okay. Whatever. But I'm still confused. And, 'resentment'? What does he mean by that?"

"You're a powerful man, Mr. Miller. You have what people want: power, money, influence, and a large happy family."

Karl sighs. "I'm not so sure about the happy family bit."

"What do you mean?"

"It's complicated. Some other time. Right now, I need to know what is next."

"Well, you need to keep thinking about what you heard from your son's spirit and see if you can find the person responsible. You also need to pay up. You owe me twelve dollars."

Karl can't help but chuckle, despite the seriousness of the moment. "A compassionate fortune-teller on the outside but a cold-hearted businesswoman inside." He leans forward and reaches for the wallet in his back pocket. As he does, he glimpses strands of dark hair protruding from Cleopatra's unshaven armpits. At the same time, in the now dimly lit room, he notices something different about the odor. Mixed in with the sandalwood and perfume is the smell of female sweat, an acrid yet compelling hormonal signal with which nature has blessed women; an odor that sends strong signals to Karl's private parts. Suddenly, he realizes his penis is demanding more room in his boxer shorts.

Sex has never been that important in Karl's life. He and Thelma had intercourse on the night of their marriage; a first for her, but not for him. That's the way it works in farm country; boys learn early, if it's only with sheep. Girls learn nothing until their wedding night, at least that's how it is for "good" girls. But, since he married, Karl has been a loyal and faithful husband. Sadly, since Sonny's death, Thelma has kept her legs crossed, at least metaphorically. She continues to be angry at her husband, believing it to be his fault that their young son died. He continues to deny it, at least in his conversations with her, but down deep he carries the guilt and wishes he had never let Sonny take the reins that day.

Just recently, in a husband-wife confrontation, Thelma shouted, "There is no other explanation for this! You let a six-year-old boy drive those dumb animals and he didn't know what he was doing, and the horses took his commands to mean there was trouble and that they had to flee. And that's what they did; right over the riverbank, and… You have got to admit it and learn to live with it! You killed my son!"

"No, I did not. And, by the way, he was also my son," Karl responded angrily.

"Okay, okay. Let's drop it and I would ask again that you leave me alone," Thelma muttered as she turned and walked away.

So, for the past few months since the tragedy turned his life upside down, Karl has been sleeping on a cot in the cattle barn, at least when the weather is reasonably comfortable. If he is forced to sleep inside, he gets into the queen-sized bed in the master bedroom with his wife. But he is careful about staying on his side of the bed and doing nothing that she might interpret as an attempt to seduce his angry wife.

Now, while this was not something he had planned, he makes a split-second decision. "Let me see that list," Karl barks at his fortune-teller.

"Come on, I'm not lying. You owe me 12 dollars," she responds.

"I know that," Karl retorts in a sharply annoyed voice. "I just want something else."

"What's that?"

"The forty-dollar thing, that's what!"

"Are you sure?" his hostess asks.

"Never surer about anything."

"Okay; as they say, 'if you've got the money, honey, I've got the time'."

Cleopatra gets up out of her chair, walks around the table, grabs Karl's right hand, and pulls her customer up and leads him into her bedroom, the only bedroom in the house. As she flips on the light switch, his eyes react to the sudden brightness, and as they adjust, he takes it all in. Walls painted in a satin pink; several suggestive yet subtle nude portraits; one of a naked couple wrapped together in a passionate embrace, a canopy bed with golden tassels dangling suggestively from its hems, a bright red shag carpet beside the bed.

It's like nothing he's ever seen; a virtual love nest designed to heighten the most benign of sensual impulses. Cleopatra pushes him into a sitting position on the bed, lights a small candle, and douses the overhead light. She stands over him as he finds himself letting go of any hesitation that he might have.

Then she asks, "Are you sure you want to do this? You are an important person, a man with means, a reputation, and a wife. I'm nothing more than a common whore. You understand what I'm saying? You have a lot more to lose here than your forty dollars. Is this what you really need right now? If you say yes, I will take you to heights of pleasure you've never known; an ecstasy you've only dreamed about. But I want to make sure you understand the potential fallout." Staring intently into his eyes, like a young man about to propose to his girlfriend, she asks, "What do you say; are you in?"

Karl does not hesitate in his response. "Yes, yes, let's do it." He grabs his wallet, rummages around, pulls out two twenty-dollar bills, and hands them to his host. She deftly shoves them into a small breast pocket on the upper-left side of her dress.

Cleopatra then drops to her knees and begins undressing her newest client. She removes his thick glasses and his well-weathered K-State cap and places them carefully on an antique nightstand that sits next to the head of the bed. Then, she unbuckles the straps on his washed-out blue overalls, throws them back over his shoulders, and begins tugging on the legs of his trousers. His pants fall gently to his ankles. She unties his boots and pulls them off; then removes his plaid stockings. As she is unbuttoning his shirt, she cannot help but see that she is being welcomed by a serious salute from under his shorts. In the final act of her undressing him, she pulls off his underpants and his anxious phallus pops up like a suddenly unleashed jack-in-the-box.

The worldly-wise prostitute smiles to herself as she ponders the paradox. A man in an old baseball cap with bib overalls that should have been tossed out a long time ago, with enough money to buy out half the farmers in the county. His almost new, light-green 1947 Packard Custom Eight luxury vehicle parked just outside her house is incongruous with the sloppily dressed farm boy lying there looking at her with a kind of innocence that belies his personal power. His humility, quiet manliness, and almost boyish innocence are turn-ons, and she feels a warm moisture oozing up between her thighs.

As he lies there naked, while his erstwhile lover remains fully dressed, Karl's ardor is dampened slightly by his embarrassment. But her dark eyes keep burning into his as though she is more interested in what's between his ears than what's between his legs. She stands up, excuses herself, and walks into the small bathroom attached to the bedroom. Moments later, she comes back with a small dishpan filled with soapy water. Once again, she kneels in front of her inexperienced client who obviously remains glad to see her. She takes a small washcloth from the basin, pulls back Karl's foreskin, and gently washes his engorged penis. She pulls down a hand towel draped across her shoulder and finishes the job, and as she does, she explains. "One can never be too careful in my business."

She shoves the wash basin to one side, stands up, and in the most seductive manner she can muster, begins undressing. The process does not take long. Her wildly bright and gaudily patterned one-piece paisley dress slides upward above her head and falls to the floor. She stands for a minute covered now by only her bra and a pair of thongs that leave little to imagination. She reaches behind her back and unhooks her brassiere and lets it find its own way to the top of her feet. Then, still staring into Karl's eyes, she slips out of her thong. "I hope you like what you see," she says, encouraging her client to take it all in. He does.

Cleopatra may be a bit older than the average prostitute, but whatever she has gets Karl's attention. Her soft, light-brown skin is without blemish. She is a little thick in the middle, but her full, sagging breasts more than compensate for that. They hang in a pendulous way, but with her nipples aiming straight ahead, not downward. As he anticipated, the area around her tits is dark brown, as are her nipples, which are large enough to suck without having to bite yet not big enough to choke on.

Karl's eyes wander down his hired honey's smooth body and look longingly at the area where her two legs come together. Her dark pubic hair is long and thick and spreads across her groin and into the inner and upper areas of her thighs. A small narrow clump of hair runs up her belly almost to her navel. As he stares between her legs, he is driven to even higher levels of sensual anticipation as he sees her clitoris and fleshy lips that hang downward from her tuft of dark hair. He imagines them having the power to grab and milk a man's privates, like the rubber grips of an electric milking machine pulling the juices from the heavy udder of a healthy Holstein. In his imagination, he can feel them at work as they massage his stiffness until he explodes.

He completes his visual tour of Cleopatra's unusually sensually inviting body. He waits. What's coming next? Suddenly, his lover is on her knees again. She leans forward and drapes her breasts across his chest and drags them south, along his hairy stomach, until she can press them against both sides of Karl's erect penis and then slides them slowly up and down. Karl fights the urge to groan as his feelings of pleasure seem to take control of his body. Then, without being asked, Cleopatra has completed the slide down his body and has put his erection in her mouth.

"Whoa. What is this?" He has heard of oral sex and stories of men having "blow jobs", but this is something radically new for him. In all the years that he and Thelma have been having sex, never have they gone down on each other. His very proper, straight, and conservative wife, when they were actually copulating, was only comfortable with the missionary position and only then if the lights are off. So this is almost too much. Just as he feels he is about to lose his load in his sex partner's mouth, she pulls back, grips her right hand around the base of his phallus and squeezes firmly, having sensed that he was on the verge of letting go.

"Not yet, Big Boy. Not yet," she gently instructs. "Relax. Think about something else; something that is anything but sensual; like pitching hay, wrestling a calf to the ground to be branded, or shoveling a pile of cow shit into the back of a pickup truck."

Karl lies quietly, trying to follow Cleopatra's advice. Meanwhile, she is reaching into the nightstand. She takes out a small aluminum package and tears it apart; separating the "Tro" from the "jan", and pulling out a large condom. She places it atop the bright red head of Karl's skyward-pointing pecker and begins rolling it into place.

"As I said earlier, you can't be too careful in this business. And you should be grateful that I have a few extra-large rubbers for times like these. Most of the normal-sized variety would not fit over a large cucumber like yours. I have to ask. Where does this large thing come from?"

Karl is smiling as he responds to this silly question. "I don't know. Maybe it's because my dad was German."

"Hell. If that's it, he must have been a German horse."

The light-hearted exchange helps move Karl's urge from the verge. He is now confident he can hold off until he has had a chance to pleasure his partner. He has always believed that sexual intercourse was a two-way street. It was only good if it were good for both parties, even though he rarely if ever felt he had brought Thelma to a real orgasm.

Karl is now armed with his rubber shield and his body is ready for action. Cleopatra works around him, pulling back the red and black, thick chenille bedspread and the black satin top sheet. Her naked body rubs against his as she maneuvers the awkward crawl into bed. Finally, they are lying side-by-side, their heads on separate pillows but their bodies facing each other. Cleopatra reaches over and softly strokes the side of her companion's face. Nothing is said as Karl responds by wrapping his arms around her and pulling their bodies together. It is for him a natural impulse and he places his lips, made rough by the outdoor life, on her softer and more sensual lips. She responds by opening her mouth and thrusting her tongue between his lips. He tastes her spittle and finds himself somewhat surprised. He'd always heard that prostitutes don't kiss their johns. They save that for their real romances, if and when they experience these.

He slides down and grasps her left breast in his hand and begins kissing and sucking playfully on its large, wrinkled nipple. He soon has both her marvelous tits in his hands and is gleefully mumbling and expressing his delight. He begins kissing her soft belly as his hand moves down into the jungle of her thick, dark underbrush. He tugs gently at her untrimmed public hair and then moves further south to stroke and fondle the most sensitive parts of her female anatomy. He is tempted to go down on her, but he is still feeling a bit uncomfortable with the whole idea of oral sex. Instead, he uses a finger on his right hand to explore the inner walls of her now wet and sticky vagina. He's heartened by the realization that her body is responding to his touch. Then, when he thinks the time is right, he rolls over on top of the naked woman beside him and prepares to thrust his one-eyed snake into her welcoming glory hole. He is gentle, moving slowly, fearful lest he hurt her. He hesitates before he pushes to far, and asks, "Are you okay?"

"You bet I am," she responds, with a grin of gratification. "You are amazing."

Karl wonders if this is all part of her act, what she says to all her johns, regardless of what she actually feels. But he continues prodding with a slow but steady rhythm, trying to keep his body in tune with hers. Finally, she hollers with a cry that sounds of a painful release, like something was hurting and now that hurt has been lifted. Her passionate outburst is the last straw. Karl lets go and in that moment the pleasure nerves from all parts of his body that have congregated in his groin combine to create an unimaginable feeling of pure ecstasy as his weeks of stored-up male jism rush to fill the end of the extra-large condom.

Karl collapses on his lover and then rolls to his left and onto his back, staring into the top of the canopied bed and working to catch his breath. She too, seems to be exhausted, as though the mountain climb and the subsequent volcanic explosion were more demanding but then more rewarding than she's anticipated. As her breathing returns to normal, she rolls over, opens the bottom drawer of the nightstand and pulls out a pack of Chesterfield cigarettes and a lighter. She puts one in her mouth and offers another to Karl. He has not smoked for a while, but has heard that this is what you are supposed to do after a good fuck. She lights both their cigarettes and they lie silently, still staring into space as though neither one of them is sure what to say or do next.

Finally, Cleopatra breaks the silence. "Karl, you may not want to hear this. But what just happened; it was different for me, really different. You know I have had sex with a lot of men; you're not the first gentlemen to cum between my satin sheets. But there is rarely any enjoyment in it for me. I mean, most of the men who come to me are ugly, fat, dirty, smelly, nasty, mean, aggressive or flawed in some way psychologically. Believe me. None of them would I choose as a lover."

"To make matters worse, some of them are abusive; as though they have paid to rent my body and can do anything they please, and if they're angry about something, they feel they have the right to take that anger out on me. Usually, when it's over and my client leaves, I climb into a tub of hot water, scrubbing myself and crying, at times cursing the gods that my life has ended up this way."

By now, Karl has rolled over on his side facing her. "Wow. I never thought about that. So, does that mean as soon as I leave, you're headed for your bathtub?"

"No, silly. That's my point. This thing you and I did was special. You made me feel like we were not just fucking; that we were actually making love. Your size; your strength; your self-assurance; your quiet charisma. All of that makes me feel safe. Protected. At the same time, you seem to focus your attention on me. You don't treat me like a whore; you treat me like a person and act as if we are making out, really making out. I feel wanted and at the same time wanting to be part of you; to hang on and not let go."

Karl does not know what to say. "Well, Cleopatra—"

She cuts him off, "No please, call me Cleo."

"Well, Cleo, as you know, this is the first time I've been unfaithful to my wife and the first time I ever paid for sex, so I really don't know how I'm supposed to feel. Guilty, maybe? Relieved? Powerful? as though I have defied the expectations of society and feel no remorse or need to apologize. That somehow, I'm tough enough not to let moral constraints stop me from doing what I want to do. Fuck the church; fuck Crossroads; fuck everybody! I've not felt this good in a long time."

"Okay, I think I get it. But do you understand what I'm saying? It's like you can keep your money. In some ways, I should be paying you. The problem is at the moment I feel you have spoiled me. It will be ever more difficult for me to have sex with strangers anymore. But, right now, I have no choice. In some ways, I should hate you for giving me a glimpse of what life and love are outside the chilly darkness of prostitution."

"Look. I'm sorry. I didn't realize I was such a cool guy," Karl quips as he smiles at this hooker-turned-friend. "Obviously, I don't understand you, your life, your work, your feelings. All I know is that this is the best sex I ever had and I don't know how I am going to live without it in the future. You are the kind of woman that serves up such a delicious meal that men have to come back for seconds, thirds, and more."

The smell of sex lingers in the air. Karl reaches over and begins gently massaging Cleo's unfettered breasts. He feels his sexual energy returning; the stud horse in him is re-emerging and while he is not stomping and snorting, his gun is reloading and getting ready for a second shot.

Cleo feels Karl's breathing slowly intensifying and notices that his still rubber-wrapped phallus is beginning to swell. "Whoa. Wait a minute. As much as I'd like to go for another round, I can't. I've got another client that will be here in less than 15 minutes. It's a woman and a regular customer who comes to me once a week to communicate with her dead husband. I can't afford to turn her away."

"Does she know everything you do? I mean, has she ever seen that list of services you showed me?"

"No. That's only for men who might want more than a brief encounter with the other world."

As Karl tries to put his arms around all that has happened in the last little bit and might happen in the future, he suddenly has a rush of emotions, including this feeling that if she is to be his woman, she needs his protection. He asks her, "Don't you worry about getting hurt? I mean, as you've said, there are a lot of mean and abusive men out there and some of them probably like the idea of beating up a prostitute. And, if they do, there is little you can do about it."

"Believe me. I think about that a lot. But, I'm pretty good at taking care of myself. And, if things start to get out of control, I know I can count on my friend, Mr. Smith."

"Mr. Smith. Who the hell is he?"

With this, Cleo rolls over and pulls out the lower drawer of the bedstand. She smiles as Karl stares at her Smith and Wesson 38 revolver. She adds, "And, in case you are wondering, I know how to use this thing and am quite willing and able should it ever be necessary."

Her new lover chuckles as he envisions Cleo shooting some out-of-control john between the legs. "Well, I hope I never piss you off."

At this point, the self-reliant prostitute jumps out of bed and begins putting on her clothes. "I'm serious," she reminds her most recent client, "you need to get dressed and get out of here."

Somewhat reluctantly and as though apologizing to his disappointed penis, he slowly pulls himself off the right side of the bed and reaches for his boxer shorts. But, before he puts them on, he removes the thin rubber balloon that protected both of them from possible disease and kept his juices from coating her uterus. "Where do I get rid of this?" he asks.

"Just toss it in the commode and please flush it down. My next client might wonder what's going on if she uses the restroom and sees that nasty thing floating there. And one more thing, I hope you heard me. I can't and won't say that I fell in love with you today, but there is something that will never again let me think of you as a customer. I don't know what's on your mind, but I want to see you again, but the next time not as a business transaction. At one level or another, I want to be your woman and I'm willing to do whatever it takes to make that happen."

Karl finishes putting on his clothes and tying up his boots. He puts his hat and glasses back on. By now, Cleo is in the restroom washing her hands. He walks up to her and leans into her face. "Does this mean I get a goodbye kiss?"

She pecks him on the cheek.

"And oh, before you go," she adds, "I want to see you again, the sooner the better. No charge; no strings attached; just me wanting to pleasure you and you to pleasure me. You have my phone number. I hope you call soon."

Karl walks out the door heading for his car, still savoring the orgasmic high of his amazing ordeal with Cleopatra. How strange. Has the unexpected happened? Has he fallen in love with a prostitute? He has heard of such things, but until right now would have bet his last dollar that it would never happen to him. In the midst of his ruminating about what has happened and what might happen with Cleo, he suddenly realizes that for at least an hour or so he had forgotten all about Sonny. But as he drives away in his new Packard, he is reminded of the real reason he had come here today. And what did he find out—that the person he is looking for is "different and resentful". Not a lot to go on.

Chapter Six
Who's Cheating Whom?

The basement of the Methodist Church is filled and alive with the banter of the crowd of farmers across the county who have come here this evening to meet with the county agent. It is late September and life on the farm is slowing down. The cooling weather and the smells of mother nature going to sleep remind most people as to why fall is their favorite time of the year. Meanwhile, in the musky confines of the lower sanctum of the aging church, folding chairs have been placed in rows facing a small platform and podium.

The county agent is a young man named Rowdy Hancock. He grew up on a farm in western Kansas and went to college at Kansas State where he majored in agronomy and minored in economics. He is of slight build, just five-feet-nine inches tall, with blue eyes, a small hooked nose, and a full head of black hair that he wears in a flat-top. Most would describe him as not bad-looking or as good-looking; just ordinary; a guy that no one would notice unless he were on fire. He, his wife and two children live on a small farm just outside of Atchinson. He's had the job as county agent for over five years now and the farmers throughout the area know him well. He is generally well-liked, but is often blamed for problems that he is not responsible for and ones he could not solve, even if he wanted to.

Rowdy gets up from the chair where he has been sitting, going over his notes and the other papers he has brought with him. He taps on the open mike and asks everyone to take their seats. As soon as he is satisfied that his audience is ready to listen, he begins by welcoming everyone. Then, in the interest of entertaining and getting the attention of this sloppily dressed, disheveled, and barnyard-appropriate group of farmers, he decides to tell a joke.

"You may have heard about this guy who had lived in Kansas City all his life, a business man who decided he was tired of being a city slicker; he wanted to be a farmer. So, he drove over into Kansas and bought a small farm. But the farm had no animals. So, one day he started walking down the dirt road in front of his house, looking for animals he might buy. The first place he passes has some donkeys in a field next to the house. He goes up to the farm house and tells the owner he'd like to buy one of his donkeys. The farmer is happy to oblige him and sells him one of his animals. 'But,' he cautioned, 'this is not your common donkey, he's actually what is called an ass. Also, you need to know, this ass can be stubborn. He might just stop on you. But if that happens, all you need to do is scratch him on the rear-end to get him going again.'"

"The guy gets on his donkey, his 'ass', and continues down the road. He sees some chickens. He wants one, but as he is paying for this addition to his farmyard menagerie, the farmer tells him, 'This feathered little girl here is not your average chicken, she's a genuine pullet.'"

"The fellow rides on down the road and has not gone far when he sees a group of roosters. He feels he has to have a rooster, so he gets the farmer to sell him one. This time the owner tells him, 'You need to know, this rooster is not just a rooster; he's a special cock.'"

"So, the city-slicker-turned-farmer gets on his donkey with his chicken under one arm and his rooster under the other. Things were going just fine until the donkey decides to stop, right in the middle of the road. Fortunately, there's a young woman walking down the road who might help him. So, he hollers, 'Pardon me, young lady. I need your help. Will you hold my cock and pullet, while I scratch my ass?'"

Half the members of the all-male, all-white audience laugh, some almost raucously. The other half groans, rolls their eyes, and shakes their heads in disproval; their religious or social sensitivities offended by this off-color joke. But Rowdy is used to this and at one level loves thrusting little zingers into the soft and sensitive underbelly of the self-righteous crowd, even when his meetings are occurring on church property. He is not a religious person or church-goer and does not share with the pious farmers their antiquated beliefs, superstitions, or moral proscriptions, but he does understand them.

The formal part of the meeting begins as Rowdy shares his data regarding this year's crop and livestock report. This has been a good year. Doniphan County farmers have sold 123 metric tons of wheat; 65 metric tons of corn; 45 metric tons of milo; 15 metric tons of hay; and two metric tons of miscellaneous crops (oats, potatoes, beans, apples, etc.). In addition, they have taken to market 850 beef cattle; 233 calves; 323 sheep; and 34 goats. These figures do not include Mr. Zimmerman's chinchilla sales. County farmers also sold 1200 gallons of fresh milk; 5600 chickens, and over 12,000 dozen eggs.

"When everything is added together, during the 1947 fiscal year Doniphan County farmers accounted for the sale of over 31 million dollars' worth of agricultural products. This compares with approximately 26 million the previous year. In short, as far as sales are concerned, you have had one of the best years ever. Are there questions?"

An older farmer with a beat-up straw hat on his head stands up and asks, "Tell me, young man. Do these figures include all garden produce, like tomatoes, sweet peas, green onions, squash? You know what I mean."

"Yes, I do; and no. They don't. Most of those sales are at things like outdoor markets or undisclosed sales to grocery stores. So, we have no way of accounting for that and no way to determine revenue."

A few other farmers get up and raise questions about the details of the Rowdy's report. Finally, Karl Miller stands and begins drilling the young agent. "Look, Rowdy, I know we've talked about this before, but we're still upset about the tax situation and feel you're not doing enough to make things right. You know and we know that we in the rural communities are getting the short end of the stick. The cities get all the money they want; and we have to beg for the crumbs. In short, we pay a lot more in taxes than we get back in benefits. For every tax dollar we give to the state and the federal government, we get back less than 60 cents. This is not fair."

The other farmers share Karl's anger and vocalize that anger by hollering "Hear! Hear!" The idea that country folk are being cheated and their money is being used to bankroll the excesses of the city is one shared by almost all the farmers and most of the other rural residents of the county. They see their dollars being used to fund expensive public schools, build skyscrapers, pay for city parks, give welfare to undeserving deadbeats, fund oversized and overpaid police forces, spend millions to attract new business; all of this in the cities. Meanwhile, the rural areas are dying of neglect.

Rowdy has heard all this before. And even though he has provided good data that proves that the farmers are wrong in the past, it is amazing how quickly they forget. So, he always comes with numbers that tell the real story and debunk the myth that rural Kansans are being cheated.

"Okay! Okay," he hollers as he tries to get the attention of the now agitated crowd. "Look, I'm sorry, but the numbers tell us something quite different. In point of fact, country folk in this state are actually taking more in tax money than they're paying."

The reaction of the crowd is a predictable one. "Boo! Boo! What are you talking about?"

Rowdy raises his right hand as a way of calming the crowd. "I'm sorry, but it's true. Let's compare Doniphan County with Johnson County, which is considered an urban area. Johnson County is one of the wealthiest counties in the United States. It is also one of the highest taxed counties, and we are talking per-capita tax burden, not a total amount. So, if we compare, the numbers are clear; that for all the state and federal taxes you pay, the county, in one form or another, gets back $1.45 for ever one dollar of the taxes paid. Johnson County, on the other hand, gets back 72 cents for every dollar it gives in taxes to the state and federal governments."

"No, that can't be. This is bullshit! You're making this up." The basement room rings with protests.

"Look, I wish I were. Remember I live in the country too, and yes, sometimes it seems like the big cities are taking advantage of us. We feed them, we send them our kids to go to college, we buy their stuff, from refrigerators to tractors. But the numbers don't lie."

Karl stands up once more. "All right, Rowdy, if we get all that money, where is it?"

"Well, look around you. Who pays for your schools? The fact is that the small schools in this county cost more to operate on a per-student basis, by far, than is the case of the larger schools in the cities. Who pays for taking care of all your roads? Look at the paving of the highway through Crossroads, for example. That comes from state and federal funds. The bridges and other infrastructure across the county. And then there are all the farm subsidies. And here, I've got to ask. How many of you got money from the AAA (Agricultural Adjustment Act) to let some of your land lie fallow?"

There's no response. No hands are raised.

Rowdy chuckles. "Come on, guys, I know you and I know who got money and who didn't. Most of you get federal funds for NOT working some of your fields. Also, the government has stepped in to buy surplus grain and other ag products in order to keep prices up. In the long run, that is like putting money directly into your pocket. So, in reality you're getting paid not to work; a kind of farmers' welfare. And you complain about the city giving money to the unemployed. You must believe me. I think the money you get is well-deserved, but let's not forget where it's coming from. Not from us; but from the urban communities of the United States."

The grumbling continues. Many of the farmers refuse to believe the numbers. One of the younger men jumps up and shouts, "Numbers do lie. Cheating us out of our tax dollars is just another way for the city folk to put us down; they call us rednecks, clod-kickers, hicks, dirt-diggers, and shit shovelers. They make fun of our customs, our traditions, and our beliefs."

Rowdy perks up as he hears the last of that complaint. "Wait a minute, did not you say that city folks make fun of your beliefs? What beliefs?"

"Well you know; like our belief in witchcraft."

"So you believe in witches?"

There is a long silence, the young farmer hesitating to respond. Finally, he mumbles, "Yes."

Rowdy looks out across the audience and asks, "Is this true? You all believe in witches? I want to see a show of hands. How many of you believe that there are witches out there who do supernatural things; magical things that cannot be explained in any other way than by their having supernatural powers?"

He waits and finally there is a show of hands. Over half of the men at the meeting confess to their conviction—that there are witches at work in this part of Kansas.

Both disgusted and frustrated, Rowdy shakes his head. He suspected this, but to see otherwise reasonable, God-fearing men admit to believing in something so ridiculous is more than he can tolerate. He has to say it, "And you wonder why city folks think you are idiots!"

Big mistake. Before he can qualify or retract his statement, two of the farmers on the front row jump out of their chairs and rush the platform, leaping up, and grabbing the suddenly terrified county agent by his clothes. One of his attackers has him by the collar and is growling loudly, "You little snot-nosed piece of shit. You think you can waltz in here, make fun of us, and walk off like nothing happened." He draws back his fist, but before he can swing, Karl and another of the more level-headed members of the audience are pulling the assaulters off the assaulted and trying to restore order. Rowdy backs up; his eyes locked in a fully open position and his mouth cocked as though he would like to scream but can't. He swipes at his shirt in an effort to straighten himself out.

Karl grabs the mike and tries to restore order. "My friends, please. Calm down. I'm sure Mr. Hancock was not calling us 'idiots'; he was just suggesting that there are those intellectual elites in the cities who look down their noses at us and suggest we aren't that bright. So what! They obviously don't know what they're talking about. But let's not take it out on our county agent. We need him on our side; okay?"

There are a few grumblings across the room as everyone returns to their respective seats. Rowdy, still trembling from the effects of his aborted roughing-up, takes over. After a few closing comments, he declares the meeting officially adjourned, grabs his materials, heads straight to his car, and makes a beeline for Atchison and home.

Chapter Seven
When a Secret Is Not a Secret

The next day, Karl is on his tractor pulling a large harrow behind him, breaking the soil of one of his large fields and preparing to plant the winter wheat. It's a pleasant October day and a few weeks since his gut-wrenching bounce in the bed with Cleo. He can't seem to get the details of that event out of his mind, and to make matters worse, his libido keeps things stirred up. Wanting a repeat performance has become an ache. On a few of the nights he has slept in the barn, he has masturbated, but clearly, that is only a temporary fix.

He wants to see his fortune-telling whore again. But how? And where will all this end? The other night, he dreamed about her. He had left his wife and was going to run off with Cleopatra. But she insisted on getting married first. Karl could see the story in the paper: "Well-Known Farmer Marries Middle-Aged Prostitute", and wondered what his family and friends would think. Nevertheless, he agreed to the wedding. They say their vows, with Rev. Craig Butler officiating. As soon as the wedding was over, they climbed into his big Packard, intending to take off on a romantic honeymoon in some exotic place. But, before he could start the car, he realized they can't move. The car is surrounded by a hundred or more men, all in black tuxes, all with erect peckers protruding upward from their zipper flies, all holding bouquets of flowers and all staring at Cleo. Suddenly, Karl realized these are all men that she has slept with—a gathering of her johns. The nightmarish terror of the scene jerked him from his sleep, and he lay on his cot trying to get the dream out of his mind and get back to sleep. But he couldn't.

Karl is determined to see his wild-and-crazy Cleo again. Even though he knows it is wrong, he finally breaks down and calls. She seems thrilled. They agree on a time, and once again, the sex is so good he is convinced it can never be better than this. She has him dancing in orgasmic ecstasy, intensely real feelings of joyful pleasures he has never known before.

So there is a next time; and even though he thought it impossible, this was even better. And now, all of this for free. After several of their special sessions, two things happen. First, Cleopatra decides she can no longer sell her body to anyone with forty dollars; for any amount actually. In other words, henceforth, she will be an honest woman; at worst, a former prostitute.

Secondly, Karl thinks it's time to put some variety into their lovemaking and they begin meeting at one of the nicer motels in St. Joe. It's easy. He drives up, checks in under a concocted alias, and pays in cash. He goes to the room, leaving the number of his room on the front seat of his car. Cleo drives up, checks out the number, and joins him. Oh, the wonder of their illicit coupling!

Karl wishes this could last forever. The racket raised by their romp in the sack on one occasion aroused the ire of an older couple in the room next door, causing the receptionist to call and ask if they could copulate without the clatter, or something like that. Otherwise, it was an ideal love nest and the good news: they never had to clean up the mess they made, which at times was almost historic.

With each of these rendezvous, Karl and Cleo became bolder. Finally, thinking no one would see or recognize them, they go to lunch together in a hotel restaurant in downtown St. Joe. They are seated in a booth facing each other. Karl is wiping the remnants of his last bite of mashed potato from his lips. Cleo is sipping her coffee. They look at each other and smile. But their smiles turn to shock when a man walks up to their table and breaks the silence with, "Well, Mr. Miller. Fancy meeting you here."

Karl looks up and recognizes Lester Porter, a fellow farmer whose land backs up to the north side of the Miller farm. "Lester." Karl almost chokes as the name tumbles from his mouth. He's not sure what else to say.

The two farmers are neighbors but have never been friends. There have been a number of incidents that strained the relationship, but they have always been cordial. Lester is suspicious that he has caught the cat with the canary in its mouth. "Hey, neighbor, why don't you introduce your friend?" His mischievous smile attests to there being more behind his request than simply common courtesy.

The philandering husband is struggling to craft an explanation, but before he can respond, Cleo reaches toward the intruder with her right hand. As Lester reluctantly grasps her hand and shakes it, she introduces herself. "Hi. I'm Jasmine Von Hussein, a seed and grain broker, with Ham and Williams out of Kansas City. I'm trying to get Mr. Miller here to let me handle some of his business. And who might you be?"

Karl's now confused neighbor pulls his hand back and seems speechless for a moment. "My name is Lester; Lester Porter. Karl Miller and I are neighbors."

"So, you're also a farmer? In that case, you might be interested in the services I have to offer. I'd give you my card, but I am out, and the new ones are in the process of being printed."

Karl is blown away by the artfulness of his lover's response. He says nothing, only nods his head.

Lester stares at Cleo for a minute and then quips, "Jasmine. That sounds like a nigger name to me."

At this point, Karl is on the verge of jumping out of the booth and pounding the pudding out of Farmer Porter. But Cleo has her right foot on his left foot and pressing as hard as she can, knowing what her clandestine lover would like to do. She responds cooly, "Funny, no one has ever told me that before."

Lester continues to push the envelope. "It's just that you look like you might have nigger blood, being so dark and all." Again, Karl bites his tongue, his hands locked tightly on the edge of his seat as he fights the urge to attack.

Cleo, again with amazing aplomb, says, "Actually, my dark skin is a result of my Egyptian heritage. My parents were from Cairo. I was born there. My father was a shipbuilder, but had his shipping empire taken from him when it was discovered that he was selling ships to the Allies during the last war. So, we moved to the United States, to Kansas City. My dad's still alive and still a wealthy and quite powerful man. I'm not sure what he might do if I were to tell him you had called me a nigger."

By this time, the nasty smile on Lester's face has been replaced by a look of uncertainty. Wisely, he backs away and as he does, he mutters, "Nice to see you, Karl", and turning toward Cleo, "and nice to meet you, whatever your name is." With his foot still in his mouth, he stumbles around several occupied tables and out the front door of the hotel.

Karl is steamed but his anger is mollified by his amazement at the way Cleo handled herself. It is a side of her he's never seen. "You are something else, my dear. I've always known you were great in bed, but never knew how great you were as a performer. That was quite an act."

"Thank you," she responds. "But there was some truth behind the performance."

"What do you mean?"

"I do have middle-eastern heritage. My grandparents were Egyptian. My father was born in Cairo but came to the Unites States as a young man. He met and married my mother who was from Kansas City. That's where I was born. I'm an only child. Unfortunately, my father was not a shipbuilder and was anything but rich."

"Are your parents still alive?"

"No. They've been dead for several years. They died a few years back when the Missouri River flooded. Somehow their car got caught in a surge that rushed across the highway and they tumbled into the river. They drowned before they could be rescued."

"Wow! I'm sorry. That's terrible!"

They are both quiet for a few minutes. Then he continues, "It's clear that there's a lot I don't know about you. As a starter, I don't even know your real name."

She smiles and quips, "Someday. Someday I'll tell you all about myself. But not now."

"Okay, I won't push. But I tell you one thing I'm going to do. I'm going to make ole shithead Lester rue the day he ran into us here and insulted you the way he did."

"What do you mean?"

"People in these parts don't fuck with the Millers. We have ways of making people pay. I'll show that bastard—"

Cleo grabs his hands and leans across the table into his face. "No, Karl. You can't do that. It will only make matters worse. Don't do anything rash. I think he already regrets having run into us and having called me a nigger."

Karl reluctantly agrees. But then he asks, "Have you ever met Lester Porter before?"

"No. Why do you ask?"

"I don't know. There was just something about the way he looked at you."

"What do you mean?"

"I don't know. Just a strange feeling, like all of that was a show."

She chuckles without pushing further. Then she asks the obvious question, "Do you think he'll say anything to your wife about seeing us here?"

"He might. But, quite frankly, I don't think Thelma gives a shit right now. It seems, as much as that's possible, she's written me out of her life these days. And Lester is not the one to be throwing stones. That asshole routinely beats his wife, roughs her up pretty bad. In my mind, that's a lot worse than having a girlfriend on the side."

"So that's what I am, your 'girlfriend on the side'?" Cleo asks with a subtlety seductive grin.

"I guess. Anything wrong with that?"

Cleo remains silent as she continues to smile. But then she adds, "You know, I've never asked you, but do you believe in God?"

"I guess," Karl answers somewhat reluctantly. "Why?"

"Because, if you do, I have to believe by your committing adultery, you are sinning against your God."

It is not as though Karl has not thought about that and at times in church he feels like a hypocrite, singing and praying with everyone else as though he were a saint. The guilt is almost always there. And, he also wonders about his eternal soul. Is this thing with Cleo going to keep him out of heaven? But over time he has rationalized it all. If God is a loving God, then he will understand and give him some slack for finding love in an unconventional way.

They finish their lunch and head back to the motel for a little afternoon delight. Another day goes by without the bereaved father thinking that much about his son. But he remains convinced that Sonny's death and the subsequent interruption of the funeral are the work of someone who has supernatural powers; someone different and resentful.

Chapter Eight
Peru Comes to Crossroads

"Hey, you can't do that," Marlene screams as one of her cousins knocks her croquet ball a good fifty feet away from the wicket. The course is set up in the Karl and Thelma Miller front yard. The event is the annual gathering of the Miller clan. The kids play croquet, chase the goats, take their cane poles down to the river and fish, or go into the barn and have hay fights. The adults sit around and chat, play checkers or monopoly. And snack. Most of the men sneak out back and enjoy an adult beverage. Items like beer and whiskey are not on the menu, but are still important to the festive atmosphere.

Karl has three brothers and two sisters, all younger than he. Between them they have 18 children. The two sisters are as different as up is to down. The older of the two is a statuesque 5'7" brunette who many think is a spitting image of Eizabeth Taylor. She is married to a wealthy developer and lives in palatial home on the edge of the Plaza in Kansas City. The younger is a woman named Greta. She is of average height, with an ample bustline and exceptionally wide hips. By any definition, she is homely, with a sad, horse face and prematurely gray hair that she keeps in a chaotic tangle of unattended curls. Born with a visual stigmatism, she wears thick, wire frame glasses which she needs for reading or seeing things up close. So, most of the time, she has her head cocked backward, looking underneath her glasses to see things at a distance.

By the time she graduated from Crossroads High she had not had a single date. But, rather than wallow around in any kind of self-loathing, she made herself popular by making fun of her aesthetic limitations and excelling as a student. She graduated and went off to college at a private girls' school in Missouri. When she finished her work there, she had dated once or twice but still had limited chances of finding someone to marry. So, she explored other options. She considered converting to Catholicism and becoming a nun. But while she was nosing around and exploring options, she discovered the Church of the Nazarene, which was headquartered in Kansas City. She was recruited and joined the church, and shortly after that she announced she was going to be a missionary. Her first assignment: Peru.

Not long after her posting in a mission just outside of Lima, she met a young man. He is a Peruvian, descended from the Huancas, a group conquered by the Incans in the 15th century and subsequently almost eradicated. His name is Alfredo Sebastian. He is dark; his skin is a burnt umber and his hair jet-black. Of medium body build, he is only an inch or two taller than Greta. His small, deep-set brown eyes seem to bulge from a surrounding sea of white in a way that makes him look as though he is perpetually frightened, even in his calm moments. His teeth are a light shade of green, apparently the result of years of coca-chewing. His upper lip is littered with a few long black hairs suggesting he is trying, though unsuccessfully, to grow a mustache.

Despite the awkwardness of his features, most would describe him as reasonably attractive, a state which might be improved with a little work. Several years younger than she, he's the man Greta thought she'd never have.

Last year about this same time, they came to the Miller reunion as simply boyfriend and girlfriend. This year they are engaged and intending to marry before they return to Peru.

At the family reunion last year, Greta and Alfredo entertained the rest of the Miller clan, by telling stories of their lives and adventures in Peru. With everyone crowded into Karl and Thelma's living room, the two most unusual members of the gathering, sat on the piano bench and entertained a room full of Millers. As though there were not enough guests to fill the room, Thelma had invited the Butlers and their two boys to join them.

Rev. Butler has a special interest in Greta and her work, since he had helped her find her calling after she graduated from college. The children in the audience seemed especially fascinated by the guy that their aunt had drug home from a far-off place that some of them had never heard of. Sonny, who saw something special in people who were different, people like Pete, seemed drawn to Alfredo from the moment he met him.

The least exciting or disturbing of their performances was their sharing slides of their life and work in Peru. The Butlers has furnished a Kodak slide projector and a portable screen. Greta, with an obvious excitement in her voice, went through the colored slides, describing each with all the details. There was one of her standing next to Alfredo, dressed in brightly-colored poncho, handmade sandals, and an Incan woven cap with flaps that hung over her ears. Alfredo is in a pair of dark trousers and is wearing a white t-shirt with the words "God is Love" inked across the front. Another picture was of a group of small native children sipping from soup bowls and smiling, some of the many people that the missionaries feed and educate, and treat when there are medical needs. There were other shots of a herd of llamas, the main chapel, the mission school, and several scenic pictures; beautiful views of the Cordillera Range, the highest peaks of the Andes, that rise high above the plain and the mission station where Greta lives and works.

After there were no more slides to show, the lights were turned back on and Greta asked Alfredo to tell the story of his life. Dressed in a bright red pullover tunic and baggy black pants, he hesitated for a moment, clearly a bit nervous. He spoke Spanish and Quechua, but his English was limited to a few basic words or expressions. Greta translated his Spanish for the audience.

"I was born in a little town not that far from Lima, a place called *Chawpi*, which means 'trouble' in Quechua. And, there's probably never been a place with more trouble. I never knew my grandparents, my father's parents. The story I was told was that they were the victims of a *pishtaco*."

"What's that?" one of the young cousins asked.

"These are normal people who fall under the influence of the devil and become monsters. They capture men, women, or children, and take them to their caves. There they are hung, split open and burned for their fat. *Pishtacos* are like vampires, only they want human fat, not blood. So, one day, one of these *pishtacos* came into town and took my grandmother to his cave and killed her for her body fat. My grandfather went to look for her and then he also got captured by the *pishtacos* and ended up the same way."

"Because of what happened to his parents, my father decided to become a *qamlaq*, I think in English you call it a witch doctor. He learned to communicate with the supernatural and do all kinds of things that ordinary people can't do. He could change the weather, he could save the people's crops, he could heal sick people, and predict the future. People came from all over to see him and seek his help. He also protected us from the eye thieves. These are people, usually gringos, that kidnap children and take out their eyes."

"Why would they do that?" one of the kids shouted out.

"Because they could sell them. There were people who would pay a lot of money for the eyes of young people. Anyhow, with the exception of my father the shaman, our family was like every other family in our small town. I had three brothers and three sisters, but three of them died while they were small."

One of the kids popped up, "Well, if your daddy could heal the sick, why did he let your brother and sisters die?"

Everyone grinned, waiting for a response. Greta, who was obviously disturbed by the question and the smart-aleck tone of the asker, answered for him, "Well, you know how when someone is sick here? We pray to Jesus to make them well, right? But Jesus doesn't always do what we want, because he knows what is best. And that's the way it was with Alfredo's father."

Her boyfriend continued, "Anyhow, we were farmers. We raised corn, barley, beans, quinoa, pumpkins. We also had a few tame animals, and we hunted rabbits, vicuna, vizcacha, and other small animals. We were poor, but so was everyone else in *Chawpi*. When I was a young boy, I decided I wanted to be a witch doctor like my father. So I began learning how to predict the future, change the weather, and protect my people from *pishtacos* and stay in touch with and appease the *apus*."

Greta translated.

"What are *apus*?" one of the members of the tightly packed audience asked.

Again, speaking through his missionary-girlfriend, he explained, "They are mountain spirits that control every aspect of life. They are the cause of weather patterns and they have the power to protect people from evil spirits." Then he asked Greta to tell everyone how he actually saved the mission station from being crushed and obliterated by a massive avalanche.

So she began, "Avalanches, what the natives call *llaqtas*, are not unusual in the uplands of the Andes Mountains. The mountains are beautiful, but the price you pay for living in their shadow is the possibility the parts of them come tumbling down on you. Well, one day, late in the spring, one of my missionary colleagues came running into the chapel where several of us were praying."

"She was screaming '*Alud! Alud! Alud!*' which means avalanche in Spanish. Then we heard the roar and realized that there was an ocean of rock and debris crashing down the mountain. We ran outside and there it came; tons of huge rocks, trees, and other debris bouncing, dancing, and picking up speed as it hurtled toward us. I knew we were dead. But, a few hundred yards up behind the mission compound, the rocky debris in the avalanche split and went in two different ways. Instead of crashing over us, it went on both sides of us. Many of us thanked God for saving us, but most of the locals gave Alfredo and his magical powers the credit."

This piqued the interest of the younger and more inquisitive members of the audience. One of them asked, "Well, can he still do things like that?"

Greta, before she translates for her friend, answers for him, "Actually, he doesn't practice that craft anymore. He has asked God for his forgiveness and turned his life over to Christ. He is a Christian now; not a witch doctor. All of that hocus-pocus is behind him."

Alfredo did not know exactly what Greta was saying, but from the look on his face, he understood enough to react. His body language suggested there was more to the story.

Despite Greta's explanation, most of the adults who were there that evening were not so sure. It seemed there were two Alfredos; one version she presented and the more believable untamed version. The guy was nice enough, but there was something strange about him, a quality that Greta could not hide.

The next day, Karl had a chance to talk to Greta alone. She had spent the night sleeping on a cot in the girls' bedroom. Alfredo slept on a mat in the room with Sonny. When the head of the Miller clan walked into the kitchen, Greta was there fixing a pot of coffee. Her hair was uncombed and disheveled as ever. She and her oldest brother sat down at the white vinyl-topped kitchen table and sipped their coffee together.

"It's good to have you back home, little sister," Karl says.

"Good to be back." Greta smiles. As always, her head is cocked back and she is looking at her kitchen companion from under her thick and uncomely glasses.

"Look, while I've got you by yourself, there's something I want to talk to you about." The brother's face morphs from playful to serious.

"Okay."

"Are you really serious about this guy, Alfredo?"

"Yes." Greta is startled by the question. "Why do you ask?"

"There's just something about him that makes me uneasy; like I don't think I can trust him."

"Come on, Karl. You're just biased because he's got dark skin and doesn't speak English that well."

Actually, there was some truth in that. He could hear it now; how his ugly sister couldn't get a man here and had to go somewhere and drag home an ignorant spic; and one dark enough to be mistaken for a nigger. But he was adamant in his denial. "No, not that. I just don't think he's the right person for you. I mean, the two of you just don't seem to fit."

"Oh, I see it now. You think he's too young and good-looking for me and that I'm too ugly for him." Greta raised her voice and tears were welling up.

"No. No. Please, sweetheart. That's not it at all. I'm just trying to protect you. I worry that you don't know this guy as well as you think you do; that you may have let your emotions blind you to the facts."

Greta lowered her head, holding it between her hands and looking down at the table, saying nothing.

Karl continued, "You know how many men there are in Peru and other countries in South America who would do anything to come to America?"

No response.

"I'm telling you, there are thousands; maybe even millions. I'm not saying that Alfredo is one of them, but I will bet that if you eventually marry him one of the first things he'll do is start pushing you to leave the mission and move back to the United States."

"You don't know that."

"No, but I do know it's something you need to think about. And, if you do move back here after you marry, what's he going to do? He has no education and, as far as I can tell, no marketable skills, unless you include witchcraft."

That hit a raw nerve. "Stop it, Karl! That's not funny."

"Sorry." The brother was silent for a moment and then added, "There's something else. It's the money you have. As far as I know, you still have a large stock account with our brokerage firm in St. Joe, money that we invested for you after Mom and Dad died. I haven't looked lately, but I'm confident there's a lot of money there. I hope whatever you do, you'll make sure this guy can't get his hands of that account."

"Are you suggesting that Alfredo is a thief?" Greta asked angrily.

"Not necessarily, but you and I both know people can do funny things when there's money involved."

*****

That was last fall. Greta and her boyfriend are back for this year's family gathering. They are now engaged and planning to marry before they return to their home in Peru. Karl had said enough last year and has washed his hands of the whole affair. His stubborn little sister is going to do things her way, regardless.

During the first night of the reunion, there is another slideshow in Karl and Thelma's living room. Nothing new. But the accounts that follow give family and friends much to worry about.

Alfredo looks different this year. He has shaved his feeble attempt at a mustache and his teeth are not quite as green. Also, at least for this occasion, he has dressed in a short-sleeved white shirt and is wearing a pink tie and a pair of sharply creased black slacks. In the past year, Alfredo's English has improved, but still, it is difficult for him to carry on a lengthy conversation or stand before an audience and tell a story. So, Greta takes the stage, if sitting on a piano bench qualifies as taking the stage. She's wearing a one-piece dress that hangs almost to her ankles. It is a soft cotton fabric that is covered with what appear to be orange roses. She has a large silver cross hanging around her neck.

"The past year has been a difficult one for everyone at the mission station, including Alfredo and me," she begins. "I hesitate to talk about these matters, but I think you should know. I have written to you about them, but have not included critical details, for fear you would worry too much. But before I say anything else, I think the children should leave the room; this might be more than their tender ears can process."

Immediately, the room is abuzz. The older children, like Marlene, are protesting; now, more than ever, wanting to sit tight; intrigued and curious as to what their unusual aunt is going to say. The younger children just look around with inquisitive faces, not really sure what's going on.

Finally, Thelma speaks on behalf of the parents, "We think all of the kids can deal with whatever you have to say. If they're old enough to understand your story and its details, they are old enough to keep it in perspective. If they are not old enough to understand, it really doesn't matter."

"Okay," Greta responds, and then, with her head pulled back and looking out from under her glasses, she scans the audience, with particular attention to the children. She can't help but notice that one important face is missing.

"Look, Karl and Thelma, I know this does not make your grieving any easier, but Alfredo and I also miss Sonny. He was special."

She drops her head for a moment as though she is praying. Alfredo is shaking his head in an expression of condolence. Finally, the missionary woman looks up and repeats, "It's been a really rough year for the Nazarene operation in Peru. As you may know, the country is in a political turmoil, one group of men fighting another group of men in an endless power struggle. Meanwhile, the rich are getting richer and the poor getting poorer. The working class is angry, but there is little it can do."

"However, there are some grassroots organizations that are leading a fight to give Peru back to the people, at least that's what they claim. One of these groups is the Aprista Revolutionary Party, the APRA. As missionaries, we are taught before we go into the field, that our business is helping the natives find Jesus, giving aid to those in need, or educating those who have no other schooling opportunities; our business is not politics and we remind folks of that every chance we get. But, despite that, one day, one of our local staff members came running into the compound shouting that the *teruccos*, the 'terrorists', were coming. We were not sure what she meant, but by the time some of us had run outside, there was a ragtag collection of well-armed young men and women in our compound pushing some of our people around."

"The first thing I saw was a woman who could not have been more than 18, with her hair cut short like a man and dressed in military garb much too large for her body, grab the barrel of her gun, swing it, and smash the butt against the head of one of my colleagues. The victim, my sister in Christ, fell to the ground. As more of the staff and other visitors heard the commotion, they ran out to join us. None of us was sure what was going on."

"Then one of this paramilitary group fired a shot into the air as a way of getting our attention. He proceeded to berate us for our anti-revolutionary activities, calling us imperialists, lackeys of a crooked government, oppressors of the masses. His anger and hatred by themselves were scary. But what came next was unimaginable, horrible. Several of us pleaded with them, trying to convince them that we were strictly a religious organization and were not involved in politics in any way. But it was as though they didn't hear us. They were convinced we were the enemy."

"Finally, they rounded us all up; I was certain they were going to execute all of us, that we all were going to die. But the man who seemed to be in charge asked about our leader, our *jefe*. Rev. Clark, the superintendent of our missionary operation, raised his hand and stepped forward. Without saying a word, one of the invaders slapped him across the face. Then they grabbed him, ripped off his clothes, and tied him to a post beside a well we had dug in the middle of the compound. We could not believe it. Right there, in front of God and everyone, the head of the militia group took out a knife and cut off Rev. Clark's privates."

One of the younger members of the audience had to ask, "What are his privates?"

His mother looked at him and tried to shush him, but at the same time, his older sister hollered at him, "It's your pee-pee."

He got it. "Oh. That must hurt," he opined.

As a result, the solemnity of the presentation was interrupted by widespread muted laughter.

Greta, however, is not laughing. She is sobbing softly as she recounts the horror of those moments. She wipes her eyes as Alfredo pats her on the back for support and then she continues, "After that, they ripped out his eyes and threw them to the ground. Then, one of the men in charge pulled out a huge knife and slit open the reverend's chest and stomach, top to bottom, and pulled out his heart. It was still beating but this butcher of a human being put it into his mouth and took a big bite. He stood there chewing on that piece of flesh like he hadn't eaten in a month. There was blood dripping down over his chin, and all the time he was grinning—an awful, evil grin. I can't describe it."

"As we watched in abject horror, the terrorists began screaming at us again, calling us all kinds of names and accusing us of having committed crimes against the people of Peru. They threatened to kill us all and burn down the whole compound, the chapel, the hospital, the school, and the administrative building. We were more than terrified. Some of the women fainted. I wet myself. Then, if that were not enough, these brutes grabbed one of the missionary nurses, a woman who had dedicated her life to providing medical care to those who had no other options. They ripped her clothes off and tied her upside down in the door to the administration building. And then…"

Again, Greta's narrative is interrupted by her emotions aroused by its telling. But speaking through her tears and choking up, she finishes the story, "Then, then…they took a broomstick and jammed it down into her privates. She screamed in pain; it was terrible! I could not take it. I had no idea what I could do to help, but along with some of my colleagues, I rushed the terrorists in an effort to come to the aid of our brutally abused colleague. But the next thing I know, something hit me in back of the head. I woke up later lying on the ground with a severe headache. Everything was quiet. Apparently, the APRA militia group had left. However, they had conscripted several of the young men who were among those whom we'd converted. Fortunately, Alfredo was away that day, so he was okay. But I still cringe when I think what might have happened to him, had he been there."

Again, throughout this woeful tale, Greta's fiancé has remained silent and almost expressionless. Immediately, as she tells the story and mentions Alfredo's absence, Karl imagines that the slimy little squirrel had probably hidden under a bed somewhere.

One of the kids asks, "Aunt Greta, why didn't Alfredo use his magic to make the bad people go away? I thought he was a witch doctor."

"No, I told you when we were her last year that he gave all that up when he converted and accepted Jesus Christ as his Lord and Savior."

At this point, Alfredo whispers something into his companion's ear. She shakes her head up and down in obvious agreement with what he has told her. She looks back at her small audience and announces, "My fiancé thinks I should tell you about another event; one that does not speak well of the American government. Do you want to hear it?"

The question is meant with a resounding "Yes!"

"Well, last year, shortly after Alfredo and I returned to Peru, we were contacted by a Lutheran missionary group working in a small community just south of Lima, asking if we would be willing to house a group of German immigrants who needed help. Apparently, the Lutheran operation was dealing with a shortfall of resources. We agreed, and a few days later about one dozen weary looking adults and three children showed up, hauling what apparently were their only earthly possessions. No one in the group spoke Spanish. I speak enough German so that I was able to figure out what was going on."

"Anyhow, we didn't ask questions. Our job is to help people, not interrogate them. They spent almost three weeks with us while they worked on finding a permanent settlement of their own. We taught them a little Spanish and did what we could to help them acclimate to their new country. They left, but not before they thanked us profusely for our help. We thought that was the end of that. But we were wrong."

"Several months later, three Americans dressed in civilian clothes showed up at the compound. They wanted to talk to the person in charge. By this time, as I told you earlier, Rev. Clark had been killed by the terrorists and one of the older medical missionaries had taken over while we waited for Clark's replacement. Anyhow, the Americans did not identify themselves, although now, we are certain they were CIA operatives working in Peru. They pushed and slapped several of us around as they asked questions about the German families we had helped. They accused us of aiding and abetting Nazis who had fled their home country to avoid prosecution for war crimes."

"Again, we argued that we were a religious organization, not a political one. They threatened us, the guy in charge suggesting they had the authority to shut down our whole mission operation. Eventually, they left. There were a few cuts and bruises, but nothing serious. However, we were really ashamed of our government. This is not the America I believe in. It was difficult trying to explain all of this to our Peruvian Nazarene staff and community."

One of the Miller brothers who had served in the military for several years jumps in, "Come on, sister, what makes you sure these guys were Americans? And if they were CIA operatives, why didn't they tell you that? Your story makes no sense to me. The American government does not involve itself in the politics of other countries." There is anger in his denial.

Greta keeps her cool. "Look, maybe so, but even now there are rumors afloat that the CIA is involved in an effort to overthrow President Bustamante."

Before she can finish, she is interrupted again by her agitated brother, "No way. That's bullshit!"

Whoops. There are women and children in the room. One of the dictates of rural morality governing the use of obscenities has just been violated. Realizing he has crossed the line, the now embarrassed uncle slinks back into his chair and remains silent.

Karl tends to agree with his brother. This does not sound like something the American government would condone, much less be involved in. He continues to keep his eyes on Alfredo, wondering if he is part of the problem; that he may be using his sister as a front for his revolutionary activities. He also is getting this sense that Greta's squeeze is not affectionately inclined toward him, her oldest brother. Karl is suspicious that Greta has shared with her lover the content of last year's discussion when he cautioned her about her relationship with the poor, uneducated Peruvian.

Meanwhile, Rev. Butler changes the subject as he asks Greta, "What do you know about 'liberation theology'? I hear stories about how in some cases the church in South America is preaching a pro-revolutionary gospel, in some ways giving the rebels and the terrorists a Biblical rationale for their activities. Is the Nazarene church and your mission involved in anything like this?"

"Absolutely not!" Greta blurts out. "However, I am aware of some of that floating around out there. We have talked about it at the mission. From what we can tell, this is coming from Catholic circles. Apparently, there are low-level priests who are directly involved with revolutionary groups and who have created an interpretation of scripture that justifies violence in defense of liberation. But we do not condone violence and we support the status quo in Peru. As I keep saying, our agenda is purely religious and spiritual. We try to stay above the ugly world of politics. We actually encourage our followers to abide by the laws of the land; 'Give unto Caeser'—you know what I mean."

Given the anti-papist attitude of rural residents of Doniphan County, this observation comes as no surprise. The predominantly Protestant population of the area is inherently suspicious of all things Catholic.

The next question comes from Thelma, the sister-in-law who is a close friend and big supporter of Greta. "I have a hard time understanding why you put yourself in harm's way like this. It seems to me you are taking a giant risk just by being there. What's the point?"

"Thelma, you know I love you like a sister, but the only way I can answer your question is to say, if you have to ask that question then there is no way you can understand my answer, no way you can comprehend the reason I do what I do."

*****

It is a perfect fall day and a great day for a wedding. The First Methodist Church in Crossroads is filling up as locals file in and are ushered to their seats. The first two rows of pews are reserved for family, which means the Miller family. Alfredo is the only Sebastian present. According to Greta, he still has family in Peru, but none of them could afford the trip to the States for this event.

It is 11:00. The crowd is seated. Mrs. Butler is at the piano playing Franz Schubert's *Ave Maria*. Rev. Butler walks to the pulpit and nods briefly at

Alfredo, who gets up and walks to the altar, where he will stand as he awaits the entrance of his bride. He is dressed in a black suit that most likely is something he found in a large shipment of discarded clothing like those that members of the Nazarene church in the United States send to their missionaries around the world. As soon as the preacher gets the signal, he has his wife begin playing Richard Wagner's popular wedding march, *Here Comes the Bride*.

Everyone stands and faces the back of the church. With the solemnity appropriate to this occasion, the bride and her escort begin the slow walk toward the altar and the nervous groom. Greta is dressed in a beautiful wedding dress that has been used by several of the women in the Miller family. Her right hand is resting on Karl's right arm, the one who will be giving her away.

As they walk down the aisle, the surrogate father cannot help but note that the size of the crowd is much smaller than that for Sonny's strangely interrupted funeral service. But the smells are the same: dirty feet, perspiration, mothballs, cheap cologne, and aftershave lotion. The head of the Miller clan remains skeptical about this marriage, with a premonition that something is wrong. He cannot ditch the feeling that Alfredo has found himself a meal ticket, and marriage is his way of ensuring he doesn't lose it.

Meanwhile, the guests, who are watching the bride marching toward her groom, are abuzz as they whisper to each other: "What a beautiful gown. She's got to be the ugliest bride ever. I can't believe she's marrying that spic. He looks like a nigger to me." Rural folks may pride themselves on their generosity and hospitality, but they can also be painfully direct, impolite, and just plain rude.

What follows is an uneventful, cookie-cutter marriage ceremony. As Rev. Butler declares Greta and Alfredo husband and wife and invites the groom to kiss the bride, the Peruvian 'gigolo' stands there with a confused look on his face. Greta mutters something to him in Spanish and, with body language suggesting reluctance, he plants a quick and unconvincing kiss on her lips. As they leave the church, folks shower them with confetti and rice and young women jostle in the effort to catch the bride's bouquet. The newlyweds climb into the back of Karl's big Packard, which is festooned with tin cans tied to the rear bumper and brief messages of chalkboard paint announcing to the world that the occupants of the car have just gotten married. The couple waves to well-wishers as one of the Miller brothers drives them away from the church and into the next phase of their lives.

The honeymoon is not a flight to Paris, a cruise through the Caribbean, or a week in Las Vegas. It's a short trip to Karl and Thelma's country home. That evening, there is an invited-guests-only dinner that includes champagne—a rare commodity among countryfolk in this part of Kansas. After dinner, the newlyweds retire to the master bedroom of their hosts' home. Karl will be sleeping in the barn; Thelma with her girls in their room.

All is quiet as the sun goes down and everyone speculates as to what is going on as Greta and Alfredo "shack up" for the first time, at least that's the story. Ideally, the bride is a virgin, and as proof of that there will be blood on the sheets of the queen-sized bed in the morning. But, few of the adults believe this to be the case. They are inclined to suspect that Alfredo and Greta have been copulating for a long time. But the idea that tonight is a first is a compelling and entertaining myth.

One of the customs among rural folks in this part of the country is something called 'shiveree'. On the night following the wedding, a crowd of well-wishers gathers outside, under the window of the honeymooners, and serenade, tease, and make a lot of noise. Tonight is no exception.

It is close to nine o'clock. The lights are off in the master bedroom of the Miller home. Several cars and pickup trucks pull into the driveway. The occupants, mainly young men, climb out and assemble quietly in the front yard underneath the bedroom window where the just-married couple is ostensibly enjoying their first joys of adult lovemaking. Some of them have been drinking and are prepared to party.

On a signal from the leader, the cacophonous serenading begins. Someone has brought a tin bucket and is beating on it with a wooden hammer. A couple of the 'shiveree-ing' gang toss small rocks against the walls of the house. The noise is enough to wake even the deepest sleeper.

As the racket reaches a roar, Alfredo leaps out of bed like a frightened grasshopper, mumbling something in Quechua that even Greta does not understand. He virtually runs to the one window facing the front yard, throws open the sash, and starts hollering, using some of the few English words he has learned: "Stop it! Get out of here!" His reaction only adds fuel to the fire, and the serenaders are laughing loudly as they increase the volume of their post-marital ritual.

Alfredo slams the window shut, and before Greta can explain, he grabs the first thing he sees—the large family Bible on one of the bedstands—and dashes out the door in his pajamas. He races out onto the porch and starts hollering again: in English, Spanish, Quechua. Whatever the language, it does not take a linguist to know that he's pissed off. Seeing that his words are not having the desired effect, he flings the Bible into the midst of the cohort of provocateurs. With that, there is a sudden silence. Desecrating the Word of God is serious, and the group's playfulness turns to bepuzzlement and a state of sober shock.

"What's the matter with this asshole?"

"Hey, man, we're only having fun." They've never seen anything like this.

One of the Miller brothers, Frederick, who helped organize tonight's shiveree, leans over, picks up the Bible, and shouts to his fellow collaborators, "Come on. There's something really wrong with this guy. Let's get out of here."

They do. Meanwhile, Alfredo returns to his designated bedroom where his newly minted bride is waiting, standing beside the door in a state of stunned silence. She can't believe what has just happened, but blames herself for not warning Alfredo that their night of bliss might be interrupted by a playful group of men and boys putting their blessing on the union by making fools of themselves. Shiveree in this area is just one more piece of the total wedding pie. She tries to talk to him, but he is wound up in wrath and consumed by the feeling that his privacy has been violated. For much of the rest of their wedding night, the odd couple simply lies in their bed and stares at the ceiling.

By the next day, everyone in the whole county has heard about the incident. The crazy spic has made an ass of himself, and even those members of the local community who had blessed this union, are now having second thoughts. Karl can only smile with a kind of cocky self-congratulations, feeling like his reservations about this character that his sister has picked up and brought home to marry are being confirmed.

Chapter Nine
Surprise!

Tonight is cakewalk night at the Crossroads school, a big night on the community's entertainment calendar. Everyone who is anyone is here. Some have brought cakes, but all have put down their five-dollar admission fee. The money will go to the school equipment fund and help cover the cost of everything from new desks and playground equipment, to supplies.

Rev. Butler is the emcee and is in the process of welcoming everyone to this annual event. Before he can finish his comments, someone walks in from the south side of the gym; someone who immediately gets everyone's attention. She is dressed like an Egyptian queen. Her bright red, sheath dress hangs to her calves and is belted at the waist. She has her dark hair tied up under a classic, feather-infested *hendu* headdress, similar to that worn by pharaohs. She is covered in costume jewelry—bracelets, necklaces, anklets, and earrings. And her face is covered in make-up: dark eyeliner, eyeshadow, and bright red lipstick.

In her hands, she is carrying the most unusual of cakes. It looks like an Egyptian pyramid with a plastic lion sitting on top glaring out at the world and daring anyone to come near. She places her cake on the table with the other cakes and turns to join the other celebrants.

The emcee stumbles as he attempts to get everyone's attention and complete the first stage of the cakewalk fundraiser. "Okay, which cake is going first?" One of the teachers who is working the event pulls up a rather nondescript cake with white icing, dusted with coconut flakes. "Our first cake is one donated by Molly Gergen. She calls it her 'Coconut Delight'."

With that, everyone gets in a line and begins walking around the perimeter of the gym as Mrs. Butler plays the cakewalk song, *Nola*, on one of the school's upright pianos. Giving everyone a chance to make at least one full turn around the gym, she lifts her fingers from the keys of the piano and everyone stops. The person closest to the small table where the subject cake is sitting is the winner.

Meanwhile, Karl Miller is beside himself with feelings of both anger and fear. The woman in the Egyptian garb is none other than his concubine, Jasmine Von Hussein, better known to him as Cleopatra. *What in the hell is she doing here?* he asks himself nervously. But she seems to be making herself comfortably at home, chatting with those bold enough to approach this strange, outlandishly attired stranger.

As the supply of unique cakes begins to dwindle, it is the pyramid cake's turn to be given away. The supervising teacher announces, "We now have a beautifully artistic cake donated by Ms. Jasmine Von Hussein."

Karl is still not sure what he should do. But he continues walking as though nothing has changed. Suddenly, the music stops and he is standing by the most unorthodox of cakes to be donated this evening. As is the custom, the maker of the cake makes the presentation. As his woman-on-the-side hands him the cake, he whispers, "I don't believe you. You have no business—"

The unconventionally dressed cake maker cuts him off, "Come on, Karl, I just wanted to get a sense of the people in your town; to get a better feel for the life you have here."

He tries to act unshaken, as though there is nothing unusual about this, and that this woman is someone he's never met. Later in the evening, he sees her in an animated discussion with none other than Lester Porter. He wants to intervene, come to the defense of the Egyptian queen, and tell the wife-beating thief to back off, or else. But, he can't.

The last cake is awarded to its lucky winner. Rev. Butler does his annual performance, singing in his booming baritone voice, his special rendition of *Ole Man River*, and then thanks everyone and wishes them a sincere "goodnight".

*****

A few days later, Karl is sitting in his little cubbyhole of an office that opens into the kitchen at the Miller home. The phone rings. He answers, "Karl Miller here. What can I do for you?"

"Mr. Miller. It's Lester, Lester Porter. Can you talk?"

"That's a dumb question. What do you think I'm doing now?"

"Okay, wiseass. You know what I mean. Will this be a private conversation?"

"Yes, but get to the point. Why are you calling me?"

"You know, the other night at the cakewalk, I had a chance to talk to your friend, the grain broker from Kansas City. What's her name? Jasmine something. I tried to apologize for the things I said when I first met her that day in St. Joe. Anyhow, she didn't say much, just thanked me. But later, I ran into an old friend of mine who was there that night. He saw me talking to your friend. He asked me how I knew her. I told him. Then he told me she was a hooker; that she calls herself Cleopatra and fucks anyone with a pecker in his shorts and forty bucks in his pocket."

Karl has been expecting this, but is still caught off-guard and is unprepared to comment. After a long pause, he asks, "Okay Lester, what is it you are getting at?"

"Simple, my friend. That small section of land of yours that you've been letting lie fallow for several years that butts up to my property. I want you to let me use it, rent-free."

"What! You're crazy. No way."

"Well, it's either that or I tell your wife what I know about your dark-skinned prostitute in St. Joe. I'm sure she would love to hear the story."

This gets Karl's attention, and a sudden rush of adrenaline brings out the angry animal in him. "Listen here, Lester. If you think you can blackmail me and get away with it, you are out of your goddamned mind. If you so much as come close to Thelma, I will rip your head off. Or better yet, I will pay someone else to do it. No one fucks with me and gets away with it. So you best keep your mealy mouth shut, you slimy little weasel!"

With that, Karl slams the phone back into its cradle, draws a deep breath, stands up, and storms out into the yard headed to the barn. He has to do something to work off his anger and frustration. While it is unlikely that Thelma would be that concerned over his infidelity, she might make his illicit relationship public and put him in an embarrassing situation, a situation that could undermine his credibility as a community leader.

Chapter Ten
Basketball Bewitched

Basketball season has begun at Crossroads High. Tonight, the Crossroads Bobcats are playing the team from Atchison that cleaned their clock last year, after the original game was forfeited and then replayed. This year, the coach and the superintendent wanted to take a stand, saying that the Crossroads team would not take the floor if the other team insisted on playing the black kid, whom they continue to believe is aided by some sort of magical power. But, when they brought it to the board, the proposal was rejected. One of Karl's nephews is the captain and leading scorer for the Bobcats this year and he appealed to his uncle on behalf of the team. They wanted to play, regardless, and felt it was insulting to think they needed to be protected.

There are over 100 persons in attendance tonight. A large number for a Crossroads game. But, over half of that number are from Atchison. The game is off to a slow start, neither team scoring that well. The Bobcats are double-teaming their opponent's black player. Without doubt the kid is good. He is listed as 6'2" but leaps to heights usually limited to those 6'6" or taller.

The first half ends with the score tied at 20 all. Karl's nephew is the leading scorer with ten points. Throughout the first half, the head of the Miller clan has kept his eyes on the only black woman in the stands, the mother of the star of the Atchison team. She is sitting in the general vicinity of the other visiting team fans, but clearly in a spot by herself—no one directly in front, in back, or beside her. Whether she is doing this by choice or whether it is a matter of bigotry, is not clear. But what is clear is that she is different.

She is wearing a long, flowing, bright orange satin dress with a matching turban-like headwrap and is weighted down with costume jewelry: necklaces, bracelets, earrings. She stands out in the crowd like a red rose growing out of a crack in an asphalt highway. Several of the Crossroads fans continue watching her, trying to be inconspicuous, but concerned lest she use her voodoo powers to affect the outcome of the game.

Karl waits for a few moments after the halftime buzzer sounds, gets up and steps down off the bleachers, and heads to the concession stand. As he walks past one of the entries to the court, he sees Marlene talking to Walt Zimmerman. Walt is still using crutches and is sitting out this semester at K. State. Karl had seen him earlier in the game, but is not prepared for this. He storms out into the foyer of the gym and grabs his oldest daughter by the arm. "What are you doing talking to this creep?" He pulls at her.

She resists. Walt is terrified, preparing himself for another beating. Karl looks at him and almost hollers, "If I ever see you again anywhere near my daughter, I will make sure that what you had happen to you the first time will look like child's play."

As he turns and walks away, he practically drags his daughter and mutters a string of obscenities under his breath. He insists she spend the rest of the game sitting next to him in the stands.

The second two quarters are a bit livelier than the first two. The lead shifts from one team to another. Finally, there are 10 seconds left on the clock. The score is tied. The Atchison team has the ball and is bringing it down court. With only three seconds one of the visiting players heaves up a jump shot from the foul line. It caroms off the rim of the basket and then off the fingers of one of the defenders. The ball ends up in the hands of an Atchison player, the only black person on the court. He is standing in the corner, parallel to and 25 feet from the basket. The ball seems to float into his right hand and all in one motion he turns and tosses up an improbable hook shot. The buzzer goes off as the ball soars high into the air and then *swoosh*, it glides through the net like a hot knife through butter. Game over.

Meanwhile, Karl has continued keeping his eye on the black player's mother. It seemed strange to him that in the last few seconds of the ballgame, everyone was standing, as was she. But she stood out in the crowd by having her head cocked backward, mumbling something up into the ceiling and arms extended out in front of her with her palms facing upward. Once more, he's convinced there is magic at work. And her performance raises, once again, the question as to whether or not the black boy and his mother had anything to do with Sonny's still-unexplained death.

Chapter Eleven
Spring 1949

It's a deary day on the Miller farm. Threatening rain clouds race across the sky. The breeze borders on a wind; a great day for flying a kite but not for having a picnic. Karl has been up since five and hard at work. He is planting seed in an area of his acreage devoted to field corn. Up until recently, he used beasts of burden to pull the planter, which at regular intervals thrust seed into plowed ground. Now, he has a relatively new John Deere tractor which makes the job so much easier. Pete follows along behind him with a team of mules pulling a cultivator, which loosens the soil around the seeds and also works to control unwanted weeds.

Karl can smell the freshly plowed earth and feel the moisture in the air. To him these are signs of fertility and positive omens of things to come. He is reminded of how dependent he is on the weather, but also how fortunate he has been. He looks across the many acres of his farm and feels a rush of exhilaration as he is suddenly aware once again that all of that is his; he owns it. It's a feeling of power, of control, and of financial security. He remembers hearing about how many years before the Pilgrims had learned to cultivate corn from the Iroquois Indians; by digging a small hole in the soil, dropping a corn seed into the hole, and then putting in a small fish before covering the hole. He smiles as he thinks about how far corn agriculture has advanced.

Lately, he has begun thinking less about Sonny and his death. He still is not convinced that there was not some element of supernatural monkey-business behind the spooking of his two draft horses. Several weeks ago, during one of his visits to his lover in St. Joe, she staged a séance and was able to contact Sonny. Again, the message from the otherworld was that his death had to do with 'resentment'. But, during the séance, Karl was overwhelmed by hearing what he thought was his son talking, and he began sobbing, his chest heaving as he asked Sonny to forgive him. It was the first time he had ever openly admitted that the tragedy was actually his fault.

Also, he knows now that the tremor that shook the church and put an abrupt, early ending to his son's funeral was the result of an explosion. Apparently, there was an illegal mining operation somewhere west of Crossroads and it conducted an underground explosion that caused the land in a wide radius to shake for a few seconds. So, it appears there was no witchcraft or sorcery here; just bad luck.

As he cruises slowly up and down the corn rows on his new tractor, the *thuka, thuka, thuka* rhythm of the engine has an almost hypnotic effect. When he has these moments of exhilaration, he usually thinks of Cleo. Their relationship has solidified into a serious romance. He finds himself in love for the first time in his life. His marriage to Thelma was a rather practical arrangement. And the sex they had together was very straightforward, methodical, and perfunctory; limited foreplay and certainly nothing oral. She might as well have simply worn a rough burlap gown with a hole in it to allow his member to do its duty.

What a change! Cleo is a sex machine. She's taught him everything: sixty-nine, fellatio, cunnilingus, around the world, doggy-style intercourse, anal sex, etc. She's a great teacher, but Karl knows why she is so good at lovemaking—for a long time, that was her job. He does not kid himself. She has never told him how many men she had serviced over the years. He really doesn't want to know. However, he likes to think of them as in one way or another part of Cleo's education, so now that she has found herself in a committed relationship, she can bring all that knowledge together to provide for him the ultimate sensual experiences.

But all of this has not come without a price. Because she gave up selling sex, which was the most profitable aspect of her business, she has been struggling to make ends meet. Karl has been giving her a small sum of cash every month. Even though she seems reluctant to take his money, she remains grateful.

These feelings of romance, of being attached to someone else at a gut level, how do you express them? How do you find the words? Karl has played around with writing a poem. He has not read any poetry since he was in high school. The only poetry he can quote is a little ditty Pete uses this time of the year:

Spring has sprung; the grass has riz,
I wonder where them birdies is.

But he appreciates the way in which poetry can encapsulate feelings; it is the language of love. It is like music, a music that sings to the heart. He is determined to find those right words, to write a sonnet that sums up the passion and emotional attachment he has to Cleo.

Karl comes to end of a row and as he is turning his machinery around, a small rabbit comes bounding out from under a pile of brush and scampers away. During hunting season, he walks the fence lines and unplowed fields of his property with one of his shotguns looking for rabbits and quail. The only other person outside his family with permission to hunt on the Miller property is Rev. Butler. Like the Millers, the Reverend and his family love to eat rabbit, which they cut open, remove the internal organs, and then peel off the skin, slice up the edible parts of the animal, and then batter and fry them. Like the others who hunt and eat rabbits, they always check the animal's liver when they open its gut. If it is runny, as opposed to solid, they know not to eat their fallen prey. A runny liver is a sign of rabbit fever and the meat can be a danger to humans if consumed. Now, however, as Karl watches the rabbit scamper away, his romantic mood trumps his thrill as a hunter, and he actually finds himself wondering how anyone could shoot something so cute and gentle.

Farmer Miller is headed down the next cornrow, driving toward the house and the main barns. As he nears the end of the row he sees his daughter, Marlene, running toward him hollering and waving her arms in the air. He stops the tractor, jumps off, and trots to meet her.

As he gets closer, he hears her. "It's Aunt Greta. She's on the phone talking to Mom right now, but says that it's important that she talk to you."

Karl climbs through the fence that separates them and together they run back toward the house. Thelma is in Karl's little study with the telephone receiver in her hand. As soon as she sees her husband, she says something to Greta and hands him the phone.

The trot back to the house has left him gasping for breath, but he manages to say, "Hello, little sister. What's up?"

"Oh Karl, I'm so sorry to bother you, I really am, but I'm in trouble and I didn't know who else to call."

"What kind of trouble?"

"You warned me and I should have listened."

"What are you talking about?" Karl responds, still breathing heavily.

"You told me that Alfredo might not be the man I thought he was and that he might be marrying me for the money."

"Yeah. So?"

"Well, it happened. A few weeks ago, he convinced me that we needed to transfer all my assets to a Peruvian bank and convert our dollars into soles. He made me believe that this was a good move, since the sole was increasing in value faster than the U.S. dollar. Anyhow, I made the transfer and then, the next thing I know, he had drained the Peruvian account and I was left with nothing."

By now, she is sobbing gently into the phone. She stops to catch her breath while Karl is now sitting down and trying to deal with this. The only thing he can say, "Damn it, Greta, I warned you! I warned you!" his voice at something close to a yelling pitch. Thelma and Marlene watch and listen nervously as they stand together in the kitchen.

Another pause. Then the apparently defrauded missionary continues, "It gets worse. I just found out that Alfredo is a member of a terrorist organization, an organization that calls itself 'Pico de Buitre'."

"What?"

"*Beak of the Vulture* in English."

Before Karl has time to get his head around all this, she continues. "Alfredo claims he and the other members of his organization are fighting for the common people of Peru; fighting to defeat the rich and the powerful and give the country back to the people; the working class who are suffering under the oppressive regime of Bustamante."

"Who's that?"

"The president of Peru."

"So, that scumbag of a human being married you, took your money, and is using it to help fund his band of killers, thieves, and idiots?" Again, Karl is having a difficult time keeping his voice down.

"I'm sorry, Karl. But yes; it's true. And also..." A long pause. "And also, the *Pico de Buitre* organization has kidnapped me."

Again, this is met with a rafter-rattling "What?"

"I know. I know. I can't believe it either. I thought Alfredo loved me, but he has been using me all along. I feel like such an idiot. But now I'm scared, really scared. My kidnappers are telling me that if I can't come up with the ransom money they're demanding, they'll kill me."

"Ransom money?" The word 'money' always gets Karl's attention.

"They are demanding one hundred thousand American dollars."

"So, you want me to send you one hundred thousand dollars?"

"I'm really sorry, Karl, but I have nowhere else to turn. And Alfredo knows you have money."

"What's wrong with your missionary friends and the Church of the Nazarene? Can't they do something?"

"No. They refuse to get involved. Like I've told you before, the mission is about religion, not about politics. And they can't afford to stray from that policy, even if it means saving my life."

"What about the police? What about the American embassy? There has to be someone there that can help you."

"I wish that were true, but the terrorists have me under surveillance around the clock. They are going to make sure I don't go to the authorities or that I don't try to escape. I would, but…"

"So what am I supposed to do?" Karl's anger has turned to confusion as he tries to envision his sister being held by a gang of thugs in the far-off jungles of Perus who are demanding a ransom.

"Alfredo's organization has an account at a bank here in Antequera, a suburb of Lima. In fact, that's where I am now. I have routing information that I can give you and you can wire the money and as soon as the transfer is complete, they will let me go and I can get back to my job at the mission."

"Look, Greta, this is a lot of money and it will take me a little time to pull it together. Also, we all know how kidnappers work. In most cases, if they get the ransom money, they don't release their victims. In fact, they are more likely to kill them or ask for more money."

"Please, Karl. I know all that but I trust Alfredo to stand by his word on this."

"Alfredo, stand by his word? You've got to be kidding me!"

"No, I'm serious. I am confident he's not lying."

The big brother thinks for a few moments then lays out his plan. "Okay. Let's do this. Give me two days to think about this and work something out. I can't call you, so you'll have to call me. Okay?"

"You've got to help me, Karl. I don't want to die." Greta sobs as she begs.

"Look. I'll do what I can, but I need a little time. Call me in two days."

With a tone of reluctance in her voice, she agrees. "All right. I will call in two days. Again, I'm sorry, but you're the only one who can help me."

"I know that and I'll do the best I can."

They swap goodbyes and Karl hangs up the phone. He sits in the chair beside his desk in a state of mild shock. He was feeling on top of the world just minutes ago, and now this.

Thelma walks into the room, having overheard enough of the conversation to know what is going on. "Well, what are you going to do?"

"I don't know."

"By the way," his wife adds, "that call was a collect call. We can expect a hefty phone bill this month."

Karl looks up at her and growls, "My sister is being held by terrorists with her life on the line, and all you can think about is our phone bill?"

Chapter Twelve
The Plan

It's late afternoon. Karl walks into Louie's Tavern and seats himself at the bar. As always, the owner is there, and several regulars are scattered around the room enjoying their beverages of choice. Karl has rarely been inside this place, so the owner is surprised to see him.

"Well, if it's not the Duke of Doniphan County. What in the hell are you doin' here?"

"Right now, I need a drink."

"Come on," Louie chuckles, "I didn't think you were a drinker."

"Actually, I'm not, but today I think a little booze would relax my nerves and help me think straight."

"So, what'll it be?"

"Draft beer will be fine."

The owner/bartender, who as usual smells of sausage and tobacco, pulls out a mug, fills it just enough so that the foam does not spill over the edge, and slides it in front of his infrequent customer. "Things are that bad, ay," he quips.

"'Fraid so," Karl admits. "But I'm here to get some advice. Do you think there's some place we can go to talk in private?"

"Yeah, but first I need to get someone to watch the bar." With that he walks to a staircase at the back of the tavern and hollers, "Karlene, I need you to get down here and help me."

And almost magically, his wife comes tripping down the stairs and sidles into the backside of the bar. She is obviously used to this. Karl cannot help but marvel at the contrast. Karlene is middle-aged with dark hair that is already streaked with gray, but still attractive, with a body that can turn heads. But she's married to this smelly, overweight, disheveled, homely slob. There's no accounting for taste.

Louie nods in the direction of a little room at the back of the bar that he uses as his office. Karl picks up his beer and follows him. When Louie instructs, he sits down in a chair facing the owner's desk. As the latter takes his place in the chair behind the desk he cuts to the chase. "Okay, big guy, what's on your mind?"

"It's a family matter. My sister, Greta, whom you know, called me earlier today to tell me that she has been kidnapped by a terrorist organization and is being held for ransom. Her captors are asking for one hundred thousand dollars."

"Wait a minute. I thought Greta was a missionary in Peru. She just got married. What happened?"

"I won't bore you with the details, but the guy she married, this Peruvian piece of shit, stole all her money and is using it to fund a terrorist group called the Vulture's Beak. On top of that, they have kidnapped Greta and are going to kill her unless I can pay them the one hundred thousand dollars."

"So, why are you telling me this?" queries the rotund Italian-American.

"Look, Louie, everyone knows you have underground connections and you understand how these things work; how money is moved from one place to another; how taxes are avoided; how gangs work and how they think."

"Wait a minute," Louie responds as though he has been insulted, "I don't know what you're talking about. I run a completely legitimate business here."

"I know that, but I think you can help me with my problem. I don't care whether or not you are engaged in illegal business deals or not. But I think you probably know a lot of things about how criminals operate and can give me some advice. I am here to ask for your help, not question your integrity or your business dealings. None of that matters. I would just like you to tell me what you think and what you would do if you were in my situation."

Louie stares at his customer for a few moments as though trying to assess whether Karl is serious. He wonders if this might not be a ploy to expose some of his questionable dealings with the less-law-abiding elements of society. But, he's a good reader of body language and intent. He's convinced Karl is sincere. Finally, he decides to cooperate.

"First of all, you know you can never trust a kidnapper. You can send that money to Peru and still never see your sister again. Or, they may decide one hundred thousand is not enough and demand more. Secondly, it is not hard to transfer money to Peru or any other place in the world. I have a few contacts in the banking world that can help you if you decide to send the money. Thirdly, I would suggest you think long and hard about this and ask yourself if your sister is telling you the truth. There are ways to hire trained operatives that have the ability to find groups like the one you told me about. What was the name?"

"The Vulture's Beak."

"Yah, the Vulture's Beak. Hire the right people and they will find a way to penetrate this organization, providing you with valuable information and perhaps even finding a way to rescue your sister, if she is actually being held for ransom."

Karl is silent as he ponders the words of the notorious tavern-owner. Finally, he addresses the issue of whether or not his sister is telling him everything. "You know, I have assumed all along that she was telling me the truth. It never occurred to me to question her honesty."

"I suspect this is something you don't want to hear," Louie chimes in, "but your younger sister has always had issues. I think being so terribly unattractive may have given her a permanent chip on her shoulder. She's angry at herself and at the world, so supporting the efforts of a terrorist group may be her way of getting back at the world that has dismissed her because of her looks."

"So, Mr. Liquor Man, if you were in my shoes, what would you do?"

"I'm not sure. But I think I would want to know if everything Greta is telling you is the truth."

"But how?"

"Well, she is a Nazarene missionary, right? The Church of the Nazarene is headquartered in Kansas City. I would contact them. I think they would know something. I mean, it's not every day that one of their missionaries is kidnapped and hauled off into the jungles of Peru."

"Good idea. I'll do that. But I still feel compelled to send Greta the money. She's my sister, I love her, and I don't want her to die because I screwed up."

"Look, Karl, I really don't have much more to say about this. If you want to transfer money safely, let me know. If you want to hire a team of investigators, I can also help you with that."

The two of them get up and head back to the bar. Karl takes a few more sips of his beer, thanks Louie, and then exits through the front door.

Chapter Thirteen
Missionary Turned Terrorist

The sun flickers through the leaves of a large rubber tree, one of the millions of trees—the cupuacu, Brazil nut, Kapok, and the Tacoma palm trees—that blanket the western part of the Amazon jungle, known as the *montana* or high jungle. Greta and Alfredo are lying in their simple string hammocks. Their rifles are leaning against the trunk of a nearby tree. The Vulture's Beak paramilitary operation has their main camp here. It has an arrangement with the Llamallosa tribe, a tribe of approximately 15,000, living in individual communities or units of some 50–75 individuals. They control approximately 12,000 square miles of territory. They speak a dialect of Quechua.

Traditionally, they survived by hunting-and-gathering. They hunted peccary, tapirs, and monkeys. They also did some fishing. Some of what they eat today is what they find in the wild. But recently, they have become horticulturalists, slashing and burning large sections of the jungle and growing manioc, maize, banana, and cocoa, until the fertility of the soil is depleted and they are forced to move their encampment, abandon their thatched huts, and start the process all over again. They are matrilocal, meaning that when a man marries, he moves in with his wife's family. Single adult males live in groups together. Sometimes finding a wife is difficult. The sex lives of these young men often involve homosexuality, but it is believed by some that their unsatisfied sex drive contributes to the violence that is a regular component of Llamallosa life.

This is both a blessing and a curse for the Vulture's Beak troops. On the one hand, this means these young men can be recruited and make able warriors. On the other hand, it is difficult at times to control their violence; violence that can sometimes turn into inter- or even intra-familial conflict. Because of this tendency toward unchecked bloodshed, the terrorist organization is careful not to let their Llamallosa troops carry firearms.

The relationship between the tribe and the troops is based on an informal agreement and trading arrangement. The Llamallosa provide food, some shelter, fish, and other wild animal meat, and pork. They also help with cooking and any routine chores that might be necessary to the daily lives of their tenants. In return, the Vulture's Beak gives them household goods, farming equipment and implements, other hardware, and food items not available in the jungle.

Greta and her husband are dressed in plain brown army fatigues: heavy cotton blouse and trousers, with leather boots. He has on a sweat-stained baseball cap. Her head is uncovered and her hair has been chopped off to within one inch of her scalp. They are surrounded by comrades in hammocks, sitting on the ground, or ensconced in the many pup tents that lie scattered about the large abandoned field of tree stumps and fallow ground. They have spent much of the morning and afternoon exercising, practicing the martial arts, perfecting their hand-to-hand combat, and taking target practice.

No one in this paramilitary group goes by their given name. Everyone is addressed as *comrada (*comrade) and everyone has a moniker or codename. Alfredo is *Comrada Guapo,* because of his good looks. Greta is *Comrada Ciega* because without her glasses, she is almost blind. As much as possible, the group tries to minimize gender distinctions.

Alfredo, staring blankly up into the limbs of the rubber tree overhead, asks his wife and now comrade, speaking in Spanish, "Do you think your brother is going to help you?"

"I do."

"Maybe you do, but I don't," her husband, and now comrade, replies.

"I understand, but I think you're still angry because of the advice he gave me before we were married. But I'm sure Karl loves me and will do all he can to protect me."

"So, is he going to pay the ransom?" a skeptical Alfredo asks.

"I guess we'll know tomorrow, if I can get to a phone."

"No problem," her mate assures her. "I know a place in a small town not far from here with a postal building that has a phone. But you'll have to call collect."

The Vulture's Beak militia has several vehicles and a small plane. With the help of the Llamallosa, they have cleared a runway and a narrow road that runs for a long way out of the jungle. The whole area is heavily guarded. To make it more difficult for federal troops to chase them down, they have cut several other dead-end roadways into the jungle and keep those looking as though they were used on a regular basis.

Just after Greta and Alfredo faked her kidnapping from the Nazarene mission station, she had her entire trust fund transferred to Peru and converted to soles. The value of the sole has fluctuated crazily in recent years from as little as three and as much as five soles per U.S. dollar. They were able to get a rate close to four which meant that when they converted their money to cash, they had approximately 800,000 soles. That money has gone a long way to pay for equipment, ammunition, supplies, gasoline, bribes, and recruitment. Flashing large amounts of cash goes a long way in the attempt to entice poverty-stricken young men and women to join a cause like the Vulture's Beak.

As dusk begins to descend on the jungle, the apostate missionary and her husband join about 100 of their comrades for the evening meal. The dining area is a scrabbled arrangement of makeshift tables and chairs: old slabs of plywood tacked on to stumps, logs as benches, stumps used as seats, as well as folding chairs and card tables heisted from churches, missionary stations, and various public buildings. The gathering has the appearance a military-uniformed band of munchkins assembled in the jungle. A host of children play in the woods, swinging on liana vines and playing army.

The towering trees and undergrowth that surround the encampment provide a sense of security and at the same time provoke awe at the wonders of mother nature. The cooks are generally the women married to the militants or those from among the Llamallosa who have been hired to help. Dinner tonight, as every night, is a combination of traditional Llamallosa, Quechua, and Peruvian dishes: *tacacho* (mashed potatoes with bits of pork), *juane* (rice and chicken wrapped in banana leaves), venison, catfish, sweet potatoes, yucca, and hearts of palm, to name a few of the menu items. The air is filled with the smell of food, smoke from the cooking ovens, and the earthiness of body odors.

Before the meal begins, the commandant of the Vulture's Beak, *El Jefe*, leads everyone in the militia group's chant:

Comemos para. vivir;
Vivimos para. pelear;
Peleamos para morir;
Morimos para que nuestra gente pueda comer.
Viva la Pico de Buitre!

We eat to live;
We live to fight;
We fight to die;
We die so our people can eat.
Long live the Vulture's Beak!

As they finish eating, the troops begin drinking *chicha*, a fermented drink made from manioc, potatoes, or palm fruit. The officers keep a sharp eye on the troops to make sure they do not drink themselves into a stupor, something not uncommon among the Llamallosa. Greta, who has until recently been a teetotaler and one who railed against the evils of alcohol consumption, has taken a liking to *chicha* and to the highs that come with its imbibing. Tonight is no exception. After not that many swigs of the potent drink, she begins to get a little giggly and unusually affectionate with her husband.

"I thought married people were supposed to have a lot of sex," she whispers flirtatiously as she leans into a more sober Alfredo and gently tickles his chin.

"You've had too much to drink," the less affectionate of the couple growls.

"But I thought you loved me and like making love to me," she purrs.

"I do, but I think it's time we do something different; put a little salsa into our routine; you know, spice it up," is his response.

As the sun disappears behind the mountains, a few naked light bulbs hanging from wooden posts bathe the area with a soft yellow aura. The noise of the gasoline-driven generator lends itself to the mild roar of the *chicha* drinkers as they enjoy the banter of camaraderie, chatting, laughing, teasing. Here and there are sounds of serious discussion as members of the organization discuss the group's mission, methods, and results.

Alfredo decides it is time to retire to the privacy of their tent. They stand up and, with Greta stumbling a bit as she walks, find their way to what has become their home. The tent covers an area of about 80 square feet with room for two cots and wooden trunks that contain their clothes and other personal belongings. They walk into the tent, shutting the flap behind them. Alfredo pulls out a match and lights a kerosene lamp hanging from the top of the tent framework.

As the lamp turns the darkness into light, much to Greta's surprise, there is a woman lying on her cot, fully clothed but conspicuously out of place.

"What is this? What are you doing here? You're not supposed to—"

Alfredo interrupts, "It's okay. It's okay. I invited her. It's okay. This is Florita, you know her. *Comarada Bella.* She's from my hometown. She's—"

"But what's she doing here?" It's Greta's turn to interrupt.

Alfredo looks at his wife and smiles. "I told you I thought we should spice things up."

At this point, the ex-missionary is not sure what is going on, but suspects it is something with which she is not comfortable. She has renounced her religion and profession and has accepted the Vulture's Beak mission and methods, although she still has problems with what she sees as the group's gratuitous violence. She carries a rifle, but has only actually used it in target practice. Alfredo has taught her to shoot and how to use a knife. As a part of the group, she has become enough of a martial artist to protect herself. But she remains reluctant to hurt, much less kill, another human being. Her mate has chided her for her passivity but has never tried to force her to shed the blood of their enemies or unsuspecting victims. But this situation does not seem to be about violence, but suspiciously different, nonetheless.

Florita looks to be in her late teens or early twenties. Like Greta, she has cut her hair short, so as to help disguise her gender. She is dark-skinned and barely over five feet tall. Her face has a masculine look to it, but this is not to say she is unattractive. Her comrades think of her as pretty. Thus the nickname *Bella.* Now, her black eyes stare without blinking at her friend's wife, but she says nothing.

Alfredo takes the initiative and asks Florita to get up from the cot. She does, and he proceeds to fold up both cots, take a large multicolored Llamallosa woven blanket from one of the chests, and spread it across the dirt floor. He then turns toward the other woman in the tent and without saying a word, points to the buttons on his shirt. Florita responds by immediately beginning to take off her uniform. She unbuttons her military-issue fatigues shirt and slowly pulls it off. She is wearing no brassiere and her manageably sized breasts flop into view, topped off with large dark aureoles with small brown nipples.

As soon as she pitches her blouse to one side, she bends over and removes her boots and stockings. Then she stands up straight again and removes her belt, unbuttons her pants, and lets them drop to the floor. All that is left is her beige jockey shorts. She looks at Alfredo. He nods. And in seconds, her undergarment is on the floor and she is standing there naked.

Greta looks, somewhat bewildered, at Alfredo. She can tell he is enjoying this, but she remains uncertain as to where this is going. She has seen the naked bodies of native women in Peru in connection with her role as a missionary who has often assisted in the health clinic and attended child deliveries. But this is the first time she has been in a situation where a woman was standing *au naturel* directly in front of her and quietly inviting her inspection. For the moment, the experience is more anxiety-provoking than sexual.

Alfredo sees the anxious look on his wife's face. But he has expected this. He pulls her toward himself and kisses her passionately on her slightly open mouth. Then, without asking for permission, he begins undressing her. Greta, although never considered attractive, has a remarkably well-preserved and sensuous female body. Her only deficit is her thick German legs, which she has not shaved in a long time. However, her tight, nicely-rounded rear-end, that begs to be pinched, makes up for her unshapely legs.

Despite the attractiveness of her body, Greta has always been almost puritanical in her modesty. She has grown used to having Alfredo see her unclothed and having him touch her anywhere and any way his desires might take him. But that's it. Even none of her brothers has seen her naked since she was perhaps two or three years old. Only her mother and her female classmates at her high school in the shower after PE class have seen her completely unclothed.

Alfredo takes off her glasses and tosses them aside. Then she removes her top, which is the same army-issue as Florita's. Alfredo gently turns her around and deftly unhooks her bra and then pulls the straps off her shoulders and lets it all fall to the floor. Florita stares at Greta's whiteness and her breasts which are a bit larger than hers, but with a smaller, pink area around nipples that are thick and larger than average.

Alfredo then has her bend over and remove her boots and socks. She cooperates, and as soon as she is upright again, he unbuttons her pants and lets them fall to the floor. Greta obediently steps out of her trousers. Her husband then grabs the hem of her beige jockey shorts and pulls them to the floor.

Suddenly, Greta is standing there completely naked, but holding her hands in front of her pubic area, which is much hairier than that of the other woman. At this point, she feels awkward but less anxious. She trusts Alfredo and is confident he is not going to do anything to hurt her. But she still is uncomfortable about what he may have done or might do with the girl from his hometown.

Again, Florita seems almost mesmerized by the details off the naked white woman's body that stands before her. The hairy legs, the wildly disheveled clump of pubic hair that extends from just below her navel down the insides of both legs. It is all new and fascinating to her.

Next, Alfredo signals to Florita to step closer. She does, and he puts his hands on both women's backs and pushes them together, face to face. Then he puts his hands behind their heads and with obvious passionate intentions kisses both of them on the lips, first Greta and then Florita; perhaps as a signal to his wife that despite the unusual nature of the situation, she remains the most important woman in his life.

As this night-in-the-jungle *menage de trois* begins taking shape, the man in the triad encourages the two women to start touching each other and eventually kissing each other fully and with sexual intent on the mouth. Reluctant at first, Greta begins warming to the idea of making love to another woman. Down deep, because of her historic inability to attract the attention of men, she has had a lingering dislike of and distaste for males, who in many ways represent to her cruelty, disrespect, and violence. She is now wondering if she has been missing out in life by not finding love with another female. She is aware of the fact that there were among the women at the Nazarene mission station, those, who while preaching vigorously against the sin of homosexuality, were involved in serious lesbian relationships. It bothered her then, but now she is beginning to wonder if she had been wrong. Yes, there was something unseemly about the hypocrisy, but finding love in the arms of another woman? Why not?

As the two women are getting acquainted, Alfredo steps back and quickly removes his own clothes without the sensual ritual that characterized the disrobing of the ladies. When he finishes, he whispers to his partners that they should lie down on the rug. They respond and he helps them get comfortable as they stretch out and then embrace each other. It is obvious that Florita has done this before. She becomes the teacher and Greta the pupil. The teacher begins touching and stroking the body of her student. Then she slides downward, wrapping her moist lips around Greta's thick nipples and eventually moving to her knees, pulling her pupil's legs apart, and diving into the most private part of her body, licking and sucking the clitoris and pussy lips that she discovers as she pushes back the heavy blanket of dark pubic hair.

Greta is squirming and moaning as she responds to the instructive lessons of her teacher. All of her passions seem intensified by the sweetness of her lover's breath and the strong, acrid, and somewhat maleness of her body odor.

Meanwhile, Alfredo is sitting on one of the wooden chests, watching; his joystick standing at attention; without a doubt, he is enjoying the show. He slowly strokes himself as his breathing becomes more labored and his desire begins climbing toward the eventually explosive peak.

As Florita continues slurping away at Greta's genitals, she swings her rear-end around and throws her leg over her partner's body. Suddenly, the pupil is staring into the most tender of her teacher's body parts. She is not sure what she should do, but decides to return the favor of her new lover and sticks her face between Florita's legs and begins working to give her the same pleasure she is experiencing. Again, this is a whole new experience for Greta but she has taken to it like a duckling takes to water. It is an ecstasy like none she's ever experienced, an ecstasy heightened by the compelling, acrid female odor that emanates from her partner's privates.

Finally, Alfredo decides it is time for him to join the party. He lies down beside the two women and begins fondling both of them in an effort to intensify their pleasure and enhance his erection. He is overcome by the raw smell of sex that floods the confines of the tent. He throws one leg across Greta's head and thrusts himself into the wet and ready honey pot of his hometown compatriot. Greta, almost instinctively, begins playing with his testicles, somehow no longer concerned about her husband's fidelity.

Minutes later, the male of the tryst pulls out of the wet and inviting confines of Florita's love lane and turns sharply to put his penis into the mouth of his unsuspecting wife. She has had oral sex with him before, but now, with the taste of another woman flavoring his penis? However, she assumes this is all an important part of her education and introduction to the world of bisexualism.

She lets go and decides to enjoy rather than resist this different way of sharing body fluids with other women.

As she sucks with limited enthusiasm, she feels him pull away and quickly he has mounted her in the traditional missionary way and is doing to her what he has done many times since they first met. Meanwhile, Florita has moved up beside them and is doing all she can to enhance the sensual experience of the copulating married couple. After a few minutes, Alfredo can no longer control his enthusiasm and lets go with a tell-tale shout of release, followed by a guttural groan of satisfaction as he falls almost lifelessly into Greta's body.

All of them remain quiet as the strength-draining effect of Alfredo's orgasm is replaced by a renewed energy and libido. He rolls to one side as Florita moves up close to Greta's side and puts the icing on the cake of the experience with touches and kisses that are more shows of tenderness than of passion. Again, all of this is new to the once self-righteous and extremely pious Nazarene missionary. She begins to wonder what her religious convictions have done to keep her from enjoying the real pleasures of life; how they have restricted her behavior to the point she has missed out on joys that might have been.

Eventually, they all roll over on their backs and fall asleep.

Chapter Fourteen
Big Brother to the Rescue

Karl has just gotten off the phone. He has called and finally gotten hold of the superintendent of International Missions of the Church of the Nazarene. All he learned was that Greta Miller was missing from the mission station in Peru; that she had left either on her own accord or because she was kidnapped by a group known as the Vulture's Beak. Apparently, the head of the mission has appealed to the U.S. federal government for help. So far, nothing has been done. The response has been, "this is simply one of the dangers of doing business in Peru." These are unsettling times and no one is safe from the violence of anti-government forces.

Subsequently, Karl has called one of his two U.S. senators whom he has helped get elected. In turn, the senator has put him in touch with the U.S. embassy in Lima. Since then, he has talked to a Peruvian embassy bureaucrat who claimed his office has no knowledge of Greta's kidnapping. However, he did say that the Vulture's Beak was a serious anti-government paramilitary operation that had the ability to strike at will and to capture and hold for ransom anyone they thought might be connected to sources of wealth. Thus, given the Miller family's worth, a kidnapping is a real possibility. Obviously, Mr. Alfredo Sebastian, the man her older brother cautioned his younger sister about, is well aware of the Miller deep pockets.

The concerned older brother then asks the obvious question, "Has anyone gone to the Peruvian police or federal government to report the kidnapping?"

The response is one of regretful acquiescence: "The authorities here are faced with so many complaints about kidnapping, some real and others concocted fairytales, that they simply ignore all of them. I can assure you they are not going to do anything to help you rescue your sister."

Later in the afternoon, on schedule, the phone rings. It's Greta. This time, she gets right to the heart of the matter. "Do you have the money? Time is running out and I don't wanna die."

"I know, Sis, and my heart goes out to you, but all of this is not as simple as it might seem. Even if I send you the ransom money, this bunch of ruthless brutes may kill you anyhow."

"Please," Greta pleads, "they're going to kill me if you don't send the money. They'll probably torture me to death since they are convinced that missionaries like me are puppets of American imperialism and enemies of the Peruvian working class."

"I know that, Sweetheart, but I need more time to get all my ducks in a row. Give me a few more days."

"Please, please…"

"Look, Greta, you have to understand," he responds with a note of frustration. "I'm doing the best I can. Call me back in four days; four days, and by then I should have a plan for getting the money to your captors."

Greta remains silent for a few moments, but knowing the stubborn resolve of her brother, she capitulates, "Okay, four days, but please, I'm desperate. I need help."

This is not the time of the year that a Kansas farmer needs to be distracted from the important work of preparing and planting fields. But Karl is determined to save his sister. It is his moral duty as the titular head of the family.

He goes again to see Louie to find out more about transferring money from the United States to another country. Louie is being careful not to implicate himself, but admits to having knowledge of how these things work. He agrees to help and make the connection with a bank in Lima that will act as an intermediary to make sure Karl's money finds its way into the hands of the group holding his sister—for a fee, of course.

Karl goes back home and calls his broker in Kansas City, asking that he sell some of his poorest performing stock in order to come up with the necessary one hundred thousand dollars. It is agreed that the money will be transferred to his bank account in St. Joe. From there, Louie will help him make the transfer.

The stressed-out farmer drives to St. Joe and spends the afternoon with his now permanent squeeze, Cleo the diviner. A little time with her in a lover's bed makes him less anxious. She works hard to calm his nerves.

That evening, during supper, the phone rings at the Miller home. Karl answers. It's the fellow from the Peruvian embassy. "Mr. Miller, I have news for you, but I'm not sure if you want to hear it."

"Of course I do. Shoot."

"Well, it turns out that a photojournalist happened to be in a small town in the western side of the country when the Vulture's Beak, the terrorist group, conducted one of its raids. He escaped with his life but also with a few photographs. One of the photos is of someone we think is your sister. She's in a military-style uniform and carrying a rifle. It also seems that she has cut her hair short, which is not uncommon among the women who join groups like this."

"Are you sure it's her?" the somewhat confused older brother asks.

"Pretty sure. We showed the picture to the preacher of the Nazarene mission here in Lima who knows your sister. He seemed certain it was her. He said he was going to alert the mission station where Greta had been posted, and that they would in turn contact church headquarters with the news."

Karl is stunned, yet something inside has told him that this was a likelihood. Louie had warned him. And he knows his sister. Her lack of self-confidence, coupled with a naïve credulousness, could easily be manipulated and let her be drawn down a path to something as radical as the Vulture's Beak. And, of course, he has been skeptical about Alfredo from the beginning.

As the reality of the situation sinks in, Karl asks, somewhat rhetorically, "So this means she is probably not a victim of kidnapping, but instead a willing volunteer as a soldier in a gang of violent revolutionaries?"

"That's how we see it," is the response.

"So, what should I do; what can I do?"

"Well, for sure, you should not send her money."

Karl realizes now that his sister has been scamming him. He still is willing to forgive her, thinking she might still be a victim, being coerced by that worthless gigolo she married, in spite of her oldest brother's warning.

"Are the authorities in Peru aware of the photo, and can they not do something to either arrest or rescue her?"

"Again, as I told you before, the law enforcement agencies in this country are slow to deal with terrorist groups like Vulture's Beak. Some of it is based on fear. In other cases, it's a matter of bribing. To be candid, if you have the money, there are very few public officials, appointed or elected, in this country who cannot be bought."

"Okay," Karl interrupts, "but what can I do?"

"Well, if you can recruit a large army of commandos and fly into the jungle and raid their secret compound, you might be able to rescue her. Otherwise, you can only sit back and hope that at some point your sister comes to her senses and finds a way to escape the clutches of the Vulture's Beak; unfortunately, not an easy thing to do."

Karl realizes this conversation is going nowhere. "Look, I really appreciate your letting me know. I would also appreciate your keeping me posted, should something come up. Meanwhile, I've got to think about all of this and decide what to do; or perhaps, what not to do."

*****

The next day, as he continues the work of preparing the fields and planting seeds, Karl cannot quit thinking and worrying about Greta. There has to be a way. As he and Pete rumble almost ritualistically and automatically from one field to another, Karl hits upon an idea, a way to get his sister out of Peru. But it will be costly and risky, and require the help of others, especially the U.S. embassy in Lima.

That evening, he goes to town and to Louie's Tavern. As before, he and the proprietor move to the office in the back of the building and Karl lays out his plan. First of all, he will need to hire his own security to protect him while he is in Lima. Louie says that can be arranged, but it will cost him. Secondly, he will make hotel reservations for himself and his security guards at a hotel in Lima. He will also alert the embassy and request that they and the Peruvian government have troops standing by, should Alfredo and his comrades be bold enough to charge into Lima.

Regardless, Karl will demand that Greta be handed over before he gives them the ransom money, which will in fact be only a leather pouch containing worthless pieces of paper. Once he has Greta under his control, he will make sure she cannot escape. He hopes that with the help of the embassy, he can arrange for her some sort of immunity, and then forcefully fly her back to the United States. From that point, he has to believe she can be brought back to her senses and settle into living a normal life in Kansas.

Louie agrees to help, but then asks, "What's in all of this for me?"

Karl smiles and replies, "I will let your son marry my sister."

That provokes a hearty laugh from the tavern-owner as he admits that he will be getting a cut of the money Karl is going to spend on the security team he has asked for. Three men, armed and experienced in the art of protection.

The two men agree on the specifics. Then Louie asks, "You do know you'll need a passport, don't you?"

Passports are a rarity in rural Kansas, since they are not required to cross state lines. Most of the residents in the greater Doniphan County area have never traveled further than St. Joseph or Kansas City.

Karl smiles. "Of course I do. I ain't dumb just 'cause I look that way." A couple years ago, Rev. Butler had arranged a trip to the Holy Land for a few members of his congregation. He had helped them get passports. The trip fell through but at least folks had their passports that were good for ten years.

With that, Karl leaves, telling his now partner in intrigue that he will get back to him with specifics as soon as he has these.

*****

The next morning, the scheming farmer is back on the phone outlining his plan with the U.S. embassy and asking for its help and cooperation. He has made reservations at the high-end Bolivar Hotel. He has also booked a flight from Kansas City on TWA and Pan Am to Lima.

By the time Greta calls him on the agreed-upon fourth day, everything is in place.

"Well, big brother, have you gotten the money together? My captors have given me the information as to where you should transfer the one hundred thousand dollars they're demanding."

"Greta, dear. I have the money, but I will not be doing a bank transfer."

"What? Look, Karl. My life is at stake here. Please don't play around with this."

"Don't worry. Alfredo and his band of crazed animals will get their money. But I'm going to deliver it in person."

Again, his comment is met with a disappointing surprise. "What? You can't do that!"

"Yes I can, and here's the plan. If this does not work for your kidnappers then there will be no ransom. As much as I love you and want to protect you, I can't risk being hoodwinked by a bunch of thieves."

There's a moment of silence before Greta, somewhat reluctantly, agrees, "Okay. I hope you're right. I don't want to die."

Karl thinks to himself, *She has played the fear-of-death card too often*. He is convinced more than ever that this is a scam. But he calmly lays out the plan. She is to meet him at the Bolivar Hotel next Tuesday at noon. He will be staying there the night before. He gives her the number so that she might call and confirm that he is actually there. Once she is handed over by Alfredo and his comrades, he will give them the money; money that he will be carrying in an unmarked leather pouch.

When he finishes laying out the details, he asks, "Do you understand?"

Again, a delayed response. "Ah, yes I guess."

"Do you think your captors will cooperate?"

"I suppose."

Karl had hoped for a more affirmative answer, but threatens, "Well, if they don't, there will be no ransom, no money, nothing, *comprende*?" He uses a little bit of the Spanish he learned in high school.

"*Si, senor*."

The farmer-turned-detective thinks, *The way she's answered is too playful; as though this were a game.*

He replies, "Okay, Dear. I hope to see you next week. Please call me if there's a problem."

With a rather terse and disappointed tone, Greta mutters "Okay then" and hangs up.

Chapter Fifteen
The Unwanted Rescue

It's early Sunday morning and Karl has all his ducks in a row. He has packed a small suitcase and a briefcase. His 38 and a leather pouch with a few 100-dollar bills masking stacks of fake bills are in his suitcase. He is carrying an ample supply of cash, he has his passport, and has reserved a roundtrip ticket to Lima, Peru, and a one-way ticket from Lima to Kansas City for Greta.

The sun is not up yet on the Miller farm, but Thelma has arisen early, as she usually does. Karl and his wife have settled into a kind of business partnership. There has been no sex since Sonny died. Thelma still blames her husband for that. Karl is suspicious that she knows about his ongoing affair with the St. Joe prostitute, but she seems not to care. She has her children, her sisters-in-law, her farmer-wife friends, and Lois Butler. Why does she need him?

Karl has explained everything about his rescue plan to his wife. Thelma wonders if he is doing the right thing. If Greta is in fact now a member of a Peruvian terrorist group and is happy, why go to all this trouble to "rescue" her when she probably does not want to be rescued?

"This whole operation is costing you, is costing us, a lot of money," she observes with an air of skepticism. "And for what?"

"She's my sister and I just can't ignore her plight. Right now, it looks like she is playing me for a fool. But I have to believe that she is being used and that, in a strange way, I have to rescue her from herself."

Karl, dressed in his *Sunday go to meetin'* dark suit and blue tie, makes the two-hour drive to Kansas City's Richards Field. He arrives with plenty of time to spare and catches the 10:00 TWA flight to Miami. The Boeing 370 plane is equipped with 38 seats, but just over half are taken. This is Karl's first flight on a commercial aircraft. He has been up in a small plane before, a crop-duster owned by a friend and fellow farmer, but this is a new experience.

The Kansas farmer arrives in Miami a little over five hours later, and after a two-hour wait, catches a Pan Am flight to Lima. This plane is a Lockheed DC-6 and a little larger and faster than the TWA plane. It's an overnight flight, and 12 hours later, he lands at Limatambo International Airport at 7:00 AM, local time.

He is not sure what to expect, but as he deplanes, he is met by a man holding up a sign: 'Mr. Karl Miller'. The man introduces himself as Juan Garcia. In broken English, he explains that he is the leader of the three-man security team that he has hired and that he will also act as an interpreter. "That sounds good for you, okay?" he asks.

The weary traveler from Kansas mumbles, "Sounds hunky-dory to me."

"*Que?*" his host replies, his furrowed brow manifesting his confusion.

Karl thinks for a moment and responds, "*yo comprendo*," using a few more words of the Spanish he remembers from his high-school class in Crossroads.

Juan smiles and grabs Karl's bag as it is offloaded from the plane. They walk through the small airport and to a waiting car with another member of the security team at the wheel. Karl is stumped. He's never seen a car like this. A traditional but luxury look: solid black with tan-colored leather seats with a new-car smell. As he settles into the back seat next to his host, the travel-weary visitor asks, "What kind of car is this?"

"A Mercedes-Benz sedan."

"Wow! Retired cops must be paid well here."

It takes a moment for Juan to get the gist of the comment, but eventually smiles. "*Si, Senor.*"

They drive to the Bolivar Hotel, where the farmer-turned-special-agent is allowed to check in early. Shortly after checking in, Karl calls the U.S. embassy to talk to his contact there. He lets him know he has arrived. The embassy has agreed to help. He is invited over to discuss the details of his plan.

Later in the day, he meets with the security team to make sure everyone is on-board with the plan. Greta is to come to the hotel with one of the members of the Vulture's Beak organization, probably Alfredo Sebastian, her husband. Karl will give Alfredo the leather pouch, containing, ostensibly, the requested one hundred thousand dollars. Then, they are to grab Greta. Since this is not a legal operation, Alfredo is not to be harmed or even detained. The goal is to get Greta and whisk her out of the country before she gets hurt, killed, or worse, put in a Peruvian jail.

Obviously, all of this is new to Karl. The intrigue reminds him of *The Shadow*, a popular radio program featuring a very crafty detective that he listens to religiously. This is exciting. Still, he is nervous. He realizes that there are a lot of things that could go wrong.

He spends much of the morning walking around Lima, enjoying the scenery while at the same time seeing occasional islands of wealth amidst a virtual sea of poverty. The stark gap between the rich and the poor is obvious; obvious to the point that Karl begins to understand the Vulture's Beak and Greta's new commitment to help the working-class people of Peru. At the same time, he keeps wishing that Cleo were here with him. He had thought about bringing her with him, but realized it would only complicate matters and possibly put her in harm's way.

In the afternoon, he goes to the embassy and meets with his contact. They discuss the plan and how it is supposed to play out. The staff member agrees to help, but cautions Karl, "If this gets out of hand and the local police or the armed forces gets involved, this could have serious consequences for you and for your sister. So be careful."

*****

It is Tuesday morning. Karl is slow to get out of bed. He did not sleep well, anxious as he is about today's planned operation. He has informed the front desk at the hotel of the anticipated call from his sister and urged them to be alert and ring his room as quickly as possible. He has his breakfast brought to his room.

Just as he is finishing his breakfast and sipping some of the best coffee he has ever tasted, the phone rings. Even though he is expecting a call, it startles him. He practically drops his cup, but collects his nerves and picks up the receiver. "Hello."

"Karl. This is me. I'm calling you just as you asked."

"Where are you?"

"I'm in Lima." And before Karl can respond, she asks in what sounds like a voice of desperation, "Did you bring the money?"

"Yeah. But I'm not handing it over until I am certain your kidnappers are releasing you."

"I understand," Greta replies.

Karl then proceeds to outline the instructions, reminding her that her captors are to bring her to the hotel where he will exchange the money that he has in a leather pouch for her release.

Greta pauses, and then explains, "Look, big brother, we have a problem. My kidnappers don't want to meet in the hotel."

"What!" Karl almost shouts into the phone. "I thought we'd agreed."

"I know, and I'm sorry, but they make the rules; I don't."

"So, what are those thieving assholes suggesting now?" the frustrated farmer asks, as he softens his tone.

"Okay, this is what they're demanding; that you come to the warehouse district, to the Del Monte building. The people at the hotel can tell you where that is. There will be a small cardboard box near the main entrance, and in that box there will be instructions as to where you are to meet us."

Karl's mind is aswirl as he begins trying to recalibrate his plan. He asks, "Are the instructions in Spanish?"

"No. They made me translate them into English."

"So what time are we talking about?"

"Two o'clock. And by the way, you are to come by yourself. If you bring anyone with you, the deal is off."

"So, what about your terrorist group? How many of them are with you? And how do I know that they won't simply shoot me and take the money and hang on to you as a captive?"

Greta replies quickly, "First of all, there are about twenty-five members of the Vulture's Beak who are with me. I had hoped that it would be only Alfredo. But the organization wants to make sure the trade-off goes as planned and it gets the money."

This is not something Karl had planned for. A small army of paramilitary nutcases, probably young and trigger-happy. The "rescue" of his sister may be much more difficult than he anticipated.

Reluctantly, he agrees to the new plan. His last words to his sister, "I hope this works. I will see you at two o'clock."

He hangs up and goes immediately to the lobby where his three-man security is waiting for him and his instructions. He tells Juan about the change of plans, who in turn relays the information to his colleagues in Spanish. They seem unmoved by the news of the change. All three members of the team have a lot of experience dealing with the criminal element in Peru. They have worked for the Lima police force, but have left that profession to assume the more lucrative role as 'security consultants'.

Karl invites the team to come back to his room where they might strategize as they adjust to the new set of circumstances. As they enter the room, he gestures to his new comrades, suggesting they find a place to sit. Before the team begins working on a new approach, he picks up the phone and calls his contact at the embassy and tells him about the conversation with his sister and the new plan for the exchange. When he tells his contact that there will be about twenty-five members of the Vulture's Beak with her, he laughs.

"There's no way that many of the terrorist group would come into Lima like that. First of all, it's a long way from their jungle hideout. Secondly, they would not take the chance of having to face local police and federal forces here. They operate largely in the countryside and in small villages. I would be surprised if there were more than one or two of the group that are here with your sister. They have a small private plane and probably have flown into a small airstrip somewhere close, so I'm betting it's at least one man, the pilot, and perhaps another one, maybe your scheming brother-in-law, what's his name?"

"Alfredo Sebastian, or perhaps more appropriate, Alfred the Bastard."

The contact chuckles, and they discuss possible approaches to the new challenge. The embassy has agreed to work with him, providing immunity for him should problems arise. Also, it will provide protection for Greta and make sure she can leave the country, despite her ties with the Vulture's Beak operation.

*****

It's time to move. Karl climbs into Juan's black Mercedes sedan along with the members of the team. It's a typically pleasant day in Lima, 66 degrees and clear blue skies. Juan knows the warehouse district like the back of his hand. The plan is that they will drop Karl off a few blocks away from and behind the Del Monte building. The team will stay out of sight until Karl has picked up the instructions from the cardboard box. He will read those instructions and then put the note back into the box.

The team will give him a little time to head toward the planned destination, then race to the box, read the instructions, and follow Karl, but far enough behind him to avoid spooking Greta's captors. Juan has assured his employer that he will be able to read the directions, which Karl assumes will have been written by Greta, in English.

Dressed in a light-blue, long-sleeved, casual, button-down shirt and blue jeans, Karl has deliberately left the shirt untucked so as to drape over the .38 revolver he has stuffed into his belt in the back. He is carrying the leather pouch which is supposed to be the requested ransom money. Nervous, to put it mildly, the mastermind behind this operation follows Juan's directions and walks to the front of the Del Monte building, a nondescript, one-story warehouse, its frontage about 250 yards in length with no opening except a two-panel metal door. The area is relatively quiet with only a few people on the street. Some look at him suspiciously; something about him tells the native Peruvian that he is an American.

As promised, there is the plain cardboard box. Karl approaches it cautiously, trying not to look suspicious and wondering if he is being watched by Alfredo or any other member of the Vulture's Beak. He bends over slowly, reaches into the box, and pulls out a small piece of paper. He reads the brief instructions.

"Walk south down the street for about 75 yards. There will be a large abandoned warehouse on your left with a for-sale sign (*En Venta*). Walk to the far corner of that building and turn to your left. You will see a wooded area not that far behind the warehouse. Walk straight back into those woods. We will be waiting there. Make sure you are alone."

Karl reads the directions several times to make sure he has them memorized and then drops the note back into the box. He stands still for a moment and takes a deep breath before striding as inconspicuously as possible toward his destination. He rounds the front of the abandoned warehouse and slowly walks toward the bright green wooded area in front of him, a virtual garden of acacia and algarroba trees. He steps under the shade of one of the trees at the edge of the woods and stops. Nothing. He continues moving slowly among the trees. In a few moments, he reaches a grassy clearing and as he does, he hears a gruff voice holler "*Alto!*"

Across the clearing, which looks like a great place for a picnic, some 20 yards away, there she is. Greta is standing there with a panicked look on her face. A large burly man with a long scar on the side of his dark, unshaved face, with a strange-looking brown hat on his head is standing behind her. His arm is wrapped around her neck and he is pressing a military-style revolver into her left cheek.

Not knowing exactly what to do, Karl holds the leather pouch out in front of him and hollers, "I've got the money!" But, before there's a response, he asks, "Where's Alfredo?"

Greta explains in a loud voice, "He's back in the woods behind us with the rest of his comrades."

"So, who's the guy with the gun to your head?"

"They call him *El Jefe*; he's the Vulture's Beak commander and he's crazy. He'll kill me if you don't give him the money."

Karl takes a few steps forward, holding the pouch in front of him. "Tell *El Jefe* to let you go and I will throw the money on the ground."

Greta relays the message to her captor in Spanish. And he immediately shouts, "*Quiero ver el dinero!*"

"He wants to see the money," Greta hollers.

Taking a few more steps toward his sister and the scruffy terrorist, Karl unzips the pouch and opens it in a way that the money is visible to Greta and her kidnapper. There are small bundles of bills inside, but only the hundred-dollar bills are genuine. Underneath each of them is a stack of fake currency.

At this point, *El Jefe* whispers something in Greta's ear. She then announces to her older brother, "He wants me to get the money and bring it to him. So, please, throw it on the ground and I will pick it up and give it to him and then he'll let me go."

Karl hesitates for a few moments, zips up the pouch, and tosses it a few yards in his sister's direction. At that point, her captor releases her and Greta rushes forward, picks up the money, and takes it back to *El Jefe*. He backs away with the pouch with his revolver pointed in Karl's direction. He turns to run away, leaving Greta behind. But, not surprisingly to the determined older brother, his sister, instead of running to his side, is racing off with her captor. This was the hoax he'd expected.

Meanwhile, his security team has circled around behind the clearing where the exchange took place. They are waiting, guns drawn, as the Vulture's Beak commander and one of his female comrades rush to what Karl suspects is a car driven by another member of the terrorist organization. But, much to their surprise, the commandant and Greta are trapped. El Jefe has put his pistol back in the pocket of his uniform. Realizing he is surrounded; he reaches for his weapon. Juan hollers, "*No lo haga o disparo.*" (Don't do it, or I'll shoot). The grisly terrorist knows his goose is cooked.

"*Suelta el dinero* (Drop the money)," Juan demands.

El Jefe looks furtively at each of the three gunmen and reluctantly tosses the pouch in Juan's direction. As Greta realizes what is happening, she turns and runs back in Karl's direction. When she sees him, she darts in another direction. But, expecting this, her brother pursues and grabs her. She screams and tries to get free, but to no avail.

Consistent with the plan, the leader of the Vulture's Beak is allowed to take off, but not before he is relieved of his revolver. Karl, at the advice of the embassy staff, has decided there is no need to involve local law enforcement. It would only complicate matters.

As Juan tells the Vulture's Beak commander he is free to go, the grungy terrorist slowly walks away. Juan fires a shot over his head and immediately *El Jefe's* stroll turns into a sprint. Moments later, the three-man security team are at Karl's side as he struggles to hang on to his sister, who continues to scream, "Let me go! You can't do this!"

In an effort to break free, she resorts to her martial arts training. She manages to land a couple of blows, but she has forgotten how strong her brother is. She quickly realizes she is fighting a grizzly and there is no way she, a mere cub in comparison, is going to win.

Juan pulls a pair of handcuffs from his pocket and, as gently as he can and with Karl's help, cuffs Greta's hands behind her back. She continues to holler and struggle as she is literally dragged out of the woods and back to the street where they wait as Juan goes to get the car.

He pulls up near the corner of the warehouse. Greta is shoved into the backseat of the car between two members of the security team. They drive to the embassy, where Juan and Karl pull and shove Greta into the compound. The liaison working with the operation meets them in front of the main building and from there they go to a basement room, where persons who are considered fugitives from American justice can be held. It is a prison cell, but a relatively comfortable one; essentially a secure apartment room with a bedroom, a sitting area, and a full bath. There is also an oven and a small refrigerator stocked with water and soft drinks. Meals are delivered on demand.

Greta's handcuffs are removed as she is ushered into her temporary quarters. Obviously, the captured terrorist is unhappy, but plops reluctantly onto the brightly-colored quilt-covered double bed with a loud "Huff!"

Karl, mustering up the calmest and steadiest voice possible under the circumstances, tells his sister, "I'm still not sure how and why you got yourself into this mess, but in the not-too-distant future, you will thank me for getting you out of it."

"Never!" she screams.

Karl looks at Juan and shakes his head in frustration. There is clearly no future in trying to reason with her. The effort is as hopeless as trying to talk a zebra into getting rid of his stripes. However, the brother still believes his little sister will eventually accept the fact that her Peruvian adventure is over, and perhaps be grateful for her rescue.

Karl and Juan leave the room and walk back to the front of the compound. Karl takes a few of the hundred-dollar bills from the pouch recovered from a defeated *El Jefe* and gives his security consultant the other half of the promised pay-out.

After a perfunctory *adios*, Karl walks back into the embassy and consults with his contact. The plan: Greta is being held as a fugitive from American justice. But she will be released tomorrow and given appropriate papers that will allow Karl to escort her back to Kansas City. Despite her association with the Vulture's Beak terrorist organization, she is being treated as immune from Peruvian prosecution.

Karl returns to his hotel. He grabs dinner at the hotel restaurant and heads up to his room, climbing into bed shortly before nine. After a long, sleepless night, he gets up, packs his suitcase and checks out of the hotel. He is picked up by one of the drivers who works for the U.S. embassy and taken back to the compound. Greta has spent most of the night ranting and pacing around the small apartment where she has been confined. One of the service staff had brought her a change of clothes and toiletries last night, but she insisted on wearing her military garb, which was dirty, sweat-stained, and smelly. It is clear she is not happy about what has happened. Karl decides not to argue over her terribly inappropriate attire as he thinks to himself, *What the hell; let her stink.*

As they prepare to leave for the airport, Greta is brought to the office of Karl's contact at the embassy, who makes sure the would-be terrorist knows what will happen if she insists on staying in Peru. The embassy will have no choice but to notify local officials, and if she is arrested, she will end up serving time in a local prison, an experience some say is a fate worse than execution. Greta has no identification: no driver's license, no passport. All of that is back in her trunk in the tent that she and Alfredo shared. But, as promised, the embassy staff has prepared special papers of introduction that will allow her to leave Peru and enter the U.S.

Karl and his prisoner are driven to the Lima airport by two members of the embassy staff. They arrive in plenty of time to catch the 12-hour Pan Am flight to Miami. Greta remains difficult. She knows it would be more than foolhardy to try to escape from the clutches of her brother and attempt to find her way back to the jungle hideout of the Vulture's Beak. She has no money whatsoever and no means of transportation. But, despite this, she seems determined to create a scene wherever she can.

The Kansas siblings board the flight, sitting across the aisle from each other. There are at least 12 empty seats on the plane. The passengers are, in general, well-dressed. Karl has put on his coat and tie again. Greta, however, remains decked out in her paramilitary outfit which begs for cleaning. This, coupled with the fact that she smells like a wet rat, is exceedingly homely, and challenged with limited eyesight that requires thick-lensed glasses, makes her an object of much attention. There are looks of disdain as passengers ask themselves, "What on earth is she doing here?"

Karl ignores the attention. His job is to get his sister back to Kansas, whether or not she wants to go or is not dressed like the other passengers.

They have been in the air only an hour or so, and Greta decides to make a scene. She looks over at her brother and hollers once again, "You can't do this!"

Karl tries to ignore her, hoping she will accept the reality of her situation and quiet down.

But she continues, "I hate you! I hate you! You have no right!"

By now, many of the other passengers are turning their heads and wondering what is going on. Karl tries to silence her, "Please. Keep it down."

But his little sister is determined to stir things up. "You're going to be sorry for this. You will pay for this! Alfredo will destroy you! You will die!"

One of the stewardesses hustles back to the aisle where the two siblings are seated and politely asks Greta to calm down. "Please, Mam, you are disturbing the other passengers."

Greta stares at the flight attendant with a blank, unfocused look, as though she does not know what is going on or where she is. But even as the stewardess is standing there, she hollers again, "Alfredo will take care of you, just like he took care of Sonny."

This gets Karl's attention. "What?"

Now in a softer voice, Greta leans into the aisle, looking around the stewardess and growls at her brother, "Alfredo put a spell on your horses. He killed your son. And he can kill you."

A skeptical Mr. Miller leans toward his sister and asks, "Why would he do that?"

"Because you told me that I shouldn't marry him; that he was nothing but a gigolo looking to take my money."

"I didn't say that. I just suggested that you needed to be careful."

"Oh no. Oh no. It was more than that," Greta responds in a threatening, low, and gravelly voice. Then she smiles and settles back into her seat.

It's a long flight to Miami. Karl is now not sure what to believe. He had pretty much convinced himself that Sonny's death was purely a fluke, a pure accident, that the horses had bolted for some strange, unknown reason. But… now… He wonders.

They get to Miami. It's late, after nine in the evening. The flight to Kansas City is scheduled for 9:00 the next morning. They check into a hotel near the airport—a room with two double beds. They go for a late dinner together. But the angry sister refuses to eat or to talk. Karl does not push her. Nevertheless, Greta seems resigned to her fate and actually bathes before retiring. Both the siblings sleep and are up and ready to go the next morning. Greta dons her unlaundered uniform once more. They catch a cab and return to the Miami airport, catch the flight to Kansas City, and drive back to Crossroads together, saying little to each other throughout the trip, unless it is essential.

Chapter Sixteen
Finding Love in Strange Places

A much-subdued Greta is living with one of her brothers on a farm that abuts Karl and Thelma's land. She is trying to put her life back together. She still dreams of returning to Peru and resuming her life as a revolutionary, but she has no money. Her life as a missionary is over. The Church of the Nazarene has essentially excommunicated her. The days go by. It is late summer. One day, she hears that the English teacher at the Crossroads school has resigned for health reasons. She applies for the position and, with her brothers' help, gets the job. She is now on the staff at her alma mater. And, because of her fluency in the language, she is given the added responsibility of teaching Spanish.

The job allows her to rent a small house in Crossroads; one that was for sale but one the owners were willing to rent, knowing how difficult it was to sell a house in the almost no-market condition of this dying community. Her new home is a clapboard, single-story cottage, constructed in the 1920s. Two bedrooms, one bath, and a kitchen only large enough for one cook at a time. Her brothers help her furnish it, largely with furniture they are not using. She gets a new driver's license and buys an old Chevy coupe with over 150,000 miles on the odometer.

She has been in the house for only a week or so and is sitting on the back porch one early fall evening, working on lesson plans for her classes at Crossroads school, when a feral cat saunters across the backyard. It is larger than the average-sized cat, with mixed black and brown, ragged, disheveled fur, and a twisted face. In short, it looks wild and ugly. Before she retreats to her bedroom for the night, Greta leaves a small saucer of milk on the steps to her porch on the back side of her house. The next morning, the milk is gone.

The next evening, the cat returns. Over the next week or so, the newly appointed English teacher is able to coax the scruffy feline on to her porch and be petted. Increasingly, the wild cat evolves toward domesticity and becomes an important part of his benefactor's life. She names the tomcat Alfredo.

Meanwhile, Karl's life has returned to normal, a cycle dictated by the demands of farm life. He continues to see and spend time with Cleo, in those times when he can get away from his responsibilities as a farmer. He and Thelma continue living together. It is a strange relationship, but they are, technically, still husband and wife. But that's about as far as it goes.

October has descended on the farming community in Crossroads. Harvest time is almost over. Temperatures are cooling. Leaves are gradually letting go of branches and falling to the ground. Farmers across the Doniphan County area are evaluating the year's return, getting their books in order, and preparing for the cold months ahead.

This month is also a time to celebrate. Every year, one of the members of the community hosts the Fall Festival. Initially, it was called October Fest, but to some, that title sounded too German. Even though the war is five years in their rearview mirror, the Poles, Swedes, English, and Dutch in the community still harbor a resentment toward the Germans.

This year, the event is being hosted by the Foster family. They own a small farm about ten miles east of Crossroads. It's a comfortable autumn evening. The temperature as the sun goes down drops into the upper fifties. The cloudless sky is a bright cobalt blue that gradually fades into a star-studded black sky. The guests bring the food, the cider, and the beer. Hard liquor is ostensibly banned, but some of the men have rum, bourbon, or tequila hidden away in their respective vehicles. There are about 40 adults and 12 children present. Several of the men have brought fireworks. The kids play with sparklers and small, lady-finger firecrackers.

The men help the children with Roman candles that blast brightly-colored balls of flame into the air. There are rockets that explode high in the air and scatter glowing, multicolored ashes across the sky. A few of the teenaged boys put cherry bombs under cans and light them, sending the cans hurtling skyward. Mothers watch all of this, entertained but fretting, nervous that their children might get hurt. Fireworks are dangerous.

Greta is here. She is dressed in a fashion not unlike that of the typical Crossroads farm wife: a light-brown, one-piece dress that hangs well below her knees, pulled tight around her waist with a large brown belt. She has a matching scarf around her neck. She has long ceased wearing the military fatigues she brought back from Peru, even though they have been washed and hung in a conspicuous location outside one of her bedroom closets. She treats them as a kind of shrine and a reminder of her life with Alfredo.

Tonight, she feels a bit strange, being the only single adult in attendance. But, many members of the Miller family are here and make an effort to include her.

As the evening wears on, the food gradually disappears and everyone is sitting or standing around a huge bonfire that Sherman Foster has constructed. Amidst the crackling of the sparks sailing into the night air, there is the sound of human chatter. Greta is sitting on a large log back some fifteen yards or so from the fire. At first, she is by herself, but after about five minutes she is joined by another woman sitting down next to her and sharing her log. It is Alexandra Porter, Lester's wife. They look at each other and smile. Alexandra, initiates the conversation, asking her log-mate about her new job as a teacher at the Crossroads school.

The conversation flows from there, as Greta takes advantage of the situation to confess to her unhappiness, how she wishes she were back in Peru, how she misses her Peruvian husband. She is grateful for the teaching position, but feels like her life lacks purpose; something she had as a missionary and then as a member of the revolutionary Vulture's Beak movement. Tears well up in her eyes as she tells Alexandra about Alfredo and how she sits at home and writes letter after letter to him, only to put them in a box where they will stay, since there is no way she can reach her beloved husband by mail.

The farmer's wife listens intently, her facial expressions reassuring Greta that she is being heard. As the newly minted high-school teacher sniffles and wipes the moisture from her eyes, Alexandra hands her a small handkerchief and in an effort to let Greta know she understands, she comments in an empathetic tone, "I understand, Dear. Life can be tough, and you aren't the only woman with a reason to be unhappy."

Greta turns her head toward her evening's companion and asks, "What do you mean?"

Alexandra throws her head back and stares into the night sky, wondering how she should answer the question. Something about Greta makes her feel safe; that her comments would go no further than this evening's discussion.

She responds, "I know what it's like to be unhappy; to be depressed and feel hopeless and helpless most of the time."

"Really?" is the only thing that Greta can say. Then, after a few moments she asks, "What do you mean?"

"I mean, being a farmer's wife is not easy. It's one long string of chores; of early morning to late night drudgery, physical hardship, and boredom. But you probably know that already."

"Yeah. I do. I see what it's doing to my sisters-in-law."

Alexandra hesitates for a moment and then adds, "What you don't know is that I am married to a cruel and insensitive man; a man who seems to delight in making my life miserable."

Greta has heard rumors about Lester, his drinking and the rough way he treats his wife; but she acts surprised by this revelation. "Wow! I mean, that's terrible. I did not—"

Before she can complete her sentence, Alexandra continues, "Come on, you probably already know this, but he has been beating me for a long time, especially in the last year or so; getting drunk, coming home, and taking out his unhappiness on me; shoving me, slinging me around, slapping me, and hitting me with his fists, although he is careful not to hit me in the face, and I'm sure you know why." By now, it is the abused farmer's wife who is tearing up. "I'm sorry," she says somewhat mournfully. "I shouldn't be dumping this on you."

"No. No. It's okay," Greta says reassuringly, as she reaches over and places her hand on her companion's leg.

Alexandra responds by putting her left hand on top of Greta's. They stare into each other's eyes for a few seconds without saying anything. Then the battered wife continues, "I guess I should have known. There was something wild and crazy about him from the beginning. At the time, I found it exciting; you might even say sexy. So, I agreed to marry him, not knowing that his craziness would eventually destroy me." She lowers her head as she talks; then pauses as she sobs quietly.

Greta continues looking at her with an empathetic eye, her head cocked back and staring under her thick glasses in a way that has become part of her public persona.

Ironically, it was at one of these October festivals that Alexandra Lombardi, her maiden name, met Lester. She was a recent high-school grad and he a bachelor farmer. Not a pretty young lady, but attractive enough to get men's attention. From a farming family in an adjoining county, she was living at home with her mother, father, and two of her siblings. There was enough to do on the farm to keep her busy, but she knew that this was not the life for her. She was intent on going to college and trying to save money from odd jobs to help pay for the education she desired. She dreamed of being a nurse.

The night she met Lester, he seemed awkwardly shy. He was older, but something about him made him seem younger. He was just over six feet tall with an athletic body: large chest, small waist, muscular arms, and a sharply chiseled face; small nose, deep blue eyes closer together than average, and a head covered with thick, slightly curled blond hair. Alexandra was smitten. Nothing happened that night, but the following week he called and asked her out. She accepted, trying hard to mask her enthusiasm. Lester took her to dinner at a small restaurant in Atchison. They were married a few months later.

Within a short time after the marriage, Alexandra was pregnant. Over the next five years, she had three children: two boys and a girl. They became her reason for living, her focus and purpose. So, once they all graduated from Crossroads school and went off to college, she found herself afloat on an ocean of chaos without a compass. Her daily life as a farmer's wife became increasingly difficult, in large part because she was married to a man who was impossible to please and who struggled to keep his head above water financially.

Sadly, he consistently took his frustrations out on his wife who felt she had no other options and thus suffered the abuse in silence, never reaching out for help, knowing that any complaint to the authorities would get her nowhere; only give her husband additional reason to abuse her, punish her for trying to make him look bad. She has thought about and considered divorce many times, but always she ends up talking herself out of it. It would be a blight on her family's reputation. The Lombardis were devout Roman Catholics and viewed marriage as a lifetime religious commitment—no exceptions. And, even if she were bold enough to flaunt her parents' dogma, she would have no way to support herself, since she did not have the education or training she would need in order to land a job that paid enough to provide a decent lifestyle, if only for a single woman.

Louis Lombardi claims to be distantly related to her family. She calls him Uncle Louie. She has considered confiding in him and asking for his help.

Louie is no friend of Lester's; quite the contrary. The notorious tavern-owner lost his older son in the war. Mr. Porter was a Nazi sympathizer during the major part of that conflict and actually continues to act like one. But Lester is now a regular customer at the bar, so the owner masks his disdain most of the time. Also, Louis is a man with a Catholic worldview, even though he rarely goes to mass and has not gone to confession since he was a teenager. But he believes firmly in the sanctity of marriage and the notion that it is the wife's role to obey her husband, regardless. It is likely, were Alexandra to confide in Louie, he would dismiss the whole thing, saying something like, "Come on, girl, Lester's a complicated man and this is just his way of showing you that he loves you."

As the women sit next to and confide in each other, the hands-on-the-leg turns to holding hands. Neither of them knows what to say next, but they both feel this sudden sense of bonding; a bonding created in the sharing of intimacies and establishing a mutual understanding. Two unhappy women finding empathy in each other, an empathy they have not felt in a long time, if ever.

Greta feels the electricity of the moment, but is not sure what to say. Finally, she murmurs, "I wish there was something I could do."

Alexandra lifts her head and quips, "Maybe you could shoot the bastard."

This unexpected response surprises, if not shocks, Greta, but the smile that comes to her conversational partner helps her understand that it was said in jest, and she chuckles.

Then the conversation turns serious again. The unhappy farmer's wife tells her companion, "You know, sometimes I think the only way out of all of this is for me to take my own life; kill myself. I often find myself in situations that remind me that there are fates worse than death."

Greta jumps in, "No. No. You've got too much to live for. Think of your children and the grandchildren that are sure to come along sometime soon."

None of Alexandra's three children is married yet, but it is assumed at some point they will find mates and have children. Perhaps that will give her something to live for. And perhaps Lester will be a better grandfather than he has been father and husband. But right now, life seems completely without meaning or pleasure—only anger and pain.

For a bit, they remain speechless, limiting their communication to body language, a language that suggests something more than casual friendship is happening, a could-be bonding, maybe chemistry.

The magic of the moment is broken as Lester walks up and puts his hand on his wife's shoulder. "Well, I bet you two bitches are talking about me."

Elizabeth turns red and rolls her eyes as she looks in Greta's direction.

"Come on, woman. It's time to go home. I've had enough of this party shit."

Reluctantly, the battered farmer's wife stands up as her husband tugs at her. He turns to pull her toward his big Ford pickup. Alexandra glances back at Greta, who mouths very distinctively, "Call me."

*****

It's mid-morning on Saturday, one week since the Fall Fest. Greta is at home seated at her second-hand desk, writing another letter to Alfredo; a letter that will end up in a pile with the other unsent missives that most likely will never reach their addressee. Her phone rings. She answers, "Hello."

"Greta?"

"Yes."

"It's Alexandra. You asked me to call you."

"Yeah. I did. I did." Greta pauses as she considers how to respond to this surprise call. "I thought you might want to talk some more; maybe finish the conversation we started."

"Actually, that's what I'd hoped. But I'd rather talk in person, you know, not just over the phone."

"Okay. What do you suggest?"

"Well, you could come here. Lester has gone to St. Joe with a truckload of feed corn, and none of the kids are here. But to be honest, I would feel safer at your place. Will that work for you?"

"Sure. Sure. It will. I'm not doing anything that important. Give me a few minutes to straighten up the place; but yes. Come on over."

Alexandra does not hesitate. "I'll be there in 15 minutes."

"Great."

As promised, the abused farmer's wife is on the front porch of Greta's bungalow in about 15 minutes, knocking on the door. The door opens and the two women look at each other with wondering eyes and then there is a spontaneous embrace. The host pulls her guest into her front room and asks, "How about some coffee?"

"I'd love it."

As Alexandra looks around the room, she sees a few pictures on the wall, largely of the Miller family. She sees one of a dark-skinned guy with a baseball cap and sunglasses. She assumes that is Alfredo. There are also a couple of scenic photos with mountains in the background. She concludes that this is Peru.

Greta returns and, minutes later, the two women sit down in the small living room, sipping coffee and looking at each other inquisitively, both uncertain as to what to do next.

Greta breaks the ice, "You wanted to talk."

"Yeah. I did." Alexandra pauses then continues, cautiously, "I'm having problems; problems that seem tied to an empty life. A life without purpose, meaning, or love."

The host is not sure how to respond, but before she can, Alfredo the cat comes strolling into the living room. He has his own rubber entry contraption on the bottom of the back door that allows him to come and go at will. Alexandra reacts with mild surprise, "I didn't know you had a cat." However, she had noticed as she came into the house the smell of breakfast mixed with a tint of cat urine, but had been reluctant to comment.

"I do," Greta affirms. "Not sure where he came from, but he wandered up onto my porch one day. I started feeding him, and at some point, he decided he belonged to me."

"Does he have a name?"

"Of course; Alfredo."

"I should have known."

At this point, Alexandra leans over in an effort to greet the still somewhat wild alley cat. Before she can touch him, Alfredo backs away, stiffens his back, bares his teeth, and hisses threateningly. The astonished guest pulls her hand back as quickly as she can.

"Not exactly friendly, is he?"

"He's not used to seeing other people here. It may be a territory thing. Perhaps he thinks you're invading his space."

"Perhaps, but I'll have to say, he's not the cutest cat I've ever seen."

"Yeah. I've tried to clean him up, but he's still a bit scruffy, and like me, he's not going to win any beauty prizes."

The conversation turns to idle chitchat. Alexandra says she has been in this house before; that she knew the previous owners. Greta explains she does not own the house; only renting.

"Well, it looks like you've done a lot of work on this place, for someone who is not an owner."

"Not that much, but enough to make it comfortable for me; to give me a sense that even though I'm just renting, it's actually mine. Can I show you around?" Greta asks.

"Sure."

There is not much to see, but Greta is proud of the way she has fixed up the place. As they look into the bathroom, Alexandra exclaims, "Oh, you have a bathtub."

"I do. Don't you?"

"No. We only have a shower in the corner of the basement. The concrete floor slopes down to a large drain; nothing fancy, but it gets the job done."

"I understand. One of my brothers has a shower like that. Not private, not fancy, but it works."

They both laugh as they return to the living room, their coffee, and their chitchat. As Alexandra swallows the last drop of her Folgers and puts her cup on the side table next to her, a piece of furniture which is badly in need of refinishing, Greta asks if she would like a refill.

"No thanks. But I would like something else," she says with an apologetic overtone.

"What's that?"

"I know you'll think I'm nuts, but I'd like to take a bath in your tub." Her faces reddens as she makes this unusual request.

Greta removes her glasses, cocks her head to one side, and looks at her guest as if to say, "Are you serious?" But quickly she realizes that Alexandra is, indeed, serious. "Well, of course. Of course. Why not?"

"Are you sure?"

"Absolutely. Help yourself. Holler if you need help."

Alexandra gets up and sheepishly walks out of the living room and into the small lavatory. Greta follows her and shows her how to use the rubber plug, points to the large yellow sponge, and puts a clean bath towel on a chair next to the tub. She also pulls a small jar of bubble bath out of the medicine cabinet over the sink and suggests that her friend add some of that to the hot water so as to enhance the experience.

As Alexandra turns on the water and begins taking off her clothes, Greta excuses herself. As she is leaving the room, she begins pulling the door closed.

"No. That's okay. Leave it open. Makes me feel less crowded. I tend to be claustrophobic. Also, things won't steam up as much."

Greta obliges her guest and walks back to the living room, retrieves the coffee cups, and takes them to the kitchen. When she finishes rinsing them out, she finds herself at a loss as to what to do next. Finally, she goes back into the living room, grabs a novel she has been reading, and tries to get her mind off the naked woman in her bathtub.

Some fifteen minutes go by and the ex-missionary's reading is interrupted, "Greta, can you come here for a minute?"

"Sure." She tosses her book onto the couch and jumps up.

As she walks into the steam-filled bathroom, she is greeted with a "Would you mind doing me a favor?"

"I guess. What?"

"Could you scrub my back?"

At this point, Greta begins to imagine where all this might be leading and finds herself becoming aroused.

Alexandra smiles at her and notes, "This is the first time I've been in a bathtub in almost five years. The last time was in a Kansas City hotel. Lester and I had gone there for a big cattle sale."

Greta kneels down beside the tub as her visitor hands her the sponge and in the process pulls herself from a slightly prone to a more upright position. In the process, her breasts emerge from amidst the bubbles which slowly slide back into the water. Taking in the exposed portion of her friend's wet body, the renter of the tub begins rubbing the sponge across Alexandra's back.

"Aah, that feels so good." Her eyes closed, the bather moans with satisfaction.

The ritual continues for several minutes before Alexandra reaches up and grabs Greta's arm and pulls it to the front of her body. "Here; why don't you scrub this side too?"

Seconds later, Greta is dragging the sponge across and around the breasts of her luxuriating guest. No longer wondering, she now knows where this is going and her excitement mounts. As the scrubbing turns to fondling, Alexandra suddenly puts her hand behind her friend's head, gently pulls it forward, and kisses her on the mouth. Somewhat caught off-guard, Greta is slow to respond and backs away.

"I'm sorry. I shouldn't have done that," Alexandra apologizes with mild embarrassment in her voice.

"No. No. I mean…that's fine." And then, without a word, Greta leans into the face of her guest and initiates a second kiss. This time, mouths slightly open, they lock their lips together, exploring with their tongues and tasting each other's saliva.

Greta backs away and removes her glasses and, without a word from the now well-bathed farmer's wife, grabs the bath towel and watches Alexandra turn and stand facing her, the water dripping off her naked body. Greta helps her step out of the tub and begins gently drying her off. It is both an act of assisting and of exploring.

As the now sensually stimulated hostess works down her guest's body with the towel, Alexandra slowly moves her right leg away from her left, non-verbally inviting Greta to dry her privates. She does, and then drags the towel down her legs. When most of the moisture has been removed, she stands up and again, without a word, Alexandra begins undressing the ex-missionary. Greta does not resist, and suddenly both of them are standing there completely unclothed, facing each other, not touching but staring into the eyes of the other—the message: "I want you."

Temperatures rise as Greta grabs her friend's hand and together, they step out of the bathroom and into the bedroom. The queen-sized bed is covered with a homemade quilt that Greta won at a local raffle—red and white squares. They sit on the edge of the bed, side-by-side; not speaking, only looking as the intensity of their passions manifests itself in their heavier breathing. As they prepare to move to the next stage of the tryst, Alfredo the cat literally gallops into the room and hissing with teeth bared slaps a clawed foot across Alexandra's ankle. She screams.

The magic of the moment is broken. Greta reacts by leaping to her feet and with amazing agility and accuracy kicks the cat across the room and then chases him back through the opening in the kitchen door. Alfredo flees, probably fearing for his life. Greta lays a wooden chair against the lower part of the door to prevent the tomcat's return and then hastens back to the bedroom where her guest is wiping blood from the small scratch. Greta goes back into the kitchen, pulls out a clean washcloth and a small wash pan, which she fills with warm water, and goes back to treat her wounded guest. The scratch is not deep and in a few minutes the bleeding stops.

Alexandra laughs. "Do you think your cat is the animal counterpart of your husband? He's apparently not happy seeing you with someone else."

"Look. I am so sorry. The last thing I want now is to see you hurt; your life is filled with enough pain."

"This is nothing. Come on. Let's finish what we started."

With that, Alexandra scoots back and lies down on the brightly-colored quilt. Greta turns and studies the freshly bathed body of her guest. Breasts the size of grapefruit that sag sideways with age lines streaked across the top and long, thin, dark nipples that droop forward. A body thick around the middle with stretch marks that tell the story of past pregnancies. White, smooth, unblemished skin with two large bruises on her left arm. Nicely shaped legs with well-defined calves. And hair... *Au naturel.* Like Greta, Alexandra apparently avoids the razor, does not shave her pubic area, her legs, or her underarms. For a woman almost twenty years older than her soon-to-be lover, she is well-preserved, still sexually attractive.

Greta climbs up beside her partner and asks, "Have you ever been with a woman before?"

"No. This is my first time; how about you?"

Greta is candid and tells the story of her experience with the female revolutionary, *Comrada Bella,* while she gently runs her hand over her friend's body. As she runs her fingers through the thick dark public hair of the woman beside her, she has to comment, "It looks like you don't like shaving any more than I do."

"Maybe. But I'll be honest. Under different circumstances, I would probably keep my body well-trimmed. However, it's about Lester. He would want me to keep my pussy and underarms shaved. He doesn't like my hair. I think it's about his whores who keep their private areas hair-free. Anyhow, it's one way for me to defy him and reduce the likelihood of his wanting to screw me. I lost interest in sex with him a long time ago."

"You said 'his whores'. Are you serious? He does the prostitute thing?"

"Well, sometimes he can't explain missing money, and on several occasions, he's come home smelling of cheap perfume. I don't like him spending the money, but having sex with other women—that's fine with me. I just want him to leave me alone. I also think he's had at least one affair with a local woman. Not sure who. Even though I've never pushed him on that, he's as much as admitted to his several infidelities. Again, I really don't care."

The two women turn on their sides and repeat the passionate kiss of their bathroom encounter. Then Greta begins moving her lips down her lover's body, sucking softly on her nipples, then caressing her belly and taking in the smell of her skin; a milky odor, sweet with sour overtones. Gradually, she works her way down into public hair and then licking the clitoris and fondling Alexandra's distended labia. The smell that emanates from the vagina is similar to the acrid earthiness of the Peruvian woman she'd lain with in Alfredo's tent.

To Alexandra, all of this is new, but she is obviously enjoying the experience as she moans and twists from side to side. Next, Greta lifts her head and turn her body around, draping one leg over her companion's head and carefully lowering her private parts into her face. Alexandra seems to know instinctively what to do next and begins returning the favor of her partner, massaging her tender parts with her wet lips and taking in the sensual odor that adds to the passion of the moment. Orgasm follows orgasm. Both women are caught up in the heat of the encounter.

Finally, exhausted and drained of sexual energy, the two women disengage and lie beside each other, breathing heavily, laughing and savoring the wonder of the experience.

As the passion cools, Alexandra is the first to speak. "Wow! I've often wondered what it would be like to make love to another woman, but I didn't imagine it would be so…" She hesitates as she tries to find the right word. "Satisfying? Fulfilling? Exciting? I'm not sure there's a way to really describe it. Wonderful? So unlike the sex I've known with Lester."

"Speaking of Lester, I'm assuming those bruises on your arm are the results of his temper."

"Yep. I haven't told you, but last week when we got home from the Fall Fest, Lester, who'd had too much to drink, started in on me. He wasn't happy that I had hung out with you that night. He said some unkind things about you. I made the mistake of trying to defend you, and that pissed him off even more. That's when he grabbed my arm and slung me across the room. Fortunately, I fell backward onto the couch. As usual, I started crying. For some reason, when

I cry, Lester seems to soften up and leave me alone. I think he realizes how wrong he is."

"You shouldn't have to put up with that." Greta squints and shakes her head as she empathizes.

"I know. But I also know that I don't want my relationship with you to stop here. I hope we can keep seeing each other. I've never known the kind of passion I've experienced today. I guess you could say I've fallen in love with you."

With that, the two lovers embrace and kiss each other with warm tenderness and an unstated commitment to the relationship.

Chapter Seventeen
Murder in a Small Town

It's Sunday afternoon on a sunny spring day in Crossroads. After church, the Butler boys go home with one of the church families, the Fosters. They have two boys roughly the same age as the preacher's sons. After a delicious roast-beef dinner, the four boys head out onto the farm to play. They choose sides and play army, throwing hedge apples at each other. They dig a small cave into the loose soil that lines the side of a dry creek that runs through the Foster farm. They look for arrowheads, which they often find, especially in recently plowed farm fields. They shoot birds with the Foster boys' bee-bee gun.

After an hour or so, they are far back in the woods that are part of the Foster farm; an area that is left largely untouched. As they are walking along the dry creek, they inadvertently spook three or four buzzards who fly off in another direction. The boys assume that they had been feeding on a dead animal of some sort; a deer, a rabbit; a coyote. But as they get closer to the buzzard's meal, they look on in horror. It is a person; a dead person. They look at each other with eyes bugging out of their heads in terror.

"It looks like a dead person," one of them observes in what is almost a whisper.

They stare at the corpse for a few moments, and then turn and run. As they near the Foster house, one of the boys starts yelling, "Daddy! Daddy! There's a dead man in the creek."

They boys rush through the back door and into the kitchen. Mrs. Foster is baking cookies. She is startled by the boys' bursting into the house. "What's wrong?"

"It's a dead man."

"What?"

"There's a dead man lying in our creek bed. He's dead! Really dead!"

Mr. Foster is in the living room reading the Bible when he hears the commotion. Before he can get up, the boys have rushed to his side, again repeating the same line.

"Wait. Slow down. What do you mean?" the confused farmer asks.

The older of the Foster boys spells it out for his father. "We were playing in the north woods and saw some buzzards and then when we got closer, we saw a dead man lying in the dry creek."

"Are you sure? This isn't one of your games, is it?"

"No!" the four boys shout in unison.

Sherman Foster puts his Bible to one side and follows the boys out of the house, along a plowed field, and into the woods. Sure enough, the boys were not kidding. There's a dead man there, and not just any man. It's Mr. Porter, Lester Porter.

"Okay boys, don't get too close. Don't touch anything. We've got to get hold of the sheriff and let him handle this."

They rush back to the house and the now stressed-out father calls the sheriff in Troy. About 45 minutes later, he shows up with one of his deputies. Shortly after that, an ambulance and two medics arrive. Together they go into the woods to examine and retrieve the body. They ask Sherman and the boys to stay away.

The kids remain awestruck. This is the first time they've ever seen anything like this and it's an experience they'll probably never forget. Mr. and Mrs. Foster talk quietly about what might have happened. Was Lester out hunting or something and maybe had a heart attack? Or did someone kill him? Certainly, there were people who didn't like him, but kill him?

An hour or so later, the medics haul the covered body out of the gulch on a stretcher and put it in the back of the ambulance. The sheriff tells Mr. Foster he'd like to ask him a few questions.

How did they find the body? Did Mr. Porter have any reason to be on the Foster property? How well did you know the victim? Did you have any issues with him? Can you think of anyone who might have killed him?

The sheriff does not say much, only that it is clear the Lester Porter was murdered. He would not comment on the evidence. He and his deputy leave and drive to the Porter farm to inform his wife. They knock on the front door.

"Mrs. Porter?"

"Yes."

"Lester Porter is your husband, is that right?"

"Yes."

"Well, ma'am, I'm sorry to inform you, but your husband is dead. It looks like he's been murdered."

Alexandra seems surprised by the news. Her eyes stare wildly at the sheriff, a hand over her mouth. She knows she should start screaming or crying, but she can't. All she can do is blurt out an "Oh no! Oh no! I don't believe it! It can't be true!"

"I'm sorry, ma'am, but it is. Some boys found his body in a dry creek bed on the Foster farm."

As she regains her composure, Alexandra tells the sheriff, "I called your office a couple of days ago to tell you my husband was missing, but was told that there was nothing your office could do; that he probably would show up. 'These things happen,' is what he said."

The sheriff responds, "I was not aware of that and I apologize. But we get missing person reports all the time and most of the time the so-called missing persons show up with perfectly logical explanations for their absence."

The now widowed farmer's wife says nothing. Just continues staring and trying to take it all in and knowing she should act more bereaved—but she can't.

The sheriff looks at his deputy and then turns back to Alexandra. "Look; we have questions we have to ask you, but we will come back later, after you've had a little time to let all this soak in and to grieve. Meanwhile, we are taking the body to Troy. After the coroner has had a chance to examine it, we will let you know and release the body to your custody. You can then move ahead as quickly as you'd like with funeral and burial plans."

"Okay. Okay. Well…thank you."

*****

The news of the murder spreads through Crossroads and Doniphan County with the speed of atomic fission. This is the biggest news since Sonny Miller's death. Reporters from newspapers and radio stations from Troy, Atchison, St. Joseph, and Kansas City swoop down on the community to interview everyone who will talk. Their questions are generally boilerplate: *What kind of person was Lester Porter? How well did you know the victim? Can you think of anyone who would want to kill him?*

The news was significant in many ways, but most importantly because, according to the myth of rural life, things like this were not supposed to happen in a small community like Crossroads.

The local gossip is filled with speculation and different reactions to his death. Few folks seem to be mourning or even suggesting that his death is a loss to the community. As one of the individuals interviewed by a St. Joe radio station puts it, "Lester Porter was a cat in the dog pound. It's like he didn't belong, but other people were generally afraid to mess with him for fear they might get scratched."

Another notes, "I doubt there will be many people crying at his funeral."

Meanwhile, the sheriff's office is conducting its investigation, studying the evidence and interviewing anyone whom they think might provide helpful information.

Alexandra and her three children make the arrangements for Lester's funeral and burial, engaging the services of a funeral home in nearby Troy. Rev. Butler meets with the family in an effort to help assuage their grief and plan funeral details.

*****

It has been a week since the body was discovered. The Methodist Church in Crossroads is filled to standing-room-only. While Lester was not that beloved or admired, his funeral is one of those events that no one wants to miss. Lester's body is lying in a cheap unopened casket. The family requested a closed casket, given the condition of the deceased one's mutilated corpse. The casket has been placed under and in front of the pulpit. Mrs. Butler is playing background music on the piano, her own rendition of *Nearer My God to Thee*. It is a somber mood, typical of most funerals. People are here, in part because they feel they need to support Alexandra and her children. Some are simply morbidly curious.

Rev. Butler sits behind the pulpit, watching. He has lived here for three years, his first experience in a small rural community. As he watches the locals walk into the chapel, he thinks about the contrast and yet similarity between the lives of country and city folk. In both cases, it seems there is a chaotic complexity to it all. Despite the myth, there is nothing simple about life in a small town. And he wonders if what many of the locals see as ties of loyalty to Crossroads are really feelings of being trapped, without the options provided by life in the city. He loves the members of his congregation, but is comforted by the realization that, unlike them, he is not stuck here. When he completes his seminary degree, he will be free to fly off to any number of places, should he choose to leave.

At the appointed hour, he stands and walks up to the pulpit and in his deep, resonant voice dives into the formal part of the ceremony. "We are gathered here today to celebrate the life of Lester Monroe Porter, a man who, sadly, was taken down before his time. Our hearts go out to his family. They have been robbed. They have lost someone near and dear. And we ask, why?"

Alexandra and her family are seated in the front row of the church. Greta Miller is sitting next to the bereaved widow. Some members of the congregation are wondering why. They see it as strange, since there has long been bad blood between the Millers and the Porters. The Miller family members present assume this is simply one of Greta's ways of demonstrating her anger over the way in which she was forced, against her will, to leave her husband and the life she was living in Peru.

Thelma and Karl are sitting together, but not touching. Appearances matter, perhaps more in a small town than in the city. It is possible to be anonymous in a large metropolitan area, but not in a tiny burgh like Crossroads. Thelma looks around at the other women in the crowd, especially the farm wives, and wonders if they, like her, feel almost enslaved by their circumstances. No education, no employment options, no way to be independent, nothing—only the day-after-day grueling routine of farm life. She feels sorry for Alexandra but is doubtful that Lester's wife is really grieving his unexpected departure from the land of the living.

Rev. Butler continues, "Lester Porter was an honorable man; a hardworking farmer, a good husband, a caring father, and a friend to all who knew him."

At this point, an old man and long-time resident of Crossroads stands up, leans on his cane and, in a shrill raspy voice, hollers, "That's bullshit! The guy was an asshole and we all know it!" With that he turns, scoots out of his pew, and walks slowly out the back of the sanctuary. Had the protester been younger, it is likely one of the Porter boys, or both, would have confronted him after the service and made him regret having opened his mouth. But he is protected by his age and the respect most members of the community have for the elderly.

Rev. Butler is not sure how to deal with this outburst, this throwing of cold water on the warmth of his remarks. As he pauses and clears his throat, there is a collective gasp from the audience, followed by an audible wave of chuckles. It is likely that a great many of those in attendance agree with the indignant, outspoken old man, but are constrained by the expectations of politeness.

The pastor is forced to ad-lib, "Everyone is entitled to his or her own opinion. I think we can agree on that. And yes, Lester did not get along with everyone, and I'm sure there are people who saw him as an enemy rather than a friend. But, come on, that could be said about all of us. I am certain there are some of you out there who don't like me and would run me out of town if you could. This is simply the nature of human society. No one is loved by all. Even Jesus had more than his share of enemies. So today, let's put aside our feelings of ill-will. Let us focus on the meaning of this ceremony, not on how we may have felt about Mr. Porter."

"Today is not just about Lester, but it is about all of us. Remember, as the poet has reminded us, 'the bell tolls for all of us.' All of us are mortal. We will all die someday. As they say, the day you are born you begin to die. And, I think all of you would agree with me; when you are gone and people gather around your grave, you would hope they would remember and talk about the good you did in life; not the fact that there were those who did not like you."

With that, Reverend Butler weighs into a boilerplate funeral sermon, quoting scripture and talking about heaven and what the Bible says about death. When he finishes, he invites family members to come to the pulpit and share their thoughts about the diseased. The older Porter brother, speaking for the whole family, reads a prepared statement in which he extols his father's virtues, while admitting his dad could be tough to deal with at times. The young man's comments end with an air of acrimony as he lashes out at whoever took his father's life. "May they rot in hell!" are his final words. He grabs his printed remarks, lowers his head, and walks off the platform and returns to his seat.

At this point, the reverend walks up behind the pulpit and asks, "Would anyone else like to say a few words about our fallen brother?"

The crowd remains silent, wishing for the service to end as quickly as possible. Some groan in frustration when suddenly Lester's daughter leaps to her feet and announces, "I do."

She mounts the platform and the preacher moves aside as she grabs the pulpit. With no visible notes, she is ad-libbing, "Look, I know my dad could be an asshole." This causes a minor shockwave among the offended self-righteous in the audience. Reverend Butler blushes. "But," the daughter continues, "my father was a good father. He struggled to keep us fed and clothed, but he did it. And then, he managed to send all three of us to college. Who else here today has done that?" She pauses as though she's asking for a show of hands. There are none, and she says with a kind of defiance in her voice, "No one. That's what I thought." With an obvious smile of satisfaction, she turns and walks back to her seat.

Reverend Butler, having recovered from his red-faced reaction to the unexpected obscenity, once again takes the pulpit and repeats his invitation. This time, there are no takers. So he brings closure to this portion of the service by inviting the audience to respond, "And all the people said…"

The crowd responds appropriately with a hearty "Amen!"

Mrs. Butler returns to the piano, and her husband leads the audience in an old church favorite, *In the Sweet Bye and Bye*. The pallbearers come forward, lift the casket, take it outside, and slide it into the waiting hearse. The crowd exits the church. People get into their respective cars and follow the hearse to the cemetery, where Crossroads residents have been burying their dead since the mid-1800s. As his casket is lowered into the ground and covered, the door on the life of Lester Porter is shut, but his murder case is still open. His death remains a mystery.

Chapter Eighteen
An Unsuspecting Suspect

One week later, it's a dreary autumn day, and Karl Miller is in one of the barns working on the older of his two tractors. Dressed in a faded blue pair of Sears and Roebuck overalls and an old green t-shirt, he is engulfed in the smell of gasoline, grease, and old dry straw. He is thinking about tomorrow. The plan is for him to spend part of the day with Cleo. But his daydreaming is abruptly interrupted by Thelma's hollering from the south entry of the barn. "Karl! Karl!"

He turns in her direction. "What?"

"You need to come to the house. The sheriff is here and wants to see you." There is a subtle note of pleasure in the announcement.

Karl drops the large wrench he's been working with, wipes his hands on an already soiled rag, and heads to the house. The sheriff and his deputy are standing in the living room waiting for him. Before he can say anything, the sheriff sticks a piece of paper in his direction. "Mr. Karl Miller. We have a search warrant and we're here to search your house."

"What!" the wealthy farmer blurts out in disbelief.

"We have reason to believe there may be evidence here that might be useful in the Lester Porter murder case."

"You're kidding! So what exactly are you looking for?"

"I'm afraid I'm serious. I'm not at liberty to discuss the details, but we have reason to believe you may have been involved in Mr. Porter's death; probable cause evidence."

Again, Karl reacts in bewilderment, "You don't really believe I had anything to do with that man's murder?"

"It's not what I believe that matters here. It's what the judge thinks about the evidence."

"What evidence?"

"Like I said, I really don't have the authority to disclose that evidence at this point. So, let's make this as painless as possible. I would like for you and your wife to wait outside while we search the house."

"You can't do this!" Karl shouts and moves aggressively toward the sheriff.

The deputy puts his hand on the angry farmer's shoulder as the sheriff calmly responds, "This warrant says I can. So, please. Don't make this difficult. If you have nothing to hide, then this will be the end of it."

Karl grabs the warrant. He peruses it quickly, and realizing there is no need to resist, begrudgingly walks out the front door and sits on one of the porch chairs, still shaking his head in apparent disbelief. Thelma joins him on the porch, but no words are exchanged. The wife is sitting on the porch swing, gently gliding back and forth. The husband is on a stiff wooden chair, leaning forward with his head in his hands.

Thirty minutes later, the investigator and his sidekick walk out the front door. They are carrying one of Karl's rifles and a small box of papers. The sheriff explains that these items will be examined and eventually returned. He also adds, "You might want to consult a lawyer. Depending on how all his shakes out, you may need one."

Karl protests once again, but to no avail.

The officers head toward their car, but the sheriff turns back and tells the frustrated suspect that he should not leave town until the investigation is complete. However, the directive sounds more like a suggestion than a command. Karl says nothing, but has no intention of changing his plans.

*****

Two days later, it's mid-morning, and Karl is in the cattle barn with Pete, treating a sick milk cow. He keeps wondering what, besides the rifle, the sheriff's office found in the raid on his house. He is angry. But having spent a good part of yesterday with his fortune-telling friend, he is feeling somewhat refreshed and at peace with the world.

Then, without warning, the sheriff and two of his deputies come walking into the barn.

Karl turns around as he hears them enter. "What the hell are you doing here?"

"Your wife told me I could find you here."

"Okay. You found me. Now what?"

"Mr. Karl Miller, I am placing you under arrest. You have been charged with the murder of Mr. Lester Porter."

"No way! No way!" The suspect shouts. "You can't do this! This is crazy!" Standing there and saying nothing else, Karl first looks at Pete and then at the men who are about to arrest him. He's not sure what to do.

The sheriff, in a calm and authoritative voice, coaxes the accused, "Let's not make this any more difficult than necessary. I'm asking you not to resist, but to come with us to the station in Troy, where you will be booked and held until the judge sets bail."

The officers have guns. The guy in charge has brought an extra deputy, knowing Karl Miller's reputation as an exceptionally strong man, most likely very difficult to subdue, should he resist arrest.

"I can handle things, boss," Pete says in his usual quiet and passive way. It is clear he is nervous. He knows the guy he works for and is worried he might be drawn into some sort of physical combat.

"I need to get my things—"

Before he can finish, the sheriff interrupts, "No need. Your wife can bring you anything you need after you are arraigned. Depending how long it takes the judge to set bail, you may not be in jail long enough to worry about a change of clothes."

"I need to contact my lawyer," Karl adds. He has not bothered to say anything to an attorney, despite what the sheriff had suggested earlier. His lawyer, who is with a Kansas City law firm, is a tax lawyer, but the wealthy farmer is certain the firm has several crackerjack trial lawyers, one of whom would be willing to take his case.

"You can do that from the county jail, after we check you in," the still-nervous sheriff explains.

"I need to tell my wife," Karl adds.

"We'll take care of that, don't worry."

The four men walk out of the barn, get into the squad car, and head for the sheriff's office in Troy. Karl can't stop thinking about what the media is going to do with this and how is family is going to react—the head of the prominent Miller clan arrested and accused of murder.

Chapter Nineteen
The Trial

Karl rolls over and reaches for his lover. She's not there. As he wipes away the sleep-induced glaze over his eyes, he sees her sitting in a simple wooden chair beside the bed, smoking a cigarette and looking at him as though she doesn't recognize this large, hairy man lying in her bed.

As he pushes the black silk sheet from under his chin and props himself up on his left elbow, he grunts, "Wow. I fell asleep. That felt good."

Cleo smiles. "You needed that. You've not been sleeping well these days. A good nap is always in order."

"What time is it?"

"Almost 4:30."

"You're kidding! Oh, man. I've got to get going." Karl swings his feet from under the sheet and onto the floor, reaches for his clothes, and begins dressing.

It's been three weeks since the well-known farmer was arrested and indicted on murder charges. He is now out on a $50,000 bail. His lawyer asked that that amount be reduced. His client was not a danger to society nor was he likely to flee and leave behind his farm and family. But the judge insisted that the amount of the bail was appropriate.

The trial is set for next week. Karl and his lawyer have spent several hours together looking at the evidence the district attorney has gathered and working on a defense strategy. On this particular afternoon, the defendant and the fortune-teller have discussed at length the ins and outs of his situation. One thing is for certain: their illicit relationship will become public. And, it is quite likely that she will be called on to testify.

Karl worries what his children will think when they find out. As for Thelma? She really doesn't matter anymore. He asks himself, *Has it been worth it?* His answer: an unqualified *yes*. The sex is no longer the unconstrained passion and volcanic explosion it was at the beginning, but it is still good. Indeed, it seems that what was once pure sensual passion has now morphed into real lovemaking. When they lock their loins and strive to give pleasure to each other, he feels he wants to be part of her, to own her, and to have her be part of him. He's never had these feelings before.

He finishes putting his clothes on, kisses Cleo goodbye, dashes out of her house and into his car. He has parked off the street, behind the fortune-teller's home, as a means of avoiding as much public scrutiny as possible.

****

Every seat in the county courthouse is taken. The trial venue is in the county courthouse in Troy. Karl and his lawyer had wanted the trial to be somewhere else, perhaps Atchison or Topeka. They thought they might have a fairer trial. Troy was too close and too much like Crossroads. There is something about the relation among farmers in an area like that of Crossroads. It's about the land and the history of land ownership. Over time, land can change hands and sometimes that change is clouded in bitterness; a feeling that the change was in someways unfair; perhaps one party taking advantage of the other party's misfortune. So, one family may harbor ill feelings about another and really not know or remember why. Such deep-seated animosity can in one way or another have a subtle but significant impact on the way a jury handles the evidence and votes on a case, whether it be assault and battery, armed robbery, or murder.

A heavy snow has fallen across the region, complicating the drive to Troy. The snowplow has removed much of the white stuff, but the roads remain slick and dangerous. But folks around here are used to this and most have chains they can put on their tires, chains that can navigate the slickest of roads. As people stand around in the lobby and hallways of the courthouse, they swap stories about other snowstorms in the past and about today's difficult journey, slipping and sliding all the way to Troy. As one of the farmers quips, "It's as slick as frog shit out there."

Why go to all this trouble? The trial looms as a major event across the entire region; Doniphan County's most successful farmer indicted for the murder of one of his neighbors. Seating is limited and unfortunately, many who braved the bad weather to be here are not allowed into the courtroom and can only sit or stand around outside. Jury selection has been completed, so the actual trial can begin.

The mood in the courthouse is a somber and quiet one, with occasional whispers, as the observers, including members of the press, wait for the proceedings to begin. The air is flavored with human and barnyard smells, mixed with those of old wood and velvet-covered benches.

Conspicuous by her absence is Thelma Miller, wife of the defendant. This is noted repeatedly as those in attendance exchange observations about the crowd, the setting, and the trial. Alexandra Porter is there with one of her sons, sitting in the section reserved for family members. Greta Miller is there on the other side of her friend who is now a widow. It is rumored that Greta is hoping that her brother is convicted and punished. She remains angry. She still believes Karl ruined her life when he grabbed her and dragged her out of Peru. She cannot bring herself to forgive him.

The 12-person jury walks in and is seated. The prosecuting attorney, his assistant, the defendant, his lawyer and a member of his staff take their places at the front of the room. All is quiet as the bailiff announces, "Please rise." Everyone stands as the judge strides into the courtroom and takes his seat behind the bench.

"You may be seated," the bailiff drones.

The judge begins, "Regarding the case of the State versus Mr. Karl Miller…" With that, he proceeds to instruct the jury, the prosecution, members of the defense team, and the audience. It is clear that he is a no-nonsense judge and will not tolerate disruptions or any other actions that might delay or derail the trial.

The first phase of the drama begins as the prosecuting attorney, the district attorney, approaches the jury and lays out the case against the defendant. The DA is a short man, maybe 5'7," no more. A slight build, a body not of an athlete but also not of one with weight problems. He is in his 50s, but is losing his reddish-brown hair. He attempts to hide his balding with an awkward comb-over. It is obvious that he has not shaved today. He is dressed in a solid brown corduroy suit, a white shirt open at the neck, with a loosely hanging tie covered with images of Kansas sunflowers.

In an annoying, high-pitched nasal voice, he begins, "Ladies and gentlemen of the jury, let me begin by thanking you for doing your civic duty and agreeing to be part of this important trial. Over the next few days, you will hear testimony and see evidence that prove beyond a shadow of a doubt that the defendant, Mr. Karl Miller, did, with premeditation and evil intent, brutally murder the victim, Mr. Lester Porter." He proceeds to lay out his case.

As the DA finishes his presentation and returns to his seat, Karl's attorney, Clyde Hartman, probably as good as any trail lawyer money can buy, stands up and walks to the front of the jury box. His appearance and presentation are in sharp contrast to those of the prosecuting attorney. He is just over six feet tall. A trim body. In his early 60s. A full head of gray hair which he combs along the side and to the back. He is donning an expensive black wool suit, a white shirt with silver cufflinks and a black and red striped tie in a Windsor knot tight against his neck. His slick outfit and strikingly good looks may not be an asset in his appeal to a jury made up largely of working-class individuals who could feed their families for a month on what he has probably paid for his well-tailored suit. Knowing this, he tries hard not to come across as arrogant or too self-confident; not talking down to but rather chatting with jury members.

Mr. Hartman stands for a few moments, just looking at and making eye contact with each member of the jury. Then he begins, "Good morning, members of the jury. I want to echo the DA's words of gratitude. Your service in this important trial is greatly appreciated. I hope you're comfortable. I suppose it could be worse. You could be outside shoveling snow. What a snow! And for this time of year. Amazing."

At this point, the judge intervenes, "Please, will the defense get to the point? This is a trial, not a chitchat session."

"Sorry, Your Honor. I was…well, you know, just getting warmed up. I-I…" He deliberately stumbles and stammers, pretending to be a little nervous. He knows this will help the jury see him as a real person and perhaps even engender sympathy.

"Okay, you have heard the prosecution's charge against my client, Karl Miller. But I am here to tell you that there is no case. Mr. Miller should never have been arrested in the first place. The state has no hard evidence at all; only supposition, speculation, and conjecture. The only evidence they have is completely, uh, what's the word I'm looking for? Circumstantial; that's it, circumstantial, which is not enough to convict a man of murder. So, I ask you to consider all the evidence and when you do, you will see that there is no way my client could have committed this heinous crime of which he is accused. At that point, your only choice will be to declare him innocent."

Again, he pauses and looks at each of the jurors and as he does, he pulls the handkerchief out of his breast pocket and wipes his brow, a tactic he uses to give juries the impression that underneath the expensive suit beats the heart of a real human being. Finally, he thanks the jury and returns to his seat.

By now, Karl is more nervous than ever. He leans over and whispers in his lawyer's ear, "What in the hell was that all about?"

"Trust me. I know what I'm doing."

Next, the DA calls his first witness, the sheriff who has been heading up the investigation. He takes the stand and is sworn in and is asked the first question: "Can you tell the court how you found Mr. Porter's body?"

"Yes Sir. It started with a call from Mr. Sherman Foster. He told our dispatch officer that his boys had found a dead man's body in a wooded area on the north end of his farm. So, I called an ambulance, and then one of my deputies and I drove as quickly as we could to Crossroads and out to the Foster farm. When we got there, the Foster fellow walked us back to the body, which was lying in the middle of a dry creek bed. He identified the person as Lester Porter. We took photos and collected what evidence we could and then supervised the placing of the corpse into a body bag and being taken away by the ambulance and its two-man crew."

"How did you determine that Mr. Porter was murdered as opposed to his committing suicide or perhaps dying of natural causes?"

"There was a gunshot wound to the head. Also, there were bruises that suggested he had been hit at least once with some sort of blunt object. However, what was surprising was that there was very little blood around his head, which suggested to me that he had been killed somewhere else and then had his body moved from the scene of the killing to the dry creek bed."

"Were you able to determine how long the body had been lying there?"

"At least three or four days. The boys said they saw buzzards on the body when they first discovered it."

"That's all I have for the sheriff for now, Your Honor."

"Does the defense wish to cross-examine?"

"No, Your Honor, but I will have questions later, after the coroner testifies, if it pleases the court."

So, with that, the judge calls the county coroner to the stand. He's a frail man, shabbily dressed, with a pair of glasses hanging by a chain around his neck. He looks like someone who might enjoy picking through the decaying remains of dead persons.

The DA begins the questioning: "What can you tell the court about the body of the deceased when you examined it?"

"Well, he was dead." Even though the comment was not intended to be funny, there is a light ripple of chuckles across the audience. He continues, "First of all, the victim had been shot in the side of the head. Appears to have been at close range. The bullet was lodged in his brain and when we removed it, it looked like a 38 caliber. At the same time, as the sheriff pointed out, there was at least one indentation on the side of the victim's head that suggested he had been struck by some kind of blunt instrument."

"Anything else?"

"Well, both his eyeballs were missing. I'm not sure, but I am guessing they were pecked out by the buzzards."

"Do you know how long the victim had been dead?"

"Hard to say; but I agree with the sheriff—probably three to four days."

"Thank you. That's all I have." And with that, the DA returns to his chair while Karl's lawyer cross-examines.

"I have just one question. You said the bullet *looked* like a 38-caliber shell; is that correct?"

"Yes Sir."

"So you can't say for certain that the bullet that killed Lester Porter was fired from a 38-caliber weapon?"

"No Sir."

"Thank you. That's all I have, Your Honor." As the coroner leaves the stand, the defense approaches the bench. "With your permission, Your Honor, I would like to recall the sheriff to the stand."

"Permission granted."

The sheriff returns to the stand and the first question is: "What kind of evidence did you have that legitimized the warrant and the searching of Mr. Miller's home?"

The sheriff looks at the judge, who had been the one signing the warrant and issuing the search, wanting to be careful with his answer. Then he says, "Well, in the first place, there were a lot of rumors about bad blood between

Mr. Miller and Mr. Porter. And then there was the call we got from Mr. Troy Ackerman, the owner of the Texaco station in Crossroads. After he heard that Mr. Porter had been murdered, he remembered seeing the two men in an altercation at his place of business. It seemed pretty serious, and according to Mr. Ackerman, some serious threats were made."

"Like what?"

"Like, 'I'm going to take you down'."

"Who said that?"

"Mr. Miller."

"And that's all the evidence you had? Hearsay evidence? And you use that as an excuse to invade a man's home? That sounds pretty flimsy to me." Mr. Hartman knows he must be careful, because in some ways, it is the judge who issued the warrant and who bears the greatest responsibility for the unusual search. So, he stops there.

Next, the DA asks to cross-examine and another shot at the sheriff. "Okay, so you searched the house. What did you find there that lead you to arrest Mr. Miller?"

"Well, we found a Smith and Weston 635 rifle; one that uses bullets like that the coroner removed from the victim's head. We found a cut-off baseball bat that may explain the blow to the head. And we found some notes, letters, and check stubs that made us suspicious."

"What do you mean?"

"It's like a lot of the stuff was related to a particular woman, a woman named Jasmine Von Hussein."

"Can you tell the court more about this woman?"

"Sure. We did some checking and found out she's a fortune-teller who lives in St. Joe. She calls herself Cleopatra. When we questioned people who know her, some of them told us that she had once been a prostitute. They also believed she was having an affair with a married man. One of the neighbors described a car that fits a car owned by Mr. Miller: a green, 1947 Packard sedan."

"So, you are assuming that Mr. Miller was seeing Ms. Von Hussein; perhaps having an ongoing affair, is that right?"

At this point, defense leaps to his feet. "This is personal information that has no bearing on the case. I ask that it be struck from the record."

"Overruled. Prosecution may continue. The witness may answer the question."

"Yes. I think they were. We found a few checks made out to her and signed by the defendant."

"Anything else?"

"Well, there's the poem. It did not seem strange to me, but after I shared the materials with you, you thought it was significant."

The DA walks back to his table and picks up a greeting card and shows it to the judge. "We would ask that this card be labeled exhibit one." He then turns to the sheriff and asks, "Is this the item you were referring to?"

"Yes, it is."

The prosecuting attorney hands the card to the sheriff and asks, "Would you please read this for the court?"

The sheriff opens the card and begins reading:

Let us to the future look
Escape our fettered past;
Sew together all we are
To weave a love to last.
Ev'ry moment that we share
Reminds us; what can be,
If our two hearts become as one
Sweet bond, eternally.
Death will someday come our way,
Erasing all that's been
And so, let's love once more today;
Do now or never do again.

He finishes and looks up at the DA.

"Anything unusual about that poem?"

"I didn't think so, until you pointed it out to me."

"Okay. I want you now to read and tell me the first letter of each line of the poem."

"L-E-S-T-E-R-I-S-D-E-A-D."

"So, what is the message there?" the DA asks rhetorically.

"Lester is dead."

"And when is the card dated?"

"There is a date at the end of the poem that indicates it was written at least several days before Mr. Porter was murdered."

"Right. So, what does this suggest?"

"Objection!" Karl's attorney interrupts. "Calling for an interpretation by the witness."

"Overruled," the judge quickly responds. "This is pertinent to the case."

The sheriff continues, "It sounds like the writer of the poem knew that Mr. Porter was dead before the news became public."

"I guess the only way to get at the facts here is to question the author of the poem." With that, the prosecuting attorney backs away from the witness stand, "That's all I have, Your Honor."

Mr. Hartman gets up and approaches the witness to begin cross-examination. "First of all, Officer, I know you know that a lot of folks in these parts have 38-millimeter weapons. In other words, that in itself is not incriminating; am I correct?"

"Yes Sir."

"Also, the poem that you read, the poem whose alliteration suggests that the writer knew that Mr. Porter was dead; are you sure about the date? In other words, could not the writer have backdated the card to make it sound like it had been written before the news of the victim's death became public?"

"Yes."

"And is it not possible that the poem was written with absolutely no intent of conveying a message? Could not that have happened by accident?"

"I guess, but—"

"That's all I have for this witness, Your Honor." Karl's attorney cuts off the witness before he can speculate any further.

At this point, the DA rises and announces, "With the court's permission, I would like to call my next witness to the stand, Mr. Troy Ackerman."

"Permission granted."

Troy stomps up to the witness stand, dressed in clean, but oil-stained coveralls, a frayed, orange sweatshirt, and rubber boots. He and his wife have been married for decades, but have no children. They live next door to the Texaco station he operates. It has only one gas pump, an ancient one that stores fuel in a large glass tub above the dispensary mechanism. He has a small shop with a hydraulic lift and enough equipment to handle routine maintenance for cars, trucks, and farm machinery. He and his wife live hermetic lives and rarely interact with other locals outside the context of the gas station. For that reason, they are looked on with suspicion by their neighbors. But the gas station is the only one for miles, so Troy is never at a loss for business.

"Mr. Ackerman, can you tell the court what you saw and heard on that Monday afternoon in question, when you saw Mr. Miller and Mr. Porter confronting each other?"

"I sure can. I was a pumpin' gas for Mr. Miller's big Packard when Lester, he drove up behind him in his old pickup. I think he was in a hurry, 'cause he didn't sit there very long before he stuck his head out the window and hollered 'don't take it all.' Anyhow, I think Karl was kinda upset by this. He jumped out of his car and went walking back toward Lester. When he seen him comin', Mr. Porter got out of his car and stood there, lookin' right disturbed. I was worried, cause from what I've heard, them two ain't had much love for each other. Anyhow, the next thing I know, they's shovin' each other and hollering."

"So, what were they saying?"

"Well, I didn't get it all, mind you, but I'm pretty sure they was talking about Karl's daughter, Marlene."

"What did Mr. Porter say about the daughter?"

"I couldn't right tell, but it was clear Mr. Miller, he weren't happy. But he backed off, and as he did, I heard him say something like, 'you better be careful or you might get hurt'."

"And that was it?"

"Yes sir."

"That's all I have for this witness, Your Honor."

"Does defense wish to cross-examine?"

"We do, Your Honor." Karl's lawyer approaches the witness stand. "Mr. Ackerman, how well do you know my client, Mr. Miller?"

"I know him pretty good. He's been buyin' gas from me for a long time now. He's also had me work on his trucks a couple times; most recently, one of his tractors."

"Do you like him? I mean, personally, do you like Karl Miller?"

"Well, I don't know. I—"

"Mr. Ackerman, is it not true that you have told people that Mr. Miller was a rich son-of-a-bitch that treated people in town like dirt?"

"I-I don't remember."

The judge steps in. "The witness will answer the question."

"Okay, maybe I did say that once, but you know, sometimes you say things before you think about it."

"Also, Mr. Ackerman, you said you *thought* you heard Mr. Miller threaten Mr. Porter?"

"Yes sir."

"In other words, you are not exactly sure."

Again, the witness hesitates. He looks nervously at the prosecuting attorney. "No, I guess it's not like I'd swear on it."

"That's all I have, Your Honor."

Next, the moment Karl has been dreading. His lady friend, Cleo, is called to the stand by the DA. She strides to the front of the court with an air of grace and self-confidence. She is dressed in a modest dark brown two-piece suit and wearing a pair of matching flats. Her hair is tied back in a bun with a small gold hairpin helping to hold it in place. She has come prepared and looks the part of a serious businesswoman, which sets her apart from most of the farm women in the courtroom.

The bailiff swears her in. The prosecution approaches the witness box and begins, "Ms. Jasmine Von Hussein. Have I got that right?"

"Yes sir."

"But you also go by the nickname, Cleopatra, is that not right?"

"Correct."

"Can you tell the court what you do for a living?"

"I'm a fortune-teller?"

"Can you be more specific?"

"I read cards, conduct seances, help clients communicate with the dead, read palms, and predict the future for those who are interested."

"Is that all?"

"Pretty much."

"But isn't it true that you are also a prostitute, in other words, having sex with any man who is willing to pay?"

Cleo blushes noticeably, even though she knew this question would be asked. Karl is staring straight ahead, gritting his teeth and trying to remain calm.

She answers, "No, I'm not."

"Remember Ms. Von Hussein, you are under oath here and can be held in contempt of court if you refuse to tell the truth. Are you or are you not a prostitute?"

"I am not." This time, she answers louder and more forcefully.

"Ms. Hussein, you are lying. We can produce any number of witnesses from the greater St. Joseph area who, under oath, would testify to having paid you for sex. So, again, are you a prostitute?"

"No."

The DA throws up his hands in frustration as the defense attorney protests, "Please, Your Honor, the prosecution is badgering the witness."

"Overruled. I must remind the witness that she is obligated to tell the truth."

"I am, Your Honor. I am not a prostitute, but I admit, I was at one point in the past; but only because it was either that or starve to death. But when I realized I could survive without selling my body, I quit; for good."

"So, you admit that you were a whore, if not now?" The DA pushes the envelope; again, the defense protests. His objection is sustained.

"The prosecution needs to watch his language," the judge warns.

"Okay. Can you tell the court why you retired from your profession as a prostitute?"

"I realized I could make a living as a fortune-teller without having to entertain male clients that way."

"That's it? But, is it not true that you stopped selling sex because you entered into an ongoing affair with the defendant, Mr. Karl Miller?"

Again, even though she knew this question would be asked at some point, she is nonplussed and squirms in her seat as she fumbles for an answer. She hesitates long enough that the judge has to prompt her, "The witness must answer the question; yes or no."

"Okay, yes!" Her response is a loud one, loaded with an air of frustration and annoyance.

"So, it's safe to say, you know the defendant very well."

"Yes."

"How would you describe his relationship with the victim, Mr. Lester Porter?"

"What do you mean?"

"Well, did Mr. Miller like Mr. Porter, dislike him? You know."

"I'm not sure how to answer that question. I may be a fortune-teller but I don't read people's minds. So, I really can't say how Karl felt about Mr. Porter."

"But is it not the case that Lester Porter on at least one occasion threatened to expose the defendant; to tell his wife about your affair?"

"I don't know. If he did, I never heard the threats."

"But surely, your lover must have told you about the threats."

"I'm sorry, but he did not."

"Remember Ms. Von Hussein, you are under oath."

"I am telling you the truth. Karl never talked about Lester Porter that much. I suspect there was no love lost in that relationship, but Mr. Porter was a Nazi sympathizer and trouble-maker, and from what I've heard, there were a lot people who disliked him."

At this point, the DA walks back to his desk and picks up the card that has been admitted into evidence. He hands it to the witness. "Did you write this poem and give this card to the defendant, Mr. Karl Miller?"

"Yes."

"You heard the sheriff's testimony. You heard him read the poem, is that not correct?"

"Yes."

"And you heard him read just the first letter of each line?"

"Yes."

"So, you knew that the victim, Mr. Porter, was either dead or was going to be when you wrote this, right?"

"No. Absolutely, not. I was not aware of how those letters were arranged like that until today; until I heard the sheriff's testimony."

"So, it was an accident? It just happened?"

"Yes. When I wrote that poem, I did what I often do: I used my Ouija board. It guides my hand to certain letters on the board as I create; it is guided by a supernormal force; one that I don't understand, but one that directs many of my choices and decisions."

"Oh, come on, that's bullshit. You knew exactly what you were doing." The DA leans into the face of the witness as the defense attorney jumps to his feet, "Objection! The prosecution is badgering the witness."

"Sustained. Again, Mister district attorney, I warned you earlier about your language."

"Yes, Your Honor. I apologize." The DA continues, "So, you want the court to believe that the poem you wrote and gave to Mr. Miller was the creation of some force over which you had little control?"

"Yes."

The DA turns around with a loud sigh of exasperation, then approaches the witness with the next question: "Do you think Karl Miller murdered Lester Porter?"

Mr. Hartman leaps up, "Point of order, Your Honor. The prosecution is calling for an opinion…" The well-dressed attorney seems angry, not happy with the way the entire testimony has gone.

"Sustained."

"Okay. Let's put it this way. Did the defendant ever confess to you that he had murdered Lester Porter?"

Obviously perturbed, she blurts out, "Hell no."

The judge reacts immediately, "The witness will watch her language."

"Sorry."

The DA immediately asks, "Do you think Karl Miller is capable of murdering anyone?"

"No. Absolutely not. He is a big and powerful man, but is also kind and considerate—"

Before she can go any further, the DA cuts her off, "Okay. Okay. This is all the questioning I have for this witness."

The defense attorney begins his cross-examination. "Ms. Von Hussein, how would you describe the defendant? Is he a man prone to violence or abusive behavior?"

"Absolutely not. He is the nicest, most gentle and caring man I've ever known."

"About the poem; have you written other poetry, besides the one in question, using your Ouija board?"

"Yes."

"And did the alliteration, the first letters, of those poetic lines ever reveal something unexpected? Something that you, at least consciously, were not aware of?"

"Maybe. I don't know. Today is the first time I realized that the first letters of each line spelled out something like that."

"Thank you. That's all I have for this witness, Your Honor."

Cleo is dismissed and the defense attorney continues, "With the court's approval, I would like to call my next witness to the stand."

The witness is a clinical psychologist, a woman with a practice in Kansas City, and a well-known expert on the psychology of the paranormal. In her testimony, she explains how the Ouija board can express unconscious feelings or premonitions of the user.

"So, you are saying that Ms. Von Hussein could have written that poem guided entirely by unconscious premonitions?"

"Yes. Exactly. I have seen many other cases like this in which the Ouija board brings ideas or thoughts from the brain of which the user is totally unaware. The unconscious mind is a powerful force."

"No more questions, Your Honor."

The DA declines the invitation to cross-examine, but moves to introduce his next witness, Mr. Homer Zimmerman. Mr. Zimmerman has dressed for the occasion: an old beige corduroy suit that smells like mothballs, a white dress shirt, and a green patterned bowtie. His feet sport what appear to be a new pair of black wingtip shoes.

He is sworn in and listens as the prosecuting attorney invites him to "…tell the court what happened to your son, Walt, that day over a year ago."

"Well, my wife and me was enjoying a cup of coffee. Our son, he was upstairs in his room, probably studying. He's a student at K-State, you know?"

"Yes. I know."

"Anyhow, there was a knock on the door and it was Karl Miller and a couple of his bothers and his hired hand. I asked them what they wanted and they said they was looking for Walt. When I asked why, Karl said he'd been messing with his oldest daughter and he'd come to our house to tell Walt to stay away from her."

"Then what happened?"

"Well, they pushed me aside and grabbed Walt, who'd come downstairs when he heard the knock on the door. They dragged my boy out into the front yard and proceeded to beat him; beat him with a baseball bat that had been cut short. They really messed him up, hurt him bad. We had to take him to the hospital. He recovered but he still walks with a limp."

The DA asks a rhetorical question, "All that because the defendant wanted your boy to stay away from his daughter?"

"Yes."

Prosecution goes back to his desk and picks up one of the items recovered in the raid on the Miller household. "Is this the bat Mr. Miller used to beat your son?"

"I think so. Sure looks like it."

"Mr. Zimmerman, based on this experience, would you say that the defendant is a violent man?"

"Violent may not be the right word. I'd say he looked not only violent that day, but like a madman. My wife called him an animal, a brute. And I think she was right about that."

"Thank you, sir." Then turning to the judge, "That's all I have for this witness, Your Honor."

Karl's attorney begins his cross-examination. He walks slowly toward the witness, stroking his chin, squinting and staring at Mr. Zimmerman, as though he is trying to craft the perfect first question.

Finally, he opens his mouth, "Mr. Zimmerman, how long have you known Mr. Miller?"

"A longtime; purt-ner 20 years, I reckon."

"How do you feel about him? Do you like him?"

"You kiddin'! After what he did to my boy, I wouldn't spit on that man if he was on fire. Guess you could say, I *don't* like him. I know it's a sin to hate someone, but I have to be honest—I hate his guts."

"Remind the court, one more time, exactly why Karl Miller came looking for your boy?"

"Like I said, he didn't think my son was good enough for his daughter and wanted to make sure he wouldn't bother her no more."

"Listen, Mr. Zimmerman, you are under oath. You have to tell the truth or face jail time for perjury. So, you may want to clarify your last statement."

"What da ya mean?"

"Is it not true that your son, Walt, who was 18 at the time, sexually assaulted and tried to rape Mr. Miller's 14-year-old daughter?"

Homer Zimmerman, whose face is now as red as a brand new Farmall tractor, looks at the DA and then at the judge who prods him, "Please, the witness will answer the question."

"Well, not exactly."

"What does that mean?"

"Well, he didn't really rape her; you know; there was no penetration."

"Mr. Zimmerman, you know and I know your son took Marlene Miller into the woods in his fancy convertible and proceeded to rip her clothes off, despite her resistance. He pulled down his own pants and was attempting to penetrate her when he ejaculated prematurely. That is attempted rape, sexual assault, and the crime of engaging in sex with a minor. I remind you: your son was 18; Karl Miller's daughter was 14. So, again, Sir, would you like to rephrase your answer?"

"Okay. Okay." Homer Zimmerman is as nervous as a frightened rabbit running away from a hunter with a shotgun. He's leaning forward, his head in his hands and staring at his new wingtip shoes.

"So, you admit your son tried to rape the 14-year-old daughter of the defendant?"

"Yes. Yes." Homer is now on the verge of crying. He blurts out, "But she wanted it. She egged him on."

"What? You can't be serious. Marlene Miller was a girl who knew little if anything about sex and did nothing to encourage your son's inappropriate advances. And, even if she had enticed him, she was still a minor and he was breaking the law. Face the facts, Mr. Zimmerman, your son is a rapist and should be in jail."

"Objection," the cry comes from the prosecutor's table. "The defense is badgering the witness."

"Sustained. The defense is advised to tone down the rhetoric."

"Yes, Your Honor. Okay, Mr. Zimmerman, you also know, I am sure, that the defendant could have turned the case over to the police, and your son Walt would have spent as many as 20 years in prison. His life would have been ruined. You know that, do you not?"

"Yes."

"The other question, and I think I already know the answer, why didn't you call the police and have Mr. Miller arrested for assault?"

"I thought about it, but decided it would be pointless. Karl Miller is a powerful man and has a lot of pull with local police. They would have ignored his beating of my son and focused on the mistake my son made."

"No, you knew that, in the end, your son would be the one to pay the price if you were to go to the police."

"Objection, Your Honor. The defense is trying to put words into the mouth of the witness."

"Overruled. Continue, Counselor."

"I thought about that, yes. But again, I knew the law would always end up on the Miller family side. They've got all of law enforcement in these parts in their pocket."

"You have no evidence to support those claims, but you are right. If you had called the sheriff that day, your son would have been the loser, not Karl Miller and his brothers. In many ways, the defendant did you a favor."

The witness does not respond. The defense indicates it is through with Mr. Zimmerman.

Before the witness is dismissed, the DA stands up and politely asks the judge if he might not ask him one more question. "Homer, you do know that what Karl Miller and his brothers did when they pulled your son out of his house and beat him to within an inch of his life is something called 'taking the law into your own hands'? This is something considered illegal in all civilized countries. Mr. Miller could have gone to jail for what he did to your son. You know that?"

The witness seems a bit surprised by the question, but answers with a timid "Yes".

The DA lets the judge know he has no more questions and returns to his desk, satisfied that he has left in the minds of jury members the fact that Karl Miller had broken the law; that he is not the saintly man that some would suggest.

At this point, the judge slams down the gavel and announces that the court will recess for lunch and that proceedings will resume in one hour.

After lunch, which for most mean a burger and milkshake from the nearby Dairy Queen, the first witness to take the stand is Alexandra Porter, dressed modestly in a one-piece, ankle-length multicolored, patterned garment with a gray, button-up sweater and a pair of brown leather tie-up boots with slightly raised heels. In short, she looks like the farm wife she has been for her entire adult life.

The prosecution begins the questioning, "Mrs. Porter, you are now the widow of the victim, Mr. Lester Porter; is that correct?"

"Yes."

"Can you tell the court how long you and Lester had been married?"

"Almost 26 years."

"During that time, how well did you and Lester know Karl Miller and his family?"

"Pretty well, I guess."

"How did Lester feel about Karl?"

"He didn't like him, that's for sure."

"How come?"

"Well, there were a variety of reasons, but I think the most obvious was the way that Mr. Miller cheated him out of the Hendrix property."

"How did he do that?"

"Well, it was after old man Hendrix died. He'd left the farm to his two children, but they were living and working in Kansas City and had no interest in farming. So they worked out a deal, leasing the 300-acre property to my husband and Karl. They had a gentleman's agreement. They would split the annual lease payment and each had the use of 150 acres to do with as they pleased. Lester used his part of the Hendrix farm to grow corn and milo. This went on for three or four years, but one day Karl tells my husband that the deal was off. He'd bought the farm from the owners without saying anything to Lester. So, just like that, we were stripped of a significant portion of our farmland. The Millers acted as though it was no big deal; no apology, no nothing. So, you can see why Lester and I came to dislike Karl Miller."

"Interesting. But did you ever see your husband in a fight with Mr. Miller or some kind of verbal confrontation?"

"I can't say that I ever saw anything like that, but Lester told me about a few incidents."

"Can you give the court an example?"

"Sure. About a year ago or so, Lester was in St. Joe and ran into Karl and his prostitute girlfriend in a restaurant where they were having lunch together. Later, he ran into Mr. Miller somewhere in town, in Crossroads, and not sure what started it, but Karl got the impression that Lester might tell Thelma, his wife, what he knew about his affair with the woman in St. Joe. So, according to Lester, Mr. Miller threatened him, warning him what he might do to him if he told people about his girlfriend."

"The girlfriend. Is she in the courtroom today?"

"Yes."

"Can you point her out?"

With no hesitation Alexandra points at Cleo, who is sitting in the second row of the courtroom benches.

"Ms. Jasmine Von Hussein, correct?"

"Yes. That's her."

"So the defendant threatened the victim; but can you be more specific?"

"I'm not quite sure how he said it, but according to my late husband, he took it to mean that he would kill him."

"Did your husband ever tell anyone about Karl Miller's affair?"

"Obviously, he told me, but otherwise, I don't think so. And I'm pretty sure he didn't tell Thelma."

"That's the defendant's wife, correct?"

"Yes sir."

"Let me ask you another question, Mrs. Porter. How would you describe your husband? The first words that come to your mind."

Alexandra pauses, rubbing her hands together nervously, then responds, "Good man, hardworking, stern, demanding, strong…"

"Did he have a temper or was he prone to violence?"

"Not really. He was a quiet and gentle man. He was a bit of a loner, but not that violent, you know." There is a kind of equivocating tone in her response.

"So do you think that Karl Miller killed your husband?"

Before she can answer, there is a quick cry of "Objection" from the defense.

Without hesitation, the judge announces, "Sustained." Then he looks at the witness and tells her she should not answer that question.

The DA steps aside and Karl's lawyer approaches the jury box. "Mrs. Porter, Alexandra, is it?"

"Yes sir."

"Do you have a nickname?"

"Not really. I'm just plain ole Alexandra."

"Okay, Alexandra. I want to go back to the question the prosecution asked you about your husband and his behavior. You said he was not a violent person. Is that correct?"

"Yes, it is."

"Well, Mrs. Porter, there are any number of folks out there who will testify to the fact that your husband routinely abused you physically, beat you up, knocked you around. He apparently also abused you verbally. Are you going to dispute those allocations? Are you going to tell the court that such things did not happen? Remember, you are under oath."

Suddenly, the witness is backed into a corner, like a rat trying to find a way out of its dilemma. "All right. There were times. He was a jealous man and sometimes got a little physical with me. But he always apologized and told he loved me. I came to believe that it was his way of showing me how much he needed and loved me. I also think alcohol had something to do with it. When he drank too much, he was not himself."

"What you are saying then, Mrs. Porter, is that indeed your husband was violent, regardless of the reason?"

"Maybe."

"In other words, yes."

"Okay. Yes."

"The prosecution is using the fact that the defendant has been having an affair as a blot on his character; as evidence of his willingness to ignore the expectations of civil society. So, my question to you. Did your late husband, at any time during your marriage, have sex with any woman other than you?"

"Objection. The details of Mr. Porter's personal life are irrelevant to the facts of this trial." The DA is suddenly red in the face, upset. It is clear he is unhappy with the defense attorney's questioning.

"Overruled. I'm sorry, but I'm confident these details have a lot to do with the facts of this case. Proceed. The witness will answer the question."

"No. I mean, I don't know."

"Once again, I remind you that you are under oath. With God as your witness, you never knew whether or not your husband had committed adultery?"

Put this way, the question is more threatening. "All right, all right. I don't see why this is an issue, but yes, I knew."

"How did you know; did he ever tell you?"

"Sort of."

"What do you mean, 'sort of'?"

"Well, there were times he would come home late, having had too much to drink and his hair and clothes were messed up; there was red lipstick on his shirt, and he smelled like perfume—perfume that was not mine. If I confronted him, he would usually deny that he had been with another woman, but sometimes he would admit it and tell me 'so what; what are you going to do about it?' Obviously, there wasn't much I could do."

"Now, I have another question Mrs. Porter. You said your late husband did not like the Millers because Karl had bought a shared piece of land out from under him. Is that correct?"

"Yes."

"But, is there not another reason; that Lester, who was a known Nazi sympathizer, thought the Millers were Jewish? And, from all accounts, he hated Jews and made no bones about it. What can you tell the court about this?"

Once again, the witness is caught off-guard, but realizes she must speak the truth. "I don't know if you could call him a Nazi sympathizer. It was only that he was a fan of Adolph Hitler. He admired him for his ability to come from nothing and eventually being able to win the support of millions of Germans and claim most of Europe, before the Americans stepped in and bombed his country into submission. He also knew that the Miller family was originally the Muellers. He was convinced they were Jewish and were simply hiding their identity. Also, the way they made money and invested that money; the way that made them richer than anyone else in the county. According to Lester, this was simply one more sign that they were Jewish, and he thought Jews were crooks and a plight on society and actually deserved everything they got during the Holocaust."

A few members of the audience look at each other in disbelief, wondering if they have heard the witness correctly.

"Do you share those biases, Mrs. Porter?"

"Not at all. But I knew better than to argue with my husband."

"Why?"

"Like I told you before, he could get a bit physical if I crossed him or if he thought I was judging his behavior. He didn't like that."

"One last question, Mrs. Porter. Can you think of anyone, other than the defendant, who might have had a reason to kill your husband?"

"Well, I know there were a lot of folks in the area who may not have liked Lester, but I don't think they disliked him enough to kill him."

"Thank you, Mrs. Porter. That's all I have for this witness, Your Honor."

At this point, Reverend Craig Butler is called to the stand as a witness for the defense. He is sworn in and the questioning begins.

"Reverend Butler, can you tell the court how well you know the defendant?"

"I met Karl on the first Sunday after I moved to Crossroads; that would have been over three years ago. Since then, I have gotten to know him well. He and his family are among the most dedicated members of my church. They attend regularly, they participate, and they support the church financially."

"Let me ask you the same question about the victim. How well did you know Lester Porter?"

"Mr. Porter's wife attended church on occasion, but I rarely saw him unless I ran into him in town or at community activities, like the annual Fall Fest or the carnival."

"Okay. Let's say that you know both men, even though you know one better than the other. I am assuming that as a pastor you have a professional ability to judge the character of people. That being said, how would you describe the characters of the two men?"

"Objection, Your Honor. I don't see how this is relevant to the trial."

"Overruled. Carry on, Counselor."

"Should I repeat the question, Reverend?"

"No, I think I know what you are looking for. Karl is what some would describe as a gentle giant; a loving father; kind, generous, soft-spoken, courteous, and a faithful member of the Methodist Church. Lester, on the other hand, was angry, loud, crude, a cynic, and what I would describe as a misanthrope."

"Pardon me, Reverend, but perhaps you should tell the courts what you mean by that last word, 'misanthrope'."

"Certainly. A misanthrope is someone who does not like people, in general."

"Objection. The reverend is not a psychologist and doesn't really have a clue as to what was going on in Lester Porter's head," the DA blurts out.

"Counselor, how do you respond to the prosecution's objection?" the judge asks.

"The reverend's suggestions are based on his own personal experiences and perspectives. These are merely his observations. He is not saying there is anything absolute about this. Nor are we suggesting he is a certified professional counselor."

"Okay. You may continue."

"Reverend Butler, you also said that Mr. Porter was crude, in that he swore a lot, made offensive comments about women, and told obscene jokes in inappropriate places. Can you give us an example of his joking?"

"Well, last summer during the carnival, he came into the old bank building where we were selling food and beverages. He ordered a hamburger. He was with a couple of men I'd never seen before. And then, in a voice everyone in the place could hear, he told a very nasty joke."

"Can you repeat the joke for the jury?"

"Absolutely not! I do not use that kind of language, even when I'm by myself, much less in public."

"Turning to another topic, Reverend Butler, is it also true that you often counseled the defendant?"

"Yes. This is one of the responsibilities of a minister who is in some ways a shepherd looking after his flock. Sometimes that involves helping them deal with grief, betrayal, loss, or any number of personal matters."

"Apparently then, Mr. Miller came to you at least once to be counseled?"

"Yes."

"Can you tell the court the reason the defendant was seeking counseling?"

"I'm sorry, but that's privileged information and I never share it with anyone, not even my wife. I am duty-bound to protect the privacy of the parishioners who seek my counsel. It's a professional obligation."

"I understand, but I think it would not be unprofessional of you if you answered this question. Did Karl Miller, in the counseling sessions you had with him, ever talk about Lester Porter?"

"Yes. I can answer that. And the answer is a categorical 'no'. He never mentioned Mr. Porter."

"Do you think Karl Miller had any reason to take Lester Porter's life?"

"No way!" the witness exclaims emphatically as he leans toward the front of the box. "Never."

"So, Reverend, do you think the defendant is guilty?"

The minister responds with a quick "No sir!" before the prosecution can object, which it does. This time, the judge sustains the objection and tells the jury to ignore that part of the testimony.

"That's all I have, Your Honor."

The judge then gives the prosecution an opportunity to cross-examine the witness.

"You said, Reverend Butler, that you thought Karl Miller was a good Christian man?"

"Yes."

"And you do know that the defendant has been having an affair with a former prostitute?"

"I do know now, at least that's what I've heard today. But I knew nothing about any of that before this trial."

"So, are you still confident that Mr. Miller is a good Christian?"

"As I said, I knew nothing of the affair until today. And, quite frankly, all of that is none of my business. That is between his wife, him, and his maker."

"But Reverend, I think everyone knows that one of the Ten Commandments is 'thou shall not commit adultery'. Does that not mean that the defendant has sinned and therefore cannot claim to be a Christian?"

"As I said, it is not in my purview to make that kind of judgment. I stand by what I said earlier. As long as I have known him, I have never personally seen him do or say anything that would make me question Karl's commitment to Christ and his teachings."

"But Reverend, are you being honest? You know—"

"Objection!" Karl's neatly attired attorney stands up and cries foul. "The prosecution is badgering the witness."

"Sustained. Counselor, I think you have exhausted that line of questioning. Do you have anything else you wish to ask the witness?"

"No, Your Honor."

The judge dismisses the witness and asks the two counselors, "Do you have any more witnesses, gentlemen?"

They both respond in the negative.

The judge proceeds to announce, "It's a bit late, but given the seriousness of this trial, the court will move forward with the summations and closing arguments. The prosecution will now approach the jury."

The DA stands up but instead of heading toward the jury, he announces: "If it pleases the court, I would like to request that closing arguments be postponed until tomorrow. I need more time to prepare."

The judge asks, "Does the defense also need more time to prepare?"

"Yes sir."

"Then the court will adjourn until nine o'clock tomorrow."

Court officers escort Karl Miller back to his cell. He has sat motionless throughout the proceedings with an almost expressionless demeanor, staring ahead into space and wondering and worrying about his fate. Now that the cat is out of the bag, he wonders how his wife, his children, his friends, and his neighbors are reacting to the news of his ongoing affair. He is confident that Thelma already knew, but for her it was only one more excuse to drive him from the marital bed, a nesting place where she feels safer by herself than with him. He also wonders if his case would have been strengthened by his testimony, but when he suggested it, his lawyer gave him a dozen reasons that it was not a good idea.

****

The next day, as scheduled, court proceedings resume at 9:00. The courtroom is packed once again, with bodies pressing on bodies. Most of the crowd are persons who sat through the first day. The key players in this highly publicized trial are in place. Karl is staring at a copy of the Kansas City newspaper his lawyer has just shared with him. A front-page story:

Murder and Prostitution in Rural Kansas

Yesterday, the trial of Karl Miller began in the Troy, Kansas, courthouse. Mr. Miller, one of the most successful farmers in Doniphan County, is charged with the murder of the owner of a neighboring farm, Mr. Lester Porter. One of the most shocking revelations coming out of yesterday's procedure was that Mr. Miller has been involved for over a year now with a hooker, who claims to be a hooker no more, from St. Joseph. In her testimony, she insisted she was a fortune-teller and nothing more. She has apparently entered into some sort of committed love relationship with the defendant.

The prosecution contends that Mr. Miller hit the victim beside the head with a sawed-off ball bat, then shot him in the head at close range with a 635 Smith and Wesson rifle, then moved the body to a dry gulch on property owned by Mr. Sherman Foster, another Doniphan County farmer.

So far, the evidence that would lead to Mr. Miller's conviction has been spotty and circumstantial. There are no fingerprints, no witnesses to the crime, or any other solid evidence.

The writer of the article goes on with a discussion of Mr. Miller's background, his success as a farmer, and his role and reputation in the greater Crossroads area. It recounts some of the most relevant testimony and ends with the announcement: *Trial proceedings resume today at 9:00 in the morning at the county courthouse in Troy.*

Clyde Hartman tries to assure his client that the article is of little significance, in that it sounds unbiased and at one level sympathetic to his cause. Besides, the jury has been sequestered and has not seen any news of or accounts about the trial.

Jury members file in and take their seats. Most of them look tired and somber, realizing the great responsibility they are facing today. The fate of a fellow human being rests in their hands. To convict or not convict. It's a serious civic duty that would wipe the smile off any normal person's face.

The bailiff, in a commanding voice, announces, "All rise. The honorable judge…"

The judge takes his seat, bangs his gavel, and asks that the audience be seated. "In the case of the State versus Mr. Karl Miller, today we will be hearing closing arguments from the prosecution and the defense. But, before we do that, does either of the parties wish to question an additional witness?"

Both the DA and Karl's lawyer shake their heads, "No."

"The prosecution may address the jury."

The clumsy, disheveled district attorney walks slowly toward the jury box, in the same corduroy suit he wore yesterday and the same loosely knotted tie. He is carrying several pieces of paper in his left hand. He runs his right hand through his thinning but out-of-control head of hair, and begins.

"Ladies and gentlemen of the jury, you have heard the evidence. There should be not an ounce of doubt in your mind. It is clear that the defendant, Karl Miller, did with forethought and malicious intent, using his wooden club and 38 rifle, bludgeon, shoot, and murder the victim, Mr. Lester Porter. He then carried the body to the dry ravine on the Foster farm, where it was discovered four days later. Unfortunately, the defense has attempted to turn this case into a trial of the victim. But remember, Lester Porter is not the one charged with murder."

"Mr. Porter had his foibles, his sins, and his enemies, but he was a hardworking and honorable man and certainly did not deserve to die this way. Karl Miller, a man of wealth and power, has used some of that wealth to keep a woman, a prostitute, on the side. There is no law against adultery, but it would have seriously stained his reputation were he to be found out. But Lester Porter, a man of principle, by sheer accident, became aware of this arrangement. He confronted Mr. Miller in a St. Joe restaurant and later at the Ackerman station, where the defendant threatened to kill him. At some point after that latter confrontation, Karl Miller made a conscious decision. He could not risk his relationship with Ms. Jasmine Von Hussein becoming public, so he decided he had to do the unthinkable—silence his fellow farmer by killing him. He knew, dead men don't talk."

"And then, there's the poem. His girlfriend knew that Karl intended to kill Lester Porter. She knew that Lester would soon be dead, so to celebrate in advance, she writes a poem with alliteration that says, and I quote, 'Lester Is Dead'. Of course, she claims she did it on a Ouija board and that the board created the poem and the alliteration. We all know that couldn't happen."

"So, again, my fellow citizens and members of the jury, I ask you to consider the facts, put those facts together, and you will see, beyond a shadow of a doubt, that Karl Miller killed Lewis Porter. Yes, Mr. Miller is a powerful man, but justice must win today; he must be convicted. Thank you."

The DA sits down and the judge recognizes Karl's attorney. Unlike his competition, Mr. Hartman has on a different, well-tailored brown wool suit, a freshly laundered white shirt, and a tie decorated with a montage of small American flags. Clean-shaven and his hair neatly combed, he appears confident and prepared to win. He has often said that he owes it to his clients to look sharp.

"Good morning." He opens his comments and smiles as he looks each of the jurors in the eyes. "Ladies and gentlemen of the jury, you have heard the testimonies and the case brought against my client, Mr. Karl Miller. Like the DA has said, you should weigh the facts carefully, because if you do, you will realize that there is not a drop of evidence that would justify convicting my client of murder. There are no fingerprints, no witnesses, no confession, nothing. Everything you have heard is second-hand, hearsay, or speculation. Why was there not solid evidence presented? I will tell you why. My client is innocent. He is completely innocent."

"Yes, he has been having an affair with Ms. Von Hussein, but as the Reverend Butler said, this is between himself, his wife, and his maker. Certainly, this affair does not make him a murderer. And the poem? You heard the psychologist. She told us that the subconscious mind works in mysterious ways and that it is quite possible that Ms. Von Hussein composed that poem without realizing that the first letter of each line, when put together, made a coherent sentence. Again, this is not the kind of evidence you rely on to convict a man of murder."

"And then there is the truth about Lester Porter as a human being. Yes, we regret his death and yes, out there somewhere there is someone who knows the truth; someone other than my client, someone who killed Mr. Porter. As you heard from the witnesses, he was not particularly a nice man; indeed, a man who had many enemies. In other words, there are many people who may have had reason to murder Lester Porter, but Karl Miller was not one of them. He and Lester had their differences and yes, they quarreled at times, but that does not mean the defendant killed him. Never."

"So, as you consider the facts and come to a conclusion, I urge you to remember, all of the so-called evidence you have heard is circumstantial and hearsay, not the evidence you need to convict. The evidence must be more than possible or even probable; it must be solid and direct and sufficient to remove any questions. The evidence must prove the defendant guilty beyond any reasonable shadow of a doubt. What the prosecution has presented does not come anywhere even close to that. Again, I ask you to consider all the evidence and I am confident you will find absolutely nothing sufficient to support the conviction of my client. Karl Miller is not a killer; he did not murder Lester Porter; and I am confident you will find him innocent. Again, thank you for your service."

Karl's lawyer's summation and challenge to the jury was much more powerful than that of the DA, who had stumbled and at times referred to the papers in his hands, as though he was not quite sure of what to say next. The defendant is confident his lawyer has done a good job defending him, but he worries that perhaps he was too slick, his style too smooth, too big-city for the small-town folks on the jury. Perhaps their feeling sorry for the awkward and poorly dressed DA will, indirectly, affect the jury's handling of the case: "Guilty! Because we country folk don't like big-time, hotshot lawyers from the city walking in here with their expensive tailored clothes and fancy talk and telling us what to do."

But now, it is too late to change the defense strategy.

The judge gives his instructions to the jury and they file into the deliberation room where the foreman will lead them in their effort to reach a verdict.

His lawyer turns to Karl, just before the defendant is returned to his holding quarters, "I'm pretty good at reading juries. I'm confident they'll exonerate you, and it won't take long for them to reach a verdict. And remember, even if they do vote to convict, it will be an easy verdict to appeal. Meanwhile, keep a stiff upper lip."

Less than an hour later, the judge is told that the jury has reached a verdict. The attorneys and their assistants are called back into the courtroom and seated. Karl is brought back into the courtroom. As soon as the announcement is made in the hallway outside the courtroom, the press and other members of the audience file back in. The judge instructs the bailiff to bring in the jury. The members of the jury file in, all with solemn, poker faces—no indication of which way the scales of justice have tilted.

"Has the jury reached a verdict?" the judge asks the foreman.

"We have, Your Honor." At that point, the bailiff takes a piece of paper from the foreman and walks back and hands it to the judge.

A few moments later, the bailiff returns the note to the foreman who, with the instruction from the judge, reads the verdict:

"We, the jury, in the case of the State versus Mr. Karl Miller in the murder of Mr. Lester Porter, find the defendant *not guilty*."

The reaction of the people in the courtroom is mixed. Some are surprised, some are not surprised; some are pleased, some are not.

The judge looks at the defendant. "Mr. Miller, you have been found not-guilty by a jury of your peers. You are free to go."

The exonerated farmer, consistent with his usual stoic attitude, shows no emotional response. He lets the verdict sink in for a few moments and then turns to his lawyer, shakes his hand, and thanks him. Again, looking neither relieved or excited by the verdict, he glances behind him at the small audience and wonders how this trial, even though he was not convicted, will affect his reputation and his stature in the community. He looks back at people he knows, people he has known for many years. It seems to him there is a new coldness in their eyes; as though they are making a conscious effort to distance themselves from him.

Despite the verdict, he knows there are those who think he is guilty and that today's decision by the jury was a mistake. They think, perhaps, that Mr. Miller, Mr. Money Bags, was able to pay off key members of the jury. Will this ever change? Will he be a pariah in his own town and county from now until his death? And what about his children? What will they think about their father cheating on their mother? Yes, he has been declared not-guilty, but the stain of the indictment and trial will never go away.

As he walks out of the courtroom and into the hallway, he is met by members of the Miller family, brothers, sisters-in-law, and a couple nephews. Noticeably absent is his sister Greta and his wife Thelma. But there seems to be exuberance all around, as though Karl had just won the Nobel Prize or a gold medal in the Olympics. He is genuinely pleased that he has been found not guilty, and grateful for the enthusiasm of his supporters, but knows that, henceforth, his life will never be the same.

Chapter Twenty
An Outside Perspective

Oliver Winstead is a reporter for the *Kansas City Star*. He has been covering and writing about the Miller trial from its beginning. Oliver is a native Kansan who has an undergraduate degree in journalism from the University of Kansas, which has one of the best journalism programs in the country. He has always fancied himself as not just a reporter, but a detective and a creative writer. He has written a couple crime novels that, while not winning awards, have sold reasonably well and gained for him the reputation as a good writer of fiction and an expert on crime.

Oliver is in his late forties. He is balding. What is left of his light-brown hair is pushed to the back of his head. He is short, having to stretch to reach 5'8". He is overweight. His kewpie-doll face is round, smooth, and plump. His strength—his dark blue eyes that are almost mesmerizing. It is as though he has trained them; eyes that penetrate and see the truth behind the façade of even the most experienced liar's pretense. He is single, lives alone. And his effeminate looks and the fact that he does not date are the source of rumors—rumors that he might be a homosexual. This is something that folks in rural Kansas talk about, but do not tolerate. So, even if Oliver is of a different sexual orientation, it is not something he is prepared to make public.

From the beginning of the trial, Mr. Winstead was skeptical. The idea that Karl Miller killed Lester Porter in the fashion described by the prosecution made no sense. A man of Mr. Miller's wealth, power, and influence? If he had wanted Mr. Porter dead, he would have found a much less crude and sloppy way to do it. And, in interviewing folks in Crossroads, he found it interesting that Karl Miller was widely respected and feared, even though not roundly loved. While the reasons expressed varied, Oliver, the journalist, is convinced it is a matter of his wealth and the vast amount of acreage he controls.

Peasant societies are often inflicted with a sometimes unarticulated but real economic principle. It is called the theory of limited means or the rule of limited goods; meaning that there is only so much wealth to go around, and if I do not have what I think is my share, it is because someone else has more than their share. So, in a subtle way, folks in Crossroads, particularly the farmers in the area, feel Karl has a lot of what rightfully should be theirs. Thus, the bias and the desire to see the king of the hill knocked off that hill. The journalist from Kansas City is convinced Karl Miller should never have been charged and tried for the murder of Farmer Porter in the first place, and that the trial was a sham.

But Lester Porter is still dead. He was murdered. Somebody out there knows how it happened, but who? This question continues to haunt the journalist and stir the ambitions of his alter ego; the detective in him is excited by the challenge of the mystery. It is like the hungry lion that has just breathed in the odor of fresh meat. He has decided to make this a priority: to find out what really happened to Lester Porter and, at the same time, share with his readers the truth about rural America. It's a great story, just waiting to be told.

*****

For Karl Miller, despite his efforts to get back to the way things were before the trial, life has not returned to normal. His wife, who probably wishes he had been convicted, is as cold and distant as ever; maybe more so, if that's possible. His children are confused. "What is wrong with Daddy and Mama?" Marlene is old enough to know what is going on and is angry at her father for his infidelity, hypocrisy, and apparent abandonment of her mother, whom she loves dearly.

It is Saturday afternoon. The recently exonerated farmer is in St. Joe, lying in bed with his illicit lover. They have just exhausted themselves in doing what they do best; driving each other to explosive passion, followed by physical collapse. They are side-by-side, staring up at the white plaster board ceiling of Cleo's rented bungalow. The room smells earthy and pungent as part of the afterglow of sexual intercourse. It is also a bit warm, and the adulterous farmer is perspiring. Sex can be ecstasy-producing, but can also be hard work.

Karl is the first to speak, "Maybe we should get married. You know, make an honest woman out of you."

"But you're already married, Karl. You do know that, don't you?"

"Well, I'd get a divorce first."

"No, you won't. I know how your family and your community feel about divorce. In their minds, divorce is almost as much a mortal sin as murder. And this time, you'd be convicted without a trial."

"I don't think so."

"Also, Thelma would take you for everything you have. She has you by the gonads, and you know it."

The frustrated farmer grunts in response, knowing his lover is probably right. He is trapped.

Cleo continues, "Besides, my friend, what makes you think I want to get married? I love you, that's true. But marriage is not for me. I don't need a man controlling my life. I hope you don't take this in the wrong way, but I certainly don't want to be a farmer's wife. What a miserable existence! I can only imagine: getting up at all hours of the morning, milking cows, picking tomatoes and digging up potatoes, collecting eggs, scraping chicken shit off the porch, and washing your filthy clothes. What woman with any other options at all would choose a life like that? And then there's the matter of having children. I have absolutely no desire to be a mother. I know, some women don't feel fulfilled unless they have a baby. There may be something wrong with me, but I'm not one of those women."

By now, Karl has pulled himself up and is sitting with his back against the headboard. He looks at his female friend with an uncharacteristic air of helplessness and self-pity. "You would not want to have my baby?"

"Not really; even though, if I had a baby, I would want it to be yours."

"But we've been taking chances lately. I mean, let's face it, we have had sex on many occasions when I was too hot and bothered and anxious to take the time to put on a rubber. If you are worried about getting pregnant…"

Cleo pops up from her prone position, sits and turns toward Karl with a big grin on her face. "You big dummy. I do worry about that. This is why I'm careful. Very careful. I'm surprised you don't know that I put a diaphragm in my pussy every time I think there's a chance we'll be fucking."

"A diaphragm? What's that?"

The sexy fortune-teller cannot believe her lover is so naïve. "You're kidding me. You don't know?"

"No."

With that, she reaches under the silk sheet draped over the lower part of her torso and deftly reaches into the depth of her privates and pulls out the thin rubber barrier that is still warm and wet in the wake of her partner's ejaculation. Cleo then explains the technology of what amounts to female condoms.

Karl listens carefully and finally asks, "But why did you not tell me before?" He sounds annoyed and surprised.

"I don't know. I didn't think it mattered. I was simply trying to protect myself."

Apparently satisfied by the response, Karl changes the subject. "I have to ask you something."

"What?"

"You may not tell me the truth, but during my trial and your testimony, there was something that told me that you had, how shall I say it, carnal relations with Lester Porter. So, tell me the truth; did you ever do Lester?"

Cleo sits still, fumbling with the edge of the top sheet, and struggles to find a way to finesse her response. Finally, she asks, "Would it matter? I mean, would it change anything if I had?"

"So, you're telling me you did. You fucked that sorry son-of-a-bitch. Jesus Christ, I can't believe it!"

"Okay. Okay. But it was well before I met you, and it was strictly a business matter. He was a client, that's all. He came to see me the first time because he wanted me to tell him his future. He was struggling. He was losing money. He'd had a bad year. He wanted someone to give him advice as to what he should do next. Anyhow, after I told his fortune he decided he wanted more. He paid me and, well…" she pauses, "…we did it. But again, it was business. You have known from the beginning that I have bedded many men. But they all, every one of them, were strictly financial arrangements. I sold my body; the only way I knew how to make a living.

"With you, it was different. With you, I sold my heart and ever since I started seeing you, the idea of having sex with any other man is actually repugnant, disgusting. So, yes, Lester was one of my johns. But he was just like the rest of them—a financial transaction."

"So the day Lester confronted us during our lunch, when you and he acted as though you'd never met, that was an act, right? You knew each other but did not want me to know? Wow. What an idiot I was."

Cleo hems and haws, not knowing what to say next. "I-I…"

Karl lifts the sheet and swings his muscular hairy legs out from under it and sits up, his feet on the floor and his eyes fixed on nothing as he stares into the wall of the small bedroom. He has suspected all of this, yet comfortable with the uncertainty. But now?

Without turning around, he asks, "How come you put on the act? How come you never told me?"

"I knew it was something you didn't want to hear."

"So why now?"

"You asked, and I could not bring myself to lie. I have never lied to you. I will never lie to you. So, I told you the truth, even though I realized you might not take it well."

"What if you had been asked that question while you were on the witness stand during the trial? Would you have told the truth then?"

"No. There would have been no reason to admit it in front of the whole world. It would only have complicated matters."

The troubled farmer drops his head between his hands, looking at his ugly bare feet. He finds himself in a dilemma, not unlike Robert Frost's divided-road challenge: there are two paths, the path toward Cleo or the path away from her. At the moment, neither choice is clear or without emotional trauma. Finally, he stands up, turns around, and in a calm voice announces, "I'm sorry. I've got to get off this bus. I need time to process all of this."

As he begins putting on his boxer shorts, his honest-to-a-fault lover asks, "Does this mean I won't see you again?" in a tone of anxious desperation, not knowing what she should say or do next.

"I don't know. Maybe."

"Okay. I get it. If this is what you want, what you have to do, I understand."

Nothing more is said. Karl finishes dressing and walks away. Cleo remains sitting in bed with the top sheet over her lower body. At this point, she has what might be described as a poker face; her emotions remain bundled up inside but tumbling in chaos, like wet clothes in a spinning dryer.

*****

Oliver Winstead is convinced that the little town of Crossroads and the larger farming community around it are a journalist's gold mine. He is also confident he can solve the mystery of Lester Porter's murder. He is now focused and in determined pursuit of the story, like a hunter who cannot give up the search for his wounded but still fleeing prey. But he wants to be careful that his interest and presence in the community are not actually seen as an effort to help solve the mystery of the murder, but rather an effort to understand small-town life in rural Kansas, at least for now.

As a first step, Oliver looks for a place in Crossroads he can rent. He plans to spend a lot of time in the area, but does not want to make the long drive from Kansas City every day. His boss has given him permission to be away from the office for two or three days a week. The problem is there is nothing to rent in the little town; at least nothing furnished and nothing but places that even squatters would find unacceptable. But, as luck would have it, when he is talking to one of the locals, he discovers that Louis Lombardi has a small Shasta camping trailer that he parks next to the two-story brick building that houses his tavern and living quarters.

He goes to see the notorious bartender and works out a deal. The place is his until the Lombardis need it, which won't be any time soon. Louie runs a large electric wire from an outlet at the rear of his building to the trailer, giving Oliver lights, heat, a small cookstove, and two outlets. A hose is run from a spigot at the side of the house to the trailer, allowing Oliver to use the small sink. There's a reasonably comfortable bed and a table with a foldout bench where he can use his typewriter. What is missing is toilet facilities. For this, Louis provides him with a portable toilet, a thunder mug, a large tin bucket with a cover that has a small handle. The plan is for Oliver to bring the bucket into the bar and empty it in the customer bathroom commode, when necessary. It's not what the investigative journalist would like, but it will do.

The day that Oliver moves into his new small-but-adequate digs, he decides that he will begin by exploring the politics of this small town. Crossroads and all of Doniphan County voted overwhelmingly for Thomas Dewey in his presidential race against Harry Truman earlier this fall. The state of Kansas was one of only four states that voted for Dewey. Oliver is curious as to why.

He walks around town knocking on doors, introducing himself, and asking questions. Among the ten or so people who talk candidly is Rev. Butler, who openly admits he's a Republican and voted for Dewey. Of course, the journalist's question is "why?"

"I'll admit, my wife and I are both from families that have a tradition of voting for the Grand Old Party. So, sometimes we let that take precedence over the details of candidate's platform, experience, and voting record. But we see Republicans as more supportive of traditional family values, of patriotism, and faith-based organizations, like our church here in Crossroads."

"What about economics? Do you think the Republicans do a better job than the Democrats in managing the country's finances?"

"That's a good question. I know it was a Republican president who ushered in the Depression and it was a Democrat who pulled us out of it. But I think that's behind us and we need to make sure people learn to take care of themselves rather than depend on the generosity of the government. I come from a Protestant-Ethic background, something I think I share with many of the farmers in this area who believe there is something spiritually rewarding in hard work. I think most of the members of my church, when they vote, vote for candidates who share their moral values rather than candidates who might do a better job of handling the economy. You might call it putting morals over money."

The journalist himself is a rather liberal Democrat, and in this exchange with the preacher, he wants more than ever to counter him with facts that undermine his argument. He is frustrated. To make matters worse, he has had a bad night and is feeling unusually irritable. It was his first night in the trailer and he woke up in the middle of the night, thinking he was in his apartment in Kansas City. In the process, he kicked over the thunder mug which he had awkwardly used before he went to bed. Fortunately, the portable toilet contained only the liquid he had deposited there before he climbed in-between the sheets. But it took time to clean up the mess, enough time to ruin his first night in Crossroads.

He bites his lip, listens to his interviewee, says very little, and scribbles furiously on the pages of his lined journal.

Even though he is not at his best, the day goes well for the investigative reporter. He is surprised how, when he knocks on doors, his reception is usually a pleasant one. Based on his limited experience, it seems that rural folks do not mind strangers coming up on their porches, banging on the door or ringing the doorbell, and interrupting their day. In a number of cases, Oliver is actually invited to come into the house where he might be offered a cup of coffee or glass of cold water. This is certainly not the case in the city, where people seem more guarded, suspicious, and reluctant to open their doors to people they don't know.

It's been a long day, but Mr. Winstead is not finished yet. He sits at the table and types up his notes. When he completes organizing today's interviews, he puts on a jacket and walks out and around the Lombardi building into Louie's Tavern. It's Friday night and things are busier than usual. The place is abuzz with chatter; men conversing with men. No women here. It is rare that a member of the softer sex comes into this establishment. But when they do, there is often a pushback from the regulars who feel as though their space has been invaded—violated by a woman. "What's she doing here?" they whisper.

All of this is consistent with what Oliver has gleaned from his questioning and interviews. The life of farm wives is tough, but there seems to be more male-female parity there than in the town itself. Less abuse perhaps, not to say that it does not happen on the farm. But in the town, it seems to be an almost accepted practice. One resident told him the story of how the Methodist preacher, the one before Rev. Butler, was walking down town one day and saw a husband literally beating up his wife. The reverend felt compelled to intervene, but when he did, both the husband and the wife turned on him and gave him a good thrashing, the woman hollering, "You've got no right to pry into our family affairs. This ain't none of your damn business!"

"Well, it's our favorite newspaper guy," Louie announces loudly as Oliver climbs on a stool and leans onto the bar. "How are things going in the trailer?"

"You don't want to know."

"Tough night, uh?"

"Yeah."

"You'll get used to it. But now, you need a drink. What can I do you for?"

"Beer."

"Coming at you."

As the exhausted journalist sips his brew from the heavy glass mug, he looks around the room and does what he calls 'passive research', simply listening to the various conversations taking place. He picks up bits and pieces. Much of the talk is about family matters, winter planting, and the topics of local gossip. For example, folks here still talk about the Karl Miller trial and speculate as to who actually killed Lester Porter and why. A couple of younger men seated at the other end of the bar are talking about the most recent NFL championship that saw the Philadelphia Eagles defeat the Chicago Cardinals in a low-scoring 7–0 game. Apparently, they watched the game here in Louie's bar, since he has one of the only two television sets in town. Miller has the other.

Oliver has not been at the bar for long when a middle-aged man with a rugged, weather-beaten face and deep-set dark eyes, dressed in blue jeans, a heavy sweater, and well-worn leather jacket climbs on the stool next to him. Louie greets him and takes his order: a beer. The tavern has only one brand of beer on tap—Budweiser. You don't like it—tough luck. The guy grabs his mug, takes a sip, and turns to Oliver. "You're that newspaper guy, aren't you? The guy that wrote them stories about the Miller murder trial."

"Yeah. I'm a reporter. *Kansas City Star*."

"I hear you're asking people questions about politics."

"I am."

"Why?"

"Because I'm curious about why people vote the way they do here in this small town. The reasons behind that vote tell you a lot about the culture of the community."

"I don't think there's anything special about Crossroads and its culture. We're just like people in any other small town in Kansas."

"Well, I agree," Oliver adds as he shakes his head in agreement. "I see Crossroads as a typical small Kansas community. So, understanding life here is essentially understanding most of the small towns in the state. And this is my interest: describing life in rural areas and comparing it to life in the cities. You might call Crossroads a microcosm."

"Micro what?"

"A small window into a larger reality; a small example of a larger collection of communities."

"Okay, so what have you learned about our politics here in our little town?"

"Well, so far, it seems to me that the majority of the folks in the greater Crossroads area are Republicans and voted for Dewey in the last election."

"Yeah, probably almost everybody but Louie. He voted for Truman; he'd vote for a damn cocker spaniel if it was a Democrat."

The journalist more or less assumed this to be the case. The owner of the tavern has a framed copy of the 'Dewey Defeats Truman' picture from the *Chicago Tribune* hanging on the back wall of the bar. But it is also rumored that Louie has connections with the mafia and does not like Dewey because of his record of going after the mob and its leaders in New York. Also, it is assumed Democrats are more tolerant than Republicans when it comes to things like operating a tavern and selling the devil's brew.

Oliver's bar mate slugs down a little more of his Budweiser and then blurts out, "I got an idea. Let's take a poll, see what folks here think about the election."

"What?"

As he slides from his barstool and stands up, Winstead's drinking buddy turns to face the men seated at the ten tables in the room. He hollers, "Listen up, guys." There's a commanding tone to his gruffy voice and almost instantly the chatter comes to an abrupt halt and everyone is looking at him.

"Here's the deal. My reporter friend here, the guy from the *Kansas City Star*, he's wantin' to know how we voted in the presidential election and why. So, I thought, what the hell, let's do a show of hands. Are you with me on this?"

"What if we feel that how we vote ain't nobody's business but ours?" one of the customers asks.

"Then don't say nothin'. I mean, if you're embarrassed you voted for the wrong guy, I understand. Okay, let's do it this way. If you voted for Dewey, raise your hand."

The customers look at each other as if to say, "Is this guy serious?" But gradually, hands began to rise. Oliver watches intently and counts the hands. Almost all the guys in the room.

"Okay, how many of you voted for Truman?"

Only one hand went up. Oliver found out later he was a history teacher at the local school. Louie, still standing behind the bar, shouts out, "I know you morons know I voted for Truman; clearly the best man for the job."

The room erupts in a chorus of verbal reactions. "Come on, man, you're nuts. That's bullshit. Truman's a loser."

As the noise prompted by Louie's announcement fades out, the man leading the discussion then asks, "How many of you scumbags didn't bother to vote?"

No one raises his hand. Oliver is suspicious that there are some in the room who didn't vote, some who really did not understand the issues anyway, but it seems to him that in Crossroads, as in other rural communities in Kansas, there is a strong sense of patriotism which brings with it a kind of moral commitment that you exercise your right to vote. To do otherwise is un-American.

"Now, I tell you what I'm going to do. I'm gonna have my friend here, the reporter…" With that, he pauses and looks at his bar mate… "Mr.?"

"Winstead, Oliver Winstead."

"Yeah, Mr. Winstead here is gonna move around the room and ask questions. He's tryin' to understand why we countryfolk have voted overwhelmingly for Mr. Dewey. I'm confident you'll tell him." With this, he turns to the journalist and says, "Okay newspaper man, it's all yours."

Oliver feels backed into a corner here, but decides to take advantage of the opportunity. He picks up his pen and journal, steps off his stool, and heads for the closest table. He grabs an empty chair and pulls up to a table surrounded by three locals.

"You okay with this?" he asks, wanting to make sure the men don't feel coerced by the charismatic character in the leather jacket and blue jeans.

"Sure, why not?" pipes up on of the three men at the table, all of whom are farmers.

For the next almost two hours, buoyed by two more cold mugs of brew, the journalist makes the rounds of the room, introducing himself, meeting each of the customers and asking questions. The questions are directed at his effort to understand why the Crossroads folks voted overwhelmingly for Thomas Dewey rather than Harry Truman. Truman grew up on a farm, lived in a small town before moving to Independence, Missouri. He has vowed to continue supporting FDR's AAA (Agricultural Assistance Administration) program, which provides important benefits to the farming community.

Dewey, on the other hand, grew up in a small city in Michigan and after graduating from law school at Columbia, became a prosecuting attorney and governor in New York, a state totally unlike Kansas. Dewey does own a farm in western New York, but his platform did not support midwestern farmers the way Truman's did.

But for most of the men in Louie's Tavern tonight, issues other than farm support seem to have guided their choice at the ballot box. Their explanations parallel those of Rev. Butler and others Oliver has interviewed today. They like to think the Republican Party is the party of family values, Christianity, and patriotism. On the other hand, they feel the Democrats are too liberal, the party of big cities, soft on crime, encourage the teaching of evolution in the schools, and are too generous with federal dollars, often helping those who are capable of helping themselves.

As he makes the rounds from table to table, the investigative reporter cannot help but take advantage of the situation and—in addition to questions about politics—ask about the murder, "Who murdered Lester Porter? Any ideas? Do you think Karl Miller was guilty?"

Most of the men in the room are reluctant to say much of anything in response to these questions. The consensus is that Lester was roundly disliked across the county so that his killer may have been any one of his many enemies. However, one of the men, the guy who teaches history at Crossroads School, quietly and as inconspicuously as possible, hands the inquiring journalist a note. "Call me one evening next week." He includes a phone number.

As the men in the bar drain that last sip of beer from their mugs and head for the exit, Oliver is busy recording interview responses and ideas in his journal. He decides it's time for him to head to bed in the rented camping trailer. But before he can leave, the owner of the tavern walks up, leans over the bar and into his face, and in an effort to sound more informative than threatening, tells him, "Look, I need to tell you. It's probably a good idea if you don't start nosing around in the Lester Porter case. It's a sore subject, you know. I mean, some folks think Karl was guilty. Some don't, and yet they ain't got a clue as to who might be. It's tearing the town apart; so, I'd encourage you not to make the situation worse. I'm sure, in time, the truth will be known and justice will be done. Meantime, it's probably best you stick to politics."

For an investigative reporter, Louie's admonition is like throwing gas on a fire. Oliver is more determined than ever to get to the bottom of Lester's murder. The next day, he goes back to his apartment in the big city and drafts an op-ed piece for the *Kansas City Star*:

Politics in Small-Town Kansas
By Oliver Winstead

Crossroads is a small town in Northeast Kansas that depends on a strong agriculture economy. Yet, in last fall's election, it went overwhelmingly for Dewey, in spite of the fact that the Truman platform promised to deliver much more for the agricultural community. One has to ask, why would a farmer vote for Dewey when Truman is the one who understands farm life and supports agricultural subsidies while his opponent does not? Strangely, it is not that the people of this small town do not understand what is in their best interests economically, but that they place core social values ahead of economic gain.

Dewey may not have put money in their pockets, as Truman has done, but he stands for things the residents of Crossroads and its surrounding farming community value most: religion, moral values, and a Protestant worldview—hard work, delayed gratification, and patriotism. The residents of this small town in Kansas see themselves as fighting for their own futures; fighting for the perpetuation of rural America and a world in which crime is rare; where the flag still means something, where folks leave their doors unlocked at night, and where people care about each other.

But, is that actually the way it is? Not really. Crime statistics, which admittedly are not always reliable, suggest that petty theft, assault, spouse abuse, and murder rates are actually higher in rural America, on a per-capita basis, than in the city. Add to that drug and alcohol abuse that is widespread in this town and others. At the same time, there is a continuous bleeding of skilled labor, as the brightest and the best who grow up in Crossroads, move away. There is nothing to justify their remaining in this small town where employment opportunities are for the most part non-existent. There is a prevailing poverty in the town itself. It seems most people who live here do so out of desperation. They may have jobs somewhere else but cannot afford to live where they work. Many residents manage to survive, but live from paycheck to paycheck.

Also, there seems to be little in the way of community pride. The town is peppered with unkept yards, vacant buildings, and enough trash to make an environmentalist cry his eyes out. Predictably, while people talk enthusiastically about what a wonderful place Crossroads is, there is really little evidence that people take pride in their community. At the same time, there is a tension between the townies and the farmers. The people who actually live in Crossroads resent the farmers who, for the most part, have a standard of living that does not exist in the town itself. In general, the farmers make more money, live in nicer homes, and are more likely to raise children who go to college and ultimately make something of themselves.

In the town itself, the young people who graduate from Crossroads High School are just as likely to end up in jail as they are to graduate from college. Folks, both farmers and town residents alike, talk of how everyone cooperates...how everyone pitches in to help when there is work to be done. Really? Not according to the farmers I talked to. Farmers may help each other out at times; For example, during the fall harvest. But rarely do any of the townies pitch in.

So, what does it mean to be a resident of the small town of Crossroads, Kansas? Not much. Residents are here because of circumstances. Some are simply squatters, people who move into a vacant home and live until they find a better option elsewhere. Others are here because it is the only place they can afford to live. There are shopkeepers—like Louis Lombardi, who owns the local bar and grill—who manage to eke out a relatively comfortable annual income. But they are like a small garden of beautiful roses surrounded by acres of invasive dandelions.

Do Crossroads residents know these things about themselves? Do they realize that the myth of the idyllic life in small-town America is just that, a myth? And do they realize that they receive, on a per-capita basis, more federal funds than any of America's big cities, Kansas City included? Maybe, but if they do, they refuse to admit it. They look at the numbers and scoff. "Some overpaid government bureaucrat's made-up numbers; all it is."

The facts don't seem to matter. It's the myth that persists and it's the myth that drives their voting patterns; often voting for the candidates that least serve their fundamental economic interests; someone who, with one hand pats you on the head and tells you how wonderful you are, but with the other reaches into your back pocket and steals your wallet. Is this the result of stupidity; of a complete lack of history; or the inability to think critically? Perhaps any one of these, but I believe it is the power of myth—this belief, this carefully constructed self-image, this need to feel that while you may be working-class poor, your patriotism and moral righteousness give you a sense of superiority; the feeling that despite your hand-to-mouth existence, you are actually better than the city-dwellers with all their money, education, and liberal attitudes.

It seems there are two rural Americas: the farmers and the folks who live in the many incorporated communities in the U.S. with a population of 5,000 or less (approximately 19,000). And, while the research and its results are ongoing, it seems there is an interesting correlation between size and commitment to the myth. The smaller the community, the more likely its residents are to tout its virtues, regardless of the facts. It is a kind of defensiveness that shapes the politics of small towns like Crossroads and on a larger scale impacts the broader political landscape of America as a whole.

Yes, Crossroads is a special place. All towns and cities are. But Crossroads is special for the way it sees itself, not for the way it actually is. The myth masks the reality. Rural America is in large part a fairy-tale, a fictional reality that ignores what is real. It is not a model for the rest of the country, as folks here would have you believe, but rather a vestige of a time when the struggle for survival kept one from having time to think, create, and define the future. It is a struggle to maintain the status quo; to impede progress; to avoid the realities of the 20th century.

As a result of what is happening to small-town economies, these communities are drying up and disappearing. Crossroads will always be here, but increasingly it will become a mere shell of what it once was; a place largely of squatters, homeless, and desperate individuals. The farmers with large fields of arable land, like Crossroads' Karl Miller, will survive. But most of the small-time famers will be bought out by large corporate farmers who have little interest in the community or in sharing its values.

So, collect your stories about the glories of life in small-town America and add them to those about Santa Claus, the Tooth Fairy, and the Easter Bunny. They are great and sometimes inspiring stories, but that is all they are: stories.

*****

With the op-ed piece behind him and in the process of being included in tomorrow's *Kansas City Star*, Oliver is at home, relaxing but still thinking about Crossroads and the mystery of Lester Porter's murder. He pulls out the note from the history teacher. It is early evening so the teacher should be at home. He calls.

"Hello."

"Yes, hello. This is Oliver Winstead with the *Kansas City Star*. We met last week at Louie's Tavern and you suggested I give you a call."

"Right. Yeah. Thanks for calling. I'm Grant Wilson. As I told you, I teach history at Crossroads High. I wanted to respond to your question about Lester Porter's mysterious death, but not while there were other men around me. You understand, don't you?"

"Sure. So, what is it you wanted to tell me?"

"It's complicated, but I should first tell you that I'm writing a history of Crossroads, so the death of Mr. Porter and the trial of Karl Miller are issues of great importance to me. I was unable to attend the trial, but my wife was there for the entire event. She obviously listened to all the testimonies and observed the presentations of the prosecutor and the defense attorney. But, more importantly, she watched the other folks sitting in the courtroom, taking note of their reaction to the proceedings of the trial. She is convinced that there were people in that courtroom who knew that Mr. Miller was not guilty, and knew who was."

"Anyhow, I cannot be more specific, but there are people here in the greater Crossroads area who know who killed Lester. I'm telling you this because I believe that if you keep looking and asking questions, you may very well discover the truth and help bring the killer, or killers, to justice."

"Can you be more specific? The people in the courtroom that your wife saw; people that she thinks know more about the murder than they would want to admit; who were they? You know their names?"

"I can't say. I'm sorry."

"But you know; you just don't want to tell me?"

There is a long pause as Grant breathes heavily into the phone. Finally, he blurts out, "Look. Like I told you, I can't answer that question. I really don't want to be dragged into the mess. I am confident you will eventually figure things out."

"So, that's it?" Oliver is obviously frustrated and annoyed.

"Yeah. That's it."

The newspaper man realizes this is all the history teacher is going to tell him, so he politely thanks his reluctant informant, urges him to contact him if he has any further evidence regarding the murder case, and says "Take care" as he hangs up the phone.

*****

It's Thursday afternoon. Oliver is back in Crossroads, this time on a mission. He is determined to get to the bottom of what actually happened to Lester Porter. He walks into Louie's Tavern. The owner is there, standing behind the bar and fixing drinks for the three or four customers who are getting a head-start on their evening of imbibing and chewing the fat with their neighbors.

Louie sees the reporter as he walks into the bar. He reacts immediately, "Well, Mister Smarty Pants, I can't believe you have the nerve to show up here, you sorry weasel, you!"

Surprised, perhaps even shocked by this out-of-the-blue outburst, Oliver's jaw drops as he asks, "What? What are you talking about?"

"Hell. You know exactly what I'm talking about!" Louie reaches under the bar and pulls out an issue of the *Kansas City Star*. "This is what I'm talking about. This goddamned piece of crap story you wrote about our town. Lies! Yellow journalism. You should be shot!"

Louis Lombardi is not one to get flustered very easily. But it is easy to see he is angry, perhaps dangerously so.

"Look, Louie. I'm sorry, but I am only doing my job: reporting the truth."

"The truth? Bullshit! The truth is that you really don't understand Crossroads and the people who live here. You arrogant son-of-a-bitch. You must think it's cool, that it's funny, making us look like uneducated fools and lowlifes! And then your nerve—showing up here again!"

Oliver is not sure what to say next. So, he repeats, "Look, I was simply being a journalist, reporting what I observed; or at least what I thought I saw. So, again, I'm sorry if my op-ed piece struck a nerve."

"Damn right it did." With that, he reaches under the bar again and this time he pulls out his notorious sawed-off baseball bat and sticks it in Oliver's face. "Now, I suggest you get the hell out of here before I do something that we both will regret."

The reporter is obviously frightened, but asks timidly and somewhat rhetorically, "I guess this means you're not going to let me use the trailer anymore?"

"You got that right, asshole! You need to go back and crawl under the rock you came from. And you better be careful. Most everyone around here has read or heard about your article, your lies, your fabrications. And let me tell you, they are pissed!"

The suddenly frightened journalist expected pushback; that locals might argue with him, but in a more civilized manner. But this? Wow! His story has apparently struck a hornet's nest, hitting a nerve in a way he now knows he should have expected. Saying nothing more, he turns and walks out of the tavern and onto the sidewalk. He's not sure what to do next. But, the investigative side of him will not let go. He decides he will check out the spot where Lester Porter's body was found.

He drives out to the Foster farm. He climbs out of his car and walks up to the front door of the white two-story, wood house. He knocks on the door and shortly Mrs. Foster answers.

"Hello. My name is Oliver Winstead, I—"

The lady of the house interrupts, "I know who you are; you're that newspaper man that has folks around here really upset."

"Well, not intentionally, Mam. I just find life in these parts interesting and would like to believe my readers would like to hear about it."

"Look," she replies, "you don't have to explain yourself to us. Sherman and I got a kick out of your op-ed piece. And quite frankly, we agree with everything you say. It's them folks in town who are upset."

Oliver sighs and smiles. "That's good to know."

"I bet you're here looking into the Lester Porter murder case, aren't you?"

There is a moment's hesitation followed by an admission, "Yeah. I am. I'm determined to get to the bottom of this. I'm convinced the jury was right. Karl Miller had nothing to do with the murder. So, who then? I think it is one of those mysteries that can be solved. It's just going to take some work."

"Listen, Sherman's out in the barn. Let me take you back there."

Mrs. Foster walks with Oliver down the steps, around the house, and into the old barn, a structure made with ancient barnwood that has shrunk and left large cracks between the slabs of siding. The smell is a mixture of old hay and horse-droppings. The middle-aged farmer is combing the broad back of one of his plow-horses. As his wife and the visitor approach him, he drops what he is doing, backs out of the stall, and meets his wife and the guest in the middle of the barn.

"Guess who wants to talk to you, Dear!" the wife asks with a bit of excitement in her voice.

"Well, if it ain't the most popular newspaper man in Northeast Kansas," Mr. Foster barks, as he wipes his hands on his denim overalls and then reaches out to shake his visitor's hand.

Oliver is not quite sure how to react, but rather timidly reaches out to shake the weather-beaten, rough, and calloused hands of the farmer. "You're being facetious, but I stand by my words, even if some folks feel offended. I hope you understand."

"Oh, I do, believe me. The funny thing is, as far as I can tell, must of us farmers in the area agree with your analysis. There is a tension between town and country folks, as you have discovered. And there is a social status gap. Us farmers are better off, harder-working, and I'd say more civilized than our neighbors in town. But I've got to ask, what you doin' out here? You got your story, so…"

The reporter sighs with relief and answers the question, "I want to help solve the Lester Porter murder case. I am by trade an investigative reporter. I believe there was some sloppy work done by the sheriff and the coroner who would also be considered the medical examiner; that they overlooked evidence and did not pursue relevant clues as thoroughly as they should have. They were too focused on convicting Karl Miller. As a result, they relied on their tunnel vision and ignored the clues that lay within their broader peripheral vision."

"So, what brings you out here?"

"I want to see the place where Lester Porter's body was found. And since it's on your property, I need your permission and, if you are willing, your help."

"Sure. Why not? I'd love to know who killed Lester. I never liked the guy, but I don't think he deserved to be murdered. Look, why don't you let me take you to the site? We can take my truck."

With that, they climb into Foster's 1943 Ford pickup and head north across a small cow pasture, through a gate and across an unplowed field of dead cornstalk stubs, and into the woods and to the site where the Foster and Butler boys found the dead body of Mr. Lester Porter.

As they pull up beside the desired destination next to a dry gulley that has not seen a stream of water in years, except during the heaviest of rainstorms, Farmer Foster turns off the engine and turns to his passenger. "This is the place, right down there." He points.

They get out of the pickup and walk gingerly along the edge of the ditch and then down a narrow path to the bottom. Sherman again points. "There. Right there. The body was there."

"Okay, but how was it situated? I mean, which way was the victim lying? Was his head—"

Before Oliver can finish, the farmer interrupts, "Yeah, it was this way. His head was here, toward the south."

"Was he lying on his back?"

"Yep. Just like he was asleep, only his eyes was missing."

"The sheriff and the coroner claim his eyes were pecked out by buzzards."

"That's right. The boys actually saw buzzards leaving the body when they first discovered it."

Oliver has had a problem with that from the beginning. But he keeps his skepticism to himself.

"So, if someone brought the body here to dump it, how would they have gotten here?" the journalist asks.

"Well, I'm thinking they came in over there on the other side of that field. There's a gate there, easy to open. And that field has lain fallow for three years now. Government pays me not to grow wheat on it. So, driving across that weedy lot would be easy."

"Okay. So wouldn't there be tire tracks?"

"The sheriff looked, but the problem is the weeds, the vegetation. There were tire tracks but impossible to identify."

The weather in Northeast Kansas has been unseasonably warm in the past week or so. As a result, all the snow has melted and the ground is fairly dry. Oliver walks around the area Sherman has identified as the exact location of the body, trying to imagine what it looked like when stumbled upon by the four boys, how the victim was killed, and how he ended up here.

"Apparently, there was little blood on the scene; is that correct?"

"That's true. That's one of the reasons the sheriff and his team believe Lester had been killed somewhere else, then his body dragged here and left."

"Were there not footprints? I mean, this creek bed is composed of a soft mixture of mud and sand. As you can see, you and I have left prints."

"Well, the only footprints that were found were mine and the boys. The sheriff assumes the killer swept his prints as he left the scene."

"That explains why the issue of footprints did not come up at the Miller trial." As the journalist surveys his surroundings, he opines, "I have to believe that it would take a pretty strong person to drag that body from the top of the gulch and down to here."

"Yeah. I reckon you're right. Or maybe two people."

As Oliver continues walking around the crime scene, stroking his chin and nodding his head, the owner of the property blurts out, "Look, I can tell you want to spend some time nosing around here. I'm going to go back to the house. You can find your way back, can't ya?"

"Yeah. Certainly. And thanks for your help. It means a lot."

Sherman mutters "you're welcome" and climbs up out of the gulley and into his vehicle. Moments later, he is gone and Oliver is alone. He continues walking around the area where the body was found, trying to visualize what happened the day Lester's corpse was dragged or pitched into the dry creek bed. It would have been difficult for anyone to toss the body from the edge of the bank. More likely, it was dragged and left to decay and ultimately feed the buzzards and the carnivorous insects that thrive on rotting flesh. The investigative reporter assumes that a vehicle, probably a pickup truck, came through the gate Sherman pointed out to him, and drove across the fallow field, into the woods, and up to the edge of the creek.

Eventually, Oliver climbs out of the dry creek bed and begins walking across the fallow field toward the barbed-wire gate. He scans each inch of the way very carefully, looking for a clue. He gets to the fence and turns around, retracing his steps and still looking. Then, out of nowhere, he suddenly sees something. Lying on the ground, some 25 yards from the gate, he sees a dark gray lug-nut. It might be something that fell off Foster's farm equipment some time ago, or it might be a clue. He picks it up and puts it in his pocket.

*****

Oliver spends the night in an Atchison motel, but is back in Crossroads the next day. He drives into Troy Ackerman's Texaco station and pulls up beside the only gas pump. He gets out of his car and looks around, waiting for help. No one is in sight. He considers honking his horn, but that might be seen as rude. He hears a clanging sound coming from the back side of the station. He walks toward the sound and finds Troy under an old pickup truck astride the car lift.

"Mr. Ackerman."

Troy's arms drop to his side and he turns to face his would-be customer. "Yeah." Troy is not one to say much.

"I need gas."

"Okay," the station-owner mumbles as he drops his wrench and walks out toward the pump. "You're that newspaper man, ain't ya?"

"I guess you could say that."

"I shouldn't be sellin' you no gas. Folks 'round here ain't happy 'bout what you said in your story about Crossroads."

Oliver does not reply. There's no point in trying to defend himself. Nothing more is said. Troy lifts the nozzle from its cradle, "Fill 'er up?"

"Yes, please."

As the gas drains slowly from the large glass tank, Oliver reaches into his pocket and pulls out the lug-nut he found out at the Foster farm. He shows it to Troy and asks, "Do you carry these?"

The station-owner reaches out, takes the nut from the reporter's hand, and studies it carefully. "No, I'm sorry. Ain't got one of these." As he hands the item back to Oliver, he rubs the side of his face and adds, "Funny though; not that long ago, someone else asked me if I had one-ah them. He needed it for his pickup; one of his back wheels, if I recall."

The reporter chuckles. "That's funny. Who was it? Probably nobody local."

"No. Matter ah fact, he was local, all right. It was Louie, the guy that runs the tavern, sellin' hooch to all the town drunks. Why'd you ask?"

"No particular reason."

*****

Later that day, Oliver walks into Ward's grocery and buys a bag of potato chips and a cold 'Coke Cola'. This is his lunch. He walks to the park across the street and sits down on a wooden bench. It is chilly, but not as cold as it usually is this time of year in Crossroads. When he finishes, he pitches the bottle and the potato chip bag into the large trash barrel on the edge of the park and wanders aimlessly down the street and around the corner. He walks past the tavern and, as luck would have it, Louie's Ford pickup is parked next to the building, in front of the camping trailer that had been Oliver's home for a few unforgettable nights.

The first thing he notices is that one of the back wheels is missing a lug-nut. The others match the one he found near the spot where Lester's body was found. Looking around furtively and hoping no one is looking, he walks up beside the suspect's vehicle. As he studies the truck bed, he sees a few red streaks that may or may not be dried human blood. But he cannot be sure. It could be the blood of a deer or some other animal that Louie may have killed. However, it does add to Oliver's suspicion that the tavern-owner might know a lot more about Lester's murder than he is willing to admit.

The investigative reporter, thinking he might be on to something critical, walks back down the street where he had parked his car, gets in, cranks it up, and pulls out into the street. He has not gone far when he realizes there is something wrong with his front tires. He stops, gets out, and, sure enough, someone has let the air out of both of his front tires. Fortunately, they have not been slashed and he is close enough to the Texaco station that he is able to get help before he ruins the inner-tubes.

Once he has the air in his front tires replaced, he hands Mr. Ackerman a five-dollar bill and thanks him for his help. As he is getting back into his car, he gets one more piece of advice from the service station-owner: "If I were you, I'd be careful about hanging out around here. Today it was just your tires; could be a lot worse next time."

Oliver says nothing, but nods, indicating that he has heard and understood the advice. He heads out of town and drives to Troy and the sheriff's office. The staff there know Mr. Winstead from prior visits. He asks to see the report on the Karl Miller case; also, the coroner's report.

"You're free to look at these things since the Miller trial, but you can't take 'em out of here," an officious clerk explains.

"I understand," Oliver politely replies.

The play-by-the-rule bureaucrat gets up from his desk and disappears into the restricted area at the back of the building. Some ten minutes later, he reappears, this time with two small file folders.

"Here they are, just as you asked. You can sit at this little table right over here and look at them as long as you like."

Oliver reads each of the reports carefully. Both are rather perfunctory. Neither report addresses the position of the body when it was found. The coroner's report is spotty and, in Oliver's experience, incomplete. Apparently, the investigation was superficial at best. It is as though all of those involved thought they knew who the murderer was, so there was no use in putting that much effort into the investigation. The experienced reporter has seen a lot of such reports. These are unbelievably over-simplified and inadequate.

The reporter returns the file folders to the clerk, thanks him, and drives immediately to his motel room in Atchison. Once there, he picks up the phone and dials the office of a forensic detective friend in Kansas City, who immediately answers the phone.

Surprised, Oliver quips, "Things must be bad. You're answering your own phone."

"Look, asshole. You do what ya gotta do. My assistant is out on maternity leave, and the temp I have hired is virtually worthless. Working on her nails and eyebrows all day, then answers the phone with something like, 'Okay. What do you want?' So, okay, what do you want?"

"I need your help."

"Doing what?"

"Well, it's a murder case. The victim was a guy named Lester Porter. Happened outside the little town of Crossroads."

"Yeah. I think I remember reading about that. In fact, it seems it was your story in the *Star*."

"That's it; so, as you know, there was a trial and the suspect was acquitted, but the killer is still at large. But I think, with your help, I can nail the real killer."

"So, what do you have so far?"

"Not much, but enough that I think I know who the killer is. Also, the sheriff's and the coroner's reports are sloppy, like the work of rank amateurs. I'm confident a lot of important evidence was overlooked."

"Okay. So how do I fit into all of this?"

"I will be back in Kansas City tomorrow. If you have time, I would like to drop by your office and discuss the case."

Oliver and his forensic specialist friend agree on a time. The reporter drives back to Crossroads. He wants to talk to the history teacher again. It is about 3:30 in the afternoon when he pulls into the Crossroads School parking lot. Students are leaving, most getting on one of the two yellow school buses that take the farmers' kids to and from school. He walks to the front door of the building, into the foyer, and checks to see if the history teacher's room or office number is posted. The classroom he is looking for is on the second floor. He climbs up the steps and heads down the hall and, sure enough, the teacher he is looking for is sitting at a desk between the blackboard and the 20 or so student desks facing him.

"Hello. Mr. Wilson. You remember me? We talked on the phone recently," the reporter announces as he walks toward the startled teacher.

"Sure. Sure. Certainly, I remember." The teacher stands up and the two men shake hands. "What do you want this time?"

"Just a few minutes of your time, if you're willing."

"Okay. Why don't we sit?" The teacher points to a couple student desks on the front row.

The journalist smiles. "This is the first time I've sat in one of these in years. Only, when I was in school, I always sat on the back row, not the front. I thought it would be less likely that the teacher would call on me, since I was never prepared."

"Not a good student, eh?"

"Terrible. Did just enough to get by. But to cut to the chase, I'm here to follow up on our discussion regarding Lester Porter's murder. I'm convinced that the sheriff and the coroner botched their reports. There is too much missing."

"Yeah, I wondered about that. But what do you want from me?"

"Right. Let me begin by asking that you say nothing to anyone about this discussion."

"All right."

"I have reason to believe that Louis Lombardi knows more about the murder than he lets on. We have some rather convincing evidence that he was at the place where the body was found. There is more, but I'm not at liberty to discuss that at this point."

"Wow."

"In our discussion over the phone, you indicated that there were folks in town who knew more about who killed Lester than they were willing to admit. So, do you think there is a feeling out there that Louie is the guilty party?"

"Yeah. There's been talk."

"Like what?"

"Well, Randy Whitehead, a farmer who has a place down the road from the Fosters, claims he saw Louie and his pickup drive by his farm four days before Lester's body was found. Apparently, Louie was in a hurry, and Randy wondered why he would be out in his part of the woods."

"How come he never said anything to the sheriff?"

"Because it had nothing to do with Karl Miller and his indictment. And he thought it was just a coincidence; that Louie probably had a good explanation, and he may have. Another thing, though, Louie has a 38 revolver and he is a master at beating people with his club. These things have made people wonder. But you have to know, people in town are afraid of Louie. He's not a guy you want to tangle with."

"Are you afraid of him?"

"In a way, yes. But if he is indeed responsible for the murder of Lester Porter, then I believe he should be tried and convicted."

"Do you think Louie may have had a motive to kill Lester?"

"Well, maybe. It's a longshot, but several of my friends have said that there was bad blood between the two of them. Of course, that was true with a lot of folks. Lester was a self-proclaimed Nazi and Hitler sympathizer. You can imagine how that might go over with folks who lost loved ones in the war. But there is one other thing."

"What's that?"

"You may know this, but Alexandra Porter is related to Louie. I think she is his niece. Anyhow, Lester was really abusive, beat poor Alexandra to a pulp; any time he was angry about something, he would take it out on her. I know Louie threatened Lester at times, telling him if he kept knocking her around, he would be sorry."

The conversation shifts away from the Lester Porter case as Oliver asks questions about the school, the students, and the history teacher's background. The fact that sticks in Oliver's mind is that there are so few students here; the history teacher often teaches classes with only four or five pupils, barely enough to make up a basketball team. But the guy loves his job. Oliver is reminded that having so few students makes the Crossroads school an expensive operation. Per pupil cost here is likely over twice what it is in larger urban schools; another indication that rural areas in the country get a larger share of the federal pie than small-town residents are willing to admit.

*****

The next day, the forensic detective friend meets Oliver in Troy. Together, they go to the sheriff's office. They look over the reports that Oliver has already seen. The detective friend agrees: there is more evidence missing in these reports than is actually recorded. Among the questions raised is one regarding Lester's missing eyeballs. According to the expert, this does not sound like the work of buzzards. There are flaws and unanswered questions.

After finishing up in the sheriff's office, they drive together to Crossroads. As luck would have it, Louie's truck is parked in its usual spot beside the tavern building and in front of the camping trailer.

"You're sure that truck belongs to Mr. Lombardi?" the detective asks his friend.

"Positive."

"Okay. Make sure no one is watching."

Oliver scouts out the area around the building. All is quiet.

The detective reaches into his backpack and pulls out a small knife and a large test tube. He leans into the bed of Louie's truck and quickly scrapes up a sample of the bloodstains from the wooden floorboard. He places the sample in the test tube and barks at Oliver, "Let's get out of here! What we are doing is against the law, you know."

With that, they jump back into the Winstead vehicle and take off.

"Where are we headed?" the detective asks.

"I think we need to have a look at the spot where the body was found," replies the reporter. "You may see something I missed."

They drive out to the Foster farm. Again, with the farmer's permission, Oliver takes his friend to the place where the body was found. The detective noses around, complaining that the time lapse between now and when the body was found has made the case more difficult. They find no new evidence.

The next day, the detective is back home. He telephones his friend Oliver. "I've run the dried blood samples by a pathologist colleague of mine. The blood is human blood and type AB-negative, a rare blood type. Unfortunately, there is nothing in the coroner's report about the victim's blood type. And I doubt the victim's family has a clue. From what you've told me, I doubt the Mr. Porter was the type who went to the trouble of donating blood. So, it seems to me the only way to make all this stick is to exhume the body."

"What! You're talking about digging up the corpse? Are you serious?" Oliver never dreamed it would come to this.

"I'm serious. The whole case seems to have been mishandled and the body, even though it has been in the ground for several months, may lead us to the person responsible for the murder."

"You're serious?"

"I am. Right now, I think we have enough evidence to indict the bartender, but not convict him. I think Mr. Porter's body might provide all we need to prove that the swarthy tavern keeper is the killer."

"But you know, in order to do that, we need the permission of his widow, a woman named Alexandra Porter. I can't imagine she would agree to anything like that."

"Well, if she wants to see this murder solved, I think she will," the detective responds somewhat arrogantly.

*****

The next day, instead of driving back home to Kansas City as planned, Mr. Winstead goes back to Crossroads and the Porter homestead. The temperature has dropped. It is cloudy, and a quiet and light snow drifts slowly from the sky but without a significant accumulation on the ground. Oliver pulls into the dirt driveway beside the two-story, white wood-siding house. He climbs out of his car and walks slowly up the chicken-shit-stained concrete pathway to the porch, climbs the three steps, and knocks on the front door. The door opens.

"Mrs. Porter. I'm Oliver Winstead, I—"

The lady of the house cuts him off, "I know who you are. You're the reporter, the guy everyone in Crossroads is talking about."

Oliver blushes. "So I've heard. But, in my business, we don't write to be liked; we write to inform."

"Well, I'm not sure what you've heard, but I found most of your article to be an accurate description of what life is like in these parts. But what brings you out here?"

"I'd like to talk to you, if I could. I need your help."

"Okay. You might as well come in." With that, she pushes the screen door open a bit further and the determined journalist steps inside.

As he walks into the living room, he sees someone he recognizes—a woman who had been in the audience at the Karl Miller trial. Before he can introduce himself, Alexandra announces, "This is Greta Miller, a friend of mine and someone who has been a great help to me as I've adjusted to my life without Lester."

"Yes," Oliver quips as he sticks out his right hand. "You're Karl Miller's sister, are you not?"

"I am," Greta responds as she throws back her head and stares at him under her thick glasses. "I am, but I can't say I'm proud of it."

"I won't ask why, but I have to say, I never thought Mr. Miller was guilty of killing Mr. Porter. The evidence was spotty at best and it never made sense to me."

Greta and Alexandra look at each other. They say nothing, but their body language suggests that, while they may not actually say it, they probably do not agree with the journalist's observation.

"Why don't you have a seat, Mr. Winstead? Can I get you a cup of coffee?" the widow asks her guest.

"Sure. That would be great."

"How do you like it?"

"Black, without cream or sugar."

"Aha. A real coffee drinker. That was how Lester liked it."

As Alexandra heads to the kitchen, Oliver turns to Greta. "Rev. Butler told me that you were a missionary to Peru. Are you here on furlough, or will you not be going back?"

A touchy subject. Greta bristles and glares at the unexpected visitor. "I'd rather not talk about that," she growls.

Oliver realizes he has struck a nerve and quickly changes the subject. "You grew up here in Crossroads, right?"

"That's right."

"You've seen the world and have had the opportunity to look at Crossroads from a more objective perspective than most folks. How would you describe your hometown now?"

"Well, I think it's a pretty backward place, a town full of idiots, and also a town that doesn't like outsiders prying into their personal lives." Again, there is an obvious hostility in her response.

Oliver gets the message. He sits quietly, keeping his mouth shut and looking around the room at the old furniture, the well-worn throw rugs, and the various framed pictures; pictures of family, he presumes.

Greta stands up and, without excusing herself, walks out to the kitchen and asks Alexandra if she can help.

They return with the coffee and everyone is seated once again. The hostess cuts to the chase, "All right. What is it you want to ask me?"

"Well, let me begin by giving you a little background. I'm a newspaper reporter and my specialization is investigative reporting. In other words, I am also a detective of sorts. I like to solve mysteries. In this case, I am interested in the murder of your husband. A forensic detective friend of mine and I have been looking into the details and we think we have enough evidence to reopen the case and bring charges. But..."

"But what?" Alexandra asks.

"We need to exhume your husband's body. The sheriff's report and the coroner's report are totally inadequate, not as thorough as they should have been; so much of the evidence, we think, was overlooked. But, in order to exhume the body, we need your permission."

"Wait a minute. You're telling me you want to dig up Lester's body? He's been dead and in the grave for months. That's crazy!"

"I know this is not easy for you. But look at it this way: if it helps to solve the mystery of your husband's death, which I think it will, then it's well worth the emotional revulsion of something like this."

"Look," the widow practically shouts, her face as red as Santa's freshly laundered suit, "I want to know who killed my husband, probably more than anyone else, but I can't approve of something so morbid, so disgusting, so sacrilegious, as digging up his rotting corpse."

Greta leans into the discussion. "No way. No way," she mutters.

"So, you would rather the murderer run free—perhaps kill someone else—than allow for a more thorough analysis of your husband's body?"

Lester's widow reacts, "Yes. Yes. Come on; nothing is going to bring him back. So, you find the killer. How does that change things? He's dead and pretty apt to stay that way." She grabs her coffee and raises it to her mouth, but her hand is shaking so violently that some of the coffee splashes out of the cup onto the carpet. She ignores it and takes a sip. Then she leans back into her chair in an effort to regain her composure. No one speaks. Finally, she blurts out, "Look, I've heard enough. There's no way I'm gonna give anyone permission to dig up Lester's remains. So, you best get up and get out of here."

In the midst of Alexandra voicing her strong opposition, a young man walks into the living room. Just over six feet tall, a trim body, a square face, and deep blue eyes that peer out from behind a pair of tortoiseshell glasses, he looks around the room, wondering what is happening. He's the older of the two Porter boys. He is at home for a few days, taking a break from working on his dissertation. Alexander Porter is pursuing a PhD in horticulture at Kansas State. "What's all this about?" he asks with a look of puzzlement on his face.

"It's about your dad. This guy wants me to give him permission to dig up your father's body. He thinks being able to study the body further might lead him to Lester's killer."

The young man is quiet for a minute. Oliver stands up and introduces himself. They shake hands as the reporter explains his presence. The journalist tells Alexandra's good-looking son what he wants and why, noting that he can do nothing without his mother's approval.

Alexander looks at his mother. "So what have you told him?"

Alexandra looks at her son with this "what do you think, you idiot" look on her face. "I told him no, absolutely not!"

The son struggles to digest this information and understand what has just happened and what he has heard. Finally, he blurts out, "But Mom, he's only trying to help. I mean, if it helps us find out who killed Dad, then I'm not sure why you wouldn't approve." Alexander turns to the guest. "Look, I think Mom is too emotional right now, not thinking straight. Let me talk to her when she calms down. Give me your phone number. I'll call if I can get her to agree. I think she'll come around."

Oliver hands him his business card, thanks his hostess for the coffee, acknowledges Greta and the handsome son, and lets himself out of the house.

*****

Two days later, the reporter is back in his Kansas City office working on another op-ed piece about farm life in Kansas and Missouri. The phone rings.

"Hello, Oliver Winstead here."

"Yes. This is Alexander Porter. Remember me?"

"For sure; the good-looking young man from K-State."

"Thanks. But I'm calling to let you know that I have convinced my mom that it is in our best interests for her to give you permission to exhume my father's body."

"That's good. I think she's doing the right thing, and if the process of a new investigation produces the evidence I think it will, then she should feel good about her approving our proposal."

"I hope so. But what do we do next?"

"Well, I've got to get to Troy and update the sheriff and get from him the document that your mother will need to sign. We will need to get a judge to issue a court order authorizing the exhumation. It is a complicated process, but one carried out with the appropriate respect for the deceased and his family."

*****

Everything falls into place, and one week later the body has been removed from its grave in the local cemetery and is lying on an operating table in the medical examiner's lab in Troy. Oliver, his forensic detective friend, a pathologist, and the local coroner are present. The rotting remains of Lester's clothed body is the subject of a much more intensive scrutiny than was the case just after his death. The room is almost refrigerator-cold. The body has been rotting for several months now, so the smell is not as overpowering as it might have been earlier. Lester Porter is lying there in his best, and only, suit—a mere skeleton covered in paper-like skin and occasional long black hair.

The local coroner is not happy. "I'm telling you. There ain't nothing here you're gonna find; nothing I ain't already reported. I still don't know why you're doing this."

His protests are ignored.

The pathologist peers into the victim's empty eye sockets. As he pokes around, he announces, "It's clear to me that this guy's eyes were not pecked out; they were cut out. There are markings here made by a knife or a razor. This is not the work of a bird's beak."

"You can't be sure about that," the defensive coroner says emphatically, trying desperately to protect his reputation.

Again, no one seems to hear him.

Meanwhile, the forensic detective is looking closely at Lester's skull. He asks the pathologist, "This doesn't look like he was hit with a ball bat, does it?" Before the expert can respond, the detective continues, "This looks to me more like something with a sharp edge. Look at the broken skin line."

The pathologist grunts his agreement.

They turn the body over and begin examining the back of the head. The detective is the first to notice what appear to be scratch marks at the edge of Lester's hairline. "Why weren't these included in the report?" he asks.

The embarrassed coroner remains silent.

"It looks like there may have been a scuffle before he was shot or bludgeoned to death; someone dragged their nails across the back of Mr. Porter's neck."

The team of examiners combs over every part of the victim's body. Nothing else unusual presents itself. The team finds no more clues. But, before they conclude the post-mortem examination, the pathologist reminds the others, "Don't forget. The major purpose of this exhumation was to extract a blood sample."

The coroner chuckles. "Good luck with that."

The pathologist and the rest of the team know it's a long shot, but they open up the chest cavity and, much to their delight, they find dried blood. They take a sample—a dried blood sample, not much, but enough to determine blood type.

As soon as the investigation is over, the body is quickly and quietly returned to the cemetery and re-interred. The family has been notified. Alexander is there to watch his father's casket returned to its original resting place.

*****

The next day, Oliver gets a call. It's his friend, the detective. "We've got a case."

"What do you mean?"

"The blood type of the corpse. It matches that of the sample we took from the back of the tavern-owner's pickup."

Chapter Twenty-One
A New Suspect

The county sheriff and his deputy pull up in the squad car in front of Louie's Tavern. It's late morning on a Tuesday and the place has just opened for business, open but without customers as yet.

A bell rings as the sheriff opens the front door. Louie hears the bell and hustles from his upstairs apartment, prepared to don his bartender hat and serve his first customer. But as he walks into the bar, he is greeted by a man in uniform; obviously not a customer.

"Mr. Louis Lombardi?" The sheriff asks, although he has met the notorious barkeep before.

"Yes," Louie responds, with a puzzled look on his face. He and the sheriff know each other well. *Why this rhetorical question?* he thinks.

"You are under arrest. You are accused of the murder of Mr. Lester Porter."

"What! This is crazy! This is bullshit! You're not serious, are you?"

"I'm afraid so, Louie. So please turn around and put your hands behind your back."

The startled bartender is still trying to get his head around what is happening. Reluctantly, he follows the sheriff's order. The deputy clicks on the handcuffs and turns the suspect around and leads him toward the front door.

"Wait a minute. Wait. Can't you give me a chance to say something to my wife and pick up a few things to take with me?"

"Not now. Maybe later."

Louie is shoved into the back of the squad car. Within minutes, the suspect and his captors are cruising along. No flashing lights, no siren; just a police vehicle that the people of Crossroads have seen many times before. A few of the locals see the car but don't recognize the guy in the backseat.

About twenty minutes later, the car pulls up in front of the county jail in Troy. The prisoner is helped from the backseat and as the three men approach the jail, who is waiting there to greet and question them? None other than the nosy reporter from the *Kansas City Star*.

"Gentlemen. Can I get a statement. Is this man under arrest? Has he been charged with the murder of Lester Porter?"

Louis recognizes Oliver and snarls in his direction, "You sorry-ass, son-of-a-bitch. You're the one that did this. When I get outta here, I'm gonna…" He stops here, leaving only a vague threat.

The sheriff and the deputy ignore the investigative reporter and march their suspect through the front door of the county jail and place him in the holding tank, where he will be interrogated.

Louie is given his one phone call. He calls his wife. She is obviously upset. One minute her husband was there and the next he was gone. She has shut the tavern for the day. The overweight suspect explains his situation and assures his spouse that he is innocent. "That god-damn reporter, Winstead's his name, he's drummed up some case against me, trying to make me out to be a murderer. That's bullshit. I should be out of here soon. Meanwhile, I need you to contact that lawyer in Kansas City, the one that defended Karl Miller, Clyde somebody. His name and number are in my address book under the phone behind the bar. Tell him what's going on and that I'll pay whatever it takes to retain him."

Louie is interrogated for over an hour. The evidence used to justify his indictment and arrest is presented to him. The lug-nut, the blood, the sighting by the Crossroads farmer. Louie continues to plead innocent. "I have no idea. Somebody must have set me up. This is crazy. I had nothing to do with that guy's death." He continues to deny that he knew or had anything to do with Lester's unfortunate demise.

The sheriff repeats what he has said before, "You know, Mr. Lombardi, you could simply confess and open the door to a possible plea bargain."

"Look, asshole. I am innocent, do you understand? I didn't do it. So why should I confess to a crime I didn't commit? Look, this is all I'm going to say. I want my lawyer to be here."

"Okay, that's your right. But you could make this so much easier if you would simply cooperate."

At this point, the suspect is returned to his holding tank. He does not resist, having concluded that there is nothing he can say or do that will alter his fate.

*****

Louis spends the night in jail. He tries, but cannot sleep. He is served a simple breakfast. He cleans up and shortly his lawyer shows up. Clyde Hartman is dressed in blue jeans and a red plaid shirt, uncharacteristically simple for the vaunted trial attorney. He explains the terms of his defense.

"Look. Money is not an issue here. I just want to get out of here and back to my normal life," Louie explains.

Hartman has arranged for Louie's bail hearing. It is set for 10 this morning. Everything is on time. The judge hears the evidence and sets Louie's bail at $50,000, even though Mr. Lombardi is not considered a flight risk.

A couple hours later, his wife, Karlene Lombardi, shows up at the jail with a cashier's check for $50,000. The check is verified, and by early afternoon Louis is free on bail. The couple heads back to Crossroads. The bar is reopened.

*****

It is late afternoon in Crossroads. Some of the regulars are already in the bar and sipping or slopping down their favorite adult beverages. By now, the news of Louie's arrest has been flying around the town's informal communication network like bats on steroids. Now, it's time for speculation. "Do you think he did it? I wondered about this. I don't think Louie could do something like that. He's a tough guy, but not a killer. I don't know. Remember what he did to that intruder that broke into the bar that time?"

Oliver Winstead, who can be described as either courageous or stupid, is back in town, talking to people. He deliberately avoids Louie's Tavern, fearing he might be clubbed to death by the angry proprietor or one of his sympathizers. He drives back to Kansas City after spending the day in Crossroads. He sits down behind his Olivetti typewriter and crafts his article for inclusion in the next day's *Kansas City Star*:

Small Town: Big-Time Murder Case

The small town of Crossroads, Kansas, is once again the focus of an ongoing murder case. Yesterday, Mr. Louis Lombardi, the owner of Louie's Tavern in downtown Crossroads, was formally charged with the murder of Mr. Lester Porter, a farmer whose body was discovered in a dry creek bed on property owned by a Mr. Sherman Foster five months ago. Shortly after the body was found, another Crossroads farmer, Mr. Karl Miller, was arrested, charged, and tried for Mr. Porter's murder. But the evidence against him was at best circumstantial and the jury had no choice but to exonerate him. But now, new evidence has emerged, some of which was discovered when Mr. Porter's body was exhumed.

As the people of Crossroads await the trial and its outcome, they are certainly not all of one opinion. Mr. Lombardi has his friends and supporters who claim he is innocent. But he also has enemies, some of whom are part of the church community. They say they believe he is guilty. After all, is he not already proving he is not a God-fearing man by selling and openly promoting the imbibing of the devil's brew?

Mr. Lombardi does have a history of violent behavior, once beating an intruder, a would-be thief, with his sawed-off ball bat. The man was critically wounded, but survived. For a variety of reasons, Mr. Lombardi is widely feared across the greater Crossroads and Doniphan County communities. It is rumored that he has ties to organized crime. However, none of these rumors has ever been substantiated. It is not unusual for an uninformed Crossroads resident to assume that, since the notorious barkeep is Italian, he must be a part of the mafia.

Louis Lombardi has lived in the Crossroads community for over 20 years. He is descended from parents who emigrated from Italy and subsequently opened a butcher shop in the Bronx in New York City. He and his wife have one son who is a recent graduate of the local high school. They live in a sparsely decorated apartment upstairs above the popular watering hole simply called Louie's Tavern.

When asked what brought them to Crossroads, he has responded, "Well, if I knew the answer to that question, I wouldn't be here."

Mr. Lombardi continues to proclaim his innocence and rail against those behind his arrest. He has engaged the services of a well-known Kansas City attorney, Mr. Clyde Hartman, and has vowed to fight this "absurd allegation".

So, the never-ending drama of life in small-town America goes on. The judge is expected to set a trial date with the next two weeks. Meanwhile, the people of Crossroads continue leaving their front doors unlocked, saying grace at mealtime, and sleeping guiltlessly through the night.

*****

Chapter Twenty-Two
The Lombardi Trial

It's April in Crossroads, Kansas. Corn, wheat, and milo planting is in full swing. But, in many ways, life stands still across the county as the Louis Lombardi trial begins.

The trial is being held in the same Troy courthouse where Karl Miller was tried and acquitted. The crowd includes many of the same people. Alexandra Porter is here, her son Alexander on one side and Greta Miller on the other. Of course, Oliver Winstead is here with his legal pad in his lap and ballpoint pen in his right hand. Louie's wife, Karlene, is sitting on the front row next to her only son, who is wearing a brown suede jacket and an open-collar, white dress shirt. As always, he is getting the attention of the ladies.

There are men in coats and ties and others in bib overalls. The women are for the most part dressed like farm wives—one-piece, boldly colored and patterned dresses that hang to their ankles. The air is pungent with a mixture of sweat, mothballs, fresh hay, dirty shoes, and inexpensive cologne.

At 10:00 sharp, the judge and the bailiff come walking into the court. As the judge stands behind his desk, the bailiff makes an announcement he has made countless times before, "All rise for the honorable judge..."

As everyone is standing, the judge slams his gavel on the desk and proclaims, "The court is now in session. Regarding the case of the State of Kansas versus one Louis Lombardi, are the prosecution and the defense prepared to move forward with the jury selection process?"

Both respond immediately, "We are, Your Honor."

"So let the process begin."

The first group of potential jurors file into the courtroom and the questioning begins. One by one, the potential jurors are accepted by both parties or rejected. The history teacher from Crossroads High has been tagged for jury duty. He is having to miss school today and does not want to miss any more days. So, he tries to act as though he has a strong bias, claiming that he is certain Mr. Lombardi is not guilty. But the tactic fails. Both the prosecutor and the defense attorney somehow know he is putting up a front and agree he would make a good juror in the case.

Jury selection takes all of one day and half of another. Finally, the jury has been selected and seated. After a long lunch break, the trial resumes with the bailiff calling the court to order. The judge and the audience are seated and the prosecution is invited to make its introductory appeal to the jury.

The DA, the same person who prosecuted the Karl Miller case, steps out from behind his desk and approaches the jury. He is dressed in a plaid wool jacket, loosely fitting work pants, and a white shirt with a paisley tie that clashes with his jacket to the point that even the bib-overalled farmers are amused. "A K-State grad," one of the audience whispers to his neighbor.

"Ladies and gentlemen of the jury, over the next few days, you will be presented with evidence that will prove, beyond a shadow of a doubt, that the defendant, Mr. Louis Lombardi, did deliberately and with malice of forethought take the life of Mr. Lester Porter. Murder in the first degree."

"Lester Porter was a decent man. Yes, he had some political views that some seemed strange, but that was no reason for him to be murdered; murdered I might add, in cold blood. Mr. Porter was a hard worker, a successful farmer, a good father, and a devoted husband."

With this, many members of the audience roll their eyes and look at each other, some shrugging their shoulders. They've heard this before, at the Miller trial, and Lester Porter, in their minds, seems no closer to sainthood now than he was then. The sunlight from outside bounces off their tell-tale eyes in a way that most certainly catches the attention of the jury.

The prosecutor continues, "In short, Lester Porter did not deserve to die, but the person who murdered him and tossed his body into that dry creek bed deserves to be convicted and put away for life."

"Again, the evidence will make it clear that the suspect, Mr. Louis Lombardi, is guilty of murder in the first degree. I am confident that you will agree and use the power of your position to make sure that justice is done and that he is convicted."

With that, one again he thanks the jury and turns toward the judge. "That's all I have, Your Honor."

The DA returns to his desk and the defense attorney, Mr. Hartman, is given permission by the judge to present his case to the jury. He gets up from behind his desk, slowly and deliberately, all the while keeping his eyes on the jury. He stares into the eyes of one juror and then another as he walks toward them, slowly but with a look of confidence. Tailored black suit, red tie, well-polished black wingtip shoes, gold cufflinks—a fashion statement that to some makes him look like a lawyer from another world. They wonder if he has the ability or the experience to understand the majority of the persons on the jury. At the same time, there are those who see the classy, professional way he presents himself as a strength: a sign of success and proof that he knows what he is doing. It's a challenge he's faced before.

After a few minutes of poignant silence, Attorney Hartman addresses the jury. "Let me begin by reiterating what the prosecution has said. We are all grateful for your willingness to serve in this important capacity The fate of Mr. Lombardi lies in your hands. Over the next few days, you will hear testimony from a variety of individuals. The prosecution will do its best to make that testimony convinces you that my client is guilty. I am sure you will listen closely and carefully. And you will ask yourself, 'Is there enough evidence to prove, without a shadow of a doubt, that Louie Lombardi killed Lester Porter?'"

"The answer to that question is simple: 'absolutely not'. Mr. Lombardi is an innocent man with no reason to kill anyone, much less Mr. Porter. There is no motive and no evidence beyond circumstantial and hearsay. So, I thank you and wish you well as you deliberate this important case."

As the defense attorney turns and walks back to his desk, the jurors look at each other with body language that suggests they are somewhat offended by this big-time Kansas City lawyer addressing them as though they were children—talking down to them. The DA smiles to himself as he sees this reaction.

At this point, the judge asks the prosecution if it is ready to call its first witness. "We are, Your Honor. We call Mr. Oliver Winstead to the witness stand."

After the bailiff swears in the witness, the DA asks, "Can you tell the court what you do for a living?"

"Yes. I am a reporter for the *Kansas City Star*. My specialty is investigative reporting."

"How long have you held this position?"

"Over 15 years."

"What sorts of events or cases do you investigate and write about?"

"A wide range of cases; thefts, corruption, kidnappings, murder…"

"Can you give us an example of the murder cases you have investigated?"

"Yes, there have been several. Perhaps the one that members of the court might best remember is the Benton Wells murder case. Mr. Wells was found dead in his car at the bottom of a deep quarry outside of St. Joe. He had been missing for months. Initially, the medical examiner concluded that Mr. Wells was a victim of suicide, that he had deliberately driven his car into the quarry where he drowned. But there was something about the case that bothered me."

"What I was able to find out about the victim suggested to me that he had no reason to kill himself. I was convinced he had been murdered. Anyhow, one thing led to another, and we finally had enough evidence to try and convict Benton Wells' stepson for the murder. He is now serving a life-long sentence in Leavenworth."

"So it is safe to say that you are an expert when it comes to solving unsolved crimes?"

"Yeah. I think so."

"Okay. Then perhaps you could tell the court how you got interested in the Lester Porter murder case."

"Sure. I sat through most of the Karl Miller trial. I was certain he was not guilty and that the real murderer was still at large. It seemed that law enforcement was no longer interested in pursuing the case, so I started asking questions. It was clear that the people who lived in the greater Crossroads area, for the most part, knew that Mr. Miller was innocent and were concerned that Lester's killer was yet to be identified."

"This led me to a visit of the Foster farm where the body had been found. Mr. Foster was kind enough to take me to the site and walk me through what he knew about the discovery and recovery of the body. I spent some time there looking around and trying to imagine how Mr. Porter's body would have been carted to and dropped in this dry gulch. It would not have been an easy task. Anyhow, in the process of looking around for evidence, I found a lug-nut in a fallow field not far from the site where the body was found."

The DA interrupts, "With the court's approval, we would like to introduce this object into evidence." He is holding a small plastic bag with a truck-tire lug-nut inside. He walks up to the witness. "Is this the item you found lying in the unplowed field near the spot where the victim's body was discovered?"

"I think so. Yes. Yes. It is."

"So what did you do next?"

"Well, there is only one gas station and one mechanic in town, Mr. Troy Ackerman. So, I went to his Texaco station and asked him if he had a lug nut like this. He said he did not, but he looked at it for a moment, and then told me that the defendant, Mr. Louis Lombardi, had come to him sometime back wanting to buy a lug-nut like that for his pickup."

"So, then what did you do?"

"I thought I should check Mr. Lombardi's pickup to see if the lug-nut matched and if one of his wheels was missing one."

"What did you find out?"

"The lug-nut was a match and one of the rear wheels was missing one. I could only conclude that, at some point, Mr. Lombardi was out in that field on Mr. Foster's farm. I could only wonder why."

"What else did you find?"

"Well, when I was looking around Mr. Lombardi's truck, I noticed something that looked like blood stains on the wooden bed of his vehicle."

"What did you do then?"

"Nothing, really. I made a mental note of it and realized I should have someone who knew how to recognize blood, take samples, and test them, handle that part of the investigation."

"And that's when you contacted your detective friend?"

"Correct."

The DA then turned to the judge. "If it please the court, I should note that the forensic detective Mr. Winstead is referring to is here today and is on the list of witnesses that I intend to question."

"Duly noted."

"I have one more question for Mr. Winstead. Do you believe Mr. Louie Lombardi is guilty of murdering Mr. Lester Porter?"

Before Oliver can answer, the defense attorney Hartman leaps to his feet. "Objection, Your Honor. The prosecution is asking the witness for his opinion."

"Sustained."

"That completes my examination of this witness, Your Honor."

The DA retreats to his seat behind his desk beside his assistant. They exchange whispers as the defense attorney slowly gets up out of his chair, adjusts his tie, buttons his suit coat, and walks toward the witness. "Mr. Winstead, correct?"

"Yes."

"Mr. Winstead, you claim to be an investigative reporter; that you are an expert at solving crimes, right?"

"Yes sir."

"Do you have a degree in criminal justice?"

"No."

"Have you taken courses in criminal justice?"

"No, not really."

"What do you mean 'not really'?"

"I mean, I've listened to crime shows on the radio, read a lot about crime in this country and about how criminal investigations are conducted. Also, I've published a couple crime novels."

"So, you're telling this court that if I listen to a few radio programs on, let's say, tonsillectomy, I'm qualified to remove someone's tonsils, even though I'm not a doctor?"

The DA interrupts, "Badgering the witness."

"Sustained. The defense will stick to the cross-examination."

"Yes, Your Honor," is the response. He turns back to the witness, "By what authority do you investigate crimes like this?"

"What do you mean?"

"Matters like this are to be left in the hands of law enforcement, not to be looked into by someone whose hobby is sticking his nose into unsolved cases. Have you been designated as a deputy sheriff or police commissioner?"

Again, the prosecution objects.

"Sustained."

"That's all I have for this witness, Your Honor."

The judge then asks, "Does the prosecution wish to question this witness further?"

"Yes, I do, Your Honor." The DA gets up and approaches the witness, wanting to give him a chance to respond to the last question from the defense.

Oliver looks at the jury, as though he wants to make sure the members hear him, and with a tone of sincerity and confidence he defends the right of the press to investigate cases like this, with or without the approval of law enforcement. "It is our duty, not just our right, to seek out the truth; to keep the public informed. This is why we are referred to as the 'Fourth Estate'. Democracies cannot survive without a free press; a press that is not controlled by the state; in fact, a press that keeps the state and all the powers that be, honest. So, no, I am not a deputy sheriff, but yes, I have all the authority I need to look into any matter that I believe to be important. In this case, it is the murder of Mr. Lester Porter."

As the somewhat angry journalist finishes the defense of his occupation and his right to investigate crimes of this nature, the DA tells the judge he has no more questions, and the witness is dismissed.

The next witness to be put on the stand is Rollie Martin, Oliver's forensic detective friend. The DA is the first to question the witness.

"Mr. Martin, can you tell the court what you do; in other words, can you explain what a forensic detective does?"

"Yes sir. Forensics is an important facet of any detective work, but some of us have more experience at it than others. We look for and often find evidence that others may have overlooked. Your average law enforcement officer or detective might dig deep but we dig deeper and are often able to solve cases that would otherwise go unsolved."

"So, how did you get involved in the Lester Porter case?"

"Well, my long-time friend and colleague, Oliver Winstead, called me and told me that he had a mystery he was trying to solve and asked for my help. The case sounded interesting, so I said I would be happy to help."

"How much did he offer to pay you?"

"Nothing."

"Nothing? How can you afford to work for nothing?"

"It's a kind of pro bono thing. These cases help my reputation and refine my skills. And there's the friendship thing, you know."

"Okay, so what did you do next?"

Detective Martin tells the court how he met Oliver in Troy one day, where they went to the sheriff's office and reviewed materials regarding the Miller trial on file there. "It was my conclusion that the sheriff's and coroner's reports were totally inadequate. In short, I felt the investigation had been botched. Anyhow, after that, we drove to Crossroads and took a blood sample from the defendant's pickup. Then we drove out to the Foster farm to study the site where Mr. Porter's body was found. We found no new evidence there."

"You claim the original investigation was botched; by whom?" the prosecuting attorney asks.

"By everyone involved: the sheriff, the medical examiner."

"Can you tell us what led you to that conclusion?"

"Yes; first of all, the assertion that the missing eyeballs was the work of buzzards did not make sense. This is not consistent with what we know about buzzard behavior. In the report, there is no mention of blood type. The hair samples that were collected were labeled as human hair, but in fact, there were a few cat and dog hairs in that sample. This and many other questions that should have been asked, were not."

"So what did you do next?"

"We decided that the way the investigation was mishandled, the way so much information was missing, it justified an exhumation of the body."

"In other words, digging up Lester Porter's body and doing a more thorough examination?"

"Yes sir."

"How did that go?"

The detective then explains how in the state of Kansas, in order to get a court order to exhume a body, you have to have the approval of the next of kin, in this case, Lester's wife, Alexandra. "At first, she said absolutely not. But her son convinced her that it was the right thing to do if they were serious about finding the killer of her husband and of his father."

"So she gave you the okay?"

"She did, and we got a court order from the judge in the case, which allowed for the exhumation. The casket was dug up and pulled from the ground and the body removed and taken to the crime lab in Troy. Here, it went through a much more rigorous examination."

"Can you tell the court what you found?"

"Well, it's not so much what I found, but rather what the pathologist who helped in this case found. I think it best if I leave the details to him. However, I will say that the finding that provided the evidence needed to arrest Mr. Lombardi was the blood."

"The blood? What do you mean?"

"The blood that was extracted from the corpse. It seems it matches the blood type of the blood found in Mr. Lombardi's pickup."

"What was that?"

"It was AB-negative, a blood type found in less than one percent of the American population."

"So this, along with the missing lug-nut, gave you enough evidence to convince the sheriff to arrest Mr. Lombardi for the murder of Mr. Lester Porter?"

"Yes sir."

"Are you convinced that Mr. Louie Lombardi is the person who murdered Lester Porter?"

"Objection, Your Honor. The prosecution is asking the witness for an opinion." The defense reacts before the detective can respond to the question.

"Sustained."

The DA backs away from the witness stand and announces, "That's all I have for this witness, Your Honor."

With that, the judge acknowledges the sharply attired defense attorney's right to cross-examine. Mr. Hartman walks slowly toward the witness stand, then asks, "Mr. Martin, right?"

"Yes sir." It is clear the forensic detective is beginning to tire and is in no mood for redundancy.

"Detective, you have stated that the blood from Mr. Lombardi's truck matches that found in the post-post-mortem examination of Mr. Porter's body? Correct?"

"Yes sir."

"Type AB-negative?"

"Yes."

"Do you know how many people in this country have that same blood type?"

"Not exactly."

"Well, I'll tell you; approximately two hundred thousand."

"Okay."

"Okay? With that number, how can you assume that the blood in Mr. Lombardi's pickup was that of Lester Porter? I mean, come on. Is it not possible that someone of that blood type had cut his finger or his leg and had lost some blood while in the back of that truck?"

"Perhaps, but that seems a stretch."

"A stretch. But possible though; am I not correct?"

"Yes sir."

"Also, Mr. Martin, I'm concerned about the way in which you extracted the blood sample from Mr. Lombardi's pickup. You see, that truck is a part of the man's space, his territory. Before one can examine that vehicle, one needs a warrant, just as he would if he were to search his home. Did you have a search warrant?"

A long pause as the detective looks at the DA. Finally, "No, I did not."

"Then you know that search was illegal, right?"

"Yes."

"Well, you're correct, and I think we could have your license revoked for having violated the legal rights of my client."

At this point, the judge interrupts the proceedings, calling the prosecution and the defense to his desk for a private and off-the-record conversation. "Look, Mr. Hartman, you are correct. The detective should have had a search warrant. But he is not the one on trial here, and I am not going to throw this case out on the grounds of illegally obtained evidence. So, I am going to allow his testimony and overlook the issue that you have raised. Is that understood?"

The judge glares at the defense attorney, who now finds himself in a hole. He can only hope the jury has heard him and understands why this evidence should not be allowed.

He turns around and walks back to his desk, telling the judge, "I have no more questions for this witness."

The judge then calls for a court recess, a break for lunch. The trial is to resume at one o'clock.

After the break, the first witness called to the stand is the pathologist who assisted Detective Martin in the examination of the exhumed body.

The DA begins the questioning, "So, you were part of the effort to exhume the body of Mr. Porter?"

"Well, yes and no. I was called in after the body was dug up and taken to the lab."

"You examined the body, right? Can you tell the court what you found?"

"Yes. There were several things that the coroner or medical examiner missed in the initial investigation."

"Like what?"

"Well, for starters, the blows to the side of the head were made with a sharp object, not a ball bat or other round instrument. Also, there were scratch marks on the back of the victim's head, just under his hairline, suggesting there was a struggle before Mr. Porter died. Also, it was clear that the eyeballs were not eaten by vultures. They were sliced out of their sockets by a sharp knife or razor."

"Have you seen this before?"

"No, but I've heard of its being a technique used by some terrorist groups in Latin America and in the Middle East. Apparently, they sometimes do it while the victim is still alive. It is said it is a way to put fear in your enemy. Mess with us and you lose your eyes—you know, that kind of thing."

"Was there anything else that caught your attention?"

"Yes. The medical examiner or coroner who handled the initial investigation had found a few hairs on the victim's shirt. These were placed in a plastic bag and labeled simply 'hair', with no further explanation. When I looked at the sample, it was clear to me that it contained not just human hair, but also animal hair; I am guessing cat and/or dog."

"How would that impact the case; in other words, what would this suggest about the killer or the way Mr. Porter was murdered?"

"Well, if it were dog hair, it might match that of the small dog that the defendant and his wife—"

"Objection, Your Honor," Louie's attorney hollers. "Speculation on the part of the witness."

"Sustained. The jury will ignore the witness's last comment."

The DA continues, "The previous witness told the court that the blood type found in Mr. Lombardi's truck matched that of Mr. Porter. Is that correct?"

"Yes. That is what I discovered when I ran the test in my lab."

"Thank you. That is all I have for this witness, Your Honor."

The DA walks back to his desk as the defense attorney gets up and moves toward the witness stand. "You are a pathologist, is that correct?"

"Yes."

"And you call yourself a forensic pathologist, right?"

"Yes sir."

"It is my understanding that pathologists are, by training, medical doctors. In other words, they have an M-D degree like any other doctor. Am I not right?"

"You are."

"So, you have a degree in medicine?"

"Yes."

"Can you tell the court where that degree is from; what medical school you attended?"

The witness hesitates, then answers, but in a less forceful voice than before, "Caribbean Medical University."

"And where is this medical university located?"

Again, in a soft response, "Curacao."

"Curacao, as the island off the coast of Venezuela?"

"Yes."

"That's a long way to go to get a medical degree, is it not?"

"I guess."

"Can you tell the court why you chose to go so far away to get your medical training?"

"Objection, Your Honor," the DA interjects. "This kind of questioning is irreverent to the case."

The defense attorney turns to the judge. "Sir, if I might. I think this has everything to do with the case. It gets to the credibility of the witness and his findings from his investigation of the victim's body."

"Overruled. You may continue with this line of questioning." The judge nods and the DA sits down with an obvious look of frustration.

Louie's lawyer asks, "Should I repeat the question?"

"No. I-I..." the witness stumbles a bit, "I guess because I thought it was a good medical school."

"Come on, you know that's not true. You chose to go offshore to get your degree because you could not get into a legitimate medical school here in the States. Your grades and test scores were not good enough. Am I right?"

The witness is blushing and looking around nervously. Finally, he mumbles, "Yes sir."

"So, after you received your degree from this Caribbean Medical University, you decided to go into forensic pathology. Was there additional training required for this?"

"Yes. I had to complete a program in criminology and investigative techniques."

"Program? You mean, course, right? You took one course in criminology at a community college in Kansas City. Is that not correct?"

"Ah, I guess."

"You guess?"

"I mean, yes."

"Since becoming a forensic pathologist, how many exhumed bodies have you examined?" Mr. Hartman continues to chip away at the credibility of the pathologist's training and experience.

Again, a muted response, "One."

"One. So the examination of Mr. Porter's corpse was the first time you've ever worked on an exhumed body; this time, a man who had been dead and in the ground for several months?"

"Yes sir."

"Regarding the blood sample, are you aware that this part of the country has a higher-than-normal percentage of individuals with AB-negative type blood, more so than almost all other areas of the country?"

"I am."

"So, it increases the possibility that the dried blood found in the back of Mr. Lombardi's pickup could belong to any number of individuals, correct?"

"Correct."

At this point, the attorney turns to the judge. "This is all the questioning I have for this witness."

"Does the DA wish to cross-examine this witness?"

"Yes, I do, Your Honor." With that, the prosecution walks quickly toward the witness stand and asks, "After one earns a medical degree, before he can actually practice, he has to receive a license from the state where he wishes to practice, correct?"

"That's correct."

"You have earned that license in both Kansas and Missouri, is that not right?"

"Yes."

"So, the fact that you were awarded these licenses suggests that your degree from the medical school you attended was as good as any other, either in the States or out, right?"

"That's right."

"Thank you. That's all I have for this witness, Your Honor."

The next witness is called and sworn in. The DA starts the questioning. "It's Mr. Randy Whitehead, correct?"

"Yes sir."

"You're a farmer and live just down the road from Mr. Sherman Foster. In fact, the east side of your property butts up against his, does it not?"

"It do."

"So, I would like for you to tell the court what you saw four days before Mr. Porter's body was discovered on the Foster farm."

"Well, I was a-sittin' on my front porch sippin' a cup of coffee my wife made for me, and I seed Mr. Lombardi come speedin' down the dirt road in front of my house; like he was in some big hurry; you know, like he were goin' to a fire or somethin'."

"How did you know it was Mr. Lombardi?"

"I recognized his pickup. I see it every time I go to town. He leaves it parked right there beside the tavern, and I figure everyone knows that big red thing."

"You recognized the vehicle, but did you also recognize the driver, Mr. Louis Lombardi?"

"I sure did. Right there in the front seat, kinda leanin' over the steerin' wheel, like he was on a mission."

"What did you think was happening?"

"Well, now, the truth is, I didn't think much about it then. Old Louie, he's always up to somethin', always in a hurry. So I figured he was just rushing back to his place so he could sell more of dat devil's brew; you know, beer and them sorta things."

"About what time of day was it when you saw Mr. Lombardi drive by your house?"

"I'd say about eleven o'clock, thereabouts. I'd done been out workin' since six and was havin' a coffee break."

"Okay, that's all."

At this point, the cocky Kansas City attorney strides up to the witness stand and begins his questioning. It is obvious that Mr. Whitehead is nervous. This is the first time he's ever been in court, much less as a witness. Also, he's slightly afraid of Louis Lombardi, an emotion shared by many in the greater Doniphan County area.

"Mr. Whitehead, you're an honest man; am I not right?"

"Why, yes, shore am."

"So you would never lie about something like this: saying you saw Mr. Lombardi when you didn't?"

"No sir."

"So, I must ask you, why have you waited so long to come forward? Why did you not testify in the murder trial of Mr. Karl Miller?"

"I don't know. I didn't think it had anything to do with Mr. Miller, and also, nobody done ask me about it till that newspaper fellow came to my house, asking me if I'd seen anything around the time that ole Lester was found dead in a ditch."

"Okay, but let me ask; you are sure you saw Mr. Lombardi, my client, driving his truck past your house?"

"Oh, yes, I ain't lyin', I did."

"But, let me ask you this. How's your eyesight? Do you have any vision problems?"

"Well, yes, maybe. I mean, I see pretty good, most things, that is."

"Mr. Whitehead, is it not true that you are near-sighted; that you need glasses to see objects that are at any distance?"

"That's true. I have glasses, but don't really need 'em that much. I can see pretty good without 'em."

"So, did you have them on the day you say you saw Mr. Lombardi?"

"No, but it ain't like I'm blind. I can see things on my road with or without my glasses."

"All right then, I see you are not wearing your glasses today, so I want to test your distance visions. Are you okay with that?"

The witness scoots back in his chair, clears his throat, looks up at the judge and, with some hesitation, agrees.

"Okay. My assistant is standing at the back of the courtroom holding up a small cardboard sign with writing on it; writing that I and probably every member of the jury can read. Can you read that writing? I want you to tell the court what it says."

Mr. Whitehead squints and stares in the direction of the sign and mumbles, "ah, something like…" A long pause. Finally, he gives up. "I ain't shore."

"In other words, you can't read the words on the sign?"

"I reckon not."

"But yet, you are sure you saw Mr. Lombardi driving past your house that day."

"Yes sir."

Lawyer Hartman turns to the judge and asks that the court record show that the sign reads, in large letters, "CAN YOU READ THIS SIGN?" He then announces, "That's all I have for this witness."

The judge asks if the DA would like to cross-examine. He declines, and the witness is told he could step down.

At this point, the judge calls for a short recess.

The trial resumes an hour later.

The first witness is a man who lives in Crossroads, a long-distance truck driver named Butch Prey. When not on the road, he's a frequent customer at Louie's Tavern. The DA begins the questioning. "Is it true that you spend a lot of time at the bar in Louie's place?"

"Yes."

"And you know the defendant well?"

"I think so, although I don't think anybody knows him that well."

"What do you mean?"

"Well, he's one of those guys that keeps his cards close to his chest, don't say much about what he's really thinking."

"But didn't you tell Mr. Winstead, the reporter with the *Kansas City Star*, that you overheard a discussion between Mr. Porter and Mr. Lombardi?"

"I did."

"Can you tell the court what you heard?"

"I guess."

"So, what did you hear?"

"Well, it was clear Mr. Lombardi was not happy with Lester. He claimed Lester was beatin' his wife, which a lot of men in these here parts do. The only problem was that Lester's wife, Alexandra, was related to Louie; his niece, I think she is. Lester said it weren't none of Louie's business."

"Did Louie threaten Lester in any way during that conversation?"

"I think so."

"What do you mean, you think so?"

The witness looks furtively in the direction of the defendant. Like Mr. Whitehead, he is nervous and somewhat fearful, his eyes darting here and there. He is rubbing his hands together as though he's trying to remove grease stains. It is likely he is worried that Louis Lombardi might come after him if he tells the truth. Finally, he mutters softly, "I mean, he told Lester that he'd better not beat his wife again or he would pay for it."

"Did he say he was going to kill him?"

"Not exactly."

"But that's what you thought."

"Objection. Objection," Louie's attorney interrupts. "Leading the witness."

"Sustained."

"Okay," the prosecution continues. "What did you think Louie meant by telling Lester, and I quote, that 'he would pay for it'?"

"I don't know."

The DA ends his questioning and Louie's attorney takes the floor.

Mr. Hartman begins his questioning. "Okay, Mr. Prey, let's see what we have here. You claim you heard my client threaten Mr. Porter, is that right? How much had you had to drink by then, by the time you heard the verbal exchange between Mr. Lombardi and Mr. Porter?"

"I don't remember."

"One drink, two drinks, how many?"

"Several."

"Now, I must remind you, you have a reputation as a drunk, an alcoholic. How is the jury to believe a man who drinks himself into a stupor and then claims he heard something, a private conversation between two men that had nothing to do with him?"

The announcement to the world that he was an alcoholic leaves the witness chagrined and speechless.

Defense continues, "Well, if you were on the jury, Butch, would you believe yourself?"

"Objection, Your Honor. The defense is badgering the witness."

Before the judge can respond, Louie's attorney announces, "That's all I have for this witness."

There is no cross-examining, so the witness steps down and the DA calls his next witness: the head of the county sheriff's department, the same officer who testified in the Karl Miller trial. A tall and somewhat distinguished-looking man, he is dressed in his freshly laundered uniform. His dark black hair swept back over his head and plastered into place with Brylcreem; freshly shaved and smelling of a cheap, fruity aftershave lotion. He seems sure of himself.

After being sworn in, the sheriff's body language seems to be saying, "Okay, ask me anything you want to know." He is leaning forward in the witness box, his hands on the railing in front of him, with his eyes wide open, like a grade-school student who knows the answer to the teacher's question and is trying desperately to get her attention.

The prosecution begins, "Let me start by asking you to tell the court how long you have held your current position."

"Sure; I've been head of the county sheriff's department for twelve years."

"And your jurisdiction includes the town of Crossroads, does it not?"

"It does."

"So, basically, you have been in charge of the Lester Porter murder case ever since his body was discovered, right?"

"Yes sir."

"I am assuming that you were the person who was responsible for arresting Mr. Lombardi for that murder."

"Correct."

"Can you summarize your rationale for that arrest? In other words, can you tell the court what gave you reason to believe that the evidence was sufficient to justify the arrest?"

"Sure. First of all, we saw the findings in the pathologist's report, the detective's report, and the eyewitness account of Mr. Whitehead. Then, when we searched the defendant's apartment and place of business, we found a 38 revolver with ammunition that matched that found in the victim's head. Also, we found dog hairs that matched those found on Mr. Porter's body. We had no choice but to make the arrest. Obviously, we're in no position to say whether Louis Lombardi is guilty or not; that's up to the jury to decide. But the evidence was sufficient to give us reason to make the arrest."

The DA asks several other questions regarding the details of the case, wraps up his examination of the witness, and returns to his table. The defense attorney adjusts his tie, and with one hand in his pants pocket, walks slowly toward the witness stand.

"Officer, you told the court you have held your current position for twelve years, correct?"

"Yes sir."

"During those twelve years, how many murder cases have you supervised?"

This question catches the sheriff off-guard. He mumbles incoherently as he struggles to answer. "Ahh, two or three."

"Can you be more precise?"

"Okay. Two."

"That number includes the Lester Porter case, is that not right?"

Squinting in consternation, the witness responds in the affirmative.

"So that means you have had very little experience in dealing with murder cases. Correct?"

The witness nods in response.

The judge steps in, "The witness will answer the question."

"Yes," the frustrated sheriff almost shouts.

"You told the court you had sufficient evidence to justify arresting my client, Mr. Lombardi, did you not?"

"Yes."

"And part of that evidence was evidence you collected in your search of the Lombardi's premises, right?"

"Yes sir."

"But that search was conducted after you arrested my client, is that not right?"

The witness squirms and bites his lip before responding quietly, "Yes."

"So, how could that evidence been used to justify the arrest?"

"I-I…don't know."

"You don't know? Of course you know. The evidence you collected during the search was not available when you made the arrest. You found that only later, correct?"

"Yes." This time the sheriff answers loudly, realizing he's been trapped.

"Also, the dog hair you found on Mr. Lombardi's premises; you said it matched that found on the victim's body. Am I quoting you accurately?"

"Yes."

"But is it not true that in a place like Louie's Tavern, a lot of men who have pet dogs hang out there, and that any one of them might bring dog hair in on his clothing?"

"I suppose."

"You suppose? You know that could happen, don't you?"

"Yes."

"And the weapon you found in Mr. Lombardi's apartment: the 38 revolver. A lot of people in these parts own 38-caliber weapons. You know that, right?"

"I do."

"So the bullet you found in Lester Porter's head could have been fired by any number of folks from around here, is that not true?"

Again, a discombobulated sheriff mumbles, "Yes."

"Also, Sheriff, not that long ago you thought you had enough evidence to arrest Mr. Karl Miller for Lester Porter's murder, correct?"

The officer responds with a reluctant "yes".

"As we all know, Mr. Miller was found not-guilty. So, you arrested the wrong man, is that not right, Officer?"

"Well, I thought—"

Before the witness can complete his response, Mr. Hartman interrupts, "You arrested the wrong man the first time, so how do you know you have not arrested the wrong man the second time?"

Again, before the flustered officer can answer, the defense tells the judge he has no more questions and strolls back to his table, takes his seat, and whispers something to his assistant.

The DA then asks for permission to cross-examine, permission which is granted.

"Officer, you told the court that, during your twelve years of service, you had supervised only two murder cases, correct?"

"Yes."

"But, is it not true that, while you were not in charge, you actually worked on other murder cases, cases you were involved in but did not supervise?"

"That's right."

"Can you give us a number?"

"Wow. I would say at least ten."

"That's all I have, Your Honor." The prosecution rests, and the witness is dismissed.

With that, the judge declares that today's proceedings have come to an end and slams his gavel to his desk and announces that "this trial will resume again tomorrow morning at nine o'clock."

*****

The trial of Louis Lombardi resumes at nine o'clock at the county courthouse, as scheduled. The judge calls the court to order. The DA calls his first witness: "Mrs. Alexandra Porter."

The wife of the victim was expecting this, since only yesterday she had been subpoenaed by the district attorney's office. She wonders why and is nervous about testifying, but tries to look nonchalant and confident.

She is dressed in her usual farmer's wife garb: soft-colored, floral-patterned, one-piece dress that just about hangs to her brown leather boots. Her hair is pulled back and tied into a bun. There is a serious and stern look to her demeanor.

The bailiff swears her in and the questioning begins. "Mrs. Porter, you are the widow of Mr. Lester Porter, the murder victim in this case; is that correct? Can you tell the court how long you and Mr. Porter were married?"

"Twenty-eight years."

"How would you describe your marriage? In other words, was it a happy marriage or maybe an unhappy marriage?"

"Objection, Your Honor." The defense contends this line of questioning has no bearing on the case. The judge overrules.

"Can you answer the question, Mrs. Porter?"

"Well, no marriage is perfect; like all marriages, ours had its good times and its bad times."

"But in your testimony during the Karl Miller trial, you admitted that you had been the subject of abuse; that your husband sometimes took out his wrath and disappointments on you. Is that not true?"

Nervously, her hands gripping her dress beside her thighs, the witness leans forward and after a short pause, responds, "Yes, but…"

"But what?"

"I mean that…that sort of thing is not unusual around here. That happens to a lot of women. It's like, well, it's like we see it as a normal practice in a marriage. A man can hit you and still love you."

This response elicits a few muted groans from some of the women in the courtroom audience.

"Some might disagree with you on that, Mrs. Porter, but whether it were normal or not, you would be described as an abused wife. But let me ask: can you tell the court how you are related to the defendant, Mr. Louis Lombardi?"

"He's my uncle."

"How so? Specifically."

"Well, let's see. Louie is the son of my Grandpa Lombardi's younger brother."

"So, he's not really your uncle; he's actually your first cousin, once-removed."

"I guess, but he's more like an uncle, maybe a great-uncle."

"Do you see your Great-Uncle Louis very often?"

"Not really."

"Is it not true that a week or so before your husband's body was discovered, you paid your uncle a visit, you went to the bar early one evening and asked to talk to him in private? That from there, you went up to his apartment where you were, according to an eyewitness, for at least 30 minutes?"

With this, the defense attorney leaps to his feet. "Please, Your Honor, the prosecution is referencing evidence to which we have not been privy."

The judge calls the DA and Attorney Hartman to the bench for a private consultation. The prosecution claims that this is new information; that a witness had come forward just the day before, claiming he would have stepped forward sooner, but he was afraid of the repercussions, afraid that Mr. Lombardi might come after him. It is decided that the person in question will be called to the witness stand and the defense will be given a chance to cross-examine.

The DA continues his line of questioning, "So, Mrs. Porter, I must ask, do you go to Louie's Bar and Tavern very often; in other words, are you a customer, perhaps a regular customer?"

Alexandra seems a bit offended by this question and responds with a self-righteous tone in her voice, "No. Absolutely not. It's not a place for decent women."

"So on the day in question, you did something you do not normally do. You went to the tavern with the single objective of talking to your Uncle Louie. Is that correct?"

Still bothered by the question, Alexandra fidgets a bit and looks at the judge. Finally, she quietly responds, "Yes."

"So why did you want to talk to him?"

"I had a few personal matters that I wanted to discuss. A few matters I thought he and his wife might help me with."

"What kind of matters are you talking about?"

"They are personal and I'd rather not discuss them here, you know, in public in front of all these people."

"But I must remind you, Mrs. Porter, you are under oath and required by law to tell the truth, to answer the questions to the best of your ability."

"I plead the fifth."

"I'm sorry, Mrs. Porter, but you're not the person on trial here today. Pleading the fifth is not an option. You must answer the question."

Reluctantly, the widow exclaims, "Okay. Okay. I went to talk to Louie about Lester and his bad temper."

"In other words, you talked about the fact that your husband was beating you, is that right?"

"Yeah. I guess so," Alexandra answers in a kind of "okay you win" tone.

"So, what did you expect your uncle to do about it?"

"I thought he might talk to Lester, tell him to shape up."

"Did you ask him to kill your husband?"

"No! Absolutely no!" The witness hollers in protest, her face a bright red. She glares at the DA.

"Did your husband and your uncle get along? I mean, were they at least friendly with each other?"

"I don't think so."

"What do you mean?"

"Well, I was not around when the two of them were together, when they saw each other, so I can't be sure. But I do know that there were a lot of people who didn't like my husband. Uncle Louie could well have been one of those. Afterall, my husband was a well-known Nazi sympathizer and that was probably the main reason that he had few, if any, friends. He was always getting cross-wise with somebody."

"All right. Given what you know about your husband's relationship with the defendant and the evidence heard in this case so far, do you believe Louis Lombardi murdered your husband?"

Before the witness can speak, defense protests and the judge sustains.

"All right. Let's put it this way, do you think your Uncle Louie would have had reason to kill Lester?"

"I don't think so."

"That's all I have, Your Honor."

The defense then gets its shot at questioning the witness. With his right hand in his pocket, Mr. Hartman strides toward the nervous widow. He stares into her eyes and says nothing for a few moments, then asks a rhetorical question, "You were frequently abused by your husband, right?"

Alexandra looks at the jury and then back at Louie's attorney. "Well, I'm not sure what you mean by frequently. It didn't happen that often; only occasionally, especially after he'd been drinking."

"So, why did you stay with him all those years?"

"Objection, Your Honor. This is not a psychological exam; it's a trial."

"Sustained."

"Okay, let me ask you this: were there times when you thought about killing him or simply wished he were dead?"

"No! Never."

"You said you asked your uncle, my client, to talk to Lester. Did he ever do that?"

"What do you mean?"

"I mean, did Louie ever follow up on your conversation and actually talk to your husband about his abusing you?"

"No. Not that I know of."

"So apparently, he saw no reason to talk to or threaten your husband?"

"Is guess so. I think he didn't think it would help; that no matter what he said, Lester was not going to change."

"So can you tell the court what Louie told you when you went to talk to him about your husband?"

Again, the witness is fidgeting in her seat and trying to decide how to answer. "Nothing important."

"Well, Mrs. Porter, did not the defendant tell you that you needed to grow up and either get a divorce, or shut up about the abuse?"

Once more, the witness hesitates; she seems to be processing the question.

"Remember, you're under oath, Mrs. Porter."

Alexandra continues to sit silently and say nothing.

"The witness will answer the question," the judge announces in a strong voice of authority.

Finally, she mumbles softly, "Yes, he did."

"So, your Uncle Louie did not think your situation was serious enough for him to get involved; am I correct?"

"Yes," she mutters, as though she has just been checkmated and must admit defeat.

"That's all I have, Your Honor." With that, the defense attorney walks back toward his seat. And just as the judge is about to ask the prosecution if it wants to cross-examine the witness, a woman's shrill, guttural scream reverberates across the courtroom.

"**Ahhhh! No! No!...Oh no!**" The source of the heartrending outburst is Greta Miller.

Alexandra leaps up from her witness-stand chair and leans into the front of the box with a look of horror on her face.

In seconds, the screams turn to sobs of "Why? Why? Lord, please." Finally, Greta collapses back on the wooden bench where she has been sitting.

Without asking the judge for permission, the witness steps out of the box and rushes back to her secret lover's side. Putting her arm around Greta, she whispers quietly so no one else can hear, "What's wrong, Dear?"

The distraught former missionary says nothing, but hands Alexandra a telegram that apparently was just given to her by her older brother:

Dear Mrs. Sebastian,

We regret to inform you, but your husband, Senior Alfredo Sebastian, was arrested and executed on January 20th of this year for his activities as a member of the terrorist organization known as the Vulture's Beak. (STOP) He was buried in an unmarked grave with several of his comrades. (STOP) We just found out yesterday, but thought you would want to know (STOP).

The Missionary Board
Church of the Nazarene
Kansas City, Missouri

The judge is caught off-guard. Chaos has overtaken the otherwise calm courthouse. He feels it would be insensitive to bang his gavel and holler "Order in the court!" So, he waits for a few minutes and then announces, "Court is dismissed until tomorrow morning at 9:00."

The jury files out of the courtroom and back to their quarters. The audience gradually gets up and files out into the hallway, many taking their time as they stare at the obviously distraught young woman.

Greta and Alexandra remain in their seats, with Alexander, who is sitting worriedly beside his concerned mother and her friend. Finally, they get up and leave the courtroom. Karl is standing in the vestibule. When Alexandra sees him, she walks at him and looks angrily into his face. "What is wrong with you? Why in the world did you have to bring her this bad news here?"

The older brother responds apologetically, "Look, Alexandra, I had no idea what the telegram said. It was delivered to our house, since they did not have Greta's address. I thought the telegram might be an emergency, but didn't feel I should open it, but rather get it to Greta as soon as possible. I'm sorry. If I had known…"

Karl really did not know until now what news the telegram brought. But when he finds out, he thinks to himself, *Good riddance. That guy was a thief, thug, and worthless gigolo. Peru and the rest of the world are better off without him*. But, so as not to seem cruel and heartless, he reacts with feigned remorse, "Oh my. I'm so sorry. Poor Greta."

Alexandra humphs and walks back to Greta's side. They walk to her son's car, and he takes them back to the Porter home where the former missionary spends the rest of the day and evening, mourning for the only male lover she's ever had. It seems that despite everything, she has never accepted the fact that Alfredo used her; that he was never really in love with her, certainly not in the way she was with him. Though she never talked about it that much, Greta still had unrealistic hopes that somehow, she and her Peruvian husband would be together again.

*****

Court resumes this morning on schedule. The judge asks the prosecution and the defense if they want to call any additional witnesses. The two combatants look each other and then answer at the same time, "No, Your Honor."

"Since there are to be no more witnesses, we will move forward with trial summations and closing arguments. The prosecution will now address the jury."

As always, the DA is not vying for a place on the cover of *Gentlemen's Quarterly*. He is dressed in the same plaid wool jacket, soiled work pants, and a white shirt begging to be ironed. And he's sporting the same paisley tie that goes with his jacket like tomato juice mixes with chocolate ice cream. This is not how he would dress for dinner at the Governor's Mansion, but—just as during the Karl Miller trial—he feels this anti-fashion statement may endear him to the largely working-class jury.

Before he leaves his desk, he pulls an old hankie out of his pocket and noisily blows his nose. He stuffs the handkerchief back in his pocket as he walks toward the jury box. He is carrying a yellow legal pad. He stops and stares for a moment at his legal pad, then begins his presentation: "Ladies and gentlemen of the jury, in this case, the State versus Louis Lombardi, you have heard the evidence. Mr. Lombardi was arrested and charged with the murder of Mr. Lester Porter, a farmer and upstanding member of the Crossroads community. You have heard the witnesses and seen the evidence. It is clearly a cut-and-dry case."

"Mr. Lombardi did, willingly and with malice aforethought, murder Mr. Porter and then leave his body in an obscure location, specifically in a dry creek bed. Let me remind you of the compelling evidence, evidence that will give you no other choice but to declare the defendant guilty."

"Let's begin with motive. Mr. Lombardi, a tavern-owner with a suspicious and questionable character, did not like the victim; indeed, he hated him. He was heard to have a heated discussion with Lester in which he threatened to kill him So, when his niece, Mrs. Alexandra Porter, called on him and told him about the way she was being abused by her husband, Louie Lombardi had had enough with Lester Porter. So, he took his gun, paid Mr. Porter a visit, hit him with a blunt object, put a 38-caliber bullet in his head, and then hauled his body away, hoping no one would discover it until the buzzards had stripped the victim's body of all its flesh."

"You have heard that Mr. Lombardi was seen in his pickup truck driving hurriedly away from the farm on which the victim's body was found, just a few days before that body was discovered. Then there's the blood; the blood found in the back of his truck that matches that of Mr. Porter, a rare AB-negative type. There were dog hairs on the body. Not surprisingly, the Lombardi's have a dog. Then of course, there's the truck wheel lug-nut that was found near the site of Lester's body. It matched with the other lug-nuts on Mr. Lombardi's pickup, which just happened to have one missing."

"So, I am confident that as you discuss among yourselves the merits of our prosecution, you will find yourselves unable to come up with any verdict other than guilty; you will make sure justice is done and vote to convict Mr. Louis Lombardi, guilty of the premeditated, first-degree murder of Lester Porter. Thank you."

The DA nods respectively at the jury, turns, and walks back to his seat next to his assistant, who leans over and whispers something in his ear. The judge hesitates for a few moments and then calls for the defense to make its closing arguments.

Louie's attorney gets out of his chair, buttons his suit coat, and approaches the jury box. Unlike the prosecution, he has no notes, no yellow pad. His approach is quite different than that of the DA. As usual, he is well-dressed. Today, he is wearing a light gray suit, with a French-cuffed white shirt, silver cufflinks, and a black and red striped tie. He is confident that this jury, at least subconsciously, is likely to equate stylish dress with credibility.

"Ladies and gentlemen of the jury, you have heard the prosecution. He is telling you that you must convict Mr. Lombardi, that you must send this innocent man to life in prison or possibly execution, based on what? I will tell you what. Nothing! Not an ounce of credible evidence."

He stops and methodically looks each juror in the eye, letting his words sink in. Finally, he continues, "I think all of you are smart enough to know that the evidence presented by the prosecution is shaky at best. Mr. Lombardi did not have an ax to grind with the victim. Yes, he did not like Lester Porter, but he was just one of many who disliked the man. The victim was a Nazi sympathizer, an agitator, and a total misanthrope. So, just because my client did not like the victim does not in any way prove that he had a motive to kill him."

"As for the dog hair evidence, the shoe does not fit. The experts admitted they were not certain where that came from. Remember there was also cat hair on the victim. The blood sample taken from the back of the defendant's truck means nothing. There are thousands of persons in this general area of the country that are AB-negative. And the fact that Mr. Lombardi was seen driving near the farm where the body was discovered? Give me a break."

"First of all, the witness who claims to have seen him has serious eyesight limitations, as we proved. Secondly, if Mr. Lombardi was actually driving down the road that day, he could have had any number of reasons for doing so. He had driven down that road many times before. The lug-nut? Again, the odds that that big screw happened to be one missing from Mr. Lombardi's pickup are impossibly low. There are millions of these manufactured every year and used on thousands of vehicles like that of the defendant."

"In short, my friends, what we have here is a murder charge based entirely on hearsay and circumstantial evidence. It appears that the State, in its desperation to pin the murder of Mr. Lester Porter on someone, has chosen to single out Mr. Lombardi, who, though he did not particularly like the victim, did not, and I repeat, did not kill him. So, as you ponder the evidence and decide whether or not to convict my client, I am confident you will realize that the prosecution's case falls far short of proving, beyond a shadow of a doubt, that my client is guilty of murder. You cannot, I repeat, you cannot send an innocent man to life in prison or the gas chamber based on the evidence that proves nothing. I am certain you will do the right thing and find Mr. Louis Lombardi not guilty. Thank you."

And so ends the second phase of the trial. The judge gives his instructions to the jury, and it returns to its deliberation room to consider the evidence in the case and reach a verdict. Will they reach that verdict very quickly, or will there be a stand-off between those who want to convict and those who feel the evidence does not justify that conviction?

It is still morning. Some members of the audience remain seated, anticipating a speedy verdict. Others leave or simply go out to find coffee. Louis is taken back to his cell, but not before Clyde tells his client, "I can usually read the jury and predict the outcome of their deliberations. I am optimistic, but don't want to guess. We'll just hope for the best."

It is clear, this does not make the swarthy barkeep feel any better. He simply grunts a muted "yeah" as he is taken away.

It has been just over an hour since the jury began its deliberations. It has reached a verdict and is now back in the courtroom. The judge instructs the bailiff to escort the defendant back to the courtroom and inform the prosecution and the defense that the jury has been reseated. Some of the audience who left the courtroom return, anxious to hear the verdict.

Once everyone is seated, the judge, consistent with traditional protocol, declares the court back in session and then asks, "Has the jury reached a verdict?"

"It has, Your Honor," responds the foreman of the jury.

The bailiff takes a piece of paper from the foreman and hands it to the judge. The judge reads it, asks the defendant to rise, and then asks the foreman to read the verdict. It is simple and to the point: "We the jury, on the matter of the murder of Mr. Lester, find the defendant, Mr. Louis Lombardi, on the charge of first-degree murder…" the foreman hesitates as he looks at the judge and then at the defendant, then with a kind of gusto, completes the verdict, "…guilty."

Louie drops into his chair, head down. A low-level buzz emanates from the audience. Some look at each other with a kind of surprise. Others simply nod their heads, apparently having expected this outcome. Lester's wife and her handsome son are silent, stunned by what they have just heard. Greta Miller, ostensibly here to support her partner, seems emotionless. Alexandra tears up and begins to sob. Alexander puts his arm around his mother and she leans into him as she continues to cry over the outcome. Greta remains staring off into space, trying to take all this in. Of course, this is not what the Porter family, particularly the children, had hoped for. The defendant, after all, is a relative, and the thought of him being convicted and facing life in prison is a lot to deal with. On the other hand, if Louie did indeed kill their father, then it is only right that he be punished.

Mr. Lombardi's high-priced lawyer is not really surprised but obviously disappointed. He does not like to lose. He puts his arm around the defendant and immediately begins laying the groundwork for an appeal. "Don't worry. It ain't over yet."

Louie turns toward his attorney, a distraught and sorrowful look on his face, and mumbles, "That's easy for you to say."

The judge carries on, despite the noisy disruption, "Mr. Louis Lombardi, you have been found guilty of first-degree murder in the case of Mr. Lester Porter. Hereby, you will remain in court custody until the date of your sentencing, a date to be determined after consultation with my staff."

Just after the judge slams his gavel to the top of his desk, Greta Miller explodes out of her trance and leaps to her feet. "No. No. This is not right. This is not right. Louie didn't do it, I did! I killed Lester Porter! I killed him!"

She is in a one-piece black dress with a veil over her face. She is mourning the death of her Peruvian husband but still is attending and watching the court proceedings very carefully.

Alexandra, who has a premonition of where this is going, pulls on her arm and admonishes quietly, "No, Greta. Don't do this. Please."

But the recently widowed ex-missionary persists, "No. I can't let someone else pay for what I have done!" She sobs forcefully.

The judge is caught off-guard. This is unlike anything he has ever seen. He stares at the protesting woman for a moment, then looks furtively at the defense and then at the prosecution with body language that seems to be asking, "What do I do now?"

Finally, he brings down his gavel and demands, "Order in the court. Please. Everyone, please remain calm." He pauses and then asks the district attorney and Louie's lawyer to approach the bench. "Look, all of this might be bogus, but we can't ignore this woman's confession. I think what we should do is have her meet with all three of us in my office." He then asks the bailiff to escort Ms. Miller to his office.

All four of them are now seated in the judge's office. Most of the audience remains seated, their curiosity and desire to know what happens next keeping them from leaving the courtroom.

In the judge's quarters, Greta is still sobbing and blowing her nose. She has removed her hat and veil.

The judge waits for a minute and then asks her for her name. Then he introduces the two attorneys, as if she is not fully aware of who they are. "Ms. Miller, you say Louis Lombardi is not guilty of murdering Lester Porter; that it was you who actually killed him, is that not correct?"

"Yes."

"You know, this is serious business and if this is simply some sort of ploy to get Mr. Lombardi off the hook, there will be serious circumstances. Under the law, you cannot violate the sanctity of the court."

"I know that, but I'm telling you the truth."

"So, tell us then, how is it that you happened to murder Louis Lombardi?"

Greta sniffles once more and then begins telling her story. "One afternoon, I was at the Porter residence, their farmhouse. Lexxy and I were enjoying each other's company."

The judge interrupts, "Who is Lexxy?"

"Alexandra. Alexandra Porter. That's the pet name I've chosen to call her."

"Okay. Proceed."

"Anyhow, Lester was not there. He had gone out of town and we thought he would not be back until the next day. But he surprised us. He came into the house, into the bedroom, and he…he…" she stumbles and hesitates.

"Yes, go on."

"Well, he caught us in bed together."

"You and Mrs. Porter were in bed together? Are we talking about women making love to each other?" The judge says this with an air of incredulity and righteous indignation.

Greta mumbles in response, "I'm sorry, but yes. We love each other."

"Holy shit!" the judge blurts out. "So, you two are homosexuals?"

"I think 'bisexual' is the appropriate word."

"Wow! All right; then what happened, after the victim caught you and his wife in bed together?"

"Well, as you might imagine, Lester was not happy. He immediately grabbed Alexandra's arm and dragged her out of bed. Just as she stumbled to her feet, he started pounding her with his fists. When she fell down, he began kicking her. It was terrible. I couldn't take it, so I went after him and stunned him with a couple karate moves I learned while I was in Peru. I knocked him to the floor, but he got up and came after me. He grabbed me by the throat and was choking me. I was scratching the back of his neck, trying to get him to let go of me. But it didn't seem to faze him."

"So, just as I was about to pass into unconsciousness, my Lexxy picked up a lamp and slammed its base into the back of her husband's head. He collapsed. It took me a few minutes, but I recovered. I felt Lester's pulse. He was still alive, so I told Alexandra to fetch Lester's revolver. She did, and I shot him. That's it. I'm the person who killed the man. And I feel no guilt or remorse. He was a mean, vicious, and despicable human being. He deserved to die."

"So why are you telling us all of this?"

"Because I am at heart a fair, honest, God-fearing woman and could not let an honest man take the blame for something that I did."

"Okay. You killed Lester, but how did his body end up on the Foster farm?" the judge asks.

"Well, that's where Louie comes in. Lexxy and I were in a state of shock and didn't know what to do. So, she called Louie, her uncle, and told him what had happened. He rushed to the house in a matter of minutes and, with our help, put Lester's body in the back of his truck. From there, he took the body away. Alexandra and I did not know where he took it until the Foster boys found it on their father's farm a few days later."

"I'm curious: do you have a cat?"

"I do."

"Okay. That might explain the cat hairs found on the body," the judge opines as he looks quickly at the two attorneys. They nod in agreement. "What about the eyeballs? Did you cut them out?"

"I did."

"Why?"

"It's a practice I learned while working with a group called the Vulture's Beak in Peru. It's a way of desecrating the body of an enemy and ensuring that wherever he goes in the afterlife, he'll never be able to see again. I was angry and it was just one of the ways I showed it."

"So, your friend, your girlfriend, Alexandra Porter, was being abused by her husband. You and Mrs. Porter were involved in an illicit love affair. Mr. Porter caught you in the act. He proceeded to beat his wife. You knocked him to the ground. Before he could choke you to death, Mrs. Porter decked him with the heavy end of a table lamp. You then, wanting to make sure he was dead, with premeditation, asked for a gun and shot him. And then you had Mr. Lombardi come and dispose of the body. Am I getting it right?" The judge asks, as he sums up the confession.

"Yes." By now, Greta has regained her composure and is no longer sniffling.

The judge pauses for a moment and then asks, "Let's say you came home and caught your husband naked and in bed with another naked man, would you not be angry?"

"I suppose."

"Would you not want to take that anger out on your cheating husband?"

"Maybe."

"Well, don't you think Lester Porter had a right to beat Alexandra in this situation? I mean, a woman who cheats on her husband, especially with another woman, deserves to be punished, don't you think?" By now, the judge is agitated, as his conservative moral values and self-righteous piety threaten to trump his sound legal reasoning.

"No. Not at all. That's caveman behavior. This is the twentieth century!" Greta retorts forcefully.

"So you think that no matter what a wife does, a husband has no right to punish her?"

"Not like that. There is no reason, no reason at all, that justifies a man beating his wife."

The DA and Louis's attorney look on, taking it all in but showing no emotional reactions. They are just working to put all the pieces together. Greta's story is both believable and unbelievable. The judge's puritanical and moralistic questioning makes it difficult for Clyde Hartman to refrain from reminding him that his personal convictions should not warp his reaction to the confession.

The questioning continues, "If you and Mrs. Porter killed her husband, why did she agree to having Lester's body exhumed?"

"Well, first of all, she thought she would sound guilty if she did not give her permission. Secondly, I did a lot of research and found that most exhumations do not yield that much additional evidence, especially when the person has been in the ground as long as Lester had been. I guess we both thought it best if we approve the request. Also, Alexander, her son, thought it was really important that his mother sign off on this; he said she should do anything that might lead to the arrest and conviction of his father's killer."

The judge turns to the two attorneys in the room. "Do either of you have questions of Miss Miller?"

Mr. Hartman responds, "Yes, I do. Greta, Mrs. Porter has three grown children, correct?"

"Yes."

"Did any of them know that you and their mother were the ones responsible for the death of their father?"

"No."

"Did anyone else, besides you, Alexandra, and Louie know?"

"I don't think so. I can't imagine how anyone else would know."

At this point, the judge retreats into a contemplative mood. All is quiet as he writes something on the legal pad in front of him. Finally, he calls in the bailiff and asks him to have the sheriff arrest and detain both Ms. Greta Miller and Mrs. Alexandra Porter. They are to be formally charged with the murder of Mr. Lester Porter. As to the fate of Mr. Louis Lombardi, he will remain in custody as an indicted co-conspirator and accessory to the crime.

After Greta has been escorted from the room, the judge turns to the DA and the defense attorney. "Are you okay with this? I mean, I see no reason for another trial. We have a confession and an account that makes sense."

"But, you don't have a confession from Mrs. Porter," Mr. Hartman notes with an air of respect, not wanting to offend the judge.

"Look," the judge says, with a pensive look on his face, "I'm going to exercise my prerogative here. I will have the sheriff's office interrogate Mrs. Porter. If he can get a confession out of her, then I will sentence her as I see fit. If she denies that she is guilty and argues she did not do the things Miss Miller has said she did, then I will have no choice but to arrange for another trial. But I have a feeling she will confess, and we can put this complicated case to rest."

*****

Oliver lets one of his colleagues write the unusual story of the Lombardi trial for the *Star*. Since he is a key actor in this story, it is better handled by someone less involved with the case. He has been too close to be objective. However, he is considering writing a book about the Lester Porter case. What a great story! Meanwhile, his experience has given him an insight into the nature of rural life. Feeling the urge to be creative, he pens the following poem. He submits it to his editor at the *Star*, only to have it rejected. The explanation is simple. A goodly number of the newspaper's readers live in rural communities in Kansas and Missouri. The editor feels Oliver has done enough to offend that population and sees no reason to rub salt into the already wounded ego of small-town America.

Little Towns That See It All
By Oliver Winstead

All hail the solid country folk
Who live in towns so small,
That everyone knows everyone,
Each name they can recall.
Like paradise; yeah, heav'n on earth,
These places claim to be.
Hard crime, abuse, and sodomy,
Of these, they all are free.
"No need to fear, to own a gun

Or lock your doors at night;
The city crowd, they got it wrong
But we have got it right."
This is the myth that bumpkins tell;
But is it really true?
The demographic facts it seems
That image does undo.
The murder rate in little towns
Is greater than you think.
And also there's a higher rate
Of folks abusing drink.
Those country towns, those rural burghs,
Breed many thieves and thugs.
And check the data, you will see,
These towns are rife with drugs.
The harmony they often tout
Is marred by lies and libel.
And though they say they love the book
They rarely read the Bible.
And then there is the piety
Their mythic story spins.
But just like people everywhere
Their lives are marred with sins.
Small towns today, so oft the case,
Are plagued by crime and blight.
And so, despite the myth, they're not
The paragons of right.
These tiny towns, these villages,
Abundant, yet so small,
Are not unlike urbanity;
These towns have seen it all.

Chapter Twenty-Three
The Truth Shall Set Thee Free

It has been two years since Sonny Miller died and six months since Greta Miller and Alexandra Porter were sentenced to prison for the murder of Mr. Lester Porter, and Louie Lombardi was convicted as an accessory to the crime. The women are serving sentences at the Kansas State Industrial Farm for Women while Louie is at Leavenworth on a five-year sentence. Alexandra will only serve another ten years, since it was deemed by the judge that she acted in self-defense. Greta, on the other hand, will be in prison for another twenty-five years before she can request parole.

Meanwhile, Karl Miller has essentially moved to St. Joseph and is living part-time with Cleo. There is now nothing to hide since the secret became public knowledge at his trial. When he's at the farm, it's business as usual. He sleeps in the barn. Thelma is adamant; she will not consent to a divorce. It is a matter of personal pride and social standing in the larger Crossroads community. So, it's a Mexican stand-off, but life goes on.

The name Louis Lombardi has become almost sacred. He was once looked down on by many as a possible mafia member, a thug, a sinner, and a lowlife seller of the devil's brew, who profited from the addiction of his alcoholic customers. But the fact that he was willing to take the blame for something he did not do, go to prison or be executed for Lester Porter's death, rather than tell the court what he knew… There is an element in the small-town ethic that frames something like this as heroic; as an act of pure altruism. And the tavern, which is now run by Louie's wife and son, is viewed as more legitimate and an accepted, integral thread in the web of the greater Crossroads community.

Karl has not forgotten about his sister, remaining committed to doing all he can to help her. But now, there is little he can do but visit her on occasion. That is what he is doing today, having driven the fifty miles from Crossroads to Lansing, Kansas. He is talking to Greta, who is seated behind a plexiglass window, dressed in prison garb, her head cocked back, and peering under her glasses as usual.

"I still can't believe you did it," Karl says.

"Believe me. I did it," is the response. "I acted out of anger, but also, in my mind, I had nothing to lose. Ever since you kidnapped me and brought me back here, my life has been shit. In Peru, with Alfredo, I felt like I was somebody, that I was doing something important. As long as I thought Alfredo was alive, I had hope that we would be together again. Now, I feel I have nothing. I'm just another disgruntled old maid…a spinster. No husband. No children. No value. I would much rather have died in Peru, fighting with Alfredo and our colleagues, than end up like this."

Karl responds sharply, "Look. I went to great expense and took great risk to save you from the horrible situation you'd gotten yourself into. Anyone looking at all this objectively would say that you should be indebted to me rather than being angry. And the chances are good to excellent that had you stayed in Peru with that terrorist group, you would have been arrested and executed alongside your bloodthirsty husband."

"Come on. Why do you talk about Alfredo that way? He was a true patriot, a liberator, a champion of the common man in Peru. In my mind, he died a martyr."

"A martyr? And a champion of the common man? You've gotta be kidding me. You yourself have told me that the Vulture's Beak and other similar militias killed women and children and actually stole from ordinary people."

"Only under extreme circumstances or by accident."

"So do you feel you're a martyr for having put Lester Porter's lights out?"

"In a way. The guy was a blemish on the face of the human race. He hated everyone; he loved Hitler; and he literally tortured his wife."

Karl shakes his head. "Look, I hated the guy and, yes, he was the ultimate asshole, but I don't think he deserved to die like that. Also, I haven't told you this, but I'm surprised you got off with just twenty-five years. It's one thing to be a murdered, but on top of that to be a female homosexual! I'm surprised the judge didn't send you to the gas chamber."

The two siblings banter back and forth. As their time ends, Greta tells her older brother that Alexandra wants to talk to him. She says goodbye, gets up, and the guard returns her to her cell. Moments later, another guard comes in with Alexandra Porter in his charge. She takes the seat facing her lover's older brother. They have not spoken since the Lombardi murder trial. They greet each other with an awkward "hey".

Karl initiates the conversation, "You look like you've lost some weight."

"Yeah. I have. You would too if you were here. They give you a lot to do and little to eat. But I must admit, I've not felt this healthy in a long time."

"Greta said you wanted to talk to me."

"I did. I've never told anyone this but Greta. She knows, but has kept her mouth shut. She wanted you to think that Alfredo's magical powers were responsible for the death of your son, Karl Junior, or Sonny. But they weren't. Lester was."

"What!" Karl leaps from his chair and leans into the plexiglass that separates him from Alexandra. "No way! No way! I don't believe you."

"You can believe what you want," the confessing inmate replies, "but I'm telling you the truth."

"But how?" the stunned farmer asks.

"Well, Lester had mounted large deer horns on the front of his car. They emitted a sound inaudible to humans but effective in keeping deer at bay. The day that Sonny died, you may remember, Lester drove by your farm, I think just to see who else was there helping with your harvest. He was angry that he never could get any of his neighbors to help him when it was time to cut, bundle, and thrash his wheat."

"Anyhow, when he saw Sonny climb up and into the driver's seat of the hay wagon, he thought it would be funny to spook the horses. He assumed they would jump and shake a little bit—that's all. He had no idea they would react like they did and gallop over the bank and down into the river to their own deaths and, God forbid, take your Sonny with them. He was struck dumb with guilt and remorse. He was never the same person after that and it was one of the reasons that he abused me so much more after Sonny's death. It was as though he was taking out his guilt on me; somehow by hurting me, he thought he was reducing the severity of the horrible thing he had done. Anyhow, I thought you'd want to know."

Karl is speechless. He sits in his chair staring at Alexandra, his mind awash with a chaotic jumble of memories, thoughts, and troubled emotions. "It was Lester? That sorry-ass son-of-a-bitch asshole of a Nazi! If Greta hadn't killed him, I would have. Sonny. Sonny." He tries but can't fight back the tears.

All Alexandra can say is "I'm sorry, Karl. I'm sorry."

Without saying another word, the shaken farmer gets up and leaves the visitation room. Alexandra is escorted back to her cell.

*****

It's a warm July day in Crossroads. There are a few wisps of clouds in the otherwise crystalline blue sky. For some, there is a reason to celebrate: Louie Lombardi has been released from prison early but remains on parole. He is again in charge of operations at his tavern. He is a new man; at least in the eyes of many locals who remain genuinely impressed, if not awed, by his altruism— his willingness to die rather than squeal on his great-niece. He's lost some weight and is once again the master of chitchat, mixed drinks, and corny jokes.

Life on the Miller farm carries on as usual. It is time once again to pull the wagon through the wheat fields and load the shocks of grain that have been left to dry. This year, the wagon is drawn by a tractor, not horses. Pete is behind the wheel of the bright green John Deere. As usual, neighboring farmers are here helping out, walking along beside and pitching sheaves of wheat into the wagon. Karl is managing the threshing machine. It has been a good year for wheat, bumper crops all around. This is both good news and bad. While the supply across the state of Kansas is up, demand remains the same. Wheat farmers will be getting less per bushel they got last year.

But Mr. Miller is not thinking about wheat prices today. It is the three-year anniversary of his beloved son's death. The grief is like a twenty-pound weight constantly pressing against his chest. However, now that he knows what happened, what actually caused Ferd and Dolly to bolt and charge over the bank and into Lazy River, he feels some relief. Only now, the mystery behind Sonny's death has been replaced by a lingering loathing for Lester Porter, the person responsible. At times, he wishes Lester were still alive so he could take him out behind a barn somewhere and beat him senseless.

The workday ends when the last sheaf has been tossed into the threshing machine and the grain loaded into the back of the weathered grain truck. Karl will drive the loaded hopper to St. Joe tomorrow to be emptied into one of the large silos at the grain elevator that sits beside the railroad. Then he will spend the rest of the day with Cleo.

Tonight, he is in his small office in the aging Miller farmhouse. He is reading the latest issue of the *Farm Journal* and drinking coffee. His stomach gurgles as it works to digest the results of his having eaten a larger supper than he should have. He continues managing the household budget and paying the bills. He eats with the family, and despite her continuing distain for Karl, Thelma still cooks for him. Technically, she is still his wife. The fact that Karl is keeping, and in some ways living with, another woman has not changed that in her mind. However, at bedtime, she insists he sleep in the barn, a fate he's come to accept. The children have a pretty good idea of what is going on and have gotten used to the nature of their unusual family life.

Karl and Thelma rarely talk about anything other than family matters and household business. But tonight, Thelma has something on her mind—personal business. She and the two girls have finished cleaning up the kitchen and washing and putting away dishes, pots, and pans. She moves cautiously into Karl's small office.

"Can I sit down?"

"Sure." The polite husband pulls a chair from the other side of the room and pushes it in her direction.

Thelma still has on the plaid apron she wore as she was doing the after-supper chores. She wipes her hands on the apron as she sits down. "What are you reading?"

Karl is caught off-guard by the friendly tone. His first thought: *She must want something*. But he answers, "An interesting article about the new combines that revolutionize the way farmers harvest their wheat. No threshing machine, no stacking and drying. Just let the wheat mature and drive through the field. The machines are expensive but the return on the investment makes it worthwhile. You capture a higher percentage of the kernels than you do with the way we do things now. Over time, it pays for itself."

"You ought to get one."

"I'm thinking about it. But you didn't come in here to hear about what I was reading. What's on your mind?"

"I'm not sure I should tell you this, but I think it's best you know."

"Tell me what?"

"I know you're still mourning Sonny's death. We all are. I also know that Sonny's death was not from any sort of spell or supernatural cause. Greta's husband Alfredo had nothing to do with it. The black woman from Atchison? Totally innocent. Her mumbo-jumbo was harmless."

"So, who did?" Karl acts as though he is clueless.

"Lester."

"Lester Porter?"

"Yes."

"But how… I don't understand…"

"It was an accident, but on the day Sonny died, Lester was here on the farm, at least briefly. Anyhow, he had these new deer whistles on his pickup and thought he would see if they would make Ferd and Dolly jump. He thought at best they would simply act startled, you know. Just lift their ears. Maybe tremble. He had no idea it would spook them the way it did."

Thelma stops and waits for her husband to react. But he just stares at her. Finally, he asks, "How do you know that?"

She hesitates and then, cocking her head to one side, she asks, "Are you sure you want to know?" Thelma knew it would come to this, but now she is nervous; worried that when her aggrieved husband hears the whole story, he might react violently. But she needs to tell her story. Whether it is to feel good about telling the truth, or hurting her blatantly adulterous husband, she doesn't know.

Karl prods his obviously nervous and troubled wife, "Who told you?"

"Lester."

"What? Why would Lester tell you something like that?"

Thelma's fists are clenched. Her whole body has tightened. Her lips are pressed firmly together as she prepares to drop the bomb. Finally, she blurts out: "Because Sonny was really his son, not yours."

"What?" Karl asks. "What did you say?" He has heard but is refusing to believe what he's heard. "No. No way. You're just trying to hurt me. That couldn't be." His face breaks into a weird and awkward smile.

"I'm sorry. It's the truth and I'm not trying to hurt you."

"I don't believe it. No way."

"Look, here's the truth. You may not remember that you and I did not have sex for several months before Sonny was apparently conceived. During that time, I was having an affair with Lester. I will spare you the details. But when I found out I was pregnant, I panicked. That's when I made an earnest effort to get you to make love to me again. You did and you asked no questions. You remember that, right?" Thelma asks nervously, still fearing a violent reaction from her ill-tempered husband.

As though he is in shock, Karl mutters, "Yeah, I do."

"Anyhow, as luck would have it, I was late in delivering, but even then, as you surely remember, we thought Sonny had been born prematurely, a month or more. I saw no reason to tell you the truth. I wanted you to think you were the father; this is why I agreed on the name, even though I wanted to name him for my father, Oscar."

"Did Sonny know who his real father was?"

"No. Never. I made Lester promise he would stay away from Sonny. I actually threatened him. It was obvious he was not happy when he found out I was pregnant. I think he was worried you would find out about our affair, and like everyone else around here, he was afraid of you."

The powerful farmer is shocked, angry, and stunned by this unexpected revelation, but he keeps his emotions in check. He would like to hurt Thelma, make her regret ever knowing Lester, much less sleeping with him. But the Miller boys were raised to respect women and never put a hand on them in anger. The alternative reaction he is contemplating is tearing through the house and trashing everything not nailed down. But instead, he looks at his wife and in a commanding voice, very calmly points to the door and tells her, "Please get out. I need to deal with this by myself."

Thelma does not wait for the command to be repeated, and with a sense of relief, she stands up and leaves Karl's little office without saying a word. She quietly closes the door behind her.

Karl leans forward and props his head between his hands and stares at the floor. As the reality of his not being Sonny's biological father sinks in, his first thought is that he has now lost his beloved son twice. But he is heartened knowing that Karl Jr. went to his grave believing the man he loved and called 'Daddy' was his real father. Perhaps that's all that matters.

Karl's contemplative efforts to sort through this raft of new, shocking information are suddenly disrupted by a violent thunderclap. The house and his calm are rattled. A heavy and much-needed rain begins to fall. Karl is reminded of a scripture verse about the rain falling on the just and the unjust alike. Perhaps this is a metaphor for what happens in the course of one's lifetime: good things and bad things happen to bad people and good people alike. There is no logic or predictability to the process. Life just happens and one has no choice but to play the cards he is dealt.

With that, he stands up, grabs his cap, and heads outside, ignoring the fact that he is getting drenched as he walks briskly toward the closest barn. "It's time to get to work."

Epilogue

It's October 1955 here in Crossroads. The area is painted in a multitude of colors—red, yellow, orange, brown—as leaves fall from maple, oak, hackberry, ash and elm trees. Black walnut trees let go of their thickly shelled nuts which lie scattered on the ground. Most of them will be picked up, shelled, and relieved of their fruit before the end of fall. The air smells of dying leaves and wispy smoke from wood-burning stoves. It is relatively quiet across the county as the harvest season comes to an end.

The year has been an eventful one for America. The struggle of blacks for civil rights has become a movement; the introduction of polio vaccine promises to eradicate polio; Albert Einstein has died; the Soviet Union and its Eastern Bloc allies have signed the Warsaw Pact in response to the creation of NATO. Significant changes for the country, but in some ways of limited significance to the people of Crossroads, who seem to pay little attention to national and international news. Right now, the most important news locally is that Fall Fest will not be celebrated this year—perhaps never again.

Much has changed in this small Kansas town over the past five years. The town's population has dropped by at least a dozen or so as a result of deaths or out-migration. A few new squatters have moved in, taking advantage of homes abandoned by those wishing to get away and unable to sell. The old train station remains unoccupied and continues falling apart—a victim of the weather and occasional vandalism.

Louie Lombardi and his wife have moved to Florida. Louie's son and his new wife are now the owner/operators of the tavern. Crossroads School has been shut down and boarded up. Local-area students must be bussed to and attend a consolidated school that serves a larger portion of the county.

Karl and Thelma are still married, but only in a technical sense. She continues to refuse to give him a divorce, and he does not wish to push too hard for fear it would cause him to lose his three children as well as half his wealth. So, he has built a cute little bungalow in a wooded area on the north end of the farm, where he now lives with his girlfriend, Cleo. She has moved out of her rented house in St. Joe and is now renting a smaller commercial space there in order to continue conducting business as a fortune-teller. She commutes three days a week. On her off days, she helps around the farm.

The farmer and the fortune-teller still enjoy a satisfying sex life, but one lacking the excitement of the first year or so of their relationship. Ironically, she and Thelma have become friends. Now that her affair with Lester Porter has come to light, Thelma finds it hard to condemn her husband for his flagrant infidelity.

Greta and Alexandra have both filed appeals. As a result, their sentences have been reduced and Mrs. Porter will be released in another year or two. Greta must serve another ten years before she is eligible for parole. The plan is to eventually move to Kansas City. Crossroads is not ready to accept, much less embrace, a lesbian couple living in their midst. Meanwhile, the Porter farm has been sold to one of the Miller brothers.

Even though most of the Crossroads residents, and those folks who farm in the general area, know in their heart of hearts that their town is dying, it is not something talked about that often. However, there is still the frequent recitation of the persistent myth: that life in rural areas like Crossroads is morally and socially superior to life in the city. It is believed that rural folks are more well-mannered and polite, more committed to the basic values of the original America and the Christian faith.

They see their community as having less crime, a less stressful social environment, and as being a place where neighbors take care of neighbors, where no one has to lock their doors at night, where men are men and women are women. Behind it all is the feeling that the rural areas of America are in competition with the country's cities, and that in that competition the small towns and country folk are being cheated. The data dispute that, but the belief persists.

Ten, twenty, perhaps one hundred years from now, Crossroads will still exist, but more than likely it will be a small wasteland of abandoned shops, buildings, and homes; with some folks still here, but only because they have nowhere else to go. Crossroads the myth will eventually become the Crossroads of reality with virtually no one there to tell its story.